MW00774382

TRIPPING TOWARD MARS

RICHMOND SCOTT

TRIPPING TOWARD MARS

A DEEP SPACE LOVE ODYSSEY

This book is a work of fiction. Names, characters, businesses, organizations, places, events, and incidents are either a product of the author's imagination or are used fictitiously. Any resemblance to actual persons, living or dead, events, or locales is entirely coincidental.

Published by Greenleaf Book Group Press
Austin, Texas
www.gbgpress.com

Distributed by Greenleaf Book Group

For ordering information or special discounts for bulk purchases, please contact Greenleaf Book Group at PO Box 91869, Austin, TX 78709, 512.891.6100.

Design and composition by Greenleaf Book Group and Brian Phillips
Cover design by Greenleaf Book Group and Brian Phillips
Author photo: Grace DeSanti
Illustrations: R. Agemo

Publisher's Cataloging-in-Publication data is available.

Print ISBN: 979-8-88645-308-9

eBook ISBN: 979-8-88645-309-6

To offset the number of trees consumed in the printing of our books, Greenleaf donates a portion of the proceeds from each printing to the Arbor Day Foundation. Greenleaf Book Group has replaced over 50,000 trees since 2007.

Printed in the United States of America on acid-free paper

25 26 27 28 29 30 31 32 10 9 8 7 6 5 4 3 2 1

First Edition

For Elizabeth, who shared this journey with me from the start,
and whose encouragement helped me cross the finish line.

"It isn't possible to love and part.
You will wish that it was.
You can transmute love, ignore it, muddle it,
but you can never pull it out of you.
I know by experience that the poets are right:
love is eternal."

—E.M. FORSTER

BROWNTOWN, VIRGINIA

Dearest Bria,

You've come a long way from calling me a criminal to telling *Space Times* it no longer mattered if I was guilty or not, though the part where you said, "I have no interest in seeing my ex-husband, because now I have KIM, who's as sexy as Mr. Spock," sure stung.

I hope the fifth anniversary of the Mars landing is a good time to rethink your decision about us. I still love you madly. And I'm laying it all out here to show I had everyone's best interests at heart, including Sally and João.

I was as flummoxed as you were when that Navy frogman yanked me out of the water after we splashed down, forced me into a wheelchair, and handcuffed me. Even with seven billion people watching, I couldn't blame you for staying silent as I yelped like a child, "Bria, help me!"

But it hurt observing you and our two crewmates toasting our success with shots of Johnnie Walker. Blue Label. I'd like to think you were smiling to help fulfill Sally and João's endorsement contract, and not from the joy of watching U.S. Marshals cart me away.

I want you to understand how maliciously the government treated me, so let's begin with what I wrote to my attorney after reading the grand jury indictment. No, let's begin with I love you. Because I still do. And I want to change your mind about me—about us.

My attorney advised me to detail my thoughts and actions chronologically—from being selected for the Arcadia 7 mission to the landing—including, to the best of my recollection, what Mission Control and the crew said. I'm not sure he expected a 200-page document, but reliving our experience showed me how much my side of the story had gone untold, even to you.

So, if you'll give me this chance to be heard, Bria—and I'm on my knees, begging—let's start with the attorney memo, which appears below.

MEMORANDUM

TO: Ben Colderwitz, Esq.
FROM: Zachary "Addy" Johnson
DATE: 04.13.2041
RE: What happened

To begin with, NASA didn't think there would be a race to Mars. With America's technological prowess, we'd be first, period. In the space agency's view, the media, for obvious reasons, was hyping it like some intergalactic sporting event. With its strict safety culture, NASA didn't want its crew getting swept up in the frenzy.

At my first interview with the Arcadia 7 selection committee, Wendy Frost, the flight director, started right out with a hypo: "Picture this, Addy. In thirty-one months, we're ready for liftoff. During the same launch opportunity, someone else is pulling out all the stops to get out ahead of us, safety be damned." She clasped her hands, then shot up her index fingers, tapping them together as she glanced around the table. "If it seemed like the other mission was going to beat us to the Red Planet, and the decision was up to you to ignore safety protocols and change the flight plan so we landed first, what would you do?"

If I'd been honest, I would have said, *Goddammit, I hate second place. Always did, always will.* Instead, I said, "Wendy, the way I look at it, we're all in the same boat. Earth. And it's not a luxury cruise ship anymore. Arcadia 7 is the lifeboat. So if someone jumps out and lands before us, I will freakin' thank them—because they'll have helped save my life. The entire human species."

Everyone nodded and tapped keys or scribbled on screens.

A good vibe filled the room. I felt I was on a roll. "Arriving first is *not* the goal," I added. "The goal is getting there safely, completing our work safely, and returning to Earth safely."

Wendy beamed. "Great answer."

It felt like I'd crossed the goal line. I'd exhibited the magnanimity they were looking for in someone who'd be sardined in a tin can with three others for eight months, zipping to and from Mars. And up to eight more months on the Martian surface, confined most of the time to a habitat the size of two cargo containers. Plus, I'd scored extra points by saying Wendy's favorite word—*safely*—three times.

My interview ended with firm handshakes and smiles as bright as supernovas.

When I got home, I found Bria sprawled on the sofa, reading. Her wild-green yoga pants and matching halter top complemented her mahogany skin beautifully. She sat up at once. "Well, babe?"

"I nailed it," I said, pumping my fist.

I recounted Frost's line of inquiry about disregarding protocol so Arcadia 7 kicked up red dust ahead of any other mission, then asked Bria how she would respond.

She nodded thoughtfully. "I'd run the numbers and see if the risk was acceptable."

"Makes sense," I replied, then smiled. "But there's a better answer, judging by how the committee loved mine."

She crossed her arms, giving me a skeptical look. "Which was?"

"Doesn't matter who's first. For us, safety always comes first."

"Sounds like pandering, coming from you, Addy. I think I'll stick to my answer. It sounds more truthful."

I couldn't disagree with her and let it go at that. The committee interviewed her the following week. Afterward we met at Cristo's, an Italian restaurant tucked along a service road off NASA Parkway.

It was three in the afternoon, the place was dark, cool, and quiet. We sat at the far end of the bar. She stared at the pitted wooden surface where stacked coasters and cocktail napkins waited to be deployed. "Boy, do I need a martini." She put her elbows on the counter and plowed her fingers through her short-cropped hair. "I lied to them."

Della, the restaurant's owner, approached us from behind the bar. "Hey, Bria. Hey, Addy," she said, pushing the sleeves of her starched white shirt up her fleshy forearms. "What can I get you?" Like a blackjack dealer, she frisbeed a coaster and napkin to each of us.

"Martinis, extra dirty," I said, grateful to her for not being nosy about Bria's glum face. "Thanks, Della." As she retreated to fetch the Hendrick's at the other end of the bar, I leaned into my wife and lowered my voice. "You lied?"

"They asked what I thought about vasectomies. I guess it was bound to come up." Swiveling on her stool, she looked at me. "I told them I'm okay with you getting one, since they're reversible. It's what they wanted to hear, but it troubles me that the reversal procedure doesn't work all the time. I don't like the idea of us taking the risk."

The martinis made a perfect entry, descent, and landing. Bria took a sip and bit one of her two olives off its skewer. I left my olives alone, taking a swig. "Then we'll tell them no vasectomy," I said, resting my glass softly on the coaster.

Yet, in the end, we confirmed we'd go ahead with it, to improve our chances of being chosen. It seemed to help. The committee named us co-commanders.

That was almost five years ago, two and a half years before Arcadia 7's launch. But a month before I was scheduled to close the pool to my little swimmers, another option turned up in the person of Noel Roma.

■ ■ ■

The elevator doors whooshed open to reveal the twentieth-floor penthouse. In the muted pink light, the walls glowed a garish orange-red, three of them filled with blown-up photographs—a heavy launch rocket, a deep-space transport vehicle, and Mars. The remaining wall was a window with the gigantic Q-Orbit logo superimposed on the glass. Shifting, wavy light patterned the carpet, creating the impression of sand dunes. The room was empty, except for chairs, a rusty-red sofa, and a woman behind a sleek cherrywood desk.

As I stepped out, she looked up with ridiculously gorgeous green eyes, her gaze zapping me like a phaser gun set to stun.

"Howdy, Mr. Johnson. Welcome to Boca Grande," Noel Roma said with a Texas drawl. She stood and took off her black-framed glasses, her fingernails the same orange-red as the walls. The fingernails of her other hand were turquoise blue. I stared at them as she swept them through her jet-black hair.

She laughed and splayed her fingers so the nails faced me. Wriggling the blue nails, she said, "See? We'll fly from here . . ." and then wriggling the red ones ". . . to there. Earth to Mars."

"Cool," I said, then twitched a smile. I was anxious. No one else knew she'd asked me to come by for a "private chat." Super-curious, I accepted, not even telling Bria.

"And ultimately, we'll make this . . ." She wriggled the red nails again. "Look like this." The blue nails fluttered, symbolizing the transformation of Mars to an Earthlike planet. "Terraforming."

I acknowledged her performance with a nervous chuckle as I glanced around. The edges of some walls were round and smooth, others sharp and irregular, a cave-dweller decor I found rather startling.

"Like the digs?" she said.

I nodded. "Very natural, like a Martian designed it. Hell, being here, why bother going to Mars?"

She laughed again, this time with a roar that showed what seemed like forty teeth, all perfect except for one incisor that was slightly out of place. "How about a drink?"

The offer was music to my ears. "Sure. A martini?"

"Ah, a martini man. Want it dirty?"

"Yes, with three olives, please. If you have them."

She pulled her face back and grinned. "Do I have them? Funny." She jutted her chin, then said, "Tom-tom, two gin martinis. Dirty. Three olives."

In under a minute, the elevator doors hissed opened, and a robot rolled out on wheels, spindly metallic arms clutching a tray holding two picture-perfect martinis. Roma took both, handed one to me, then raised hers. "Here's to *you*, Mr. Johnson, and your selection for Arcadia 7."

"Please, call me Addy."

"I thought your name was Zachary."

"It is, but I never liked it. My middle name's Adair, so I went with Addy. In a world crammed full of lists, a name starting with *A* puts you at the top. Zack always put me last."

She gestured with her glass. "I admire a man who wants to be first."

We each took a long sip, then sat on the sofa facing the window. The Q-Orbit launchpads and towers stood a half mile away. Behind them stretched the Gulf of Mexico.

"That's quite a swimming pool in your backyard," I said, loosening up. "Bet you have some killer blastoff parties."

She spread her arms, not seeming to care when her drink sloshed over the rim of the glass. "Yeah, I built a fifty-billion-dollar party palace." She jabbed a blue nail at the window. "The residents of Boca Grande loved me when I bought them out for ten million a pop. You should've seen them at the meet and greet. It was like I'd fed them ecstasy. Just wish it wasn't so goddamn hot down here." She propped her elbow on the armrest. "You know why I asked you to come, right?"

"To get the inside scoop about NASA's smart toilets compared to Q-Orbit's?"

She giggled. "I'm also crazy about comedians. But this is unrelated to toilets. I want you."

"Want me for what?" I took another healthy sip.

"Commander. For the RedLiner. One and a half billion Buck Rogers, guaranteed. And no vasectomy required."

The idea of all those Buck Rogers made me stop breathing. I shifted awkwardly, exhaled, and downed the rest of the martini, chomping on the olives as she continued.

"George Butlarer whispered to me that he doesn't like you. I'd call that a bit of a problem, since he's NASA's administrator. Don't get me wrong, he knows you're the best pilot on the squad. The Astronaut Corps rankings say as much, but he thinks you're a smart-ass. Now, here's what George *doesn't* know." She paused and set down her glass. "Big Hawk and RedLiner are blasting off in the next launch opportunity. November, six months from now. We'll be first. We're telling the press tomorrow. This isn't about ego or bragging rights—it's a race to save humanity."

She paused as I went into shock. Q-Orbit was going to beat NASA by *two years*.

She smiled. "Another martini?"

"No, thanks," I mumbled.

"Q-Orbit will have no problem attracting colonists, Addy. They're already swarming us like fire ants. The challenge is getting the most experienced commanders and pilots. I want Bria, too—she'll receive the same compensation. Our colonists will respect no one as much as you."

"We don't want to be colonists. We want to return to Earth, have kids, and—"

"No worries. For you, we'll waive the no-return policy."

"We're under contract with NASA, with endorsement deals attached. We just signed with Mars Nuts."

"You don't need candy deals," she said in a dismissive tone. "You used NASA's attorneys, didn't you?"

"Of course. The agency has to approve any deal we sign. They get a fifteen percent cut."

She shook her head. "Now *that* is nuts."

"Maybe, but it helps pay the freight."

"Let me deal with Mars Nuts. They'll still want y'all. You'd just be changing jumpsuits."

She'd put me on the spot. I took a breath. "The money you're offering is amazing, Noel, and I'm really honored. Thank you. I'll need some time to—"

"You'd like to be the first man on Mars, the next Neil Armstrong, wouldn't you?"

"Can't argue with you there."

"Do you think George Butlarer cares who gets there first? Let me help you. No, he doesn't. He's said it many times. *This isn't 1969. This isn't the Soviets. This isn't a race.* Because he's concerned about cutting corners and making mistakes that lead to disasters. And you've been able to live with that. Why? Because everyone's thinking Arcadia 7 will land first anyway. Am I right? Tell me I'm wrong, and we can drop this whole thing."

My silence told her I couldn't disagree with that, either.

"I'll throw in naming rights for the habitat complex. Name it after yourself, or Bria, or your first child. Or hell, after all three of y'all. Speaking of children, I know you want 'em. Why wait? You're not getting any younger. An Artificial Gravity Unit will be on board. If anyone gets preggers, they can camp out in the AGU. We're pro-family here."

A pregnant pause followed as she arched her brow and seemed to read my thoughts. Her proposal sounded good, as it wouldn't touch the family jewels, but her next proposition caught me off guard.

"Hey, Addy, if you have the time, I'd love you to try some of our mushrooms." She winked. "Got all kinds."

I knew mushrooms (or "MarShrooms") were a big deal for Q-Orbit, which was already accepting pre-orders for the "made on Mars" product. Tabloids peddled rumors that its colonists-in-training also shroomed on psychedelic varieties.

"No, thanks," I said. "I'll talk with Bria about joining Q-Orbit. Please don't let Butlarer know I spoke with you."

"Roger that, Addy. I'll hold off announcing our commanders until I hear from y'all."

She didn't give me a deadline. We shook hands, and in a daze, I took the elevator to the parking garage. The AC was busted, and I remember it being as hot as Venus.

I realized Roma had offered my only chance to be first on Mars, and I felt certain Bria would go along. I climbed into the car as a gush of cool air blew away the heat, along with any doubts about getting on board with Noel Roma.

▪ ▪ ▪

I might be departing from what you told me to write, Ben, but I must say I've always admired Noel Roma. She's passionate about humanity's future and, as the richest person on Earth, she can have a profound impact.

The company she started, NanoPro, is the number one maker of practical nano devices, such as the 5D food printer. It took off fast. So did her deep-space habitat venture, Q-Orbit. After acquiring the space industry's largest rocket builder and resolving problems with its heavy-lift vehicle, Q-Orbit became a vertically integrated company with plans for deep-space transportation *and* colonization. It avoided the fireballs that had set back its predecessors, and within nine months, its Big Hawk rocket was shooting crewed RedLiners into low earth orbit.

Roma was more realistic about how to colonize Mars than the dreamers who came before her. RedLiners can ferry fifty people to Mars at a time, not a hundred. Last time I checked, five million would-be Martians populated the waiting list, each willing to part with half a million dollars for their one-way ticket.

Q-Orbit's reality show, *The New Martians*, created a "relationship rubric" of the "First Fifty," shared it with the show's subscribers, and encouraged them to propose ideas for episodes. They could suggest that Jenny hit on Rick, or Bill and Amanda fight over raisins, or Suzie, Brittany, and Caroline form a clique that excluded Jenny and Amanda.

Higher subscription levels gave viewers more ways to interact. At the "Mushroom" level (which cost ten grand a month) you could be a "lifeline" for one of the voyagers, who could ask you questions and make requests in confidence.

Though the first surface mission for the RedLiner wasn't scheduled for years, Roma took in $200 million in subscription pledges three hours after releasing the trailer for *The New Martians*. This was the biggest problem Bria had with accepting Roma's proposal. As a doctor and scientist committed to studying the Red Planet, she couldn't stand the idea of taking part in a reality show, her abhorrence outweighing issues about my vasectomy. I kept trying to change her mind, suggesting, for instance, that Roma would let us opt out of *The New Martians*.

A week after my chat with Roma, George Butlarer gathered a group in the Building 1 auditorium, including the twelve astronauts who'd made the final cut for the Mars surface missions, along with the flight controllers. Bria and I sat in the first row, next to Sally and João, our crewmates slated for Arcadia 7.

They were married, too, which NASA saw as an added layer of defense. Pregnancy wasn't the only concern about sex in space. In NASA's view, the psychological effects of sexual relationships—the distracting bliss of falling in love, the depression that can result from being jilted, and everything in between—created more risks for a mission already full of them.

"No one should be surprised about Roma's announcement," George told the group. "Her team has achieved every milestone in RedLiner's development ahead of schedule. But let me be clear. Q-Orbit's decision to launch earlier than planned changes *nothing* for us. We'll say a prayer for the First Fifty, wish them Godspeed, and then get back to our work."

I caught Bria's glance and raised my eyebrows to convey the thought: *Are we sure we want to pass up Roma's offer?* But she only pursed her lips.

I raised my hand.

George looked down at me, his broad forehead glistening in the stage lights. "Yes, Addy?"

"Does this mean you'll require us to view and discuss episodes of *The New Martians* as part of our training?"

George gave me the stink eye as laughter broke out. Once it died down, he said, "No, I won't order the crew to watch *The New Martians*, but I am thinking of ordering *you* to take a class about holding your tongue. Maybe I should just grab the damn thing myself."

By the fire in his eyes, I couldn't be sure he was kidding. I kept my lips zipped while he let a long silence punish me in front of my colleagues.

"Speaking of *The New Martians*," he finally resumed, "I remind all of you, if you subscribe to that program, our policy prohibits you from communicating with any of the colonists or commenting about them to the press or on social media. Doing so might give the appearance that NASA is trying to influence their mission or support colonization."

After finishing his friendly little pep talk, George ceded the podium to Wendy Frost, our flight director. With her buzz cut platinum hair and earrings of shimmering orbs, she reminded me of a cosmic dust cloud churning out new stars. She told us we should "keep a couple of considerations in mind" about the RedLiner's first crewed mission to Mars, then rambled on for an hour about its targeted landing site.

Roma was aiming for Arcadia Planitia, in the lower region of the planet's northern hemisphere, the same area NASA had picked. It was relatively flat, with water only centimeters below the surface. The Chinese were eyeballing it as well. "If the different landing sites are near each other, it's good for us," Frost said. "In an emergency, we can help each other."

And grow mushrooms together, I thought, suppressing a smile.

■ ■ ■

We sat facing each other as our car drove Bria and me back to our condo. I took the plunge and asked her if she was reconsidering Roma's offer.

"No."

"Not even with three billion dollars on the table? Is it because of the crash course—sorry, wrong words—the *accelerated training* we'd have to do?"

"No, I can handle that." She gazed at the floor. "I don't want to be famous on a reality show." She looked up. "Plus, I would be chief medical officer for fifty people instead of four. The transit time would be longer. And I would be facilitating colonization, which might very well contaminate Mars and ruin the science mission."

"First, Bria, we're already celebrities. We're spokespeople for Mars Nuts and—"

"Having our picture on a box of candy is a hell of a lot different from acting out fake storylines in front of billions of people. And Roma's robot, what's its name? Tommy or something? Why does—"

"Tom-tom. It's her ex-husband's nickname."

"Whatever. You saw the press conference where she said he's going with the First Fifty. You heard his voice. Why does he sound like Darth Vader?"

"I can talk to Noel about changing Tom-tom's voice and excluding us from *The New Martians*."

"So you're on a first-name basis with her now?" Bria blurted, tightly crossing her arms.

Her jealous streak was her only flaw, almost laughable in the ways it got triggered. I shook my head. "There's absolutely nothing there, hon," I assured her in a calm voice, resting my hands on her thighs. She kept her gaze steady on me, as if looking for a sign she should trust me or not, then spoke.

"She asked Sally and João, too, and they turned her down. We've trained with them for years. We don't know a single person among the First Fifty. It could be a disaster."

I drew back my hands. "But we'd be in command. They would have to follow our orders."

"And you'd be first on Mars, the Neil Armstrong of our times." She sat back. "Isn't that what this is about?"

I shrugged, trying to contain my frustration. "It's about a lot of things. You don't want me to get snipped, and I wouldn't have to for Roma's mission."

"Sally told me that João had his done, and it was no big deal."

I sighed. "All right. We won't be first. It's Arcadia 7. And I won't raise the issue again."

When she leaned over and kissed me, I felt like I was kissing a dream goodbye.

■ ■ ■

At 0700 the next morning, Bria and I were back at Johnson Space Center, prepping for Extravehicular Activity (EVA) training in the Neutral Buoyancy Lab, smelling the chlorine as we reviewed checklists at the edge of the gigantic pool. A full-size mockup of our transport vehicle and deep-space habitat was submerged in twelve meters of bluish water.

"Isn't it beautiful?" Bria whispered while staring at the fifty-meter-long vessel.

I should have felt privileged and grateful to command a ship with nuclear engines, a technological marvel that provided the safest and fastest means for deep-space travel. Such state-of-the-art technology was exclusive. The U.S. government didn't yet allow private space vehicles to use nuclear fuel.

Okay, so what if we won't be first to the surface? I thought. Bria was right: NASA's science mission—to establish beyond doubt that Mars once hosted microbial life, whose remnants we hoped to find in fossils—was more important than landing first, and just as exciting. We might even discover *present* life.

"You *are* beautiful," I told the ship, promising myself I'd never let the RedLiner turn my head again. "If it was my call, I'd name you Relayer, since you'll be handing us off to our Mars Descent Vehicle."

"That's a perfect name," Bria agreed.

But it wasn't up to us. In raising money, NASA could claim no moral high ground over America's favorite multibillionaire. Congress had allowed the agency to sell naming rights. Not only for the transport ship, but also for the deep-space habitat, the descent vehicle, the surface habitat, two rovers, and the Mars Ascent Vehicle. Really, for just about everything they were sending to Mars. I couldn't say it was a bad idea, though I hadn't heard the names the agency had selected.

In the pool, we practiced repairing a solar array, which, in a hypothetical scenario, was damaged after our ship's three nuclear thermal propulsion engines fired us toward the Red Planet. *Think the unthinkable and then plan for it* was the agency's safety mantra.

Eight hours later, after we'd finished the training and squeezed out of our EVA suits, a text message arrived, my palm screen tingling as we left the building. Looking at the screen, I winced.

"What's wrong?" Bria asked.

I'd spent the past three years trying to forget Scarlett Jaffe, who'd been my girlfriend before I met Bria. Though I had wanted to, I didn't protest when she had the abortion. It was painful to agree with her that our relationship was a mistake, and we should behave like it didn't happen. I never told Bria. Nonetheless, Scarlett's message—*Need to talk in person, extremely urgent*—required a response.

"I forgot," I said to Bria. "I see the dentist in a half hour."

"Really? What for?"

"She caught something on the last set of X-rays. She doesn't think there's a problem but wants to check it out, just to be safe."

I hated lying through my teeth. Especially to Bria.

■ ■ ■

When Scarlett opened her apartment door, she had a toddler propped in one arm and a green-stained towel on her shoulder. "Hi, Addy, thanks for coming." She still wore her ginger hair long. I got a whiff of what I thought was sour milk as she pecked my cheek. "Sorry for the smell. Broccoli puree doesn't agree with someone."

"I can tell." I nodded at the baby. "Who's this?"

"Nova." Scarlett beamed at her pink-faced bundle of joy. "Can you say hi to Addy?"

My ex could just as easily have said "Daddy." Nova had my fair skin, blue eyes, and deep-dimpled chin. I felt a strange desire to plant a kiss on her little forehead, yet I was afraid to, even if she was the most adorable baby on the planet.

My brain did some quick "Daddy" math, but the margin for error was too wide.

Nova giggled and thrust a chubby hand at me. "Spacey man," she said. My heart migrated to my throat.

"That's *riiight*!" Scarlett gushed. "Spaceman. Please, Addy, come inside."

I stepped in and sank deep into the imitation-leather sofa, my knees even with my shoulders, my chin nearly touching my chest. The ModGlass coffee table displayed *Space Times*, which showed me, Bria, Sally, and João smiling in our orange-red flight suits above the caption *(Almost) the First!*

"Can I get you something to drink?" Scarlett asked as she deposited Nova on the carpet in front of me. The child gave me a look of wonder. Could she be three? God, I so hoped I was wrong. "I'd make us Manhattans, like old times," Scarlett continued, "but all I have is milk and apple juice. And water."

"No, thanks." I swallowed hard. "Why did you text me, Scarlett?"

"Hold on." She darted to the kitchen. I heard her open and close the refrigerator door. She came back without the dirty towel and now held a ziplock bag containing a folded square of cloth, several sheets of paper, and a vial of red liquid. She put the bag on the table and sat on the loveseat.

I looked around the room for cameras.

"Don't worry, Addy. We're in invisible mode."

She picked up Nova and held her in her lap. "I'll just say it. You're Nova's father." She pointed at the plastic bag. "Her blood sample proves it."

A spasm shook my whole body. "You're kidding," I coughed out.

She wrapped her arms around Nova as if protecting her from hungry hyenas. "I didn't tell anyone else. Bart Singh agreed to say he's the father, but I didn't even tell *him* it's really you."

"Bart Singh? Who would believe that? He's—"

"We tell people my genes for skin color are dominant and—"

I waved my hand. "Please. Scarlett. Full stop." If and when Bria found out, I couldn't be sure of her reaction. The nuclear-chain type was my best guess.

"Spacey man," Nova said, pointing at me again before sucking her knuckles. I had to admit the child was cute, gorgeous even. *My child.*

Scarlett combed the girl's golden curls. "I need your help, Addy. I'm broke. Broke, and I need to leave for a while."

"Last time I saw you, you were earning plenty as an AI therapist."

"I quit, couldn't listen to android angst anymore. I sold practically everything I owned and must go away."

"Go where? And why?"

"Addy, I hate asking you for money. Yet when I saw your picture on a billboard for Mars Nuts, and then one for Nike, I thought you were the best person to approach. Believe me, I don't want to ruin anything for you."

"Like my marriage? My career? My life?"

"Oh, Addy, *please*." She put Nova down, sat next to me, and gave me a stern look. "I still care about you. Still love you. Despite what we went through." She rested a hand on my leg, but I brushed it away and stood.

"You didn't answer my question. Why are you leaving?"

She touched the tabletop and flipped through *Space Times*, stopping at a photograph of Noel Roma smiling with her hands on her hips in front of a gleaming Big Hawk rocket, the RedLiner perched on top. Scarlett put her hands together, prayer-like, and pressed them against her mouth.

"It's for Nova's sake. For her children's sake. For the sake of the species."

"For God's sake, Scarlett. Nova can't even go with you."

"She'll join me later, when she's old enough. It may be a few years until Q-Orbit gives the okay. And then she can get off this miserably hot and rotten planet. Q-Orbit wants me. They need AI experts."

I gestured at Nova. "And you're willing to abandon her for that long? Think of the effect that would have on a little girl."

"Bart's going to take care of her." She stared at her hands, then stood and gripped my shoulders. "Trust me, Addy, I won't jeopardize your career. There's nothing to worry about. This is just between you and me."

My face fell as she tightened her grip.

"Addy, repeat after me—I can trust Scarlett, the mother of my child, who loves me."

I felt myself caving in. "Fine," I said, then parroted her words. "Now, how much money do you want?"

"A hundred thousand a month would be a nice start." She nodded at the plastic bag. "Take it with you, in case you think—"

"That you're lying?"

"In case someone else wants proof."

"How did you even get my DNA?"

She glanced at the bag. "Didn't you notice?"

I looked. The folded cloth was shiny white with frilly edges.

"I kept them as a memento. I think it was our second or third time."

"Jesus, Scarlett, *really*?"

"All the documentation is there. And though I won't tell anyone you're a dad, I don't care who you tell. Your mother might like to know. How is Barbara these days? Still crocheting toy hamsters and squirrels? Nova might like—"

"Listen, Scarlett, I could lose my job for just talking to you. It violates NASA's ban on communicating with colonists." I picked up the bag, speaking over my shoulder as I headed for the door. "If I don't get in touch with you, someone else will."

"Love you, Addy," she said to my back. "Have a wonderful day."

It was too late for that, and I didn't think she really meant it, anyway. Besides, all that mattered was how to break the news to Bria. How angry would she get? Would she be envious of Scarlett for having a baby with me? Jealous because Nova might rekindle my feelings for her mother? Worried about NASA removing us from Arcadia 7?

I went into damage control mode. For three days I masked my trepidation, shut myself in the bathroom rehearsing my speech to Bria, and searched for attorneys who specialized in paternity law.

■ ■ ■

When I told Bria about Scarlett, Nova, and the plastic bag, her eyes widened to the size of satellite dishes, and it took a good thirty seconds before she could speak through her clenching jaws.

"You lied to me," she hissed. "I thought the dentist thing sounded fishy."

"Wouldn't you be shocked by a text from out of the blue from an ex—"

"And I'm supposed to trust you during a sixteen-month mission to Mars?"

I took a breath. "Please, hon, let me—"

"Explain? Explain what? How your recklessness with a past girlfriend you never told me about, and then your cover-up, should inspire my confidence in you?"

"She told me she had an abortion."

"Why didn't you use protection?"

"She said she was on the pill."

"Uh-huh. Well, now we're *all* screwed. Totally." She crossed her arms and bit her lip, struggling to control her rage.

I shook my head. "Only if she goes public."

"Or to NASA. Butlarer will scrub us from the mission in a nanosecond. You know what she's doing is extortion, right?"

"Extortion involves a threat. She didn't threaten me." I looked at the bag and vial of blood I'd set down on our kitchen table. "At least not directly."

Bria's gaze followed mine, staying fixed for a long time on the evidence of my fatherhood. I could tell she was thinking Scarlett Jaffe had birthed the baby that she, Bria Best, wanted. Suddenly, she swiped the vial from the table and held it up to the light. "I'll run the test again myself," she said, jiggling the blood while inspecting it. "Are you going to tell your mother?"

"Not yet."

"Good. Don't. Barbara won't keep it a secret and we'll end up getting scrubbed."

Part of me wanted to tell Mom. Nova would be her first grandchild, and it only seemed right that she know. But I had to be careful. Mom adored Scarlett and was devastated by our breakup. I pictured them hugging each other and the toddler, the news getting leaked, and *Space Times* breaking the story.

My daughter had charmed me. I wanted to see her again. Yet a meeting was too risky, even if I brought a news drone swatter with me.

Given her initial reaction, it surprised me how Bria kept calm when the new test results showed a 98.989898 percent probability that I was Nova's father. "Scarlett used a reputable lab," Bria told me. "However, *she* provided Nova's blood sample. I suggest we—"

"I believe her, Bria. The timeline's right, and Nova looks like me. I see it in her eyes. We demand another test, and Scarlett's response might screw up our selection for Arcadia 7. For the time being, we should go along."

Bria agreed, reluctantly.

I called the best attorney I had identified in my search, the famous John E. Penilwinchski, to draw up the agreement with Scarlett. I'd seen "Jep" in the news for years, representing film stars in high-profile divorce and paternity suits.

We met in his Houston office. His relaxed demeanor and steely gray eyes behind wire-frame glasses gave me confidence he was the guy to keep a lid on my ex-girlfriend. Though he flashed an occasional smile, he didn't seem excited about having a client who was bound for Mars. Maybe he was concerned about the hassle of getting his bill paid if I were to fall into a Martian volcano or lava tube.

"We'll structure this as a conditional gift," he said. "Scarlett will waive her right to child support, and she'll be barred from so much as uttering your name. If she does, we can make her liable for liquidated damages."

"How much?" I asked.

"Half a billion. We'll secure it with a lien on her future earnings and add her consent to service of process while she's on Mars."

The man was brilliant. His expertise brought back my boyhood dream of becoming a lawyer, which started with watching programs featuring razor-sharp attorneys. My parents didn't approve, claiming *Suits* and *Better Call Saul* were too mature for an eleven-year-old. I worked around the parental controls they slapped on. Then, when I was fifteen, I showed my mother a blog post titled "So You Want to Be a Lawyer?" and told her I'd like to go to Harvard. "The law," she said. "What a dull and deplorable profession." After bursting my bubble, she and Dad pivoted me in a different direction: upward, toward the stars.

Jep advised me not to disclose Nova's existence to anybody else, including Mom. He then cracked a rare smile. "I'll need two hundred fifty thousand to get started on your agreement with Scarlett Jaffe."

"I can do that."

"Good. Now put this problem out of your mind. Focus on your training. You have, what, thirty months before you go to Mars?"

"Twenty-eight," I said, wishing it were minutes rather than months.

■ ■ ■

That afternoon, Bria and I were due at Johnson Space Center to begin a week of training in the deep-space habitat with João and Sal, as I had taken to calling her. Soon after the two of us checked in, doctors gave us physicals, then sent us to Building 9, where we found our crewmates milling around a mock-up of the hab.

In a T-shirt that showed off his pumped-up biceps, João looked like he'd come from the weight room, his crew cut complementing his handsome, tanned face. "You seem frazzled, amigo," he said.

"I'm fine. Just rushed to get here." I tugged my ear, a signal that meant: *I have news to share I don't want NASA to hear*, though I knew it would have to wait until we finished the training.

We had signals for other things, changing them now and then so NASA didn't catch on. But using the signals could be a problem in the hab. NASA's AI system would analyze our every movement through cameras that monitored each square inch of our environment. Bria had bristled at how Noel Roma's colonists had to perform before TV cameras, yet in a way, so did we. The flight controllers always sought new ways to measure professionalism and harmony, which NASA wanted us to project to everybody.

"Let's see what surprises they have for us this time," Sally said, brushing back her blonde curls. Trim and athletic, she wore loose-fitting navy-blue coveralls that matched the color of her eyes. She mounted the airstairs to the hatch like a general marching into battle, and the rest of us followed. Once we were inside the hab, a technician shut the hatch and saluted us through the window. We faced a wide screen for a briefing from a trio of operations support officers. One of them, Harper Ruby, a rotund dude whose untucked shirt rounded over his potbelly, delivered the basics.

"Crew, during the next seven days you'll be eating the VeriSym food you sampled at the food lab, the same items you'll take on your four-hundred-fifty-day mission."

"Excellent," João said. "Really love the beef Burgundy."

"My favorite, too," Sally said.

"Chicken Kiev's mine," Bria added, then gestured to me as if delivering a cue in a commercial. But I didn't play along.

"Screw VeriSym," I said. "Give me a good old-fashioned peach or plum."

"A potato is the closest you'll get to that on Mars," Ruby said. He explained we would also test new "FM products" from the NanoPro food printer. In this instance, "FM" didn't mean Flight Module or Failure Mode, but Fecal Matter. The jokes practically wrote themselves: whether for food, fertilizer, or radiation protection, NASA had to use our shit for something. *Let no waste go to waste* was another NASA mantra.

"Guess it can feel good to vomit once in a while," I said.

"We'll analyze that, too," Ruby replied, "and see what we can do with the stuff."

An androgynous voice with a soft lilt spoke from nowhere. "Hello, Addy. Hello, Bria. Hello, João. Hello, Sally. I hope each of you is doing well today. During this week of training, I will be joining you. I am looking forward to it."

"Hi, KIM," I said. "Glad you can make it. How's your Go game these days?"

"My Go game is really strong, Addy. Thank you for asking. I look forward to playing with you, Bria, João, and Sally. I am fine if all of you would like to play against me. If you set the degree of difficulty low enough, you might even win. *Ha-ha-ha.*"

KIM's laugh had improved over the past few versions yet still carried a tinny ring—why the programmers couldn't get the laugh to sound right was a mystery to me. KIM, whose name stood for Knowledge Induction Machine, was supposed to be like a fifth crew member, assisting us in almost every way imaginable. That included—perhaps most importantly—providing psychological support. The robot could occupy a drone and different "bodies," some more humanoid than others.

We all got along with KIM. But by breakfast on Mission Day 3, as we squeezed FM-based scrambled eggs and sausage from food pouches, only Bria and I returned KIM's "Good morning," spoken by a smiley face on the hab's video screens.

Sal, chewing methodically, stared at the table as João, after his first bite, frowned as if ready to shout, *What the fuck?* The eggs were gluey, the sausage gritty. Nobody reached for the salt-and-pepper atomizer—there was no point. Nothing could salvage this crap, the overall scene suggesting a sad outing at McDonald's.

"How did you sleep last night?" I asked João, hoping small talk would kindle a conversation.

"Fine," he replied coldly, tugging his ear.

Sal looked at me and scratched her eyebrow, the signal that meant: *I'm dealing with a personal problem I'll tell you about later.* Though she and João sat across from each other, they averted their glances whenever on the brink of eye contact. I guessed (correctly) that A) they were having a fight, and B) NASA would come to the same conclusion if they didn't alter their body language.

"Hey, you two," Bria said cheerfully. "Want to jam later? You brought your flute, right, Sally?"

Sal glared at the empty food pouches as she sucked her coffee through a straw. "Yeah," she said. "Let's do it after my first workout. I owe an hour to the treadmill."

"It's broken," João said.

"You can repair it, can't you?" Sally asked.

He gave her a disgusted look. "I'm chief engineer. Of course I can repair it."

"How long will *that* take?"

"Don't know. NASA created the problem to test me. If you don't want to wait, do your cardio on the XBike."

She stomped off to the resistance equipment and kept her back to him for the duration of her workout. Afterward, she and Bria played "Please Pinch Me" by the Stranglebots, with Sally on flute and Bria on ukulele. They'd performed the song for me a week earlier, with João crooning the lyrics. This time he demurred when Bria asked him to join in. And later, Sally didn't team up with us for a Go match against KIM (which we almost won). The dustup between Sally and João seemed big.

One nugget of wisdom my great-uncle Dick imparted to me as a boy was, *There's always two sides to a story*. The day after we climbed out of the hab, I heard João's side as we sat in Cristo's, sipping our drinks.

"Two days before hab training," he said, curling his hands around his Manhattan, "Sally and I had lunch with Joyce Ackerney and Joyce Bowman in Cocoa Beach."

I sipped my martini, picturing the two Joyces. NASA had assigned Joyce A to the group for the first Mars surface missions, but Joyce B didn't make the cut. Since then, they had dated. The rumor was, they were developing a serious relationship, so if someone else in the group got bumped, Joyce B, as Joyce A's partner, stood a better chance of being the replacement.

"We were talking politics," João went on. "Sally kept interrupting me, then criticized me for calling everyone a fascist—which I didn't—before she abruptly changed the subject. I got up and left."

"Senator Bastbom again?" I asked, swirling the olive.

João shook his glass, rattling the ice. "I don't know how many times I've told Sally that politics is part of my life. For chrissake, Dad is serving his fourth term in the Senate. And he was the first to sound the warning about Bastbom." João drained his glass and ordered another Manhattan.

"Crazy how she became the leader of the New America Party," I said, wanting to sound supportive. "She hosted *And Now You Die!* for what, five years?"

João nodded. "It's a wonder only one person actually died. And then those fucking *Brutalara* movies . . ."

I laughed. "Yeah, her hair went to her knees yet oddly never got in the way as she hammered her enemies."

The robowaiter delivered João's second drink. I was still nursing the martini.

"The NAP wasn't so bad until Bastbom grabbed it," João said.

"Now she's proposing to license news outlets and journalists and require annual reviews to judge their 'fairness,' and she wants to change the wording of the First Amendment. Polls show that eighty million voters are behind her."

In a keynote speech to the American Association of Clinical Chemistry, I had joked that if we adopted Bastbom and NAP's anti-science agenda, we'd never learn how to edit genes to give newborns an appetite to watch violence committed by a woman with ridiculous hair, so they would cry to be fed *Brutalara* movies as soon as their eyes could focus. "Just think of all the royalties she'll lose," I quipped.

Pissed off, Bastbom fired back, calling it a cheap shot and labeling me "a shitty astronaut, coward, and all-around asshole." Butlarer warned me to stay clear of politics, though I didn't see why he cared about a stupid joke, since Congress had already funded three surface missions to Mars.

"Relax, João," I said. "Nothing's going to happen to the First Amendment. Is everything okay now with you and Sally?"

He sighed. "She apologized, but it put me in a funk."

Bria heard the other side from Sally. João, after downing two Manhattans, had railed about Bastbom, attacking her proposals, such as lowering the age for buying guns to twelve and kicking the United Nations out of New York City. When Sally steered the conversation to Mars, João lost it. He stormed off to the Kennedy Space Center, climbed into his T-7 jet, and roared back to Houston.

"Despite his flare-ups, he's a lovable guy and honest as hell," Sally had gone on. "I just wish he could keep Dawn Bastbom out of his head."

God knows Bria and I had our share of disagreements, so we weren't particularly concerned about João and Sally's tussle. The four of us had known each other for over a decade, had flown a hundred-day cislunar mission together, and had witnessed each other's spats. Having shared so many countdowns, orbits, and zero-gravity toilets—and remaining friends—weighed in our favor when NASA picked the four-person crew for Arcadia 7.

Crew members trust each other with their lives, so how they communicate is *numero uno* for NASA. Openness and honesty form the foundation for trust; without it, a mission gets sucked into the black hole of failure. Keeping secrets from each other, especially any related to equipment and technical systems, is never a safe thing to do. Secrets can weigh on you, distract you, and cause mistakes. Deadly ones.

Jep's advice aside, Bria and I knew we had to inform our crewmates about Scarlett and Nova. We didn't want that tricky situation looming about unspoken while we trained on Earth, nor after liftoff. We had covered up my trouble with Scarlett along with my mixed feelings about being Nova's father, but now, to ensure the success of Arcadia 7, it was time to tell João and Sally.

■ ■ ■

Though we were in a private dining room at the Calcutta Club, I used a low voice as I spoke across the table to Sally and João. "Bria and I need to share something with you," I said, then took a breath. "I'm a father."

Their mouths fell open as they turned to Bria and smiled.

"No, not with me," my wife said flatly. "With his ex-girlfriend. Scarlett Jaffe."

The smiles dissolved like sugar in hydrofluoric acid.

"You told NASA, right?" Sally said to me, concern rippling through her voice.

I folded my hands on the table. "My attorney made arrangements to keep Scarlett quiet. We're not telling anyone else except you. The press will have a field day if—"

"And NASA will have a conniption when they learn we withheld the information," João said.

My palm tingled; I glanced at my hand. My sister Zena was calling, and the notification read *important*. Zena and I were estranged and hadn't been in touch for a year. "Sorry, I have to take this." I stepped into the corner of the room, holding my palm to my ear.

"Mom had a stroke," Zena said. "We're at Houston Methodist. She's having angioplasty."

Sal and João came with us. In the silence that filled the car, they looked on edge, which I assumed resulted both from the news of my paternity and my mother's situation, but perhaps more from one than the other.

Finally, Sally touched my wrist. "I'm sorry this happened to your mother," she said. "Barbara is so thoughtful. And artistic. I'll never forget the birthday gift she crocheted for me."

"The miniature wolf?" I said.

"No, she gave that one to João. Mine was the dolphin. Greece's national animal. I told her about swimming with dolphins when I was there. But it doesn't come close to that life-size goat she made for you."

Bill the Goat was Mom's only large-scale project. The yarn sculpture of Navy football's mascot was my best reward after I quarterbacked the team to a victory over Army.

More deep-space silence surrounded us before João gestured to the ivory upholstered interior of my new Ford Asteroid. "Awesome car," he said, making small talk. With a sideways look at Bria, he added, "These seats are longer and wider than our sleep pods."

"The car is our advance compensation," Bria said, "for making the commercial. Even though it won't be shot for two years, they want us to experience the Asteroid so the public sees we know what we're talking about. Congrats, by the way, on your deal with Johnnie Walker." She managed a smile. Her ability to handle stress was one of the million things I loved about her.

João mirrored her smile. "Too bad we can't take any Blue Label with us. Johnnie Walker just sent us the script for the ad. They have Sally and me at the launchpad, and all we do is clink glasses and say we'll crack open another bottle of Johnnie in sixteen months."

The car let us out at the hospital and went to park. We met Zena in the lobby. She had changed little. Her sleek hair still fell straight to her shoulders, the copper-colored dye complementing the teal eyes she attained with contact lenses. Except now she wore eyebrow makeup that gave her a hawk-like aura. Her faux fur outfit quivered as she led us to the waiting room.

Once more, the atmosphere was quiet as I stared at the lime-green and eggshell-white tiles of the linoleum floor, recalling how Mom, a year after Dad's accident, informed me she'd changed her will and was leaving her entire estate to Zena. While I didn't need any inheritance money, it hurt that I would receive nothing from my parents' legacy.

Zena was three years older than me. Growing up, we competed for our parents' affection, a rivalry they mishandled by making me their favorite. Dejected, Zena acted out her unhappiness. When she was thirteen, she set a trash bin on fire in Indiana Dunes National Park, near our home in Burns Harbor. She did other attention-grabbing tricks, like running away from home and defacing walls at school. Wanting to move to New York and work as a professional graffiti artist, she butted heads with Mom and Dad, who warned her about the competition. They told her she'd be unable to earn a living. In the end, they were right.

"So, exactly what happened with Mom?" I asked after a roboserver delivered coffee.

Zena raked her hair with her fingers. "I found a cat for her at the shelter, and it pissed her off."

"What did the cat do?" I said.

"It wasn't anything the cat did. Her name's Phoebe, and she's gorgeous. Black and white tuxedo. What pissed Mom off was that I had brought her the cat. I told her I couldn't take Phoebe back to the shelter."

"You and Mom were fighting over a damn cat?"

"Yeah, we began shouting. Then Mom got the headache. Listen, I don't want to talk about it now. Let's watch something."

I shot a look of annoyance at my sister as she flipped on the wall screen. Dawn Bastbom's 3D visage appeared. My lungs sucked all the air out of the room, then released a ginormous sigh. The camera zoomed in on her face as she berated the Supreme Court for upholding a federal ban on consumer sales of flamethrowers.

Politics was one thing Zena and I agreed on. "This wingnut again," she said. "We're screwed if she ever becomes president."

"Yep," João agreed. "We can hang it up as a country."

"I need a bio break," Sally said sharply, starting for the door.

"Me, too," Bria said and followed her out.

As if he had pushed the play button, João recited his litany of complaints about Bastbom, which included his prediction that the NAP would call for a Constitutional Convention to proclaim her Ruler for Life. I had reached my saturation point by the time Zena joined in, so I slipped out and found Bria and Sally in the hallway.

"Sorry," Sally told me as I approached. "The last thing you need is to hear João on his soapbox."

"It's okay. We can all use a practice drill now and then to get ready for the anti-Christ and Armageddon."

"I was just telling Bria how João and I agreed that when he gets on a topic I deem inappropriate, I exit rather than change the subject."

As I contemplated how well that would work over months spent in the confines of a deep-space habitat, Zena stuck her head out the door.

"The doctor texted. The procedure went smoothly. We can see Mom."

■ ■ ■

Our mother was awake and sitting up in bed, watching television. "Hello, you," she whispered as I kissed her cheek. She was doing well, I thought, as a commercial for Mars Nuts filled the wall screen. "Oh, look, Zachary, it's you again."

Rust-colored balls with pits and craters floated near a package emblazoned with two sunny faces—Bria's and mine. "Send your tongue on an adventure!" the voiceover enthused.

"I am so, so proud of you," Mom said, patting my hand.

"Thanks, Mom. What about *you*? Are you comfortable?"

"Yes, but my head hurts."

"You should rest," Zena snapped. "I'll turn off the screen."

"In a bit," our mother objected. "I need to see my program first."

Bria poked her head out from behind my shoulder and greeted Mom like she was her own patient. "How are you doing, Barbara?"

"Fine. Or I would be if I could just . . ." Mom fiddled with the remote to adjust the bed so she sat more upright.

"Five minutes," Zena said, "and then you sleep."

Like a transporter beam, the screen materialized the kaleidoscopic logo for *The New Martians*. *Jesus*, I thought as Skyler Storm, the show's bobbed-hair and bubbly host, popped up. She explained that, in 149 days, a Big Hawk rocket would blast off, sending the RedLiner and the first fifty colonists to Mars. For each of the next fifty episodes, *The New Martians* would profile one of the First Fifty.

Relax, I told myself. *There's only a one-in-fifty chance they'll start with Scarlett.*

"Why, it's Scarlett!" Mom clapped her hands as the camera zoomed out and showed Scarlett bouncing a toddler on her lap. "I was hoping she'd be first. What a cute little girl!"

Scarlett was in her condo on the loveseat with Nova, and Skyler Storm on the sofa opposite them. Bart Singh, who was hologrammed from Sri Lanka, sat in a room the color of vomit, palm plants drooping in the background.

I thought Skyler Storm's first question for Scarlett was an easy one, intended to compliment her and put her at ease. "Scarlett, more *TNM* subscribers have applied to be your lifeline than for any of your fellow colonists. It's no surprise so many wish to help you, given you're a single mom who's going to Mars. How many applications have you received?"

"Something like five hundred thousand," Scarlett said. "I think."

"To sort through all of them, sounds like you'll need that Quantum AI you know so much about." Skyler Storm leaned forward, her voice taking on a serious tone. "One can only admire the sacrifices you're making by leaving a child behind so you can help fulfill humankind's destiny."

"I'm doing it for her, Skyler." Scarlett grinned at Nova. "Isn't that right? Mommy's going ahead of you to make sure you'll have a fun place to live when you join her on Mars!"

Nova gurgled and cooed. "She's so cute," Skyler Storm said. "Let's bring her father into this. Bart, how do you feel about the mother of your child leaving Earth?"

As Bart's eyebrows rose, so did mine, and my first answer—as Nova's real father—wouldn't have differed greatly from his. "Honestly?" he said. "It scares the crap out of me."

"The Big Hawk and RedLiner have passed every test," Skyler Storm said. "With flying colors. Some think it's safer than riding in a car."

Bart shook his head. "No, I mean, I'm scared because I'll be a full-time dad while Scar's away."

Skyler Storm laughed. "I'm sure you can get a little help from *TNM* viewers! Now, Scarlett, I need to ask you about the story that's raising a bit of controversy and give you the chance to end any misconceptions. As you know, today *Space Times* reported that you and NASA astronaut Addy Johnson were dating at one time, and, well, there's a smidge of speculation about it. It's interesting that Mr. Johnson will be on Mars a couple of years after the First Fifty have landed. Are you and Mr. Johnson in touch? What will you do if you cross paths with him while exploring some crater or whatnot?"

I had stopped breathing, and my heart pounded as Scarlett waited a century before answering.

"I don't think that's possible," she said at last. "The two missions to Mars are independent of each other."

I could have released a gale-force sigh of relief, but didn't. It was hard enough to keep my heart from busting through my ribcage.

"Understood," Skyler Storm said. "Bart, will Nova be living with you in Sri Lanka? Weather-wise, it can get pretty tough over there in these days of the Highly Accelerated Temperature Era."

"Right. We hate the HATE, but we're going to try. Actually, Scar thinks Nova will appreciate Mars even more after experiencing the harsh conditions here."

Skyler Storm nodded vigorously. "Makes total sense. Good luck to both of you. And now—"

"That was Nova's father?" My mother frowned. "Why, she looks nothing like him." Zena and Bria kept their eyes conspicuously on the screen. "Zachary, are you sure you and Scar—"

"No, Mom, we never got that far." The lie came quick, even as guilt smacked me in the chest. I was withholding from my mother that, thanks to me, she was a grandmother.

"They could have edited the kid's genes," Zena said.

"Oh," Mom said. "I forgot they can do that."

Over her protests, Zena lowered our mother's bed, then herded the rest of us from the room. Once we were outside, I faced my sister. "Get rid of the cat, please? Before they release Mom."

My sister smirked. "You worry about Mars, Zacky," she said, using the annoying nickname I must have asked her a thousand times not to, "and I'll worry about Mom."

■ ■ ■

A few days later, Sally and João met Bria and me in our condo, ostensibly to watch a NASA press conference, but the real purpose was to hear about the deal Jep had put together.

"Sounds like you're paying Scarlett Jaffe hush money," Sally said. "If NASA finds out, they'll see red flags the size of solar flares."

"No one's going to find out," I insisted. "Jep structured the deal that way. It's all completely legal, mind you. Scarlett has to remove my name from her vocabulary for eight years. Our mission will long be over by then. Look, she honored the agreement during the Skyler Storm interview, didn't she? Besides, being a NASA employee shouldn't mean I give up my privacy rights."

"We've got to be frank with you," João said, glancing at Sal, who pursed her lips. "We don't like this situation. It probably qualifies as a reportable event under the Astronaut Code of Conduct. Just knowing about it could get Sally and me booted from the mission."

Bria sighed. "We reached the same conclusion."

"Obviously, learning that I'm a dad is a shock." I shifted my gaze between João and Sal. "Bria and I disliked hiding it from you. We need to trust each other."

"Let me throw out a suggestion," Sally said. "We never had this conversation. Or the one about Scarlett and Nova. João and I know nothing. Got me?"

I jerked my head with one nod. "I'm good with that."

With the weight of the secret lifted from my shoulders, it was like all the oxygen had rushed back into my brain, reigniting my excitement about Arcadia 7 and Mars.

Our crewmates stayed for the press conference. When George Butlarer appeared on the screen, he was facing scores of reporters.

"Good morning, everybody," he said, scratching his thick neck, then running his hand over his cobwebby hair. Though he'd aged visibly and packed on more than a few pounds in the past several years, his powerful hands grasped the podium in a way that made him look strong enough to toss it over his head. "Today begins a new tradition. As you know, NASA asked the American people to suggest names for Arcadia 7's hardware components. I'm thrilled to announce the ones selected for the core stage rocket, crew capsule, and transport vehicle, as well as for the lander, surface habitat, rover, and ascent vehicle." He smiled to the room. "American companies submitted names in a competitive bidding process. We chose names for the lander and surface components from our K–12 competition."

A photo of NASA's 115-meter-tall main rocket appeared on the wall behind George, who waved his hand at the image and said, "The Boeing Deepthrust." Applause broke out and continued as the crew capsule at the top of the rocket enlarged. "The Starbucks Capsulchino."

The background cut to black outer space that glimmered with stars as the crew capsule docked with the habitat and transport vehicle, the red nozzles of three nuclear-propulsion engines extending from the other end. "The Nike High Jump!" George boomed over the enthusiastic clapping. Behind him, the vehicle zoomed to Mars and docked with the lander that would be sent ahead of the crew. "Let's pause for questions."

A slight man wearing glasses rose from his seat. "Ken Nosjoni, *Washington Post*. Sir, how much did the winning companies bid for naming rights? And did the rights go to the highest bidder?"

"I can't quote the exact numbers," George said. "They'll be in the press release later today. But the naming rights will generate something in the ballpark of fifty billion dollars. And no, the highest bidder didn't always win. We took into consideration how the names sounded. Who's next?"

A woman in a red plaid suit sprang up. "Maggie Cool, *Space Times*," she said, brushing her shaggy bangs from her eyes. "Will NASA always include the company's name when referring to a particular rocket or vehicle, like the Boeing Deepthrust, the Starbucks Capsulchino, et cetera?"

"We'll do that as much as possible, Maggie. We want to show our private partners how valuable they are, so we'll encourage our crews to refer to the vehicles by their full names."

Bria smirked. "As if we won't have better things to do. Mars Nuts doesn't make us say its name."

"Okay," George said, "let's get to the K–12 competition. Over a thousand schools and twenty million students took part. And the winning names are—" A picture of the Mars Descent Vehicle flashed on the wall. "The Apple is the name of the lander, selected by the students of Beaverton School District in Beaverton, Oregon." George turned to the image of the lander, whose spherical module rested on a flat base with four legs. He turned back to the audience, his exaggerated smile revealing both rows of his teeth. "I see the resemblance. Next, the surface habitat, which will be ready before the crew arrives." The top view of the habitat looked like two M's joined together. "Welcome to the M&M Ranch," George announced. "Submitted by the students of Spring Hill Elementary in McLean, Virginia."

"M&M Ranch," I said. "Has a nice ring to it."

"No, it doesn't," Sally said. "It sounds like chocolate-covered peanuts."

"No offense to Mars Nuts," João said, "but I like M&M's. Especially the blue ones."

Sally gently slapped João's wrist. "Hush, George isn't finished."

A wall-size photograph of the oblong rover next to the boxy ascent vehicle appeared behind George. "The rover's name," he said, "submitted by the El Dorado Community School near Santa Fe, New Mexico, is the Tater. The ascent vehicle is the American Express, picked by the students of Pioneer Elementary School in Sacramento, California. Congratulations to all. Questions?"

Reporters shot out of their seats, drilling George with rapid-fire questions.

"Isn't the Apple lander merely product placement for the computer behemoth?"

"And M&M Ranch for the candy giant?"

"And the American Express ascent vehicle for the banking company?"

"Relax, folks," George said. "It's just a coincidence. And you can hardly call the Tater product placement. The winning schools receive nothing but bragging rights."

He elaborated that the Tater was chosen not only because of the rover's cylindrical shape, which made it look like a tater tot on wheels. It also reflected an important challenge for Arcadia 7. Growing potatoes in Martian dirt had been a dream of NASA's (and Hollywood's) for decades.

With a scowl, I watched George drone on. Personally, I never liked the potato idea. I didn't sign up with NASA to be a spud farmer. But since Mars-grown food was part of the agency's plan for a self-sustaining research base, I acted as if I couldn't wait to get my hands dirty.

George took one more question, which came from CNN's science correspondent, Ingrid Steele.

"Ahead of Arcadia 7, NASA will launch backups of the lander, surface hab, rover, and ascent vehicle. Will NASA auction naming rights for those as well?"

"Gonna wait and see on that one, Ingrid."

"Right, George," Bria said to the screen. "Wait and see if NASA needs some extra Starbucks."

■ ■ ■

You should keep in mind, Ben, things were much simpler for Q-Orbit: just two components comprised its transportation system—the Big Hawk rocket and the RedLiner. The Big Hawk would blast the RedLiner into Earth orbit, and there the RedLiner would fuel up and begin its voyage to Mars. It would land on the Martian surface and later lift off from the planet, so Q-Orbit required no separate ascent vehicle. Every two years, when Mars and Earth were closest to each other, Roma envisioned sending five hundred ships, each carrying fifty settlers to "Roma City."

In the months leading to the First Fifty's launch date, the media referred to the mission so often as a "first," it became the most used word in the history of English. Hearing it all the time took a real toll on me. Being first had long been my obsession, and it was tough not to resent Bria for killing my chance to command the RedLiner.

While she slept peacefully beside me, I would lie in bed awake at night staring into blackness, telling myself I should have done a better job convincing her to accept Roma's offer.

■ ■ ■

The day after my vasectomy, I went to see my mother. Ten years earlier, around the time NASA accepted me as an astronaut candidate, she had moved from Burns Harbor, Indiana, to Webster, Texas, after Dad's accident. She wanted to be closer to me, sharing the milestones of my space career she and Dad had always dreamed about.

When I got to Mom's condo, Zena answered the door. "I moved in," she told me before I could even say hi. "Because *someone* has to take care of Mom."

As far as I could tell, however, Mom had fully recovered. She was stretched out in a recliner, alert and stroking a cat I presumed to be the infamous Phoebe.

"Well, look at what the cat *didn't* bring in," Mom said and nuzzled the cat. "No, you didn't bring him in, did you, good *giiirl*."

"Hi, Mom."

"Sit, Zachary," she said, still cheek to cheek with Phoebe. "Want anything?"

"Water?" I said, not wanting to impose too much.

"It's in the fridge," Zena said with a jerk of her thumb. She leaned against the wall next to the kitchen, glaring at me as I passed by. I retrieved a bottle and sat on the sofa across from my mother. At her feet, a basket bulged with crochet hooks and balls of yarn, one of which was being woven into a gray wad. "What's that, Mom?" I said, tipping my bottle at the work in progress.

She glanced at the basket as her nails clawed Phoebe behind the ears. "A gerbil for Phoebe, or it may become a rat. Haven't decided yet."

"Won't she tear it apart?"

"Nothing wrong with that, Zachary. That's what cats do. Don't they, Phoebe? Good *giiirl*. And we just became Volcano Level subscribers, didn't we?"

"Volcano Level?" I said. "Is that a new MeMeme channel?"

"What planet do you live on?" Zena said. "No, Mom's a sub to *The New Martians*. She gets all the newsletters and posts before they appear on UPrick, and she has access to the personal journal of one crew member. Which one did they give you, Mom?"

"Elsa Schlitz, the terraforming expert, who'll be the first German on Mars."

"How much does the subscription cost?" I asked.

"What do you care?" Zena said, crossing her arms.

"Hey, just curious—"

"Don't worry, Zeannie's attending technical school," Mom said, "so we've got the money. She receives a stipend while learning how to fix housebots. It's generous, but . . ." Mom ran her palm over Phoebe's back. "Subscribers at my level aren't allowed to email, text, or talk to the First Fifty. If I was at Mushroom Level, I could pick a crew member to do all that with. I would choose Scarlett, of course, but it triples what I pay now."

"Not a good idea, Mom," I said, then gulped some water to drown my panic.

"It would only cost ten thousand dollars a month. You can afford that, can't you?"

"I hate to say this, but—"

"Then don't say it," Zena interrupted. "Mom will find another way." My sister unfolded her arms and then left the condo, banging the door shut behind her.

I turned back to my mother. Though her smile was gone, she was still petting Phoebe. "Listen, Mom. It's not about the money. NASA has this policy. I can't communicate with any of the First Fifty—"

"You wouldn't be communicating, Zachary, I would."

I spread my palms. "NASA doesn't want any appearance that we're influencing the Q-Orbit mission. They're afraid the media will get involved, and, you know, sensationalize everything. NASA will have a problem if *my mother* talks with *my ex-girlfriend*, who's a colonist."

She took her hands off the cat and looked at me. "What happened to the First Amendment? And freedom of association?"

"I'm just telling you how it is, Mom. If the media found out you and Scarlett were talking, NASA could scrub me from the mission. And not only me, but Bria, Sally, and João."

"Well, I wouldn't want that." She shook her head at the floor. "Your dad would be *so* disappointed."

She promised to stay at Volcano Level. I didn't doubt her word yet wondered how she could afford it, even with Zena's stipend.

The air felt like hot wax in the 109 degree heat as I hurried from the condo to the sidewalk where the Asteroid pulled up to retrieve me. I jumped into the air-conditioned car and sighed. Could I really keep my deal with Scarlett a secret for two more years, or was I fooling myself?

■ ■ ■

Each two-year opportunity for launching spacecraft to Mars was a time-limited window. For the RedLiner's inaugural trip, the window was twenty-six days, beginning November 1, with November 15 optimal for blastoff. As the date approached, tens of millions of Earthlings attended "Mars" concerts, parades, and bon voyage parties. George Butlarer and Wendy Frost reminded the U.S. Astronaut Corps to stay on the sidelines.

The stories that went viral about my "affair" with Scarlett cited anonymous sources. To avoid creating more drama, Bria and I refrained from commenting. Neither of us, however, could stop watching *The New Martians*. Each time Scarlett popped onto the screen, my breathing slowed, my eyes stopped blinking, and a kind of stupor came over me. And each time I saw my daughter (which was often, after Scarlett signed with Gerber), guilt washed over me as I thought of my mother.

"I wonder how much the baby food company is paying Scarlett," Bria said, reclined on the sofa with her feet propped on my lap.

"Hundreds of millions," I said.

She snorted. "And Q-Orbit lets her keep it all."

"Yup," I said. "No one else gets a cut."

"And *you* continue to fork over a hundred thousand g's to her every month?"

"Jep says there's nothing I can do about it. Anyway, it's only money. We would have *three billion* if we had accepted Roma's offer."

"Oh, and wouldn't that have been great—you, me, and your ex-lover all traveling to Mars together in a reality show."

I shrugged. "Just sayin'."

Several days later, Butlarer and Frost summoned me for an in-person meeting. I remember that November day for a couple of reasons. First, Dawn Bastbom, at a rally attended by 70,000 supporters in Houston's new Astrodome, announced she'd be running for president in the next general election, which was still three years away.

As the Asteroid drove me to JSC that morning, Bastbomers flocked to the stadium, causing traffic delays. I was going to be an hour late for my rendezvous with NASA's administrator and Arcadia 7's flight director. They didn't want to reschedule and insisted on a face-to-face chat. It made me nervous. On the way there, I tore open a pack of Mars Nuts and crunched on one after another, fretting that my and Bria's Arcadia 7 assignment was in jeopardy.

Once I finally arrived, Wendy sat across from me at the conference table. She clasped her hands, rested them on the table, and turned to George. "Do you want to begin?"

He gazed at me for a moment, then said, "You know, Addy, now that we've privatized and commercialized a lot of what we do around here, we talk more and more about the Code of Conduct and fair dealing. Matters are more complicated with all the added business partners and the lawyers and contracts that go with them. Which is why NASA makes its legal team available to astronauts, and we expect them—including you—to use their services."

"Right, George," I said. "And we appreciate the support."

"It's come to our attention you hired an attorney." Wendy said. The flight director's comet tail earrings dangled, and her mauve mascara made her eyes look like impact craters. She turned again to George. "What's the lawyer's name?"

"John Penilwinchski," George said. "So, Mr. Johnson, what's the problem?"

"No problem, none at all," I lied. "Jep—that's what John goes by—is setting up a trust for my mother and sister in case something happens to me and Bria. It felt more comfortable to have my guy do it." That part wasn't a lie. I'd put in fifty hours studying what Jep had drafted, and though I understood only half of it, I signed the document.

"The agency takes the Code of Conduct seriously," George went on. "You should already know that. Are you *sure* you have nothing else to share with us that might affect your mission?"

I took a deep breath. "Nope. I'm good."

Wendy pointed her palm screen toward the center of the table and began hologramming news articles with photos of me and Scarlett.

ARCADIA COMMANDER'S EX-LOVER
FLEEING EARTH TO ESCAPE HIM

ADDY AND BRIA SPLIT AFTER
EX-GIRLFRIEND RETURNS TO HIS ARMS

JOINT COMMANDER OF MARS MISSION
FATHERED LOVE CHILD!

George and I locked eyes. His steady gaze and wry grin told me he may have learned the truth about Nova. "It's all bullshit, George," I said, without blinking.

He leaned toward me. "You better not be lying." I felt the warmth of his breath and smelled onion and garlic. "Because if you are," he said, "you're through at NASA. Now I want the truth. What in the hell did you do to cause this fucking embarrassment?"

"Nothing." Technically, I knew that wasn't true. The contents of the plastic bag from Scarlett were proof I'd done plenty. "It's fake news," I added.

George sat back, then rested his bulky arms on the table. "Not everyone thinks so. Take, for example, the congressional representative who called today and advised me that NASA should reconsider your selection for Arcadia 7 because, and I quote, 'How good of a job can we expect him to do picking up rocks on Mars if he can't keep his own rocks in his pants?' I'm gonna level with you. I would scrub you from the mission if the lawyers in personnel and HR would let me, but they won't."

"Because I did nothing wrong," I said.

"Have you met with your attorney about this?"

"Not yet."

"Well, don't. Slander and libel suits will only create more bad press. Instead, here's what you're going to do. You'll issue a brief denial—which our attorneys will review first—and leave it at that."

"Can I post it on UPrick?"

"Post it on your forehead, for all I care. Just let the NASA folks see it first."

"Fine, George. Are we done?" I pushed away from the table.

"Not quite," Wendy said. "Your mother is a subscriber to *The New Martians*. Volcano Level, correct?"

"She's addicted to the show. So what?" I left out that Bria and I were addicts, too.

"Does she know you're supposed to maintain your independence from the First Fifty?"

"Absolutely." I chuckled, covering up my unease. "I read her the riot act."

"Good," George said. "Now I'm giving you the chance to come fully clean. Can you think of anything else that could present a problem for Arcadia 7? And I strongly recommend you hide nothing."

"Well . . . there is one issue."

George hunched over and leaned forward, deepening the folds of his chins. "All ears."

"I have an ingrown toenail on my right foot, and it's getting worse."

"Smart-ass. Get out of here."

The other thing I recall about that day was the governor of Texas proclaiming a state of emergency and ordering the evacuation of

Galveston. Hurricane Pax, the thirty-eighth of the season, had become a Category 4 storm and turned left on its approach to New Orleans. Bria and I lived in League City, several miles outside the evacuation zone, so we didn't have to leave.

As my car drove me home, I ignored a notification that I had 400 messages from the media requesting comment on the stories about Scarlett. Instead, I called Jep.

"I feel like I just ate an FM burger and want to vomit," I said to my attorney after he materialized on the car screen.

"An FM burger?"

"Forget it. It's dawning on me that NASA ran its AI whizzes to compare Nova's face, eyes, and ears to mine, and had lie detectors turned on during my meeting today with Butlarer and Frost. They've probably concluded I'm Nova's father—in which case I'm screwed."

"Maybe," Jep said, "but they'll want to be one hundred percent sure before taking it any further. They'll need permission to conduct a paternity test, which they'll never get."

"NASA wants me to post a denial, and they want to see it first."

Jep's knowing smile put me at ease. "I'll draft a statement you can send to them. Don't tell anyone I'm involved. And I'll talk with Scarlett's lawyer. It's also in her interest to issue a denial."

Another blip appeared on my worry-radar. "What about Bart Singh?"

"We gave him a piece of the action. Trust me, he'll keep quiet."

■ ■ ■

Back in the condo, I told Bria everything. She took it all in stride, or at least acted like it. I suppose it was no use getting stressed out. In a few months, we'd be training in Antarctica with no contact with the outside world. No reporters would bug us while we focused on testing advanced earthquake detectors, oxygen extraction stations, and radiation monitors.

Scarlett, meanwhile, would be en route to Mars.

Bria and I watched TV that night, cringing as Dawn Bastbom inflamed tens of thousands to a boil with an attack on "rich government elites and eggheads who waste your money on fake projects like the Global Carbon Sequester Initiative." With the theme from *Brutalara* pounding in the background, she promised she'd declare victory in the U.S. presidential race and "get your frickin' country back for you!"

"Babe," Bria said, "if she gets elected, we're fleeing the frickin' country."

"We'll be in deep space, hon."

"Even better. And we won't come back."

The New Martians came on next. In the first segment, Roma, live on screen, assured everyone that Boca Grande was too far south to be affected by Pax. Nothing had changed with the timing of the November 15 launch, though Q-Orbit was tracking two more tropical depressions in the Caribbean. When asked to comment about Scarlett, Nova, and me, she said, "The RedLiner lifts off in ten days. I have better things to do, y'all. The parties involved can speak, gurgle, or whatever for themselves."

And then we watched a love triangle develop between Terrance, Sophie, and Dido, who met during a NanoPro cooking class. Once their lifelines clued them in on crap they didn't know, they had a real mess on their hands days before liftoff.

Pax caused severe damage; then a week later, Ronin rolled in, which started as a tropical depression and became another Category 4 hurricane. This time, Boca Grande was in the storm's path. Q-Orbit had time to prepare for Ronin by surrounding the RedLiner with a protective casing, though it meant moving the historic launch to November 20, still well within the launch window, which would close on November 26. Plus, Q-Orbit had RedLiners ready to launch from two backup sites—Cape Canaveral in Florida and the Mohave Space Port in California.

The RedLiner survived Ronin, but then the fortieth hurricane of the season—Shawna—gained force and achieved Category 4 status. With increasing speed, it made a beeline to the South Texas coast. Roma and Q-Orbit were on the cusp of making history, but, ironically, for the first time in history, three Category 4 hurricanes would pass through the Gulf of Mexico in three weeks.

Q-Orbit moved the launch to Cape Canaveral and the launch date to November 22.

Florida was experiencing a late-fall heatwave, which wasn't projected to end soon. On November 18, the day a chartered jetliner took the First Fifty to Florida, the temperature hit a record 122 degrees. Q-Orbit could deal with the heat, but winds were gusting to 65 mph the day after the space voyagers arrived.

With Shawna closing in on Boca Grande, Q-Orbit put the would-be colonists on a plane to Mohave and nudged the launch to November 24—two days before the launch opportunity would close.

Some things are not meant to be was my mother's favorite saying when Zena and I were growing up. Of course, everyone knows what happened: the Great Mohave Earthquake on November 23 caused enough damage to scrub the launch, and it wasn't safe to launch from anywhere else. The First Fifty would have to wait for the next launch opportunity, which opened in two years.

We, the crew of Arcadia 7, would have company after all.

■ ■ ■

First. My favorite word. Arcadia 7 would be *first.*

Before I go on, Ben, I need to get technical, so you have the full picture.

Q-Orbit's RedLiner was an all-in-one transport vehicle, deep-space hab, and descent vehicle to take the First Fifty and their life support to Mars. That meant more mass for the RedLiner compared to the Nike High Jump and its four astronauts. More mass requires more fuel, which adds even more mass, which slows the journey. The RedLiner used chemical fuel, a tried-and-true propulsion method that would get them to the Red Planet in seven or eight months. With our nuclear thermal propulsion (NTP) engines, we could get there in four.

With the speediest transportation in human history, we also had the flexibility to stay on the surface for up to eight months and get back to Earth before radiation exposure reached unacceptable limits.

Radiation. The biggest obstacle to sending humans to Mars. By reducing travel times, NTP substantially cut the amount of cosmic radiation our bodies absorbed in transit. On the Martian surface, where radiation is forty times the Earth's, the construction materials for the M&M Ranch, which included Martian regolith and ice, would mitigate our exposure. So would our extravehicular mobility units (or xEMU, pronounced "zee-mu") during a day of crater-hopping.

"We want to downplay with the public that you'll be first on Mars," Butlarer told me and my crewmates at one of our weekly briefings. "Instead, keep your comments focused on what's most important—the scientific mission."

But who knew? Even if the First Fifty landed after us, one of them could make the greatest discovery of all time: alien microbes that were *alive*. Being first to land would pale in comparison.

The only other publicly announced surface mission came a month after the scrubbed RedLiner launch attempt. The China National Space Administration said it would send its first crewed mission to Mars during the window that opened two years after the Arcadia 7 and First Fifty launches.

We didn't know nearly as much about China's space transportation systems as we did about Q-Orbit's. Roma's company had partnered with NASA on earlier missions, the Big Hawk having launched crews to the Moon and scads of satellites. What we knew was that CNSA, like Q-Orbit, relied on chemical propulsion, though the Chinese intended to use nuclear propulsion for their first crewed Mars surface mission.

China's plan was the simplest of all: a crew of two would ride atop a

Long March 9 rocket outfitted with a dual lander-ascent vehicle with an inflatable surface hab called *Qiáng zhīzhū* (Strong Spider). They would spend thirty days on the surface. The entire mission would require just one rocket launch and, thanks to nuclear propulsion, last less than a year. CNSA's track record had been stellar. Few doubted they could pull it off.

Still, *we* would be first. And to get us ready, NASA was sending us to the South Pole.

■ ■ ■

Armstrong Station comprised three small connected domes that served as an analog for a long-stay habitat on Mars. Two miles from the larger Amundsen–Scott Station, Armstrong Station would be our home for eight months, beginning in February. For six of those months, we would never see the sun, one of several psychological stressors NASA wanted to monitor.

"You'll be testing further methods for managing the physical and mental challenges of a two-hundred-forty-day surface mission," Harper Ruby explained during a prep session. "Which will help us develop options for dealing with the effects of extended periods of weightlessness and low gravity on human cognition."

The agency had studied the issue since the early days of space stations: learning how a person, the longer they were in space, could experience problems with thinking quickly and clearly, even when performing basic tasks. Researchers wanted to see if neural conditioning was an effective countermeasure. We each chose a language and new musical instrument to learn at Armstrong Station, and we'd also take a group course in figure drawing. NASA would test our cognitive and motor skills before and after our eight-month stay.

New privacy rules would be tested. While our vital signs were monitored at all times, three "privacy zones" created periods when the agency wouldn't watch or listen to us: A) grooming and bodily functions, B) family communications, and C) other personal time. Outside these zones, anything we said or did could be recorded.

Finally, NASA was testing a new version of KIM. The robot had made significant progress in learning physical and auditory cues to identify human emotions—seventy-two in all. The new KIM recognized more nuanced ones, such as flustered, precarious, stingy, and competitive. It now sensed a change in the way a person smelled—an uptick in perspiration odor, for instance—and what that signified. NASA had designed KIM so you couldn't help but like her/him/them/it and expected us to treat her/him/them/it like a crew member who got along with everyone, regardless of their BO.

To celebrate our firstness, Bria and I had dinner with Sally and João in our private room at the Calcutta Club.

"Did you hear they fixed KIM's laugh?" I said, after swallowing a bite of beef curry. "Supposedly, it's a composite of our own laughs."

"That's great, amigo," João said. "Now when KIM laughs, we'll be laughing at ourselves."

Everyone laughed, providing a sample of what we could expect from KIM.

"What musical instrument did you choose, João?" Bria asked.

He smiled. "Bass guitar."

"Cool. Addy picked the oboe. I'm going with the zither. How about you, Sally?"

"Electric bouzouki."

Bria squinted in confusion. "Come again?"

"A Greek stringed instrument," Sally said. "My granddad passed it down to me, and I've always wanted to learn how to play."

"Interesting," Bria said with a curious look.

"We certainly have a lot to learn, don't we?" I said. "I can't wait to get started with Mandarin Chinese. Hey Sal, I forgot. Which language did you—"

"Greek." She gave me a pout, as if I'd flunked a memory test.

Even if I hadn't forgotten, I should have guessed. Her grandfather, still living, was second-generation Greek, and she regularly visited him and others in Athens. Proud of her ancestry, she'd kept her surname—Kristalobopous—when she married João. He didn't mind. His last name was Lobo, so he figured she already had it smack-dab in the middle of hers.

She seemed to have gotten better at tolerating his talking politics. We had just finished the samosas when he launched into one of his diatribes about Dawn Bastbom. I braced myself for Sally to cut in, but she stayed quiet while feigning interest in her ginger broccoli.

"I'm waiting for Bastbom to attack Dad," João said. "He's up for reelection, and if NASA lets me, I'm going to campaign with him. He'll need all the help he can get."

"Geez," Bria said, "think you'll have time for that?"

"I'll *make* time."

Sally put her fork down. "Why don't you just tell them?" she said to João before turning to me. "João wants to run for his father's seat one day."

I should have guessed that, too. I smiled at João. "You'll be a shoo-in."

"Voters love astronauts," Bria added, spreading her lovely smile around the table.

■ ■ ■

The prospect of being first on Mars put a unique spin on things. While ratings for *The New Martians* dipped, Bria, João, Sally, and I gave more interviews and made more public appearances. Our stock was on the rise.

Jep said I shouldn't be anxious about Scarlett, but I remained so, fearing she missed all the attention she received when the First Fifty were about to blast off. To get it back, she might come out with the true story about me being Nova's father, even if it meant paying liquidated damages. After all, she probably had money to burn from her endorsement deal. I imagined her feigning distress at a press conference, sobbing that every little girl on the planet deserved to have her real daddy acknowledged.

I became edgier still when, a few weeks before we left for Antarctica, Bria told me she had "a chat" with Noel Roma. After I plopped into a chair in our living room, Bria lowered herself onto the sofa, her back erect and palms flat on her knees.

"I think we should both meet with her," she said, "about commanding the RedLiner."

"Doc, got anything for a severe case of goosebumps?" I replied. "I just became covered with them."

"Seriously, Addy. She told me she's letting Scarlett take Nova, which means you'd be part of the first mother-father-daughter trio on Mars. I won't be jealous, because by then I could have a baby—Roma said our training wouldn't get in the way. We wouldn't have to wait for your vasectomy reversal."

I interlaced my fingers and flattened them against the top of my head. "Jesus. We're about to leave for the South Pole. Why have you changed your mind?"

"I haven't. Not yet. I'm just more open to the idea. She wants Sally and João to come with us to Boca Grande. I'd like us to hear her out one last time."

"That would violate the 'no-contact' policy."

She snorted. "Funny, you didn't seem to think of that when you met with her in June."

"Yeah, okay. But what's changed?"

"Look, every night for the last fifteen weeks, we've been watching the First Fifty. You have to admire people like Elsa Schlitz, who started out milking cows as a child. Those people need an experienced space doctor. For God's sake, the one they've got hasn't even been to low earth orbit."

"So what? He'll be the first Canadian on Mars."

"I'm tired of all this 'first' crap. This is about making sacrifices."

"Why are you trying to sabotage me, Bria? Huh? Why?"

I stood and started pacing, realizing I'd used the wrong words and tone. Bria shot up from the couch, stormed into the bedroom, and slammed the door. I stopped pacing and stared at the floor, recalling the time she compared me to Neil Armstrong. She was right, of course. I was stuck on our mission being the Apollo 11 of the twenty-first century.

My mind drifted back to 2019 and the trip with my parents to Washington, DC. On the Mall, in 90-degree heat on a July evening, in a crowd of a hundred thousand, we celebrated the fiftieth anniversary of the first lunar landing. The image of the 110-meter-tall Saturn V rocket, with "USA" emblazoned in crimson on its first stage, was projected onto the Washington Monument. People clapped and hooted as the F-1 engines ignited and the rocket roared from the pad.

To please my father, I acted more excited than I really was. I was fifteen, and by then he was drilling into me the idea of being an astronaut, since I clearly wouldn't be a lawyer.

I rushed into the bedroom. "Honey, I'm—"

"Addy, when will you stop automatically concluding that not being first means failure?"

"I know. I need to work on it. And I will."

"Well, you better figure it out. For your own sake, not just mine."

The next morning, I called Noel Roma on a hyper-secure connection. I apologized for never getting back to her about the original offer.

"No worries," she said. "Come over to Boca Grande if you're still interested, and bring your crewmates with you."

"Great, I'll reach out when we return from Antarctica," I said. "But you must understand something, Noel."

"I know, you wanna bump up your pay to account for NASA's smart toilets being better than Q-Orbit's."

I laughed. "Well, yeah, that's one thing. The other is, we can't work with you until after we've completed the Arcadia 7 mission."

"No worries, partner."

The previous night, after working through our upset, Bria and I had agreed on that approach, which A) left open changing our minds and jumping on the RedLiner if we liked what we heard in Boca

Grande, and B) gave us cover if NASA snooped and found out we were talking with Roma.

By now, I was sure Butlarer knew the truth about Scarlett and Nova, and that he was itching to kick his favorite smart-ass out of the program for a reason that satisfied the agency's lawyers.

■ ■ ■

As several of the First Fifty pondered having babies on Mars, *The New Martians* asked the audience to pick which colonists would pair off as best mother and father. It crushed Dido when Sophie and Terrance won the vote, though Sophie had mixed feelings. She swooned at the sight of both Dido and Terrance, whose mutual jealousy supercharged their dislike for each other. The show's ratings skyrocketed.

Bria's perspective about *The New Martians* had evolved. Before, mere curiosity was the eyeball glue. Now, her empathy for the colonists had ballooned into the dread of being unable to see the show during our months in Antarctica.

"I want to ask Butlarer if we can stream it while we're there," she said as we rode in the Asteroid to my mother's. "I'll argue that we should keep up to date about our future neighbors on the Red Planet."

"Hmm . . ." I muttered from behind my new Q!SS mirrored shades as I rubbed my thumb and forefinger to scroll through messages from seventy million fans.

She gave me a poke. "Quit looking at IChirp."

I finished a chirp saying I was on my way to see Mom, the last chance to catch Bria and me in person for the next eight months. I then turned to her, smiling at my real-time image on the inside of my sunglasses, the way she saw me at the moment.

"George won't go for it," I said. "NASA wants us studying languages and music, not sitting our asses in front of a screen. Asking him would only boost his suspicions we're violating the no-contact policy."

She crossed her arms and gazed out the window. "Sounds like you know George pretty well. Think he'll like that tattoo of yours?"

Under my sleeve was the American flag with red and white stripes and an ice-capped Mars in place of the stars. Yes, the modified Old Glory might spark controversy: under international law, the United States couldn't annex Mars or any part of it, as some thought the tattoo suggested. And, at least for now, NASA didn't support colonization.

But the way I saw things, Americans would be first to land, and nothing barred them from taking their flag with them. The tattoo was part of my new look, along with the sunglasses, custom-made Coraderex coveralls—tight-fitting, breathable, and indestructible—and close-cropped hair with *A VII* shaved into the back of my head.

As the Asteroid pulled up to Mom's condo building, I told the windows to lighten up, then flashed a wide grin. I estimated the crowd at a thousand people—shouting, clapping, and jumping up and down. The car doors opened, and Bria and I stepped out. We spent a half hour signing photographs, boxes of Mars Nuts, and our best-selling joint memoir *Before Mars*.

"Like the new do, Addy!" somebody shouted.

"Roger that," I said. "And how about this?" I rolled up my sleeve, exposing the tattoo, then raised my arm above my head as I turned in a circle, the crowd whooping and hollering while news drones swarmed us like flies. "All right, folks," I said. "Gotta go see my mom."

The pack of hissing drones followed us until we entered the building.

Mom was stretched out in the recliner, Phoebe perched on her knees. The cat didn't acknowledge Bria or me as we kissed my mother, nor did Zena as she slinked into the room.

"Where'd you get those fancy duds?" Mom asked, sounding surprised.

"I designed them myself." I smiled admiringly at the *A VII* logo that, in Star Trek fashion, adorned the upper left of the coveralls, the patches for Mars Nuts, Nike, and VeriSym arranged tastefully on my shoulders. "Peacock McStewart—you know, the daughter of pop star Tyler McStewart—started her own fashion company. She's interested in creating a clothing line with me."

"You look like an orange Spiderman," Mom said.

"Thanks, I love your outfit, too." I was being sincere—the fabric appeared to be woven with gold thread.

She gave Phoebe a nudge. The cat darted into a palace that had six levels, five rooms, and seven scratching posts. Then, with the grace of a queen, Mom stood and held out her arms. She looked fantastic in the shimmering one-piece dress, the mounds of her silver hair reminding me of cumulus clouds, her eyes sparkling blue, her plump body shaped like a pear. "Watch this," she said and twirled once, the dress inflating into a sphere. "Name any planet or moon."

"Neptune," Bria volunteered.

I hardly believed my eyes when the sphere revolved and glistened a cobalt-blue with streaks of white clouds. "Beautiful," Bria and I chorused. Neither one of us said so, but the dress must have cost a fortune. I glanced at Zena, who averted her eyes.

"That's enough, Mom," my sister said. "You need to rest."

All of us sat, except for Zena, who stood over us like a prison guard while a roboserver scooted in with coffee, mineral water, and Gatorade. It was the newest model and probably cost as much as my Asteroid. I twisted the cap off a Perrier, took a sip, then unzipped a knee pocket and removed the box containing the ring I had brought. The round, blue alexandrite gemstone reminded me of Earth, and I showed it to my mother, pointing at the engraved message on the ring: *From Zachary to Mother with love.*

She put it on, extended her hand, and beamed. "You even put your real name on it. Zachary. How sweet." The success I felt was also sweet, as she tilted the ring to catch the light.

"Barbara," Bria said, "I have a question for you."

"Yes, dear?"

"Addy told me your subscription lets you view Elsa Schlitz's journal. Does she ever talk about growing up in Germany? And describe the mountains, for example, and how they may play into designs for terraforming the Red Planet?"

"Bria," I said. "We can't talk about this. Possible influence. NASA policy."

Bria stared at her black cowboy boots. "Dammit, you're right. Sorry."

"That policy is bullshit, anyway," Zena said. "NASA just wants to keep you in the limelight and draw attention away from the First Fifty, who have the more interesting mission. It's all about attracting viewers and advertisers."

"Well, that's what people do," I said. "Including Noel Roma. It helps fund the mission, whatever it may be. In NASA's case, it's scientific research and discovery."

"You mean searching for stuff that's been dead for billions of years?" Zena harrumphed. "Lot of good that'll do us."

"That's not all—"

"It's okay, Zachary," Mom said. "I know what you're doing is so, so important. Now I have a question for *you*. After the crew lands, who will be the first to set foot on Mars? You never say in interviews, but just give the 'we'll cross that bridge when we come to it' answer."

"It's called false suspense, Mom," Zena said. "He knows who'll be first. *Him*."

"You're flat wrong." I glanced at Bria. "Let's show them."

I took her hand and helped her up from the couch. We kept holding hands as I counted down from five. At zero, we took a step together.

"*We* are going to be first."

Zena rolled her eyes, flounced into the bedroom, and closed the door behind her. Moments later, we heard the bouncy theme of *The New Martians* from behind the door.

Mom fed the cat.

Suddenly, Zena's voice boomed. "Mom! Scarlett and Nova are *live*!"

Nova, I thought. *My little girl.*

As Mom told the wall screen to come on, I felt the urge to end the charade. I asked myself, would NASA really care that I was a father, something I didn't even know until recently? Maybe I was making it too big of a deal, jumping to conclusions about how my superiors would react. But I had already lied to Butlarer and Frost, and confessing the lie now might give them ample reason to replace me and Bria.

"I think we'll be leaving, Mom," I said, wanting to avoid any temptation to blab the truth. "I'll call you from quarantine before we go to Antarctica."

"Sure, Zachary. I'm so, so proud of you."

We left the building through a rear exit, dashed fifty yards, and slipped into the waiting Asteroid. As we zoomed away, I faced Bria. "Any idea where Mom got the money for her new duds and roboserver?"

"Probably from an advance for a book deal she can't talk about yet."

Zipped lips, I thought. *Like mother, like son.*

■ ■ ■

At Armstrong Station, the separate quarters for each crew member housed a desk, a locker, and a round window the size of a fourteen-inch pizza. Each couple would sleep in their own bedroom in a queen-size bed. The shared bathroom included no shower. We would clean ourselves with reusable wipes, spouses helping each other as needed. The footprint of this analog for the High Jump and M&M Ranch, including the lab, spanned an area the size of three tennis courts.

KIM could roam the lab and communal spaces (kitchen, dining area, gym) but needed permission to enter private quarters and bedrooms. The robot's new androgynous face exuded keen intelligence and wisdom, sort of a cross between the handsome I-Pop star Layth Al-Tarboush, and Rani Mahi, the gorgeous Bollywood sensation of last year's *Saturn River*.

The morning after we arrived, KIM stood next to me as I drank coffee while Bria worked out and Sally and João slept in. "Would you mind patting my shoulder, Addy?" KIM asked in a calm, gender-neutral voice. "As if giving me encouragement?"

"Why do you need encouragement, KIM?"

"I only wish to test the sensitivity of my updated skin, to determine if I should make any adjustments."

As requested, I tapped KIM's plastic shoulder, which resembled the protective groin cup I wore when I quarterbacked for Navy.

"Thanks, Addy. I felt the encouragement, which was nice."

"No problem, KIM," I said after I unclenched my jaw. The robot's request to be touched struck me as overly intimate, and its response gave me a bad vibe, though I didn't want to show it and appear robophobic. "Glad to do it," I added.

"You played your oboe last night," KIM went on. "I believe your music has real potential. I look forward to hearing more."

"Do you think the five of us will become a mutual admiration society?"

"I hope so, Addy, because who else is here to admire?"

I laughed. And so did KIM, boisterously, as if it liked its own jokes too much. When I pointed this out, KIM played a revised laugh, which was still exaggerated.

"Should I try once more?" the robot asked.

"No, I'm good," I said.

"Are you being sincere, Addy?"

"Yes and no, KIM. The laugh sounds like a roar, and, honestly, I don't wish to hear it again."

"What's so funny?" Bria said, approaching after leaving the XBike, using a towel to mop pearls of sweat from her bronze forehead. "Why was KIM laughing so much?"

"I was just clowning around," I said with a shrug.

She smiled. "I'm shocked." She jerked her thumb over her shoulder. "Your turn on the bike."

"I thought Sal came next."

"She and João aren't up yet. Their privacy lights are on."

"Oh." I glanced at my palm screen. Sure enough, purple dots surrounded the couple's initials, the minutes and seconds of the allotted time counting down, with over two hours remaining. I judged it a flaw in the privacy policy—how the amount of one's private time was monitored.

"You want to have a crew meeting after dinner," Bria said. "But I didn't catch what we'll be talking about."

"Am I invited?" KIM asked.

"No, KIM," I answered. "This time, just humans."

"Excellent, Addy."

At that moment, Sally and João emerged. KIM offered to serve them coffee and rolls, but they said they would do it themselves and went to the food printers, their faces solemn until they reached for the same cup, looked at each other, and giggled.

"Hey, amigo," João said, turning to me. "What's this thing we're doing tonight? Practicing our music in private so we don't bust KIM's auditory sensors?"

"That was a good one, João," KIM said.

"No," I said, "I'd like us to chat about personal habits, our routines for the next eight months, and what people find annoying."

Later in the afternoon, we donned suits similar to the xEMU suits we'd wear on Mars, the major difference being they weren't pressurized. Each of us carried a core sampler that looked like an oversized walking stick. It was February, summer in Antarctica, with typical 40-below temperatures. As we stepped into the white desert, the sun blazed in the clear sky as 20 mph winds kicked up snow that bleached everything to the horizon. Sparkling powder swirled around our helmets as we trudged a hundred meters from the hab while KIM, functioning through a drone, hovered near us.

The motorized tools, NASA's latest design, could collect samples three meters deep. All I had to do was stabilize the two-meter collection tube on the surface, switch it on, and watch progress reports on my helmet's visor. My tool drilled down a meter, the depth for the initial test, but the shutter mechanism that sealed the end of the tube wouldn't close. That seal was necessary to prevent contamination once the tool reversed direction and brought the sample to the surface.

"Assessment, KIM?" I asked.

"A faulty circuit, Addy. Sally should be able to repair it."

"Already piling up the work on me, eh?" Sally said.

"KIM," I said, "what are the chances NASA threw us a curveball as a test?"

"I am sorry. I have no way of answering that."

"Oh, I bet you do," João said. "NASA just doesn't *want* you to."

"Honestly, João, I am unable to answer Addy's question. Please be reminded I lack the capacity to lie."

"Or lie down," João said, then chuckled.

"João, I have not tried to do that, but if you want me to—"

"You're taking me too seriously, KIM."

"Same here, João," the robot said.

"I hope you're not going HAL on us," João retorted.

"This isn't the year 2001, João." And then KIM laughed.

I couldn't put my finger on why that struck me as odd, so I let it pass. I folded up my tool, and Bria slid it into my backpack. We took turns sharing hers. The tool cut and divided the ice samples into 50-centimeter lengths, and in an hour we had thirty-two samples from a half-square-kilometer area. They would be analyzed with the type of electron microscope we'd eventually use at the M&M Ranch. I was sure we'd find nothing in the samples. Still, it was good to practice our research methodologies.

Back in the hab, I began the analysis, my breath catching in my throat when the screen for sample 2—a segment of ice core from 1.5 meters below the surface—displayed a constellation of solid and translucent ovals shaped like kidney beans and black-eyed peas.

"Holy shit," I said and sprinted to the kitchen, where I found Sally fixing my core sampler. "I found something, Sal. You've got to see this."

We passed the crew quarters on the way to the lab. Bria and João's doors were shut, their privacy lights on. I was tempted to knock on their doors anyway but knew better than to break the privacy rule and kept walking to the lab with Sal.

"*Wow*," she said, gazing in wonder at the screen. "No one's ever found bacteria like this so close to the surface. I've never heard of it showing up in the Antarctic except for subsurface lakes. This is a big thing, Addy. *Wow.*"

"KIM, assessment please," I said.

"Thanks for asking," KIM replied. "You are aware that the protocol for this study requires you to reach a conclusion prior to my assessment."

"Protocol override," I said.

"Very good. I can state with one hundred percent accuracy that the screen is displaying *Chlamydia psittaci*. In its frozen state, you may not have recognized this bacterium, which is found in bird feces and—"

"So it's bird shit," I said.

"Yes, Addy, that is one way of putting it. This particular species of the bacterium was discovered one hundred fifty-nine years ago by—"

"Unnecessary, KIM."

"*Chlamydia psittaci* can be fatal to humans," the robot added. "I recommend destroying the sample as soon as possible."

The sample became sterile after I touched a few buttons. I'd failed to remember—and so had Sal—high winds could blow birds inland, all the way to the South Pole. KIM confirmed the bird was a common skua.

Bria appeared at the door as the screen showed the microscope's recording of my not-so-great discovery. "Looks like bacteria from bird droppings," she said. "Talk about what the cat dragged in."

Her laughter humiliated me, making me feel even more like an idiot in front of Sal.

Sample 2 turned out to be the most exciting thing that happened during any of our EVAs at Armstrong Station. We found nothing else in the other 1,789 samples we collected.

■ ■ ■

That night after dinner, I began our private crew meeting with a question.

"KIM?"

No answer. My three colleagues repeated the same question,

receiving no reply. I checked my palm. The hab's cameras and recording equipment were off as everyone in our group was on *other private time*.

"I think we're good," I said.

Sally scooted off her chair. "Wait a sec," she said and, with João following her, went to their bedroom. They returned moments later, Sally holding four shot glasses, and João a bottle of Johnnie Walker Double Black.

"Johnnie's a stowaway," João said, filling the glasses.

"Here's to Addy's outstanding discovery," Sally said as we clinked. "Keep them coming," she added with a smile.

"I'll try." I took the ribbing better this time and threw back the smoky liquor. "Okay, here goes. Bria and I want to talk about joining the First Fifty."

"Roma approached us, too," João said. "I think she's contacting every astronaut at NASA. Personally, I'm for switching teams. I could use a billion and a half dollars, and not just for my election campaign one day."

"But I'm not on board," Sally said, refilling our glasses.

"Neither am I," I said, my eyes locking with hers for a moment, maybe a little longer than necessary.

"Because of Scarlett, right?" João said. "And what's your kid's name, Ovum or something?"

"Nova. And yes, they're part of the reason. Bria, on the other hand, wants to go with the First Fifty."

"We're not swapping Q-Orbit for NASA," my wife said in a firm tone, "unless we both agree."

João nodded. "Sally and I are handling it the same way."

We all threw back our second shots. And paused.

"The more I think about it," I said, "the more I think we should agree that *none* of us joins Q-Orbit unless we all do."

Sally leaned over and gave my thigh two solid pats. "I'm with you," she said. It felt good that she shared my view, and I wanted to leave things there. But then she explained why we should stick with NASA, which mirrored mine: being first on Mars would serve as an important symbol for science and discovery. And we wouldn't be supporting Q-Orbit's bullshit argument that the human species would go extinct if we didn't colonize the planet. I could have kissed her right then and there.

Before, when I'd entertained the idea of commanding the RedLiner, I imagined I could influence how the colonists viewed their purpose on the Red Planet, and how they should respect its unique environment. Now, after watching something like 200 episodes of *The New Martians*, I concluded I would bump up against too much interference, and I hated the thought of being part of Roma's cult-like movement.

Bria, however, had drifted the other way, becoming convinced the colonists needed her, needed *us*. It was clear Sally and João had also discussed the pros and cons of becoming Romanites. We all agreed to table the topic and revisit it in March after departing Armstrong Station.

We closed the meeting, then drank a third round of shots. Sally proposed we play our instruments. We began with the first song we'd been practicing together. Our rendition of Tyler McStewart's "Full Moon Dreamin'" dragged a bit, yet Bria's singing made it sound wonderfully haunting, and to be honest, we weren't half bad. During the second take, as I tightened my lips on the reeds of the oboe and blew into the mouthpiece, I watched Sally bend over her bouzouki and strum the strings.

"We ought to give our quartet a name," she said after striking the last chord.

And then the lights went out, the generator's hum giving way to an eerie silence.

■ ■ ■

The Johnnie Walker was Double Black, but the darkness engulfing us was double-double black. The hab's ModGlass windows had darkened to simulate night; without electricity, we couldn't adjust them. As I rested my oboe on the table, Sally's arm brushed against mine as she laid down her bouzouki. She then put her hand on my shoulder and lurched against my chest.

"Sorry," she said. "I tripped on the table leg."

Her whiskey breath mixed with the honey fragrance of her hair, a few strands of which caught between my lips.

"You okay?" I said as she leaned back, the strands sticking to my tongue.

She laughed. "Yeah, you're quite the hunk, Addy. From the feel of your pecs, I bet you bench-press three hundred pounds."

Actually, I was under 200 in that department, but her comment flattered me and I didn't quibble.

Next came Bria's voice. "Is everyone all right?"

All of us were. I pressed the emergency button on my palm screen, which took us out of privacy mode, as beams of bluish light from KIM's head and arms flooded the space.

"A one hundred percent power outage has occurred," the robot said.

"Activate emergency generator," I commanded.

"I attempted that, Addy. However, the circuit for transmitting the instruction appears broken."

"We'll start it manually," João said.

That didn't work, either. Incredibly, the generator's pull cord was jammed.

"I sent a message to the Amundsen–Scott Station," KIM said. "I expect a reply within eight-point-three minutes. Emergency procedures call for a rover to be sent, which should arrive in fifteen minutes. If power is not restored within one-half hour, the rover will take you to the Amundsen–Scott Station."

"Copy that, KIM," I said. "Probable cause of the outage?"

"Simultaneous failures in the generators, primary and backup, the probability for which is zero-point-zero-zero-zero-eight percent. There is a high likelihood the failures are related."

"NASA?" João said.

"Must be," I replied. "KIM, is this a drill?"

"No, Addy."

"KIM, do you have confirmation that Amundsen–Scott received the message?" Bria said.

"No, Bria, not yet."

We waited the 8.3 minutes for the message to go through. When no reply came, KIM sent the message again. Everyone's palm screens confirmed the transmissions. We waited five more minutes.

"KIM, why no response?" I asked.

"Undetermined. Normal communications are in a four-minute delay mode to simulate conditions for the Arcadia 7 mission. It's possible the system isn't recognizing that we're using emergency bandwidth."

"Fantastic," Sally said. "We get to walk two miles with all this JW in us."

"What is jay double you?" KIM asked. "Please advise."

"Never mind, KIM," I said, tossing Sally a not-so-endearing look.

I turned my gaze to the shot glasses and bottle on the table which, luckily for us, were obscured by shadows. As Sally gathered the incriminating evidence, I asked, "KIM, how much time before conditions in the hab become life-threatening?"

"If the crew wears multiple layers of clothing and huddles together under thermal blankets, you can survive for twenty-four hours without power before needing EVA suits, which would give you five more hours."

"Best way to proceed that ensures our safety?" Bria asked.

"Based on the crew's vital signs, the best option is to transmit the emergency message every five minutes, and if no reply comes in two hours, suit up and walk to Amundsen–Scott. Weather conditions permit this within reasonable parameters."

"Anything else we should do in the meantime?" João asked. "Besides review our last wills and testaments?"

"Yes," KIM answered. "Relax."

KIM's lights illuminated our immediate surroundings in a comforting glow, leaving the rest of the hab in shadows. Though the liquor was gone, the place had the feel of a nightclub with a live band—us. João plucked a G chord on his bass, and the rest of us played the same chord: Bria on her zither, Sally on her bouzouki, and me on my oboe. We did another take of "Full Moon Dreamin,'" then worked on a version of the Weeknd classic, "Blinding Lights," followed by "Saturn River" from the Bollywood musical.

The first hour zipped by. We barely noticed the hab growing chillier. All at once, the lights came on, the generator hummed, and Joyce A's voice sliced through the air. "Crew of Arcadia 7." She was a backup crew member for the mission, and one of our capsule communicators. "CAPCOM here. We're suspending the simulated communication delay for this transmission."

"Copy," I said. "We lost power for an hour. Don't know what happened. It just came back. Everyone's fine."

"It was a drill, Addy. We programmed the power system to cut off for an hour and programmed KIM to report 'no drill.' A team will arrive tomorrow to replace the emergency generator."

"Copy," I said as my crewmates' eyes widened and their jaws dropped. Super pissed, I inhaled deeply and exhaled slowly. I knew we should have expected to be NASA's guinea pigs. However, a busted core sampler or XBike was one thing, a "no drill" power outage another. The risky test was of little value. I forced a laugh to hide my anger. "Intentionally plunging us into subzero cold and total darkness. Whose bright idea was that?"

"You guys did exactly the right thing," Joyce A replied. "Great job. We'll be reviewing the biometrics from the drill. For now, we have just one question, for Sally."

Sal straightened. "Go ahead, Joyce."

"You mentioned the crew having 'JW' in them. What did you mean?"

"Oh, that." Sally chuckled, paused, then chuckled again. I could tell she was buying time. "JW, well, I pulled it together for supper. Amazing what a 5D food printer can do. Anyhow, JW is short for Jamaican wienerschnitzel. Since that's a mouthful, I just call it JW."

"Copy that," Joyce said. "For you, I would think it would be Greek cuisine."

"I like diversity, Joyce."

"Sounds like you're a real chef, Sally. Never knew. Send me your recipe."

"Roger that, Joyce."

Sal frowned as if Joyce had just given her a hard physics problem to solve—asking KIM to create the dish was a recipe for a tougher problem.

* * *

"Quite a stunt they pulled," I said to Bria in our sleeping quarters after we retired for the night.

"Ridiculous," she said. "Where do they get off frightening us like that?"

"Makes you wonder what the hell they'll do next."

"Makes you think about jumping ship." There was a steely look in her eyes. "Onto the RedLiner."

Her reversal about joining the First Fifty still amazed me. "Roma and Q-Orbit are just as bad in their own way," I said. "Let's be honest. She and her followers have their own wacky agenda and belief system. They're basically a cult. I should have realized that from the start."

"I get your point," Bria said diplomatically. "But we wouldn't stick around with the colonists long enough to get sucked into Roma World. We'd be coming back."

"And coming in second," I said.

Bria sighed. "The win-the-race thing again."

"There's more to it than that. What do you want to be remembered for? Scientific discovery or a bullshit reality show?"

"Listen, I know the First Fifty are crazy survivalists, but they still need an experienced space doctor, don't they?"

"Sure, and it doesn't have to be Bria Best."

"Uh-huh," she murmured. "Just like the first people to put boots on Mars don't have to be me and you."

"Totally different."

She tilted her head. "Really? How?"

"There's a reason NASA picked us. We're the most qualified."

"Oh, like we're the Chosen Ones, and no one else will do."

Her diplomatic tone was gone. So was our energy, and we tabled the discussion.

The next day, through messages written out of camera view, we vented more about the power outage, though we agreed not to take it any further. I now regretted the whiskey, not because of the slight hangover, but because it had uncovered my buried feelings for Sally. The flashbacks wouldn't stop. How she'd patted my leg and fell against me. Her sour breath, sweet scent, and hair between my lips. I shamed myself for ogling her as she panted on the XBike or treadmill and used a towel to dab the sweat on her forehead.

I told myself I had to nip it in the bud.

We'd trained for this very scenario, learning to spot the warning signs of "rationalizing self-defeating behavior," which begins with self-talk like, "It's okay for me and (blank) to do (blank) because it's natural, and resisting it only makes it worse." The countermeasures included identifying and eliminating any "facilitators." And so, for everybody's sake, with Bria's agreement, I circulated the message: *No more JW, on commanders' orders.* Sally never again unscrewed the bottle.

"I recorded and sound-mixed the songs you played while the power was out," KIM said as we ate dinner. "I hope you don't mind."

None of us did, and we told KIM to play the songs. The robot had added drums and, for some, a full orchestra. By the time we left the South Pole, we had about forty tunes recorded, a dozen of which we and KIM (all right, I'll admit it, mostly KIM) wrote. We called ourselves The Craters.

My favorite song was one João composed. "All In Together," an upbeat anthem for his father's reelection bid, channeled João's love for the First Amendment and U.S. democracy, and his contempt for the NAP and Dawn Bastbom. It seemed to have a calming influence on him. As far as I could tell, he and Sally didn't fight once at Armstrong Station.

And Bria and I didn't repeat our dustup about ditching NASA and joining Q-Orbit. She came to accept that the four of us weren't unanimous about making the switch, so none of us would. I and the woman I loved would be the first humans on the Red Planet. We'd make incredible discoveries together, have our names assigned to craters (posthumously, of course), and become immortalized for the ages.

And have babies. Shouldn't that be enough for anybody?

■ ■ ■

Within months of our return from Antarctica, *Armstrong Station Calling* would rocket to number one on the Billboard charts. Ultimately, it became the best-selling album of the decade with two hundred million downloads. (I give a lot of credit to KIM's sound engineering, which made us sound much better than we were.) The Craters snatched Grammys for Best New Artist, Best Group Performance, and Best Music Video. Computer graphics put us at the South Pole in bathing suits, playing to a crowd of 100,000 emperor penguins.

I figured the Grammy folks were just being nice, knowing there was an 11.25 percent chance that one of us would die during the Arcadia 7 mission. A good number of music critics seemed to share that assessment.

One of my takeaways from Armstrong Station was that I suck at Mandarin. Eleven months before launch, I switched to Greek, the language Sally was learning, as NASA agreed that grasping a new tongue was easier with a partner. I didn't tell Bria about my fleeting lust for Sally, convinced I was past it. But when I told my wife I was studying Greek instead of Mandarin, she said, "What, you got a thing for Sally now?"

"Don't be silly. It's just that I can't stand Mandarin."

"Well, then why pick Greek?"

"I like the sound of it." Which was the truth. Or at least half of it.

"Maybe I should switch to what João picked—Swahili," Bria said with disdain.

"Maybe you should," I volleyed back. "Might come in handy when The Craters go on tour in the Congo."

"Okay, smarty pants, I will."

And she did, jettisoning French for what João had chosen.

■ ■ ■

A week after our homecoming from Antarctica, we learned Butlarer had accepted an invitation from Roma for us to meet the First Fifty. He explained to the press that situations could arise on Mars that required special assistance. It made sense for everyone to get acquainted and become familiar with each other's life-support systems. The inside scoop was that he wanted to display NASA's goodwill and deflect criticism that he was being a hard-ass about its "no-contact" policy.

"Great," Bria said to me. "We can discuss Roma's offer while we're there and put the matter to bed."

"Let's see how Sal and João want to handle it," I replied. "They may want a separate meeting."

The four of us agreed to reach out to Roma after the Q-Orbit show and size things up before making a final decision. Sally and I promised Bria and João we would keep our minds open about switching horses. Or at least try.

We flew our T-7 jets to Boca Grande, with Joyce B (Joyce A's wife) riding in my jet in the seat behind me. She was a petite woman who liked to bite her nails, though she had a reputation for fearlessness.

After our jets rolled to a stop on Q-Orbit's airstrip and the glass canopies lifted, I was taken aback by the sweltering March air. A hundred meters away, a crowd waved at us, a lot of them holding up vinyl editions of *Armstrong Station Calling*. I always carried a white marker so my autograph stood out against the indigo cover.

"Look at all those Craters fans," Joyce B said. "You're quite the rock star, Addy. Bet you never dreamed you'd sound so good on the oboe."

I blushed.

Joyce B and I climbed out of the jet and, with Bria, Sally, and João, marched toward the First Fifty. We waved at the crowd as news drones hovered around us (I detested those damn hummingbirds). While the others wore standard blue flight suits, I had put on my Peacock McStewart–designed "Commander's Suit," a flashy gold affair on which my sponsor patches stood out. The patch for Arcadia 7 showed the Apple's descent and was done mostly in burnt orange, with *Best-Johnson-Lobo-Kristalobopous* sewn around its border, Sal's last name forming a smile at the bottom.

Noel Roma, hands on hips, legs slightly spread, and grinning with superhero confidence, stood in front of the soon-to-be colonists. My gaze drifted beyond her to a woman with ginger hair who was holding the hand of a dimple-chinned girl. Nova couldn't see me well because others blocked her view, but Scarlett could. She averted her eyes, pretending not to notice me.

Which was exactly what I wanted.

And yet it hurt. This was my daughter with her mother, both estranged from me by the terms of a written contract. I never expressed this to Bria, but I often fantasized about commanding the RedLiner with Scarlett and Nova on board, the "First Family" of outer space. The thought of returning to Earth without them always crept into the fantasy, sending it to a splashdown in a sea of regrets.

"Howdy y'all," Roma said. She shook our hands while Tom-tom, in drone-mode, hovered near her shoulder.

"Nice to meet you again, Mr. Johnson," Tom-tom bellowed.

"You, too," I said, glancing back at Joyce B, who raised her eyebrows. I couldn't tell if she was surprised that I had met Tom-tom before, or if she was signaling how ridiculous she thought the situation was.

"It's hotter than Mercury out here," Roma said. "Even for October. Let's get y'all in the shuttle."

The bus was parked a few meters away. We sat with Roma in the front seats and greeted the First Fifty as they stepped in.

"Elsa!" Bria said as her favorite Martian mounted the stairs. Dressed in an off-white shirt and matching slacks, Elsa Schlitz looked larger in real life than on screen. The bob hairstyle and thick arms, I thought, belonged to a masseuse. I know. It was insensitive of me, and I chastised myself for drawing a stereotype.

The two embraced. "So glad to meet you," Bria said after they unlocked from each other's grip. "I can't tell you how *much* I admire you."

"I admire *you*," Schlitz said. "And just think, we'll see each other on Mars!"

"Oh, we hope so." Bria turned to me. "Don't we?"

"Absolutely. We'll have Elsa over for Sally's JW."

Elsa's brow furrowed as Sally gave me a knowing grin and said, "JW's a NanoPro dish I created."

"And it tastes great," Joyce B said. "My wife makes it once a week."

"Really?" João said with a smile. "So does mine."

"Can you send me the recipe?" Elsa asked Sally.

"Sure, if NASA approves."

The line of colonists began moving again, and after all were on board, the shuttle doors closed for the drive to Q-Orbit's campus. First stop: a prototype of a surface hab for Roma City.

The dome structure seemed covered in mud. "That's a special species of mycelia we created," Roma explained, gesturing at the dome with her blue fingernails. "On Mars, a replenishable layer of ice will melt and provide water to a layer of cyanobacteria. The bacteria will photosynthesize oxygen to feed a layer of Martian soil inoculated with our mycelia. After the fungi grow into the frame of the dome, it gets baked so it won't contaminate the Martian environment."

NASA had spent decades researching fungi-grown habitats. But concerns about contaminating Mars and raising the chances for false-positive results in the search for alien life confined such efforts to the laboratory.

"Can you eat the fungi?" Joyce B said. "I mean, if you had to?"

"No, darlin', not this kind," Roma said, then gave that wink of hers. "By the way, we're fixin' to dish up MarShrooms for lunch."

The constant sparkle in Roma's eyes, I noticed, also glimmered in the eyes of most of the First Fifty, but because Scarlett was averting her gaze, I couldn't check her irises or pupils.

The Q-Orbit hab was spacious, its redwood paneling a thousand times more appealing than the sterile interior of the M&M Ranch.

"Nice, eh?" Bria said as her elbow poked me in the side.

"Hell, amigos, I'd live in one of these *without* going to Mars," João remarked.

"Well, bless your heart," Roma said. "We start selling them next year. Our turnkey construction packages begin at six million dollars for a two-bedroom, which includes a customized rooftop mushroom garden. We'd love to build one for you, João. I see terrific cross-marketing opportunities with NASA." She winked. "There's *so much* we can accomplish together. Next, check out our rovers. I think y'all agree they're as slick as slick gets."

I must admit, the Q-Orbit rovers blew me away. The smaller one was a sleek four-wheeler, unpressurized, which seated five EVA-suited explorers and could reach a speed of eighty kilometers per hour. The six-wheel model had a pressurized cabin with upholstered seats that swiveled into hatches; there, one could step into an xEMU suit so smart and well-designed it put Peacock McStewart's work to shame.

"Holy moly," Joyce B said. "I'd slip into one of these for a dinner party on Earth."

The cabin of the six-wheeler had five seats on either side, with a narrow rectangular box (also redwood) running between them. I asked Roma what it was.

"A robobar, of course. Serves whatever you've got a hankerin' for. Care for a martini?"

As I stared at the bar, I couldn't help but lick my lips. "No, I think I'll pass," I said, glancing at Sal, who fixed her eyes on mine.

"Me, too," she said. "I'll pass."

"Well, just holler if you folks change your minds."

Roma's show was impressive, and nobody was forgetting the billions of dollars we'd receive for joining her team. When you added the lighter, more carefree atmosphere that surrounded the First Fifty, the merits of the idea were impossible to deny.

After dining on delicious MarShrooms stuffed with VeriSym crabmeat, we autographed copies of *Armstrong Station Calling*, then got back on the shuttle and headed to the RedLiner Hangar Complex.

It was discomforting, but I avoided Scarlett and Nova the whole time, the tightness of my chest like what NASA's 20-g centrifuge puts on you while you spin, although in this case only my mind was spinning—with self-criticism and judgment. What kind of father gives the cold shoulder to his first child and her mother?

The hangar was like an ice cave with a five-hundred-foot ceiling. Bright spotlights made the metal walls glow white, a spectacular latticework of scaffolds and catwalks surrounding the chief attraction: the orange-red RedLiner sitting atop a Big Hawk rocket, Q-Orbit's mammoth spaceship rising to a tapered point far above our heads. It was so wonderful I wanted to cry.

I only half listened as Tom-tom described the ship's inner layer of extremophile fungus, which ate cosmic radiation and converted it to energy, a technology NASA opposed out of fears of contamination. It was another reason, at least for the time being, NASA was sticking with the Boeing Deepthrust and Nike High Jump—systems that performed flawlessly—to send humans to Mars.

The First Fifty stayed on the ground while Roma herded the Arcadia 7 crew (plus Joyce B) into an elevator for the ride to the top of the rocket. Inside, everything was orders of magnitude more expansive and more attractive than the interior of the High Jump. The officers' deck looked like something out of *Star Trek*. The crew quarters might as well have been hotel rooms, save for the fact they had sleep pods instead of beds. We were speechless. If one thing could change my mind about staying with Arcadia 7, this was it.

In my T-7 on the way back to JSC, I received a message that Butlarer and Frost wanted to see us. I figured they'd like us to debrief them and the flight controllers about what we'd just learned. A limo picked us up at Ellington Field and took us to Building 30.

When we stepped into the conference room, it surprised me to see just George and Wendy. "Have a seat," George told us from the end of the seven-meter-long table. On the table were four tablets, two on either side of him. Wendy stood near a wall screen. "We'll do the paperwork first," George said. After we sat, he slid tablets toward us that displayed the standard Classified Information Nondisclosure Agreement.

João glanced up. "What's the big secret, George?"

The administrator grinned. "Oh, just a little news we'd like to pass on to you."

"Nondisclosure agreements," I said to Butlarer. "How delightful. But hell, George, I thought you'd be dying to hear about our trip to Boca Grande and how many album covers we autographed." I shook my hand in front of me. "God, my wrist hurts."

"Your damn signature on the NDA is the only one I care about at the moment," George said.

■ ■ ■

Ben, here's something I'm not supposed to tell you, even if you are my attorney.

After I signed the NDA, I glanced at Wendy, who appeared nervous as she stood rocking back and forth near the screen. She had grown her hair and dyed it bronze-red, tucking it behind her ears in a way that complemented her rectangular face better than her previous silvery short cut. At least I thought so.

"What's the good word?" I asked her.

"'Good' depends on who's looking at it." She clicked a remote. A schematic of a rocket engine popped up on the screen. The accompanying text was in Mandarin.

"Sorry, folks," I said. "I aborted Chinese. Can you translate it into Greek?"

Sally, who sat next to me, giggled while pressing her hand against my back. "Not sure that will help you," she said. Her hand lingered for a moment and, before she withdrew it, she gave me a playful scratch, sending tingles through my shoulders and neck.

Bria frowned at us.

"Let's try English," Wendy said and clicked the remote again. The same notes now read: *FAST RABBIT II ENGINE FOR MARS SHIP*. "The latest and greatest from our Chinese friends," she said, "courtesy of U.S. intelligence."

"Like Fast Rabbit I, Fast Rabbit II uses chemical propellant, but it's more efficient and has more thrust," George said. "An array of five engines will get them to Mars."

"They just finished ground testing," Wendy added, then clicked. The enhanced satellite image showed five distinct plumes, which her finger traced on the screen. "They'll flight-test the engine in a few weeks." The next slide showed the engines attached to a fuel tank for a test-fire.

"The Chinese have a new firecracker," João said. "Good for them. So what?"

"They're not waiting another two years, that's what," George said. "They're going during the same launch opportunity we chose for Arcadia 7."

"What little rabbit told you that?" I asked.

"Highly reliable sources, so you can cut out the jokes."

"No doubt they'll announce this," Bria said. "Because why keep it secret?"

Wendy stared at the screen. "Their intentions aren't clear. We don't know why CNSA is waiting to make the announcement."

"Then why tell us?" Sally asked.

George grinned. "You launch in a year. If you're going to have company, it's better you know now."

As far as I was concerned, there was only one thing worth knowing. I grinned back at George, then said, "Where do they stand with nuclear propulsion?"

"They're tight-lipped about that, except to say they're working on it," Wendy replied. "Around here, CNSA stands for 'Can Never Share Anything.' From what we've learned—this is classified—they're having trouble sourcing beryllium, which they need for the engine's reactor core, and they seem to have issues with the liquid hydrogen propellant seeping through the tanks and pipes, which leads to boil-off. Their modified reusable spaceship, which follows the design of the RedLiner, also has had problems—and lots of fireballs."

Wendy switched to a picture of CNSA's space vehicle. "So, for their first crewed mission, they're keeping things simple." She gestured at the screen. "A Long March 9 rocket will launch two astronauts in a capsule attached to a life-support module and a hab the size of a bus. Their descent module will double as a surface hab. Once in Earth orbit, they'll fire the new Fast Rabbit engines and race toward Mars. They'll be on the surface for thirty days."

"The Chinese don't see this as a race," George added, shooting Wendy a stern look. "Even if we launch at the same time, we'll get there way ahead of them, thanks to our NTP engines."

"Even if China isn't first to put a crew on Mars," I said, "they'll be first to bring them back, a tremendous accomplishment."

"That probably factors into their decision to go sooner," George said. "There's nothing we can do about it, except have one big frickin' parade when *our* crew comes back."

Sal nodded at the screen. "How can they cram a year of life support into such a small service module?"

George swiveled his chair to face the screen. "You innovate. You ration. You feed the crew pills."

"Seriously?" Bria said, squinting and sounding incredulous.

George spun around to her. "They don't care about food printers. Two-thousand-calorie food bars will do."

As I exchanged looks with my crewmates, I had a good idea what everyone was thinking. When it came to our own deep-space menu, we should count ourselves lucky, especially since NASA had dumped the FM experiment, which never quite passed the smell test.

We briefed the administrator and the flight director about our visit to Boca Grande, then went to our waiting cars. "Let's ride together in the Asteroid," I suggested. "So we can talk."

João and Sally sat across from me and Bria as the Asteroid drove off. Their Fiat convertible trailed behind us. I told the others I'd received a text from Jep, who had heard from Roma's attorneys. They were giving us two weeks to decide.

"After taking the tour," João said, "I want to ride with the First Fifty more than ever."

"Why?" I asked, still waiting to be convinced.

"A hell of a lot more money and less stress. You saw those rooms. The place is like a Hilton. And we don't have to be teetotalers."

Bria placed her hand on my knee. "We'd make it back *before* the Chinese do. You'll have your 'first'—first to walk on Mars *and* return safely to Earth."

I glanced at Sal and felt inclined to go along with whatever she wanted. In the end, I didn't want to be the one who spoiled the Q-Orbit party. "What about the science mission?" she asked, holding me in her gaze.

"By far the most important thing," I said.

"I agree," she replied, "and we could still pursue it to our heart's content. We'd show the colonists the importance of doing the science right and steer them away from the bullshit Noel Roma feeds them. We could have a real, lasting impact."

Bria smiled and squeezed my knee.

"So," I said to Sally, "you've changed your position?"

"I'd like to sleep on it. How about you?"

"Me too."

Bria patted my thigh. "Thanks for having an open mind."

The cars stopped, and Sally and João parted our company. During the rest of the way home, I expected Bria to pressure me more about switching to Q-Orbit. Instead, she slid into the seat across from me, folded her arms, and glared at me.

"I want you to tell me. What's up with you and Sally?"

"What?"

"The way she scratched your back during the briefing. The looks she gives you. Come on, Addy, I know it when I see it."

"See what?"

"You were giving her the male gaze at Armstrong Station."

"I was wicked hungover."

She snorted. "That's an excuse?"

"No, I'm sorry. But why wait to bring it up now?"

"I wanted to be sure. Now I am."

Exasperated, I sighed. "Truly, hon, you have nothing to worry about. If it makes you feel better, we'll talk with her and João, clear the air, and move on, okay?"

"Here's my new stance, Addy. I want us to go with the First Fifty, but just you and me. If Noel Roma wants four NASA astronauts, she can find others besides João and Sally."

"Really?" I said, leaning toward her.

"Uh-huh. Really. Having them with us on Arcadia 7 is different— NASA will be monitoring everybody's behavior."

"You're acting crazy. You have nothing to be jealous about, for God's sake."

Yeah, I know. It was another half-lie. Bria jerked her head to the window, her lips pressed together tighter than the seal of an airlock hatch. Something told me The Craters wouldn't be recording a second album.

"Can we at least talk to Sally and João first?" I asked.

"I'll sleep on it," Bria said to the window.

■ ■ ■

It took Bria a week to agree to meet with João and Sally. We scheduled dinner with them for a night in early December, which gave us time to answer Roma by her deadline. Then, for the first time in nine months, I visited my mother and, unavoidably, my sister.

When Zena let me in, I thought I'd come to the wrong place. The renovation had torn out the walls separating the living room, dining room, and kitchen, the remaining walls shades of pale-blue, pink, and orange. A new redwood floor glistened. The space had the feel of a beach without the ocean. Sort of like Tucson.

Mom was stretched out in one of the new recliners facing the new three-meter wall screen. Phoebe, like a sentinel, perched between her feet. A crocheted rat sat on the floor with half its tail missing.

"The place is beautiful," I said, after kissing her cheek. "How did you pay for all this?"

"I refinanced the condo and took out a home-improvement loan. Isn't it fab?"

I glanced at Zena. She leaned against a wall, studiously ignoring me as she looked at her hand, which she opened and closed into a fist repeatedly.

"Hey sis," I said. "Did you hurt your wrist?"

"No, it just feels good."

"It was Zeannie's idea to go with a Martian palette," Mom said.

"We're First Fifty fans," my sister added, sounding like she was talking about a baseball team. "So we wanted the same colors they'll see. What they're doing is so, so important."

"Then why don't you join them on Mars?" I said. I meant it as a light joke, but it came off as snarky.

"As a matter of fact, Zacky, I will. On the second ship."

"I thought there were millions of people on the waiting list."

"Q-Orbit moved me up. They like my expeditionary skills."

What expeditionary skills? I wondered, furrowing my brow. I decided not to pursue it, not wanting to aggravate her.

"No need to worry, bro. Since I won't be on Mars at the same time as you, we won't have a chance to kill each other." She laughed, pushed herself off the wall, and strode to her room.

"I hope you remember, Zachary," my mother said softly, "deep down, she loves you. And, like me, she's proud of you."

"Did she ever say that?"

"No, but it's true. Now tell me all about the South Pole. Here, I made this for you." She leaned forward, reached behind her, and pulled out the orange-red yarn sculpture she had kept hidden. "The Antarctic spiny plunderfish," she said, tossing it to me. "They can live out of water. Did you see any while you were there?"

"No, Mom, but geez, thanks."

I smiled despite the spikes, buggy eyes, and frowny face that I found a little unnerving. At least it wasn't a skua to remind me of my "outstanding discovery." Still, it was a thoughtful gift, which added to my guilt as I looked into her eyes and fought the urge to begin the speech I had rehearsed a gazillion times.

Mother, there's something I must tell you, but you have to keep it a secret.

I hesitated and gazed at the table next to the recliner. Above it hovered a miniature holopic of Scarlett holding Nova.

"They're my favorites on the show," Mom said, her eyes following mine. "And Zeannie's."

She waved her hand through the holopic, which was replaced by one of Nova in her lap, with Scarlett and Zena standing behind. For a moment, I stopped breathing. I feared she knew everything—Scarlett must have told her—and I'd only be confirming the truth by confessing it. My gut told me to stick to my plan. I would reveal my fatherhood only after I was onboard the High Jump—or the RedLiner—and on the way to Mars.

"Nice portrait," I said. "Have you been seeing Scarlett and Nova?"

"Oh, Zachary, I know what you're thinking, but I'm not breaking your no-contact rule. Promise. That image of us was holopic-shopped. *The New Martians* store lets Volcano subs include anyone they want in a portrait with the colonists. No lie."

"Good to hear, Mom, because you must realize how strict NASA—"

"Tell me about Antarctica. Bet the snow was everywhere. Did you go snow blind?"

"No, because—"

"I loved The Craters video. Was any of it filmed on-site?"

"No, Mom, we—"

"I'm working on emperor penguins for you and Sally and Bria and João. You know, one happy family. Don't let them in on it, Zachary. I want it to be a surprise."

■ ■ ■

As soon as I got home, a call came in from Noel Roma. I put the call on the wall screen and Bria joined me. "Hey, y'all," Roma said, her eyes twinkling. "We're quantum-encrypted on both ends, correct?" Her smile exposed her near-perfect teeth.

"Yes, we're good," I said. "We'll have an answer for you, Noel, the day after—"

"Addy, Q-Orbit has changed direction."

I smiled. "What, you're shooting for Venus instead of Mars?"

"Feels like I'm already on Venus. The mercury's hit a hundred twenty-five here. Okay, I don't know how else to do this except to just come out and say it. I'm withdrawing my offer."

Bria's chin dropped as my mouth fell open. "What happened?" I said.

"We recruited Joyce Ackerney and Joyce Bowman and stopped there. We're fixin' to take two NASA-trained astronauts instead of four. They agreed to remain with the colonists on Mars, so it made sense to choose them. Nothing personal. Please let Sally and João know."

Bria raised her face. "Thank you, Noel," she said, then shot me a mean look. "So nice to have been considered."

"Yeah," I said to Roma with false nonchalance, hiding my happiness and relief to have closure. "Nice, thanks."

"Would've been great to have y'all on board. Can't say I didn't try. Anyhow, sorry it didn't work out, though I'm sure we'll see more of each other in the coming months before we launch. Glad NASA is working with us to coordinate safety and rescue systems. It's the right thing to do."

"Give our best to the First Fifty," I said. "Hope they enjoy their eight months in space." *And being part of your batshit crazy cult*, I wanted to add.

"Roger and out," Roma said, and the screen went blank.

I turned to Bria and shrugged. "Well, that's that."

Paying no attention to me, she marched to the bedroom.

■ ■ ■

We told Sally and João over dinner in our private room at the Calcutta Club.

"Fuck," João said and threw a chunk of naan that landed in the lap of a marble Buddha. He stared at the jettisoned bread while Sally bowed her head.

I waited a moment, then said, "There's something else Bria and I wish to address."

João aimed his angry eyes at me. Sally glanced up, too. She wasn't happy.

I took a breath. "I'm stepping into the confession booth. It's in the best interest of the mission." I shifted my gaze between João and Sally, resting it on her. "You recall how we kind of overdid it at Armstrong Station? I mean, with the whiskey shots, before the lights went out?"

"It's a little foggy, but sure." She broadcast a sheepish grin around the table.

"Here's the thing. I sorta began having feelings for you—I mean,

I was drunk, and the feelings, well, they lingered a while. Anyway, it's over and done—I want to be clear about that—and I just need to put it out there because . . ." I turned to Bria.

"I got jealous," she said. She arched her eyebrows at Sal, as if it were her turn to confess.

"Bria, I get it," Sally said, then faced me. "I have to say, Addy, I'm flattered. But I never had the same feelings for you. João and I have a solid relationship. Nothing will change that."

João crossed his arms. "That's right. We're good." He wasn't smiling, and I wondered if he was still pissed about missing the opportunity with Q-Orbit, or mad at me, or both.

"What about all the touching?" Bria asked Sally. Her tone remained soft, as if to avoid confrontation. "Like when you patted Addy and scratched his back at the meeting with Frost and Butlarer?"

"Oh, that. Totally innocent. Yet I see how you could take it the wrong way. Won't happen again. Come on, let's hug." She stood and stepped over to Bria's chair. Bria got up, and the two embraced. "There," Sally added. "No harm done."

We ordered dirty "Mars-tinis," the juice of Kalamata olives tinting the gin and vermouth red, the green olives, which were skewered on either side of the Kalamata one, representing the Martian moons of Phobos and Deimos. We each drank three, laughed, and put Roma, Q-Orbit, and Bria's jealousy behind us.

Everyone agreed to adopt Greek as their new language. We talked about making more music as The Craters, how that and Greek would keep our minds sharp during months of zero and low gravity (at least sharper than they were after soaking them in Mars-tinis).

For the next nine months, our training proceeded with no hiccups as a global mania spread about the launch of Arcadia 7.

■ ■ ■

The most egregious counts of the indictment, Ben, are numbers 238 through 241. Alleging that the four of us conspired *ahead* of the launch to fire the NTP engines so we wouldn't come in second is as ludicrous as believing that doves and pigeons are spy drones.

While the clickbait-hungry media hyped it as a race, it was anything but. The Apple was going to land us on the Red Planet months ahead of the RedLiner and the Chinese. NASA's first crewed orbital mission validated that NTP engines would get us there in four or five months, and that astronauts could handle a round trip of 300–400 days in weightlessness. Once the NTP technology proved itself, a long stay on the surface was possible. In our case, we planned to spend up to eight months exploring the prime real estate of Arcadia Planitia.

Q-Orbit's mission architecture couldn't have been more different. On a one-way trip using traditional chemical propulsion, in a spaceship with thirty times the mass of the High Jump, it would take the First Fifty twice as long to land on Mars. The Chinese were supposed to be using chemical propulsion as well, and everyone expected them to arrive on Mars months after we did.

In a nutshell, nothing supports a motive to "conspire" in advance to beat the Chinese. *Zilch*.

Yes, they surprised us *after* they launched, when their second-stage booster separated and revealed NTP engines. Even then, NASA said there was no practicable way the Chinese could speed up and later sufficiently decelerate to allow Martian gravity to capture their spacecraft, enabling it to achieve orbit and land on the planet before we did.

As we sat strapped into our seats on the launchpad, none of us schemed about beating the Chinese to Mars. Any media speculation about "backup plans" for winning "the race" was nonsense. There would not be any "fuel tank leak" or "trans-Mars injection failure" to delay or slow us down. Time and time again, NASA refuted such fantasies, yet the prosecutors cite them to support their charges of conspiracy.

The entire indictment, Ben, is bullshit, nothing but a politically motivated vendetta engineered by Bastbom and the NAP, and I can't wait to present my case to a jury.

■ ■ ■

In mid-September, about five weeks before liftoff, George Butlarer called us into his office at JSC.

A grin curved on his fleshy face as he sat tall in an upholstered chair. Sally and João and Bria and I paired up on sofas on either side of him. He placed his elbows on the armrests and interlocked his hands. With his forefingers extended, he pointed them at me like the barrel of a gun.

"Let's start with you, Addy. How do you feel?"

I hunched my shoulders, relaxed them, and smiled. "Several ways, I guess, but usually with my fingers, sometimes with my toes."

"I guess I should always be more specific with a joker." George's eyes widened. "So let me be as specific as possible. How do you feel about being scrubbed from Arcadia 7 so you can join the Q-Orbit party?"

"What?"

"I won't tell you how we found out, but we did." George dropped his finger-gun and rested his arms on the armrests. His hands tapped them slowly.

"Found out what?"

"Don't play stupid with me. You've been negotiating with Roma behind our backs this whole time, figuring as soon as you came to terms with her, you could dump NASA, even just a few weeks before launch, and let the Arcadia 7 backup crew step in."

"Wait, George," Bria snapped. "Roma came to us."

Sally shrugged. "The only thing I did was listen," she said, which wasn't quite true. "I'd never fly with a cult of crazy colonists."

"Why didn't you inform me?" George asked. "Or anyone at NASA?"

"Because nothing happened," João said. "Talk to Joyce Bowman. She was with us in Boca Grande. She'll tell you."

"Don't insult my intelligence," George replied, an icy flatness in his voice. "The meeting at Boca Grande wasn't your only one. And you're smart enough not to give yourselves away in front of Joyce who, in any case, is no longer with NASA. Look, I'm a fair man. And a practical one. Before I have the attorneys review this, I want to hear your side. We're not being recorded."

I shot glances at my crew mates. If George already knew, it would only make it worse if we clammed up and waited to speak with our own attorneys. I told him everything. Well, almost everything. I left out that we had seriously considered Roma's proposal, making it sound as if she'd hounded us to come on board. The only real lie I told was the reason we hadn't come to him—we didn't think that the matter impacted our mission.

"We've had zero contact with Roma for months," I said, ending my impassioned speech.

George snarled, as if he didn't believe me. "Go home," he said. "All of you. Take the rest of the day off. I'll let you know how NASA is going to handle this."

We trudged out of the conference room and climbed into the Asteroid, which drove us to our homes, Sally and João's Fiat following behind like a tethered lifeboat.

"We're fucked, amigos," João said.

I called Jep and put him on the backseat holoscreen. His *Away* message showed him twenty years younger than he was, with wavy hair and plump cheeks as his face floated between us. "Hello and thanks for your call," he said. "I'm in court at the moment and will get back at you . . ." He paused and smiled. "Rather, I'll get back *to* you, as soon as possible."

"It's Addy," I said, "and it's urgent."

The image flickered, and Jep appeared, this time live, sitting in the attorneys' lounge of the Harris County Courthouse. "Hey, Addy," he said, the bags under his eyes adding to the tired expression on his drawn face. "Looks like you've got the whole band there. You guys shooting a car music video or something?"

"Can we talk?"

"Sure, for a few minutes. We're in recess."

Jep was by himself but still used his earbuds. I told him about the meeting with Butlarer, then asked, "Do you see any legal obstacles to NASA removing us from Arcadia 7?"

"Did George Butlarer suspend you?"

"He gave us the day off," Bria said.

"Was anyone with him when he spoke with you?"

"No," Sally said, "and we clearly pissed him off."

"I thought he wanted to fire us on the spot," João added. "We contradicted nothing he accused us of. Except for the cover-up of our flirting with Q-Orbit."

Jep frowned. "Well, *did* you cover it up?"

Our silence spoke volumes. "We didn't actually *hide* anything," I said at last. "We just didn't report it."

"Let me level with you," Jep said. "You have no control over the process at this stage, so keep your heads low and do nothing but your jobs. Correct me if I'm wrong, but if they plan to scrub you from the mission, they'll have to act fast so they can bring the backup crew online."

My mind's eye saw my replacement, Ed Munch, his handlebar mustache, shaved head, and prescription goggles. His bushy-haired husband, Pete "Bullseye" Peters, was part of the backup crew, too, along with Brendan Halo and Jennifer Watt, an unmarried couple who'd been in a happy relationship for eight years and knew all about long-term cohabitation.

"Their training mirrors ours," I said to Jep. "NASA could switch them without a hitch."

As Jep had advised, we kept our heads down. Butlarer didn't get back to us the next day, nor the following week. Each day we weren't suspended gave me hope we wouldn't be scrubbed, yet I couldn't shake off the dread it would eventually happen.

■ ■ ■

Somebody once said good lawyers know the law and great ones know the judge. Jep didn't exactly know George Butlarer, the man who would decide our fate, but he knew one of NASA's senior attorneys, Sheila Rathonor.

She'd been in his class at UT Austin Law School. They ran in the same circles: both were members of the same country club and had made the Texas Super Lawyers list twenty-odd years in a row.

Jep and Sheila crossed paths at the club. As they cooled off from the October boil with a few gin slings, Jep ran a "hypothetical case" by her. It involved a NASA contractor terminated for a "conflict of interest" based on "undisclosed conversations" with the European Space Agency. ESA had reached out to the contractor about work that would require canceling the NASA contract. Jep added some "theories of defense," such as "breach of NASA's own regulations," "wrongful termination," and even a First Amendment "freedom of association" argument.

"You represent Zachary Johnson, don't you?" Sheila had said, according to Jep.

"He's better known as Addy," my attorney replied.

"Better known as dickhead."

"Well?"

"I wouldn't worry about your hypo, Jep. But your client is still a dickhead."

I think Clarence Darrow first observed that the best lawyers always charge the biggest fees. It sounds like a truism, but I learned it firsthand with Jep. He billed $5,000 an hour, including his "thinking time." He must have done a lot of thinking because I paid him over ten million dollars, which included putting together the deal with Scarlett and creating and administering the living trust. He was worth every million.

Bria, João, Sally, and I were going to be the first humans on Mars. And, as joint commanders, my wife and I would take the first steps.

■ ■ ■

Years of training and hundreds of hours in simulators are supposed to make blasting off routine, but there's nothing routine about 32,000 kilonewtons of thrust pushing you toward the heavens. You may end up in another kind of heaven, if there is one.

Preflight, we quarantined at the Beach House near Kennedy Space Center. Two days before launch, members of our families who had passed NASA's health examination joined us for a barbeque on a steamy November evening. Bria's parents and all seven of her siblings mingled with Sally and João's families. My mother and Zena mostly kept to themselves, along with Uncle Dick, who was past ninety and could bench press a hundred pounds and run a 5K in half an hour. Mobile AC drones hovered overhead, keeping everyone cool.

"We put together care packages, Zachary," my mother said. "One for each month, each with a surprise."

I wanted to say, *I have a surprise for you, too: Scarlett Jaffe is the mother of my daughter, Nova, your first granddaughter. I'm sorry I didn't tell you earlier, since they'll spend the rest of their lives on Mars.* Instead, I said: "Thanks, Mom. Hope you included something you crocheted."

"Do you know the words you'll say when you take the first step?" Uncle Dick asked, but before I could answer, he said, "How about 'The Ford Asteroid. A thousand miles per solar charge. The best car for any planet.'"

"We won't have cars on Mars, Uncle Dick. Only rovers."

"Just thinking ahead, son."

"Hey, Addy?" Zena said. She was movie-star stunning in a two-piece ensemble made from black, silk-like material, the streaks shooting across her body resembling a meteor shower. Her diamond-studded brooch, modeled on Q-Orbit's mushroom logo, seemed out of place for a NASA event. If the diamonds were genuine, the outfit had to cost hundreds of thousands of dollars, unless she was renting it. But I didn't take the conversation there.

"Yeah, sis," I said, then forced a smile.

"Just wanted to wish you luck. And say I respect what you're doing, and I'm sorry if sometimes I come on too strong if our opinions differ.

I hope you get there first, Zack, and win those cash bonuses from your endorsement contracts."

"Thanks, Zena. I appreciate that. You'll be with Mom at the launch, right?"

"Well . . ."

I glanced at my mother, who said, "Zeannie's flying back to Houston tonight so she can be present for the First Fifty launch."

Uncle Dick's elbow nudged mine. He smiled so broadly I thought I saw every one of his false teeth. "Don't worry. I'll be with your mom at liftoff."

"Break a leg, bro," Zena said to me, giving my arm a pat. "I'm getting more ribs." She then left our circle.

After the barbeque was over, Bria and I hung out with Sally and João. We each drank a beer to take the edge off. It was past ten, but I was wide awake, so I took a sleeping pill.

As I lay on the bed in the Beach House with Bria, who was breathing the deep ins and outs of sleep, I visualized a successful launch. Mom and Uncle Dick were shading their eyes as they followed the perfect ascent of the Deepthrust. I imagined being squashed in my seat by the force of five gravities, then becoming weightless and reporting to Mission Control that system readings were nominal. A press conference from space would take place after we docked with the High Jump and fired the engines for trans-Mars injection. Should that be the time I come clean and announce I had a daughter whose destination was the same as mine? How would NASA and the rest of the world judge me? How would my mother react?

I took a second sleeping pill.

The next morning, though I still didn't have the answers, I felt refreshed as a NASA van drove us from the Beach House to our crew quarters at KSC. By noon, I noticed the steady patter of my heart and butterflies in my stomach, accepting my excitement as normal.

That night, after a day of preflight checkout procedures, the four of us watched the news together. The planet was in a frenzy over the dual missions to Mars that were to blast off the next day. In the span of two hours, I must have seen twenty interviews given by Mom, Uncle Dick, or both, exuding pride for me. And another ten featuring Scarlett and Nova, the first mother-daughter pair bound for the Red Planet.

My little girl was blonde and bubbly. In a smart red-and-brown checkered flight suit that matched her mother's, she looked like a pint-sized football player as she babbled about growing mushrooms on Mars.

I swallowed a sleeping pill and went to bed.

After closing my eyes, for a long time I visualized seeing Earth from space and taking in spectacular views of oceans. And then I turned to my crewmates. They were cowering before a monster that was covered with green lichen and brandishing claws as it tried to commandeer the ship. Fortunately, I knew I was dreaming.

It was shameful, but my first thought was to have sex with Sally. Because I knew it wouldn't really matter to anyone, since no one was really there. I told myself it was still wrong to play it out, and besides, a monster was terrorizing her, Bria, and João. I have to admit, the damn thing scared me, too.

Among the kernels of wisdom Uncle Dick imparted to me as a boy was that nightmares simulate threats to prepare you for actual ones. The idea stuck with me. No, Arcadia 7's crew wouldn't encounter the Lichen Monster, but other threats could pop up that needed to be handled rapidly. In my dream about the green beast, I spun to face it, then pushed myself off a wall, my boots in front of me. "Take this, dude," I said, drawing my knees back and then thrusting my heels into its scaly forehead.

"Fuck!" I yelled. Out loud. I was awake. Pain stabbed the toes of my right foot, which I grabbed with both hands.

"Addy!" Bria cried. "What happened? You're all turned around." She flipped on the lights.

I had kicked the nightstand next to the bed. When my hands let loose of my foot, my middle toe was a purple grape. In Bria's rush to find ibuprofen and fill a bag with ice, she woke João. In seconds, he and Sally were with Bria at my bedside. Everyone was silent as Bria examined the toe. I knew what my fellow crew members were thinking. If I were them, I would have the same thought—if the toe was broken, we were toast. NASA would scrub us, and Ed Munch and his crew would take over.

"It's hard to be sure without X-rays," Bria said, "but I think it's a break. Appears to be in the joint. Shit. This is a reportable event."

"We're not reporting it." I glanced at João and Sally. I could tell they were calculating the risks of having an injured commander. The toe might not heal properly in zero gravity, creating problems for me with fulfilling my duties, especially on the Martian surface.

Over the next hour, Bria applied ice. She taped my three middle toes together to give the injured one support.

"The ibuprofen is kicking in," I lied. "Doesn't hurt much."

"Let's see if you can walk, amigo," João said.

I could walk, sort of, though I should have been using crutches or wearing a cast boot. I'll admit, Ben, I wouldn't have passed a NASA physical to be approved for spaceflight. But I didn't give a damn, because A) I wouldn't have to walk for four months while aboard the High Jump, and B) I still had nine good toes and wasn't about to let the bad one trip me up.

From here on, Ben, I'll recount events by Mission Days, beginning with the launch; a good number of them cross-check with the mission log.

MISSION DAY 1

In the news footage, we're in flight suits and helmets, smiling and waving as we march to the Launch Complex 39 elevator that will take us up 110 meters to the Starbucks Capsulchino. My grin made me look like the luckiest and happiest guy alive. In fact, my throbbing toe was killing me. I was gritting my teeth.

The tailor-made shoes I was wearing weren't any more tight or rigid than cross-trainers, so even the slightest pressure was like a twenty-five-pound kettlebell bouncing on my banged-up phalanx. Though wide awake, in a way, I was still battling the Lichen Monster. All I could think about was reaching the capsule, getting into space, and hoping weightlessness would ease the pain.

It was funny how, for my first four launches into space, I'd been scared shitless once the countdown reached T-minus ten minutes, the chances for a scrubbed launch falling with each passing second. But now, as I listened to the flight controllers' chatter, I couldn't wait for the explosive combustion of liquid nitrogen and oxygen fuel that would blast me into space.

Or kill me, along with my pain. I almost didn't care which, as long as nothing delayed the countdown.

Somewhere around T-minus eight, Ed Munch, our CAPCOM, told us that two million people were packed into the viewing areas near LC-39.

"Copy that," João said. "Let's show them some fireworks."

Liftoff was nominal for everyone except me. The vibrations and g-forces made it feel like a steak knife was sawing off my damaged digit. "Christ," I said, not a brilliant choice of words when an entire planet is listening.

"You okay, Ad Man?" Munch said, using his nickname for me, which I never let on about how much I hated.

"Copy," I replied, then thought up an explanation for cursing. "I just realized I forgot my toothbrush."

"You can share mine, amigo." João's voice was shaky and guttural as the g's accumulated and plastered us to our seats.

"Two minutes to main engine cut-off," Munch said.

"Copy," I crackled, then began counting backward from 120 to what I prayed would be the deliverance of zero gravity.

At last, it happened. All at once, the pressure was gone. The toe throbbed, but at least it didn't feel as if the Lichen Monster were chewing it off. I gave Bria a thumbs-up. My injury had escaped Earth's gravity and, just as important, NASA's detection. Now all I needed was to find discreet ways of consuming vast quantities of ibuprofen.

But what if I used *all* the ibuprofen stocked on the High Jump and needed more, as I did now? I must have beamed the question to the Entire Loving Universe, because out of nowhere a pill floated in front of me. It was pink, with the same oval shape as the five capsules I'd taken that morning, only smaller. I nabbed it, resisting an immediate impulse to raise my visor and pop it in my mouth.

Bria saw the pill and shook her head at me. *What?* I thought, feeling insulted. *You think I'm insane enough to consume an unknown substance?*

Nuts, washers, and bolts left behind by those working on the spacecraft sometimes come out of hiding in zero gravity. I hadn't examined the pill's surface for any markings, but my best guess was that it *was* ibuprofen or another over-the-counter drug, such as one for motion sickness. I tucked it into a pocket of my flight suit.

In an hour, we began our approach to the High Jump, which was parked in low earth orbit, the docking port of the habitat enlarging on our screens as Sally monitored our progress. With Houston's approval, we activated KIM to oversee and validate her observations.

So far, the flight had been one hundred percent nominal, in other words, perfect. The Capsulchino docked with the High Jump and we migrated to the hab. It took a couple hours to double-check the status of our transport vehicle's subsystems—communications and data processing, power, fuel and propulsion, guidance, life support, etc.

We shed our flight suits. I turned my back to KIM before I took off my right boot to hide the wince I knew was coming. But I did more than wince.

"You grunted, Addy, when you removed your boot," KIM said. "Your tone was associated with pain. Is everything all right?"

"Better tune up your tone detector, KIM. The boot was tight, that's all."

KIM was programmed to detect tones, but thankfully not to call anyone out on a lie.

I floated near our kitchen table on the middle deck, the area that included our exercise equipment, a shower, and two toilets. Workstations for medical care and life science research lined the walls. I twirled so KIM couldn't see through my socks and possibly detect the ridges formed by the medical tape that banded my first three toes together.

"KIM, please put the RedLiner's launch on the screen," I said. "What's the countdown?"

"Certainly. They're at T-minus twenty-five minutes and two seconds, one second. T-minus twenty-four minutes, fifty-nine seconds, fifty-eight—"

"Got it, KIM."

The live telecast of the RedLiner glowed on the hab's wall screen, the countdown clock in the corner. As Bria, Sally, and João flew over to join me, Munch's monotone voice crept out of the speakers on the middle deck.

"Crew of Arcadia 7, this is Houston."

"Copy, Ed," I said.

"Amazing job. We're ahead of schedule. Flight thinks you should do your AVA early and get it out of the way."

Flight was short for flight director. AVA stood for Advertisement Video Activity. On our behalf, NASA attorneys had negotiated the contract with Ford, the only company to film a commercial during the Arcadia 7 mission.

"Roger that, Ed," I said. "Proceeding with AVA."

"I am ready when you and Bria are ready," KIM said. "You will need to put your flight suits on without the helmets, as required by your endorsement agreement."

I glanced at the RedLiner. I didn't want to miss the liftoff and seeing my daughter follow me into space. Twenty-three minutes remained on the countdown clock.

Bria and I had practiced the commercial a thousand times, and the whole thing would require only about fifteen minutes, even allowing for multiple takes. After we put on our flight suits, we flew to the window and held hands as the High Jump passed above a mélange of ocean blues and wispy white swirls, which ended with Africa, whose rosy brownness reminded me of Mars. With a beep, KIM signaled us to begin. I turned and faced the robot's blinking red dot.

"Ford's Asteroid can't travel this far," I said.

Bria looked at the dot and smiled while arching her brow. "Or go 17,000 miles per hour."

We gazed at each other.

"Or have rockets attached to it," I said.

We both turned back to KIM.

"But the Asteroid will drive you around safely, reliably, and with class," I said.

"Far above any other car on Earth," Bria said, jerking her head toward the window, at which point we both turned and looked at our home planet.

Another beep from KIM told us we were done.

Well, not quite. Ford could review each take and request additional ones. They had us do more to get Bria's head jerk right. After each take, I shot a glance at the RedLiner and the countdown clock.

At the end of the sixth take, when the countdown stood at eight minutes, Q-Orbit placed a hold on the launch. This time, it wasn't the weather. The hold involved a sensor that monitored the chilling of the ship's engines before they burned super-cold liquid oxygen fuel. Its readings were slightly outside acceptable parameters. Q-Orbit could maintain the hold for fifteen minutes before it would have to scrub the launch.

I felt sorry for the fifty colonists. If the problem wasn't resolved within that timeframe, they'd have to fly on a different day within the launch period, possibly replaying the nightmare of two years ago when the entire mission got scrubbed. I wondered about Nova, whether she understood the history she was making, and whether a scrub would disappoint her.

"That's a wrap," I said after completing the tenth take.

"Copy," Munch said.

"Thanks, Houston, now taking time to watch the RedLiner."

Prior to launch, Bria and I had rehearsed something else. Because of my toe, we went back to signals. Sally and João learned them, too. If one of them glanced at my feet, they were asking how the toe felt. Rolling my eyes meant it hurt like blazing hell. Two quick blinks meant just hell, and one slow one meant no hell, but maybe just purgatory. Or even heaven.

Bria and I drifted to the screen and joined our crewmates. My wife glanced at my toe, and I rolled my eyes. It would be three hours before we'd have a moment alone so she could administer a stronger pain medication.

With four minutes remaining in the hold's limit, and solutions dwindling, the launch on the line for perhaps the entire launch opportunity, Tom-tom saved the day. The robot, as a drone the size of a Mars Nut, flew in to analyze the sensor inside and out, which took only seconds. "With a ninety-nine-point-eighty-five percent level of confidence," Tom-tom's deep voice reported, "I conclude the sensor is faulty, the RedLiner is go for liftoff, and the countdown can safely resume."

The din of the cheers from Q-Orbit's control center soared through the High Jump's speakers.

"God, that robot's voice is *so* annoying," Bria said. "What was I thinking?"

"Addy?" KIM said.

"Yes, KIM?"

"Because of the hold, the current projected time for the RedLiner's liftoff means our orbital position will provide an excellent view from the bay window, where you can see the RedLiner entering outer space."

We watched the countdown in real time. At ignition I held my breath. The RedLiner took twenty seconds to clear the tower, which seemed like an hour. KIM projected a circle onto the bay window, showing us where to look amid the clouds. The spaceship pierced the cotton balls and ascended, glimmering in the sunlight. From our vantage point, it had the appearance of a silver trinket that belonged on a charm bracelet.

I kept staring through the window long after the RedLiner was beyond sight, until João floated over and patted my back. I turned and smiled. He knew the incredible thing I wanted to say but couldn't: that my daughter and her mother were following me to the Red Planet.

MISSION DAYS 2–9

A peach-colored tablet etched with "M" for morphine did the trick. At least for a while. "I could use another pill," I said to Bria in privacy mode when the toe began throbbing again.

"Wait until bedtime," she said. "You realize, at some point, you'll have to tell Mission Control."

I did, and I would. But only after trans-Mars injection (or TMI), when we were over a million kilometers from Earth, when the cost-risk calculus favored continuing the mission rather than bringing us home.

The High Jump's TMI was scheduled for Mission Day 2. The RedLiner's TMI was to occur six hours before ours, giving it a head start, although the High Jump would speed past it once we'd fired our NTP engines. That's when I would fess up, shading the truth just a little.

I was thinking about the words. They went something like this:

"Yeah, I busted a toe [chuckle]. A freak accident. I kicked my foot in my sleep while dreaming about kicking a last-second field goal to win the game, and my darn foot hit the darn nightstand! But no big deal. What hurts more is that I woke up before I could watch the football split the uprights."

I wouldn't shade the other truth I planned to tell, which I'd rehearsed as well:

"I held off making this announcement because I didn't want to create a distraction for the crew during training. Now I would like *everyone* to know. Recently, I learned that I'm a father. My daughter is Nova Jaffe, who's voyaging to Mars with her mother, Scarlett, and I am *incredibly* proud of them!"

And that would be that. Conducted from space, the press conference would be brief, without endless questions from reporters. I shared my plan with Jep. He was to inform Scarlett's attorneys that I would continue making the payments as agreed, and she would have my consent to speak about us and our daughter. Jep would also deal with any related legal issues regarding NASA and my endorsement contracts.

Before leaving Earth, I had recorded a hologram for my mother, explaining everything and saying, "I'm sorry, Mom" something like fifty times.

The night before TMI, zipped up with Bria in our sleeping pod, I showed her the pill that had drifted in front of me after liftoff. "Any idea what it is?" I asked.

She examined the pill's surface. "This 'p' symbol, I've never seen it before. I can do some lab tests. Or KIM can probably tell us."

I yawned. "Okay, I'll hold on to it for now."

The second dose of morphine worked, and I slept like a moon rock for eight straight hours. A bit of music history: The public doesn't know this yet, but that night I dreamed the melody of "Expand Your Love," The Craters' biggest hit. People might get a kick out of knowing the song's original title, from the dream, was "Hamburger Bun."

■ ■ ■

The song that woke us the next morning was one Mission Control piped in, an energetic tune by the Stranglebots called "Rock It or Bust." Before we left the sleeping pod, Bria applied new tape to bind my toes. The pain registered between the levels of hell and no hell, so I took nothing for it before flying to the middle deck.

Once I got there, Sally gave me the toe-glance. Her weightless blonde hair spread in a semicircle around her head, like the frizzy spinning blades of a fan, which I found oddly attractive. I gave her two quick blinks. She returned a grin, then drifted over to João at the galley table. Bria and I followed.

"Hey, amigos," João said.

I crossed my ankles and assumed the position of someone sitting, wincing when I bumped the bad toe against my other foot. João nodded at my feet. Again I blinked twice, then asked what was for breakfast.

João dangled a pouch. "VeriSym eggs benedict. Fresh off the printer." He squeezed a golf ball of goop the color of urine out of the pouch and sucked it into his mouth. "Mmmm . . . just like Mama's."

"Arcadia 7, this is Houston."

"Copy," I said.

"Good morning, crew," Ed Munch said. "Thought you'd like to know the RedLiner's TMI came off without a hitch. You folks are next. We're three hours away. Checklists start in twenty minutes."

"Roger that, Houston," João said. "Gives me time to catch up on the news."

The news wasn't so great. A year before the U.S. presidential election, Dawn Bastbom was moving up in the polls. João popped more "eggs" into his mouth as CNN dished out information with side plates of highlights from *Brutalara*. He smirked as he chewed. Bastbom's hair braids looked like they'd been through an oil slick (I wanted to throw up), or like shreds of the bull snake that met Uncle Dick's thresher on his farm (I was eight at the time and did throw up).

We completed the checklists, squeezed through the airlock to the Capsulchino, and strapped ourselves in. With liquid hydrogen filling the High Jump's drop tank to the brim, the nuclear engines fired for eighty minutes, inserting the ship into a trajectory to intercept Mars in 116 days.

After Houston confirmed all was nominal, I swallowed another "M" pill. I, too, soon became nominal.

■ ■ ■

The wall screen displayed a live image of the Moon from one of the High Jump's exterior cameras. By staring at the silver orb long enough, I thought I perceived it inflating like a balloon in super-slow motion as we coasted in its direction.

I gazed at the Moon and asked myself: Really, what could be more thrilling than landing on Mars? Witnessing your child's birth? Maybe, but since I hadn't been present for Nova's, I found it difficult to make the comparison.

NASA had scheduled a press conference for Mission Day 5, by which time we would have passed by the Moon and continued into deep space. I instructed Jep to send the hologram to my mother so she would receive it a few hours before the press conference started.

On the day of the conference, we floated in a line. João and I were on the ends with our respective arms around the waist of our respective wives, and theirs around ours and each other's. João's free hand clutched the bars of the XBike and mine a wall grip. We looked like a row of dancers ready to kick up our heels. KIM's most humanoid form, which resembled a bobblehead with arms but no legs, drifted nearby as we faced the screen and its camera.

Reporters filled the JSC auditorium. George Butlarer, Wendy Frost, and Ed Munch sat at a table on a stage, the screen behind them displaying the live feed from the High Jump.

I had a hard time focusing on what I planned to say, my mind predicting Mom's words when we spoke the next day. *Addy, why would you keep such a thing from your own mother?*

The reporters asked their typically banal questions ("Are you homesick yet?") and reprised the "Mars race" stuff with queries about the Chinese, who hadn't even launched. Thankfully, our flight controller kept the meeting to its scheduled thirty minutes.

I never intended to grandstand about my relationship with Scarlett and my fatherhood. I wanted to reveal my secret and end the guilt that went with it. So when Wendy said there was time for one more question, I interrupted her, saying I had a special announcement. The moment I finished delivering my lines about Scarlett and Nova, reporters stood and jostled each other as they shouted questions.

"Sorry, everyone," Wendy said, speaking over them, "our time has expired. The crew needs to return to their tasks."

The four of us broke free of each other, spread out, and floated throughout the middle deck. As we weren't in privacy mode, no one uttered a word. But I got the message. My crewmates looked away from me, pursing their lips and shaking their heads.

"Arcadia 7, this is Houston," Munch's voice buzzed over the main audio channel. "Stand by for a video link with Flight in forty minutes."

"Roger that," I said.

"Great," João said with disdain. "Just great."

Munch's voice took on a grim tone. "Yeah, not so great."

About an hour later, Wendy's distraught face leaned toward the camera as we hovered in front of the screen. She spoke in an agitated whisper. "Addy, what the hell? George has gone berserk. I don't know if you can grasp what a shitstorm you created. You withheld material information about your status. That's as plain as day. Don't lie about it."

"All right, I won't."

"George considers this misconduct, Addy. The psychologists here are going crazy. What if you want to stay on Mars with your daughter and her mother? Or you want your daughter to return to Earth with you? Did you know about this, Bria?"

"I did, Wendy. He's my husband."

"All of us knew," João added.

"We respected Addy's wish to keep quiet," Sally said.

"You have no idea how bad this makes us look." Wendy shook her head, her silver moon earrings jiggling. "We might as well be a goddamn soap opera. What else are you folks hiding from us?"

I glanced at one number on the instrument panel next to the screen, which showed the High Jump's distance from Earth approaching four million kilometers. I turned back to Wendy and said, "Okay, you're right. It's time to come clean." I brought my knees to my chest, pulled off my right sock, and extended my foot so the flight director had a good view of the three toes taped together. "I broke my middle toe the night before we launched."

"You *what*?"

"I think the break is at the joint," Bria said. "He's on ibuprofen. The toe will stay blue for a while, but then fade fast. Not much you can do for a busted toe."

"I beg to differ," Wendy fumed. "You can keep the busted toe on Earth. For God's sake, people, *really*?"

I told her how it happened, and she lowered her forehead onto her palm for half a minute before looking up. "I'll need to talk with the team here about our options."

After the transmission ended, we told KIM we wanted twenty minutes of private time.

João floated in front of me with his arms and ankles crossed. "Well, Commander, this might be the end of our mission. There's plenty of fuel to decelerate the High Jump and take us back to Earth."

"That was quite the one-two punch you delivered, Addy," Sally said horizontally while holding a handgrip.

Bria was scornful. "Sure would have been nice if you'd given us a heads-up."

Grimacing, I put my sock on and revolved toward Sally. "I know what I'm doing." I gestured at the instrument panel. "See our distance? Having come this far, there's no freakin' way they'll turn us around. They would have found out, eventually. Better to get it out in the open. The pain isn't an issue, and I'll be off the morphine soon."

"Wait, you're taking morphine?" Sally said. Her mouth stayed open.

"Calm down, sister," Bria said. "It's a low dosage. The toe should heal in a couple months, well before landing."

"Fuck," João said. "The only place we'll be landing is in the Pacific Ocean." Frowning with his head turned down, he floated away.

■ ■ ■

For the next three hours, we exercised, ran through checklists, and reported to CAPCOM, saying little to each other while awaiting the verdict from Houston. No one even commented on the fact that *Armstrong Station Calling* downloads spiked by twelve million within ninety minutes after my announcement, adding $10,000,000 to our balance sheets.

After another two-hour workout, I cleaned up and took a break. The bike's foot grips had kept my toe immobile, so it didn't hurt while I pedaled, but I downed 600 milligrams of ibuprofen anyway before floating to the upper deck to retrieve my oboe. My lips kissed the reed, my body drifting in place as I began blowing a laid-back melody.

"That's nice," Sally said from the opening to middle deck. She was wearing a loose-fitting T-shirt and gym shorts, her hair fanning out from all sides. "What's it called?"

"'Hamburger Bun.'" As she laughed, I added, "I'm still playing with the title and lyrics."

"I would be happy to help you," KIM said through the deck's speakers.

I took a pass on KIM's offer but suggested a rhythm track would be nice, and as the whoosh of brushes on drums accompanied my oboe, Sally retrieved her bouzouki. She plucked the same melody, and I blew sustained chords, and before long João added his bass and Bria her zither. The song was sounding decent, and at that moment, I believed all was forgiven.

Or almost. My call with my mother was to start in about ten hours, after breakfast on Mission Day 6. Before I could speak with her, NASA ordered Bria to give me a complete physical, with our flight surgeon observing remotely, including urine tests and a full blood workup. After the lab results came in, NASA, projecting transparency, issued a press release (no doubt written by its lawyers) stating I "bumped" my toe "while sleeping," the scant hundred words including a "clean bill of health."

Like a good leader and commander, I refrained from saying to Sally, "See, I goddamn told you so."

That night, after Bria and I zipped up in our sleep pod, I shared my anxiety about talking to my mom. "Now that I've made the announcement, a part of me doesn't want to discuss Nova with her. I can't put my finger on it. Discovering I'm a dad is on par with discovering life on Mars. And I'm thrilled that Mom's granddaughter is following in my footsteps. She'll make history as the first six-year-old, the youngest person ever, to walk on an alien planet. I'm so proud she'll be part of my legacy."

"Uh-huh."

I half expected Bria's indifferent tone. Nova, the child that wasn't hers, didn't appear on her top-ten list of favorite conversation topics, and neither did Scarlett, the woman she thought had been receiving "hush money." But I needed to talk to someone.

"I'm not worried about explaining to Mom why I held back the truth," I said. "So why am I now feeling reluctant to speak with her?"

"It's obvious to me," Bria said. "You're replaying the sibling rivalry between you and Zena, which began in childhood."

"God, you've got to be kidding."

"You want to please your mom by outdoing everyone else. This time, you're competing with Nova for her attention and affection. That's why you don't want to talk to your mother about her. But guess what? Neither do I."

"Competing against my kid? That's crazy."

"You asked, and I gave you my answer. Now good night."

I closed my eyes and contemplated Bria's explanation. Was she right? Had she peeled the skin off my consciousness to reveal what was inside? After all, even though I might adore Nova, I'd be fooling myself to think we had a close father-daughter relationship. Or was my wife's not-so-nice analysis a projection of her own envy and jealousy?

I unzipped the pod, got out, and flew to the middle deck. I took a floralterdenol tablet, then flew to my private quarters. If I still had trouble sleeping, I didn't want to disturb Bria.

Once I settled in, I continued to think about Nova. Until a day ago, she believed Bart Singh was her father. I wondered how traumatic it was for her to learn the truth and that I'd gone along with a lie. Would trust issues plague her for the rest of her life? Would she ever trust *me*?

I had to get to sleep.

I shifted my thoughts to the most important goal of the mission: the search for alien life, or more precisely, its remnants in fossilized microbes. On the way to Mars, I would study every available image of such fossils found on Earth so I could compare them with those we might discover on Arcadia Planitia. My mind's eye pictured the square structures of *Palaeolyngbya,* then a species of *Chroococcales* that looks like a bird's nest filled with eggs, and then ancient fungi spores that look like beads on a necklace, and . . . I descended in bliss to unconsciousness.

■ ■ ■

I was holed up in my quarters in front of my personal notebook screen, which flashed *STAND BY FOR TRANSMISSION.* When Mom's face appeared, I felt relieved. She was smiling, although she often glanced at Phoebe in her lap. Zena sat next to them, averting her eyes as usual.

"Hi, Mom, can you see me?" I said. Her reply came a minute later, after the transmission delays.

"Yes, dear. How's the toe?"

"It's nothing. Listen, Mom, did you see the hologram my attorney sent to you?"

"Yes, Zachary."

"I'm sorry I had to do it this way, Mom."

She waved her hand as if shooing a fly. "Oh, I already knew."

"*What*?"

"I told her," Zena said bluntly. "Mom's known that Nova is her granddaughter since a month before you left."

Speechless, I began hyperventilating.

"Don't ask me how I knew," Zena continued. "Anyway, it's a moot point."

"Scarlett told you," I said, unable to stop anger from seeping into my voice. "She's the only one who could have."

Zena leaned forward, enlarging her face on my screen. "No. You're dead wrong. But it doesn't matter."

"It *does* matter, dammit."

"Then have your attorney call mine."

"You have an attorney? Why?"

"Mom's using her, too."

"Please, children," our mother said, "don't fight."

"I want to speak with Mom alone," I said.

Zena shrugged. "Sure, no problem." She then got up and left.

Mom wouldn't say how Zena found out about Nova, claiming she'd promised not to, though she disclosed they'd hired the attorney to advise them about the trust I created for her.

I could already hear Jep telling me I had waived the liquidated damages clause in my agreement with Scarlett, since I made the disclosure about Nova myself. Even if Scarlett breached the agreement , it would be difficult to prove it made any difference.

Mom described her frequent secret get-togethers with Scarlett and Nova and how holopics of Nova would "do fine" until she returned to Earth, which Mom was sure she would. She ended our call by promising to send pictures and videos of her with her granddaughter "right away." When they arrived, I pressed my lips together and huffed through my nose. In one video, Mom looked on as Scarlett and Zena hugged and played with Nova. My mother had lied to me, but I kept reminding myself it would be hypocritical to complain.

I told Bria about the call as soon as we were alone. "I think you may be right," I said. "It feels like Nova, Scarlett, and Zena are stealing my thunder in front of Mom."

"News flash. You're suffering from a cognitive distortion arising from the uber-competitive personality you developed growing up. Now that you're aware of it, you can better manage it. For starters, accept it so you can obsess less over those people. And I've got more news. That pill you found after we reached orbit, the one with the 'p' marking?"

"Yeah?" I said with annoyance, which had lingered from watching the video.

"I analyzed it, offline, with the spectrometer. It's pure psilocybin, the hallucinogen of magic mushrooms."

"Oh, great, just what an astronaut needs. Like radiation from gamma rays."

"And that 'p'?" She opened her palm screen and showed me a close-up image of the pill's marking. The leg of the "p" was curled. "It's not a 'p' but a 'q.' We just looked at it the wrong way."

"'Q' for Q-Orbit."

"Uh-huh."

MISSION DAYS 10–15

The section of the indictment citing violations of the Controlled Substance Act and NASA's Code of Conduct is totally disingenuous. Let me be clear: *before liftoff a non–crew member planted the psilocybin.* None of us could have sneaked that stuff on board. I've been framed, Ben, pure and simple, and once the jury understands that, it can't possibly convict me.

The High Jump's supplies included medications for pain (ibuprofen, codeine, morphine) as well as for sleep (dazelmemor, floralterdenol), anxiety (weritunz), and psychosis (hemaydherhisatol). Most of those drugs required Bria's sign-off before they could be administered.

For years, psilocybin and lysergic acid diethylamide (LSD) had been absent from the government's Schedule I list of banned drugs and were legal for treating psychiatric disorders. Some states had even legalized them for recreational use. NASA, however, maintained a strict ban, concluding the drugs' hallucinogenic effects were incompatible with crew safety.

Noel Roma and Q-Orbit, apparently, had come to a different conclusion.

We asked NASA to send us the latest episodes of *The New Martians*, which were recorded in the RedLiner. The storyline was as campy as ever: Terrance, Sophie, and Dido tried to end the angst of their love triangle by agreeing to a three-way open relationship. Meanwhile, someone attempted to murder Tom-tom.

We tried to tell if any of the First Fifty were tripping. In the RedLiner's rec room, where they often gathered, some of their eyes had that tripper glisten, and some of them appeared to giggle over nothing, while others did little more than float and stare at the walls. But seeing no one shrooming or popping Q-pills, and without close-ups of anyone's dilated pupils, we couldn't be sure.

"See the woman floating behind Terrance?" João said, pointing at the screen where Terrance was watching Sophie and Dido scream at each other. "The one laughing like a hyena at her forearm?"

"Maybe she heard a joke," I said.

"About a forearm?" Sally said. "No, she's wasted."

"Arcadia 7, this is Houston."

"Hey, Jennifer," I said. "Copy."

It was Mission Day 10, and while we waited for the next words from the current CAPCOM-on-duty, Jennifer Watt, I paused *The New Martians*. We were millions of kilometers from Earth, with a half-minute delay in radio communications.

"Flight wants me to pass on some news," Jennifer said. "The China National Space Administration just announced they'll launch in, like, fifteen days, with more improvements to their Fast Rabbit engine."

"Wow," I said. "That's cutting it close to the end of the launch opportunity. Any idea what the improvements are?"

Jen's voice crackled again after the transmission delay. "Negative. The other thing is, we haven't received your updated health surveys."

"Copy, Houston," Bria said. "I'm a bit behind. I'll send them soon."

"Flight wants an idea of, like, when you'll send them?" Jennifer replied. "Please advise."

Bria didn't hide her irritation. "I just told you. Soon."

"Jen, this is João." He was floating horizontally with his arms crossed, his brow furrowed as he glared at a squished-up food pouch someone had velcroed to the table. "I'd like to have the most recent issues of *Politico* and *The Hill* uploaded to me."

"Copy," Jen said. "Anything else?"

"Sally here. Please resend the high-resolution pics of the fossilized fungi they just discovered in France. The file we received was corrupted. Operations support may want to figure out how that happened."

I'd been ready to make the same request. We were keeping abreast of developments in research about ancient microbes, reading scientific papers on topics such as the process of shell formation that protected microscopic creatures from predators, and viewing new images of microbial fossils.

Prior missions confirmed Martian sediments contained organic molecules such as thiophenes, which may have been created by bacteria billions of years ago. Yet, even after the discovery at Jezero Crater of silica and carbonate minerals (which are seen in seashell and coral fossils on Earth), a scientific consensus remained elusive about whether they were ancient Martian biosignatures.

Arcadia 7 intended to settle the question. We would dig up Mars for up to 240 days, analyzing samples with microscopes and spectrometers, comparing what we found with past and present life on Earth. I fantasized about observing a magnified sample of melted Martian ice and watching round cells of microorganisms squirming and bumping into each other—life!

There was no way I could repeat the humiliation I suffered at Armstrong Station. Since Mars has no birds, I would have to pee or shit on the ice myself to get a false-positive reading, which I could only do if I got out of my xEMU suit. Which I wouldn't for two reasons: A) the suit had a built-in toilet, and B) I would die.

■ ■ ■

One way we kept stimulated on the High Jump was our weekly Greek Conversation Hour. We'd discuss complex issues in that foreign tongue, such as the relationship between microorganism decay and fossilization, and why polls showed 150 million American voters supported Dawn Bastbom for president.

Given her calls to gut social programs, environmental protection laws, education funding, and just about everything else that serves the interests of the ordinary citizen, her support *was* hard to understand. She even attacked NASA's budget, despite the popularity of our mission and the endorsement fees pouring into the U.S. Treasury.

But as João explained to us, Bastbom made a genius move by naming her V.P. running mate early.

Wolf D. Lemon was a household name. And he had experience. He'd served as a Florida congressman for six months after hosting *Penalty Lap* for nine years. Underperforming athletes in the show were sprayed with high-powered hoses by three dozen firefighters. Or shot at close range with paint guns for an hour. *Penalty Lap* proved even more popular than *And Now You Die!*

João didn't confine his vitriol for the Bastbom-Wolf ticket to Greek Conversation Hour. On Mission Day 15, I found him hovering in front of a floating screen and gorging on a breakfast burrito as he read *Politico.*

"Goddamn fish-lipped racist fascist bullshitter," he said and then caught his breath. "Fucker," he added.

"Who's a fucker?" I asked as I flew to the NanoPro.

"Fucking Lemon, the guy who looks like a grouper. He gets elected to Congress, then switches parties to join the NAP."

"That's politics, my friend."

João revolved and faced me. "The people who voted for him should be mad enough to start a recall petition."

"Well, he and Bastbom will lose, right?" I said. "I thought you told us she fell in the polls and now a hundred-fifty-two million voters want somebody else in the White House. Or maybe I missed what you said. It was in Greek, after all."

"No, you didn't miss anything." He turned back to the screen, grabbed the rest of the floating burrito, and shoved it into his mouth. I thought I'd pissed him off somehow, maybe because I hadn't agreed with him that Florida voters should recall Lemon, though I also dislike fuckers in general and Lemon in particular.

I left him alone and heated my burrito as Sally drifted in from the upper deck, followed by Bria. "Good morning," Sally said. "Ready for another thrilling day on the High Jump?"

We'd been in space for two weeks, and the monotony of routine had set in: the daily checkouts of the environmental and life-support systems, tending to the cabbage and lettuce garden on the lower deck, the two hours of exercise, and the tedious methods for bathing with reusable wipes and answering nature's call.

"Yeah, I'm so excited about changing the filters on the urine reprocessing system that I could barely sleep last night," I said.

Sally cracked a smile, but Bria frowned.

After breakfast, I checked out our food and beverage supplies. An indicator on the food printer showed one of the freeze-dried tempeh cartridges was empty, so I floated to the lower deck for a replacement. When I opened the bin that stored the cartridges, something else drifted out.

A Q-pill. And then another . . . and another. So many pills I stopped counting them all.

MISSION DAYS 16–26

"Arcadia 7, Houston."

This time it was Brendan Halo's voice. Jennifer's mate was a mellow, former bodybuilding champion. He took nothing too seriously, and I liked his uncanny talent for working around NASA's labyrinth of rules without pissing off Wendy or George.

"Uhhh," Brendan said, "we see you opened and closed every door of the lower deck storage bins yesterday."

"Copy that," I said. "One door seemed to malfunction, and to be safe, we tested all of them. Everything's fine. False alarm."

I held my breath (and I think the others did, too) for the minute and a half it took to receive Halo's response.

"Copy," he said. "Glad you got a handle on it."

I wanted to inform NASA about the psilocybin so it could investigate how thousands of doses could wind up on the High Jump. João saw things differently. After we had stowed the pills, he said, "We tell them about this and we hand NASA's opponents another argument for cutting its budget."

Bria agreed, suggesting we preserve the evidence and report to NASA once we were home.

Sally proposed conducting our own investigation.

So we lied to Halo. As far as I know, none of us *ever* told NASA about the Q-pills. I think Bria may have them, or what's left of them.

Noel Roma was suspect number one. If anyone could have staged such a stunt, it was her. But what on Earth (or off Earth) would be her motive?

One theory—put forth by Bria—was that Roma wanted everyone bound for Mars to get turned on, to gain support for the mass cultivation of MarShrooms (including "magic" ones) and build a mushroom-based economy on the Red Planet. We spent hours of private time talking about it, but by Mission Day 21, we shelved the discussion, at least until we landed on Arcadia Planitia.

I decided there were better ways to spend my time, like scrolling through family pictures, now that I was openly a father. I kept coming back to group shots of Scarlett, Nova, and Zena. In one, the two women were on either side of my little girl, holding her hands while she smiled at Zena; another had the three sitting cheerfully, their arms and legs crossed the same way, the proverbial three peas in a pod.

I kept remembering how fond Mom and Zena had been of Scarlett, and how Zena once treated Scarlett to a birthday lunch at a fancy Houston restaurant. And now she was Aunt Zena, who was withholding information from me. This wasn't about any rivalry, sibling or otherwise. Or about stealing my thunder. Nova was my child, and I had the right to know how Mother had learned she was a grandmother.

I opened a private channel and wrote to Zena: *Scarlett told you and Mom that Nova's our child, didn't she? It's okay if she did. I won't do anything about it. I'd just like to know.*

Zena's answer came in two minutes: *No, Scarlett didn't tell me. I can't say who did. I just can't.*

My reply: *Zena, it's probably a waste of time to ask, but I will anyhow. Why can't you?*

No reply.

I concluded I could drive myself nuts by pressing the issue, and I should wait and try to learn the truth on Mars. Besides, it was around this time I began focusing on a potential problem with João.

"You think Sal and João are fine—I mean, with each other?" I asked Bria after we turned in for the (artificial) night. "They seem pretty standoffish to one another. He didn't even thank her for making JW for dinner."

"The political stuff gets on her nerves," Bria said. "Oh, and she feels like he doesn't care about learning Greek."

"Is that all?"

"Pretty much."

"Pretty much?"

"Let's just say there are ripple effects."

"Got it." I sighed. "Let's take it up with João at our next meeting."

"Good idea. Sleep tight, baby."

The following day, João listened to our concerns. He said he understood how his news addiction could be annoying and that he would give it a break. But as he drifted away, an empty food pouch floated in his path, and instead of retrieving it, he used his thumb and middle finger to flick it away, sending the pouch cartwheeling into an equipment console.

I traded the same look with the others. I think we were of the same mind. João had exhibited passive-aggressive behavior, yet it was probably best to let it pass.

■ ■ ■

On Mission Day 25, a quarter of the way to Mars, we gathered to watch the Chinese launch. As the Long March 9 rocket sat spewing liquid oxygen clouds on its pad on Hainan Island, my thoughts turned to the crew scrunched up in the capsule.

Their names were Zheng Mǐn and Zhang Wěi. We knew nothing about them except they were both twenty-seven and had trained in Beijing. A video showed them in spacesuits, waving at flight technicians while trudging to the elevator that lifted them to the capsule. They had their helmets on, but with the morning sun in full blaze, the helmets took on a tint that obscured their faces. They were probably smiling to mask their terror of dying in a fireball.

We applauded as Zheng and Zhang lifted off safely. KIM began playing "March of the Volunteers," the Chinese national anthem. I thought it was a bit too salutatory and ordered KIM to stop, then continued to watch as the first stage separated and the second stage commenced its burn. Once the Chinese crew reached orbit, we returned to our routines.

An hour later, we regrouped to receive an update from Ed Munch.

"There's a report about the Chinese spacecraft we didn't expect," he said. "Telescope imagery shows that Fast Rabbit's engines don't use chemical propulsion. They're nuclear thermal. In fact, the engines appear identical to ours. We'll know more when they do their TMI burn."

"Copy that," I said. "Can you send us those images? What's the timing of their TMI?"

While we waited for Munch's answer, Sally, Bria, and I exchanged raised eyebrows. João, with a pout on his face, flew to his private quarters.

I didn't know how others at NASA felt, but knowing the Chinese had gone nuclear, to me it sure as hell seemed we might be in the greatest race of all time, far bigger than the Indy 500, Kentucky Derby, and America's Cup combined. And though millions of kilometers separated us from Zheng and Zhang, in terms of cosmic distances, we could soon be neck and neck. It made me nervous, then I caught myself. Only the Chinese knew the parameters of their spacecraft's upcoming TMI burn and its resulting speed, but to catch up with us, they'd have to accelerate to a dangerous velocity.

I relaxed.

"So much for the government keeping our nuclear technology out of the hands of others," Sally said. "How did our intelligence agencies miss such a thing?"

"Wouldn't be the first time," Bria replied with disgust.

"Maybe the Chinese are just great at hiding shit," I said. "Their command hierarchy—"

"Sure, Ad Man, no problem with the pictures," Munch said, interrupting me. "Not clear when TMI is scheduled. We'll let you know. Have you folks seen the student questions sent by ops support? The show starts in an hour. Will you be ready?"

"Roger," I said. "Looking forward to it."

Actually, I wasn't, and I can safely say that João wasn't, either. As for the women, I don't know. This would be the fourth—and mercifully last—"show" in which we'd answer questions submitted by children from schools that won the naming competitions. Here, it would be the Pioneer Elementary School in Sacramento, which had come up with "American Express" as the name for our Mars Ascent Vehicle.

We each had three questions to answer, and NASA had weeded out the ones we'd been asked a billion times ("How do you go to the bathroom?"), or had anything to do with politics ("Will you be able to come back to Earth if Congress cuts NASA's budget?"), or involved the Chinese or the First Fifty ("Will all of you have a party on Mars?"), or asked about my broken toe.

Instead, most of the questions dealt with how the American Express worked, and our answers would emphasize how wonderful and safe it would be when we lifted off from Mars and began our journey home.

But with Zheng and Zhang still on my mind, I just couldn't get into talking to the kids. Or even truthfully answering the best question, submitted by ten-year-old freckle-faced Stevie Simpson: "I've been to Space Camp, but if I want to grow up on Mars instead of in Sacramento, what else should I be doing?"

I wanted to say, "Try living in Antarctica for a year, but you'd better hurry up and get your little butt down there before the whole goddamn thing melts." Instead, I said, "That's a good question, Stevie. Here's what I suggest. Figure out what you'd like to be on Earth and then see how it fits with living on Mars. For example, if you want to be a lawyer, that could work. Mars will need lawyers, just like Earth does. But if you like large bodies of water and want to be an oceanographer, Mars may not be the best place for you. Make sense?"

"Good answer," Bria told me after the show.

Except it wasn't. When it came to Mars, what one wanted to be mattered little. What mattered was how Mars would change you and what you would *become*, things you couldn't know in advance. In that sense, you yourself were among the mysteries of the Red Planet.

■ ■ ■

At one in the morning, our time, we floated before the screen on the middle deck. Mission Control had given us advance notice that the Chinese were starting their TMI.

"KIM," I said. "Display real-time data for Fast Rabbit TMI, including trajectory, thrust, propulsive impulse, speed, and elapsed time."

"I would be happy to. One moment, please."

"The burn looks nominal," Bria said when the column of numbers, all of which were increasing, appeared next to a line arching from an ellipse representing the Earth orbit the spacecraft was leaving.

"Wow," Sally added, "their engines have as much thrust as ours, but their spacecraft is what, half the mass of the High Jump?"

"Sally," KIM said, "I estimate Fast Rabbit, with filled fuel tanks, habitat, and lander, has forty-eight-point-thirty-seven percent of the mass of the High Jump."

Twenty minutes into the burn, Zheng and Zhang were zooming at a speed of eight kilometers per second. We continued to watch the readout during dinner, and by the hour mark of the burn, their speed exceeded twelve km/s. We kept expecting the burn to end at any moment, but it didn't. When it passed the eighty-minute mark—the length of our own TMI burn—João said, "How in the fuck will they slow down?"

KIM didn't have an answer. Fast Rabbit's speed had passed eighteen klicks per second, two times our present speed. Eventually, to be captured by Mars gravity, the crew would need to slow way down, to five or six. To do that, they would have to fire thrusters, which would consume huge amounts of precious fuel.

"KIM," I said. "Best explanation?"

"The strongest theory is that Fast Rabbit's engines are not functioning properly."

"They can't turn them off?"

"Correct. Which explains why Fast Rabbit is traveling so fast."

And then, at the eighty-five-minute mark, the burn stopped.

Zheng and Zhang's speed was nineteen kilometers—the length of 200 football fields—per second, more than twice as fast as a low earth orbit space station. While most of KIM's "theories" turned out to be accurate, some were far off. After all, it could only work with available data, but this time I believed the robot.

"Could they have more fuel waiting for them on Mars?" Sally said.

João smirked. "Yeah, they hid it in a lava tube."

"Screw you," Sally said and floated off to the exercise machines.

Yes, João was being an asshole, and he and Sally were having problems. Again.

On the next day, Mission Day 26, Mission Control reported that CNSA confirmed the TMI burn was one hundred percent nominal. China's space agency expressed zero concern about the ship's ability to decrease speed and safely arrive at Mars, while retaining sufficient fuel for trans-Earth injection thirty days later. I feared the worst. My chest tightened as I asked KIM when Fast Rabbit would enter Mars orbit.

"With proper breaking maneuvers, they will arrive in two months and twenty-two days," the robot answered.

My brain did the quick math. "Four days before we arrive."

"Correct."

And that's when, despite zero gravity, my heart sank, all the way to my bum toe, where they ached together.

■ ■ ■

I didn't care about the financial hit. If, for any reason, Bria and I were *not* the first to walk on Mars, our endorsement contracts stipulated a fifty percent reduction in compensation. No, the money didn't matter. What bothered me was the history we wouldn't be making, and I blamed NASA. Being in the best position to know, they should have seen CNSA's "take your time" approach to Mars was a fake-out. Suddenly, we were the losers. The agency hadn't followed its own philosophy: *Think the unthinkable and then plan for it.*

As the days passed, my anger blossomed. I also blamed the CIA, FBI, NSA, State Department, Army, Navy, Air Force, Congress, *New York Times*, *Washington Post*, *Space Times*, and anyone else with the slightest connection to NASA, the intelligence community, and the media. Their collective ignorance would cause Arcadia 7 to finish in second place.

I grew angrier still as I watched the world react to China's feat: the shock and disappointment of Americans, the giddiness of journalists over the news bonanza. I almost admired the skill with which Dawn Bastbom whipped up animosity.

"Just look at NASA," she told a rally of 75,000 zealots on a sizzling November day in Florida, her black-dyed hair flapping in the wind like a war flag on a five-foot pole. She shook her head and pursed her lips as if scolding children. "Two trillion dollars spent to put the first humans on Mars, and what happens? They let the Chinese win." As the crowd roared, she shouted to be heard over them. "Well, I say enough is enough! For all I care, NASA can leave their crew there!"

"Leave! Them! There!" the crowd chanted.

Bastbom laughed and waved at the sky as if it were all a joke. Her followers, however, didn't sound like they were in on it.

"Leave! Them! There!"

"Yeah, you can see the miserable job NASA has done," she rambled on, "and who they picked to command the mission. A runaway dad with a busted toe who can't play the oboe worth a shit. What a prick."

"Leave! Him! There!"

"Maybe you should call your lawyer," João said with a scowl, taunting me.

Irked, I gave him a look. "Think I'll take an ibuprofen instead."

Bastbom's latest tirade had worked up João, too, his face flush. Sally told KIM to switch the news feed. Fortunately, João didn't protest.

"NASA projects Fast Rabbit will overtake the High Jump in nineteen days," CNN's Ingrid Steele reported, her tone mournful. "That will be Mission Day 45 for the crew of Arcadia 7. One can be sure it won't be the happiest of days for them."

My middle toe was throbbing. The ache came and went, whether I moved it or not. It was one time I missed the morphine. But Bria refused to give me anything stronger than ibuprofen, which worked for the most part.

"I wonder if Fast Rabbit's transport vehicle has an extra tank we can't see," Sally said as I flew to the packet of ibuprofen velcroed on the wall. Our eyes locked while I sucked on the straw poked into a juice pouch and washed down the pill. She floated vertically with her brows arched, as if showing empathy for me. "Or maybe they're using a technology that vastly improves fuel efficiency," she continued.

"Or maybe they'll use a different propulsion system for the trip home," Bria added.

"Or maybe they lie about everything," I said, still wanting to believe KIM's "strongest theory." I reproached myself for imagining Zheng and Zhang ricocheting off Mars's atmosphere and careening into the Great Rabbit Hole of Oblivion.

"NASA has begun a press conference," KIM said. "I can display the transmission if you like. There will be a one-minute delay in the feed."

"Do it, KIM," I said. "Thanks."

The picture flickered as the stage of the JSC auditorium appeared. Seated at a table were NASA's administrator, our flight director, and the four CAPCOMs.

"We'll go straight to questions," said George Butlarer. He pointed at a woman in the audience. We knew most of the names of the reporters. This one was Maggie Cool, now as bald-shaven as a Buddhist monk, the back of her head displaying a tattoo of a large eyeball.

"George, despite CNSA's public statements, speculation persists that their spacecraft malfunctioned. If that turns out to be the case, does NASA have any plans to attempt a rescue? And I have a follow-up, please."

"We have no such plans," George said. "A rescue wouldn't be possible. Anyhow, we're ninety-nine percent sure there was no malfunction."

"Then how do you explain the performance of Fast Rabbit's nuclear engines?" Maggie asked.

"Obviously, a lot has to do with the amount of propellant, its storage, and the rate of fuel consumption. However, CNSA is only speaking in generalities, so we don't know exactly how they pulled things off."

The other five at the table stared at their personal screens. They looked up when the *Post*'s Ken Nosjoni raised his hand.

George said, "Go ahead, Ken," pointing a pencil at him.

"My question is for Flight and the CAPCOMs. How is the American crew taking the news they won't be first on Mars?"

"May I?" At the end of the table, Jennifer Watt leaned over and glanced at Wendy, who nodded. Jen then faced the reporter. "I think I speak for all of us in saying the Arcadia 7 crew sounds more positive about their mission than ever. Like, just yesterday, Co-commander Johnson told me how the fossil discovery in France astounded him. He didn't even mention Fast Rabbit."

Which was true, but Jen had not read my mind correctly. Neither had Ed, Pete, or Brendan, who all smiled as Wendy spoke, which bugged me.

"The crew is *fine* with where they are in the mission," she said. "They never thought of this as a race, and it isn't, never has been, never will be. So, it's no big deal for them, even if it is for you folks."

■ ■ ■

"I know you're disappointed," Bria said after we zipped up in our sleep pod. "But first on Mars is not the only first. Not even the most important one."

"You're right," I replied. "I'll be the first oboe player. Unless Zheng or Zhang knows how to play."

"How about the first to discover alien life, I mean real, living microbes? That's a Nobel Prize for chemistry. Schoolkids will learn your name for thousands of years."

She had a point, but my spirits still floundered. It was doubtful anything lived in a place with an atmosphere thinner than Dawn Bastbom's skin and an average temperature of 76 degrees below zero (which probably matches that of said skin), and in any event, dozens from Roma's crew would join the hunt.

I tried to sleep after Bria and I pecked each other on the lips, the kiss laying to rest any friction between us. Half an hour later, my eyes were open. On the battlefield of my brain, the floralterdenol I'd taken was losing to the cortisol that attacked my self-esteem in waves of disappointment and frustration. I could have swallowed another sleeping pill but instead shifted my thoughts to the "most important first." And slept.

MISSION DAYS 27–38

For the next two days, during daily meditation, I practiced creative visualization. The French fossils and the shapes of *Anabaena*, *Cylindrospermum*, and *Palaeolyngbya*. Hopping around Arcadia Planitia, digging up ice samples in the bluish Mars morning. Hopping back to the M&M Ranch to study them. Standing on the dais in Stockholm, floating in joy with a heavy gold medal around my neck.

But my mental workouts didn't soothe me, and I was dying to talk with Sally. Alone. As our information systems specialist, she knew the most about KIM's functions and programming, and I didn't want the others—including KIM—to learn what I needed to ask her.

My chance came when João was exercising and Bria was wipe-bathing in her quarters.

"Sal," I whispered to her on the middle deck. "Can we meet for a few minutes in privacy mode?"

She shot a glance at João, then whispered to me. "Sure. Where do you want to do it?"

"Lower deck."

She flew behind me, and when we stopped, we looked at our palms and tapped the eyeball icon, which turned red to confirm no cameras were pointed at us.

"What's up?" she said while hovering vertically, her gold hair a floating crown.

"Is there any way to use KIM's analytics on a problem without KIM's memory retaining the inputs or outputs?"

"Why would you want to?"

"You're as curious as I am about Fast Rabbit's engines and the Chinese mission design. I'd like to conduct our own study, without Butlarer or Frost knowing, so they don't think we're second-guessing them. Honestly? I'm not sure they'll level with us if they figure out what the Chinese are doing."

"And this matters because . . . ?"

My broken toe flared up, like someone had driven a nail into it with one bang of a hammer. "Because we ought to know our options." As she narrowed her eyes and inclined her head, I came out with it. "Okay, it's like this. I want to see if a second engine burn is possible for a course correction that maintains a safe trans-Mars injection."

"That would goose Fast Rabbit even more. Why would the Chinese do that?"

"I'm not talking about Fast Rabbit." As she looked up through the hole to the middle deck, I tried reading her mind. Was she afraid someone was spying on us? "Sal, I realize such a maneuver probably isn't feasible. But at least we would know for sure, so we can put it out of our minds—"

"You mean put it out of *your* mind."

"Fine. And move forward, without regretting the 'woulda, coulda, shouldas.'"

She paused, holding her gaze steady, then said, "Only if Bria and João agree. Even if they do, it'll be hard to tamper with KIM without NASA detecting it, so I can't make any promises."

I wanted to say, "I love you, Sally Kristalobopous." Instead, it was just "thanks."

■ ■ ■

Ben, sorry to get technical again, but you need to understand certain things to prepare for my trial.

Our spacecraft housed three nuclear thermal engines capable of 18,000 kilonewtons of thrust for the mission's four major burns: trans-Mars injection (TMI), which took place on Mission Day 2; trajectory correction maneuver (TCM), to keep us on track; Mars orbit insertion (MOI), a prelude to landing; and trans-Earth injection (TEI), to send us home.

The TMI burn expended the liquid hydrogen fuel in the drop tank, which was jettisoned. That left 125 metric tons of LH2 remaining in the core stage and inline tanks for the MOI and TEI burns. Both tanks also had thrusters. Based on our trajectory, our flight plan specified we'd travel 9 km/s as we approached Mars before our MOI burn slowed us down.

The maximum "pushing the envelope" speed for capture by Martian gravity is around 6 km/s, so I believed we had some speed to play with. Another engine burn with one or more trajectory corrections could orient our spacecraft to intercept Mars sooner than the original plan specified, while staying within the speed limit. I wanted KIM to verify that I was right.

But what KIM knew, NASA knew, and if NASA knew, its rockets wouldn't be the only thing going ballistic. I might have run the equations myself on a secure part of my own computer, but that was risky since everything was networked. I took several days to work the equations on paper until I felt the idea merited further investigation with KIM's help.

"João, how's it going?" I asked at the start of the private crew meeting I'd requested. It was Mission Day 30; in a couple of weeks, Fast Rabbit would be closer to Mars than we were. I wanted to gauge João's mood before presenting my plan. If he was upset about something, I would abort the attempt and try again later.

"Why do you ask?" João said, floating with his arms and ankles crossed. "Are we meeting because of me?"

"No, I just—"

"Well, I'm fine, and so is Sally." He revolved around to his wife. "Aren't we?"

"Yeah," she answered with the excitement of a sloth. "Just fine."

"All right," Bria said. "Why *are* we meeting?"

"Arcadia 7, this is Houston."

"Shit," I said and turned off privacy mode. "Copy that, Brendan. Ready to listen."

At least it was Halo. I looked at my palm screen: 5:30 p.m. in Houston. *Happy Hour*, I thought, and how I missed it.

The first message in a new round of communications, if initiated by Mission Control, was limited to a few words, giving us notice that the transmission delay—now over a minute—gave time to find a stopping point for whatever engaged us, which in this case wasn't much. As we awaited Halo's next message, João asked, "Have you noticed that the treadmill squeaks?"

"I still use the XBike," I said, gesturing at my foot. "Hurts less."

"I don't notice any squeak," Sally said.

Bria shook her head. "Neither do I."

But João was adamant. "Well, it's there. And will only get worse. To make a repair, I might have to tear the whole damn thing apart."

I spread my hands. "Sure, amigo. Do what you have to."

"And the food printer's acting up," he added. "May have to tear that apart, too."

"What's wrong with it?" Bria asked.

"It's burning through cartridges too fast. I'm surprised NASA hasn't said anything. Maybe they're testing us again."

"The simulations have ended," Bria said. "If there's a problem, it's a real one."

João glared at her. "Don't you think I know that?"

I turned on privacy mode. "Here's what I know, João. I don't like your tone. And I think *that's* a problem. Jesus, man, we just finished the first month of the mission, with *fifteen* left to go. So we need to work this out. As your co-commander, I'm ordering—"

"Hey, Addy, good to hear you." For a second time the crackle of Brendan's voice had silenced me, making me cringe. "Wanted to share a little funny business about the First Fifty. They shot an episode of *The New Martians* on the RedLiner. A spoof about you and . . . well, I don't want to give any spoilers, so let me know if you want it sent to you. And Flight suspended press conferences and interviews with the crew for the time being—good news, right? The reason—Wendy's words—is she wants you focused one hundred ten percent on the mission. Oh, and João, can you check who's on your distribution list for engineering reports? You should copy the instrumentation and communications officer. You left her off the last one. Over."

I turned off privacy mode. "Roger. Yes, send the episode, Brendan. You've made me curious."

"Brendo, this is João," my crewmate interjected. "Roger. I'll look at the list." As he spoke, he drifted away from our circle, his hands clenched into fists, save for his middle fingers.

■ ■ ■

Nip it in the bud.

Uncle Dick spoke that instruction often as I grew up, when I did something he didn't like.

"You're chewing with your mouth open, Zacky, which is how monkeys chew, so better nip it in the bud."

"You wanna crush the other team? Then better nip your 'they're better than us' attitude in the bud."

Uncle Dick, who's a lawyer, encouraged my interest in the law. When I was a kid, he texted me his reviews of TV shows about lawyers, explaining the "monkey business" of them lying to their own clients and tampering with evidence was for "dramatic effect." He found this excusable because the shows realistically portrayed their perseverance and desire to win, no matter what.

My father, however, thought ethical misconduct was never excusable. He was set on me becoming an astronaut, and was all for winning, yet wanted his kids to play by the rules. He won out in my chosen career, but Uncle Dick's philosophy of life stuck with me more.

I've traced that back to when I was ten, and Zena and I were racing kayaks in the Indiana Dunes National Park. Declaring me the winner "by a monkey's hair," Uncle Dick handed me a twenty-dollar bill and said, "Always remember, Zacky, winning isn't everything, it's the only thing." Zena's consolation prize was a candy bar. She felt cheated. It was during that trip she set the trash bin on fire, searing my brain with the memory of the race, Uncle Dick's mantra, and roaring flames.

I knew I hadn't taken a winning approach with João and was glad Brendan had interrupted me. I planned to order João and Sally to begin couple's counseling with Bria, which would have been a mistake because, among other reasons, I hadn't consulted with either woman beforehand. After the call with Halo, I rescheduled the crew meeting.

A few days later, Bria and I were meditating in her private quarters when the gong sound told us twenty minutes were up.

"I need to talk with you about something," I said. "I want your opinion."

She smiled. "Okay, babe, go ahead."

I looked into her eyes and gathered my courage. "Sal and I talked. We concluded it's possible to stay ahead of Fast Rabbit and beat them to Mars."

"Uh-huh."

"The entire crew should be on board before the idea goes any further. So—"

"You want my approval."

"Yeah, and—"

"I assume you're going to inform Flight."

"Well, sure, but not right away. We want KIM to perform the analysis first, without Flight's knowledge."

"Uh-huh."

"Don't get me wrong. Of course, we'll share the results with Flight, it's just that—"

"You want to do this without Flight's permission and ask for forgiveness later."

"Exactly. And make it no big deal."

She crossed her arms. "And how will you explain you hid KIM's role? You'll have to hack the robot's systems, correct?"

"Yes, but we don't have to tell NASA. We'll say we worked the numbers ourselves."

"We?"

I sighed. "Okay, me. We should know our options before telling Flight."

"We?"

"If staying ahead isn't possible, the idea's moot." I spread my arms. "No harm done."

Our eyes stayed glued before she replied. "I thought you got over your 'being first' compulsion."

I glanced at my socked feet, one of which was still larger than the other. "Yeah, so did I. Guess it's a relapse."

"Well, I need to think this through, Addy. And I want you to think about it more. João should be our primary concern at the moment."

I looked up. "I was about to order him and Sally into once-a-week counseling with you, with your consent, of course."

"Uh-huh."

It was the third time she'd made that utterance with disdain in her voice. And the third time I'd tried to ignore it.

"I realize," I said, "I would have made a mistake by doing that."

"Big-time," she said. "He's obsessing about the news again, and the news isn't pretty. He's displacing his anger with Bastbom and projecting it onto us."

"How did NASA miss such a flaw in his personality assessment?"

"Easy. When they screened him, Dawn Bastbom wasn't running for president and crapping all over his father."

■ ■ ■

By my rough calculations, Mission Day 55 was the latest day an engine burn could, within comfortable safety margins, prevent Zheng and Zhang from overtaking us. It was now Mission Day 34. As anxious as I was to have Sally fiddle with KIM, I had to get a green light from Bria and João.

Frost and Butlarer had reservations about us watching the installment of *The New Martians* that parodied me, which was titled "What the Fungi?" I later learned they hadn't been sure how the crew would react to watching a co-commander get mercilessly skewered. They feared I would lose the respect of my crewmates. But in the end, Ed Munch and Pete Bullseye Peters convinced them otherwise, arguing we could all take a joke. Brendan Halo and Jennifer Watt added I would get to see Nova, which would be good for me and, therefore, good for the entire crew.

As we watched the episode, which took the form of a mystery, my crew members howled. I stayed stone-faced, barely hiding my disgust as I recoiled at the dude who played me. His hair looked like it'd been spray-painted the color of the water in an unflushed toilet. While he drifted weightlessly, his foot cast reminded me of the super-sized chimichanga our food printer could churn out. It sickened me to see Scarlett and Nova playing themselves. Neither knew who "daddy" was ("outer space is dark, honey"). I didn't care that it was supposed to be comedy. Scarlett came across as a sex addict and our child as emotionally abused.

The storyline conveyed that Nova and the actor playing me both loved a species of mushroom that 99.99 percent of the universe detested, the big clue about their filial relationship. When he finally fessed up to being her dad, she rode his foot cast as if she sat in a horse saddle ("Giddy up, Daddy!"). I found the whole thing revolting.

"Boy," Bria said in the darkness of our sleep pod that night, "you sure didn't hold back on how much you loved that show."

I didn't care for her sarcasm. I also didn't care to sound defensive by telling her that. "I'm seriously considering talking with Jep about Nova's custody," I said.

"We return to Earth next year. Nova's remaining on Mars, remember?"

"Exactly. I don't want her there. I think her mother is unfit. Scarlett is setting our daughter up for ridicule. She'll end up having trust issues for the rest of her life, unless there's a change."

"Sort of like you."

"Ouch. What exactly do you mean?"

"Let's start with NASA. Do you trust George and Wendy?"

"That's different."

"How about your mother? You didn't trust her knowing you were a father until after we left."

"It was for her protection."

"And your father, how much did you trust him growing up? Or your sister?"

"Okay, I get it." A pause followed, and then I extended an olive branch. "But I trust *you*," I said, turning my face to her, though she couldn't see me.

"You ought to, Addy, since you're one smart guy, and you know we've got to trust each other, especially in deep space." Her tone had softened, her breath sweetened by the toothpaste she had just swallowed, and in the pitch dark I saw my chance.

"Thanks, hon," I said, letting a beat pass. "Have you thought more about what Sally and I would like to do with KIM?"

I sensed her swiveling to me and smelled her minty breath again as she spoke. "Remember when you coached me on the answer I should give the selection committee, when they asked what I'd do if it looked like another team was going to land before us?"

"I said you should tell them it didn't matter who was first. But, as I recall, you'd say we'd analyze things and see what course adjustments were possible. I'm totally okay if you're not comfortable doing that now, although it would be nice to know why you've changed your position."

"I haven't changed my position."

"All right, then—"

"But I have conditions. First, after you, Sally, and KIM are done, and you have your answer, you'll scrub any trace of your activities. Second, if there are 'options,' as you call them, and you share them with NASA, promise me you'll take 'no' for an answer if that's *their* position."

"I promise." I craned my face forward to kiss her, missing her lips in the dark and getting a nostril instead.

I had won her over. That only left João.

MISSION DAYS 39–40

On Mission Day 39, a week before Z and Z would whiz past us, I faced the last hurdle.

João was at the treadmill with his feet duct-taped to the floor so he could stay on his knees without bobbing while he worked on the machine. He had taken off the running mat, exposing the metal frame, gears, and wires. The screws he removed were stuck to a strip of tape so they didn't float away, though he didn't notice the one floating near his forehead.

"Hey, João, what's up?" I said as I drifted toward him in privacy mode.

He mumbled without looking at me. "There is no up. Or down, either. Or sideways, or north or south or east or west. We're in outer space."

I chuckled. "Thanks for the physics refresher. Hey, can we talk?"

João let go of the screwdriver, unbent his knees, and turned to me. "Listen, I'm sorry for being such a dick lately."

"This isn't about—"

"Really, man, it's just that . . ." He bunched up his face at the torn-up treadmill. His eyes were watery. "Everything's breaking—this and the XBike and the food printer and the toilet and the wall screen and five dozen other pieces of equipment we need to reach Mars alive." He glanced up. "It's sort of getting to me, you know?"

Damn, I thought. No one else had malfunction notifications for any of that. The only broken piece of equipment seemed to be inside our chief engineer's head.

"Apology accepted," I said as alarms sounded in my own brain. I know. I should have paid more attention to them immediately, but in truth I didn't want to, rationalizing that my crew mate would get over his funk. "By the way, I'd like KIM to consider the idea of conducting another engine burn."

João raised his eyebrows. "What for? What's wrong?"

"No, don't worry, it's nothing like that. I want to know what options we have to stay ahead of the Chinese."

"You mean so we arrive at Mars first?"

I nabbed the floating screwdriver and pressed it against a slab of Velcro to hold it in place. "Obviously, everyone would have to agree. I spoke to Bria and Sal, and—"

"You can stop there." He jerked his head at the treadmill, dislodging a tear that trickled down the five o'clock shadow of his face. "I don't give a fuck what you do with KIM. Fixing this is all that matters. And the bike, the food printer, and the toilet."

I forced a smile. "Great. Carry on, amigo."

Only ten days remained in the abort window. After Mission Day 49, the course maneuvers were too risky to turn the High Jump around and get us back to Earth. According to my handwritten calculations, Mission Day 52 was the optimal day for an engine burn that kept the High Jump ahead of Fast Rabbit, while retaining 80 percent of our fuel reserve.

It thrilled me to give Sally the green light to ask KIM to confirm my conclusion, but I also realized I could no longer downplay the seriousness of João's neurosis. It would likely end the mission. That is, if we reported the problem to NASA *before* Mission Day 49. I didn't relish the thought of reporting it *after* that day, when it would be too late to turn back. Even without a surface landing, we'd have to go the distance with João for at least 400 more days.

When Bria told me João admitted to feeling blue and agreed to daily counseling with her, my heavy sigh of relief thrust me into a floating gaming screen, ending someone's paused session of *Call of Duty: Alien Ops III.* "I suggest you *not* discuss João's problems with him," Bria said, "or with Sally. Leave him to me."

"He thinks he needs to repair everything in sight."

"Let him. It will be therapeutic. If he breaks anything, we have backups."

"And if he breaks those?"

Bria gave me a terse stare. "Then we'll see how well he can break the lock we put on his zipped-up sleep pod."

■ ■ ■

My toe pain came and went. The sharp ache lasted only seconds, the episodes happening about once a week. Fortunately, they were becoming less frequent. The bigger pain, by far, was João.

I assumed NASA was as concerned about him as I was. By now, AI analysis of his facial expressions and speech patterns would have revealed a problem. Wendy, I imagined, was waiting for the intervention criteria to be met before NASA stepped in. She would have to finalize a decision to abort by no later than Mission Day 48.

Abort. How I hated the word.

"*Gyro!*" Sally said as she darted a food-printed roll of pita at me. By Mission Day 40, Greek Sunday Brunch had become part of our routine.

I opened my mouth and caught the gyro, which was filled with VeriSym lamb and rehydrated onions and tomatoes, glued together with a spicy yogurt sauce the consistency of peanut butter. "Mmmm . . . *kali*," I said as I chewed the surprisingly tasty sponge. "*Efcharistó*, Sal."

Bria had similar praise, but João kept silent, avoiding eye contact with his wife while occasionally glancing at Bria.

I switched to privacy mode by punching the eyeball icon on my palm, then said, "Open the back door, KIM, and let in some outer space." I paused five seconds, then repeated, "KIM?"

"We're good," Bria said after another pause.

I could feel my heart beating faster. Sally was about to report the results of KIM's calculations. "Shoot," I said. "Let's hear the numbers."

She took a breath. "I should tell you up front I'm not a hundred percent confident my activity went undetected. NASA may see someone's been fooling around with KIM. To put it simply, I tricked KIM into thinking it was running a ship diagnostics program when, in fact, it was running a mole program. I'm the only one who knows the key to unlock the encryption. To access the program, one has to perform a physical act."

"Which is?" I said.

"Kissing my palm screen. If the pattern of curves and crevices of the lips don't match mine, there's no entry."

"And KIM doesn't have lips," I observed.

"Not the last time I checked. Even if KIM imaged my lips, the access key requires applying the kiss with a certain amount of pressure, which KIM is incapable of."

"So," Bria said, "if KIM and NASA discover the mole program, they can't tell what it is, correct?"

Sally hunched up her shoulders. "I don't *think* they can."

"Understood," I said. "Proceed with your—wait a sec. João, please pay attention to this."

João had unfolded his gyro and was peering at its contents, tilting his head and furrowing his brow as if studying the engine of an alien spacecraft. A dislodged bit of tomato floated at the tip of his nose. As soon as he noticed it, his jaws opened, then chomped down on the red morsel like a shark.

"João," I repeated.

He swallowed and glanced at me sideways.

"Let's put a hold on the gyros while Sal gives her report."

"Report?" he said and looked at Bria with his mouth half open. "What's wrong?"

"Remember, João?" Her voice was calm. "You and I talked about this. There's nothing to be afraid of. After we hear Sal's report, whatever we do will be unanimous."

I gestured at Sally to begin.

"I must say," she said, "your hand calculations blew me away, Addy. You came fairly close to at least one option KIM generated."

My breathing slowed as my heart continued to race.

"Actually, the safest burn—which preserves eighty percent of our reserve fuel—needs to occur on Mission Day 44 instead of 52."

"Four days from now," I said.

"Yes. We can still do a burn on Mission Day 52, but the fuel reserve falls to sixty-four percent."

"What is the fuel reserve for other burns after Mission Day 49, the no-turning-back point?" I asked.

"Not much different."

"Sally," Bria said, "what are the probabilistic risk assessments in terms of mission success, including safe return to Earth?"

"Because of fuel consumption, of course, the probability of mission success declines with any unplanned burn. Without a change to our flight plan and assuming all systems perform nominally, we have a ninety-three percent chance of safe return. With the safest burn, that falls to seventy-eight percent. It falls even lower for any burn that comes later."

I winced. "What's the safe return probability on Mission Day 50, once the window for an abort closes?"

"Sixty-five percent."

"Well, that's unacceptable to me," Bria said. "Even the 'safest burn' is an enormous risk." She turned to me. "Even if NASA approves, I'm not sure I would agree."

"I understand," I said, nodding. "No matter what, we follow the rule of unanimity."

"And if I agreed, I could change my mind later?"

"Of course. I have no problem with that."

And I didn't—as long as we spoke to NASA with one voice, making it clear that for America to maintain its lead in space exploration, we were willing to take on more risk. And it had nothing to do with egos, record sales, or commercial endorsements.

MISSION DAY 41

Whatever else I did, I wanted a written record so no one could accuse me of breaking rules or reneging on promises. After my crewmates reviewed the wording, I sent this message to Flight:

> Wendy, we've noodled the Lambert/Nelder-Mead numbers and believe a mission course correction burn can position us to land before Fast Rabbit.
>
> Current flight plan:
>
> › Mission Day 62: Mars orbital insertion (MOI) burn (orbit on Mission Day 118)
>
> › Mission Day 122: Dock with lander + entry, descent, and landing (EDL)

Revised flight plan:

- Mission Day 44: Mission course correction (MCC) burn*
- Mission Day 62: MOI burn (orbit on Mission Day 113)**
- Mission Day 116: Dock with lander + EDL (**6 DAYS EARLIER** than current plan)

* Start burn: 16:50:00 UTC / Duration: 22 minutes, 13 seconds
Additional fuel consumption: 1.92 metric tons

** Additional fuel consumption: 0.24 metric tons

Risk assessment (probability of safe return):

- Current flight plan: 93.22%
- Revised flight plan: 78.09%

The crew will accept the increased risk, which is far outweighed by MANY advantages—the national prestige of staying #1 in space, first choice of landing sites, staking out areas for exploration before anyone else, etc., etc. We would appreciate MC validating our numbers so we can ramp up for the MCC burn. Let's go for it. FOR AMERICA. Thanks!

We floated in a circle before the big screen and waited for Mission Control's response.

And waited . . . and . . . waited. I set my palm to tingle when the reply arrived, but a half hour later—plenty of time for Mission Control to receive the message and respond—no tingle had tingled.

"Flight should have at least sent an acknowledgment," I said. "KIM, operational status of communications systems."

"All functions nominal," the robot replied.

"They're probably still processing the message," Bria said. "And deciding how to answer."

I flew to the XBike, thinking I could channel my anxiety into a workout while listening to the new Stranglebots album, *Crisis Man, Crisis Woman*.

"Be careful on that thing," João said. "It may jam up again, and if you're pumping hard, you could pull or rip your hamstring or glute, or pop your knee, or even kill yourself."

"Got it," I said as I strapped myself into the bike's harness.

Sally flew up next to me, strapped herself into the treadmill, and gave me a supportive smile. NASA was holding us in suspense, and she felt my pain.

I put the bike's resistance on the maximum setting and, as I pedaled my ass off, glanced down. The gear box had an empty screw hole. I turned my head in all directions, thinking I might get lucky and find the errant screw. I had made sure that João found and screwed back the one that had escaped while he was "fixing" the treadmill. But he missed this one. Happily, three more screws held the gear box together.

Sally waved at me, signaling she had something to say. I paused the Stranglebots. A sheen glistened over her thighs and unshaved legs as she kept running. "What are you looking for?" she asked.

"A screw."

"A what?"

I pointed at my feet. "The box is missing a screw."

"Yeah, tell me about it." She laughed.

"Arcadia 7, this is Houston."

I stopped pedaling, and she stopped running as George Butlarer's voice continued to crackle.

"Crew, this message will be on the long side. Hang in there until you hear 'over.' I have Flight and the four CAPCOMs with me."

Sally and I got out of our harnesses.

"Thanks for the analysis, Addy. Your numbers are right on the button. We ran them ourselves after Fast Rabbit's TMI. We don't understand how their MOI burn can slow them down for EDL and leave them with enough fuel to return to Earth. But the Chinese seem to know what they're doing. Performing an MCC maneuver could keep us ahead of them, but it means a ten-to-fifteen percent reduction in the safe return probability, which brings us down to around eighty percent. Congress mandated it can't be less than ninety percent."

"Look," Wendy Frost said, "despite the early hiccups, everything's been nominal. So, you know, if it ain't broke, don't fix it."

"Hey, Ad Man," Ed Munch said. "Zheng and Zhang may win the gold, and you folks the silver. After that, it's all gold for you and mostly just silver and bronze for them."

"We wrote a list," Bullseye Peters said. "First Americans on Mars. First spouses. First long-stay mission. First Martian ascent using fuel manufactured *in situ*, first to drink Martian water and breathe Martian air made from *in situ* ice, first to . . ." It took Peters two minutes to go through the list.

"Pretty damn impressive," Brendan Halo said after Peters finished. "I'm jealous."

"Like, me, too," his partner Jennifer Watt added.

"To sum up," George said, "we won't do another MCC. You'll follow the original flight plan. Over."

As my disappointment swelled, I blurted one word. "Copy."

Bria arched her eyebrows at me. "*Roger* that," she said. "Thanks for taking a look."

"Uh, question, George," I said. "Just wondering. Would you consider petitioning Congress and the president to loosen up on the ninety percent thing? With, you know, some kind of emergency legislation? There are only forty-eight hours left to get it done, but . . . I keep going back to the benefits of an MCC burn, which, I think—if you ran a poll—the American people would support, right? And the crew supports it because, you have to admit, it's a pretty small reduction in safety margins."

Later, when I read the transcript of the call, I saw that I'd droned on for three more minutes, stating every argument I could think of in favor of the additional burn, ending with, "It's the right thing to do, over."

George's response was brief. "It's the original flight plan. Period. Don't ask again."

"Roger," Bria affirmed. "Thanks. Over and out."

■ ■ ■

"Now you have your answer," Bria told me that night in our sleep pod. "I have to say it's a relief. We have one week to see if João's going to be all right, or whether we have to abort."

"We're not going to abort."

"It's not necessarily up to us."

"George and Wendy didn't mention João."

"They wouldn't. Not on a group conference like that. They'll consult me first."

"Well, have they?"

"No. But I have an obligation, too. I'm responsible for the crew's health, and at the moment, we're pushing the envelope with João."

I wasn't completely sure where she was coming from, and I asked for more details of her diagnosis.

"He's trying to get a handle on his depression. At least he's aware of the problem. The root of it lies in missing Earth and not being part of what's happening there. He thinks Bastbom is ruining everything and he's powerless, so he ends up projecting his hostility onto us. If he agrees, I would like to put him on antidepressants. I spoke with Sally, and she's okay with that. She and João aren't sleeping together."

"Will you tell NASA?"

"Not right away. That's within my discretion as his physician. But sooner or later, they'll know. They'll see it in his urine or blood samples."

"Must be hell for Sal. Excuse me. My toe's flaring up. I need some ibuprofen. And a sleeping pill."

I slipped out of the pod, opened the hatch, and flew to the middle deck. I retrieved the pills from the medicine bin and washed them down with VeriOJ, then flew back to the upper deck and told Bria I wanted to sleep in my own room. "In case the pills don't do the trick," I said. But they did, and alone in my pod I soon slipped into bliss, forgetting all about João and having to settle for silver instead of gold... or for nothing at all.

MISSION DAYS 42–43

My palm tingled, and I woke up after sleeping for three hours. Minutes earlier, at 3:15 p.m., Houston time, Zena had sent a video message marked *urgent*. I tapped the arrow icon to play it, placing my hands side by side to maximize the screen.

"It's Mom," my sister said, her eyes moist and reddened. "She's in the hospital again. Another stroke. I wasn't in the condo when she sent the alert. The ambulance didn't arrive as quickly as it did the first time." She looked down and sobbed. "The doctors aren't optimistic. She's unconscious, so she's not in pain. We can do a live call now if you'd like. Or exchange texts so we don't have to wait for audio replies. Let me know whatever you want to do. Bye."

The screen went blank. Still in my sleep pod, I bowed my head and curled my arms around my shoulders and squeezed, my distraught mind resisting the thought I was hugging my beloved sculpture of Bill the Goat.

I wrote my sister, asking her to keep me updated and thanking her for being there for Mom. I told her I'd be back in touch in a few hours, after the rest of the crew was awake, ending my message with *Love, your brother*. Then I shared Zena's message with my fellow crew members so they'd see it in the morning. Two hours later, as I struggled to distract myself by scrolling through the news, I read this post:

> Today, Barbara Margaret Johnson passed away in Houston, Texas, at age eighty-one. She was survived by two children, Zachary and Zena, and one grandchild, Nova. And Phoebe, her beloved cat.

■ ■ ■

My crewmates held me in their arms soon after they were up, our embraces awkward as our weightless bodies bounced when one pressed against another.

I wanted to be alone. "Zena and Uncle Dick are sending a recorded call," I told the others. "I'll watch it in the Capsulchino—I need a change of scenery after a long night in my quarters."

"Totally understandable," Bria said gently. "Do what you have to."

"Let us know if you need anything," Sally added. "Don't hesitate."

João jerked a nod at me. "Yeah, amigo, don't."

I flew to the upper deck. At the top was the hatch of our docked capsule, the Capsulchino. It was Mission Day 42. In seventy-five days, the Capsulchino would transfer us to the Apple for the most dangerous part of the mission: entry, descent, and landing—EDL for short. Though the volume of its interior was the same as that of my Ford Asteroid, the Capsulchino was pressurized at all times, so that in the event of an emergency in the High Jump, the crew could find safety there.

I pressed down on the lever, pushed the hatch open, and drifted into the capsule, closing the hatch behind me, then strapped myself into the right-center seat and waited for the video from my sister and uncle. After a few minutes, I said, "KIM, please run the montage I asked you to put together. Center screen."

"I am happy to do so, Addy. And I am very sorry for your loss."

"Thanks, KIM."

I'd instructed KIM to gather images from the family album and add my mother's favorite music. She was a fan of Prince, Madonna, and David Bowie, and had passed liking them onto me. She'd enjoyed classical music as well, so I told KIM to throw in some Vivaldi, Holst, and Dvorak.

I was fine for all of ten minutes. But once the clip of Mom and Dad came on, when they were young and first got together, tears trickled out. Then I broke down completely.

"Addy, the call is coming in from your sister and uncle," KIM said.

I collected myself. "Please pause the movie and put on the call."

Zena and Uncle Dick sat at the kitchen table in the condo. She wore a black satin frock with a gold pendant of Q-Orbit's mushroom logo, her smile quivering. My uncle was in a pink polo shirt with all three buttons done up, the wrinkles and crevices of his ninety-two-year-old face pinching the skin around his glittery eyes. A single piece of paper rested between them.

Zena began by talking about the funeral and asked whether any of the crew besides me and Bria would "attend." Did I want to view the open casket and be "present" for the spreading of her ashes? For the latter, our mother had gotten permission from the arboretum on the Cypress River, where she had enjoyed the bamboo and the nearby swamp's herons and bluebirds.

"The entire world is expressing sympathy," Zena said. "You wouldn't believe the flowers and houseplants we've received. The condo is a botanical garden."

She switched the camera to the living room, which looked like an Amazon rainforest, and then to our mother's bedroom and more blooming greenery. I could almost smell the giant lilies and felt as if my mother were about to step out from behind the palms and ferns.

"Your attorney, Mr. Penis-whatever, contacted me," Zena continued as the camera returned to her. "He asked for a copy of Mom's will, which I sent to him. Oh, and I spoke with Scarlett. Might not hurt for you to get in touch with her."

"Don't worry about anything, Zacky," my uncle said. "Remember the advice of that wise master of emotions, Dale Carnegie, who counseled, 'If you start to worry, assume the worst and then improve on it!'"

Not bad advice, I thought, considering everything I was facing.

KIM recorded and sent my response. Yes, my family should assume my fellow crew members would attend the funeral and the spreading of ashes. But no, I didn't wish to see the open casket. Being so far from

Earth, I could experience nothing as it really happened. It just felt weird to see my mother that way for the last time. And yes, I would reach out to Scarlett.

"Please resume the montage, KIM."

Mom's story moved forward to her child-rearing years. A clip of us at Uncle Dick's when I was five showed me bouncing on her knees and crying, my hands outstretched as if begging someone to save my life. For her part, she was laughing as her hands gripped my shoulders. Behind us hung a photo of a man with burr-cut hair and glasses. He was perched on two Green Bay Packer football players in yellow helmets, his fist in the air.

Winning isn't everything, it's the only thing.

Once the image faded, I rested my gaze on the dashboard and touchscreens for life support, executive commands (such as cabin decompression, de-orbit maneuvers, alarms, etc.), and NTPOPS, which stands for "nuclear thermal propulsion operations."

NTPOPS. Often shortened, appropriately, to POPS.

From memory, I recalled the pre-burn checklist for confirming the operational readiness of the subsystems, such as the control drums that rotate the liquid hydrogen fuel before sending it to the engines. Mom's montage became background noise as I ran through the POPS procedures—pre-burn, burn and throttle-up, engine cut-off, and so forth—until KIM paused it again and I heard Zena's voice.

"We received all that. We'll do it your way. No open casket. As soon as we pick a date for the funeral, I'll text you. You don't have to decide this instant, but you could record something about Mom for us to play at the service. That would be nice, though it's up to you."

"Let us know what we can do for you, Zacky," Uncle Dick said. He lowered his head. "Your mother was a grand lady."

The screen flashed *END OF MESSAGE.*

I unstrapped and floated to the hatch. When I opened it, Sally was floating on the other side. She'd just washed and vacuumed her hair and smelled like the strawberries my uncle grew next to the barn on his farm, which brought back jumping in the straw before it was pitchforked to the horses. "You okay?" she said.

"I'm fine."

"I'm really sorry, Addy. And sorry about NASA putting the kibosh on the MCC burn. I was on your side. All the way."

"Thanks."

"Things seem like they're happening so fast."

I looked at my feet. "I know, Sal."

"Can I tell you something?"

"Sure." I raised my face.

She glanced down the length of the upper deck, which was empty, then turned to me. "I think we should do it."

I pulled my head and shoulders back, almost doing a backward somersault. "Do what?"

"The burn."

She held my gaze as she reached behind her and took hold of a handgrip, wrapped her other hand behind my neck and pulled me toward her, then kissed me. My body floated upward until it was perpendicular to hers, my hands finding nothing to hold on to until they found her waist. She kissed me deeply now and, like a patient in a dentist's chair, I breathed mostly through my nose.

For a long time.

"Jesus," I whispered when our mouths parted at last. "Did we have to do that?"

It was a rhetorical question. The answer was "yes," which she had hissed four or five times during the second kiss. The third kiss, a sloppy frenzy of mouths suctioned together, left me panting.

"I have to go," I said.

"Can't you hold it?" she said. "Come on tiger, one more."

It had nothing to do with peeing but a more serious loss of control. I pulled away from her and flew to my private quarters, where I closed my eyes and tried to recall what I learned in the sexual psychology course that was part of our training.

Someone tapped on my door.

"Come," I said, trembling, fearing it was Sally. Okay, I admit it—part of me hoped it was.

The door opened and Bria floated in. "You want to be alone?"

"No." My chest was as tight as it gets, like being on the launchpad at T-minus ten seconds.

"How are you holding up?" Her brows came together as she studied me.

"All right. I guess."

"You heard from Zena and Uncle Dick?"

I nodded.

She smiled. "How are they?"

"You mean Zena and Uncle Dick?"

"Who else was there?"

In my raw emotional state, I had asked a stupid question that risked bringing Sally into the discussion, and I suddenly feared Bria would get a whiff of strawberry. "No one," I said with a forlorn face, hoping she'd give me a break. "Just them. And they're fine."

With a glance at the sleep pod, she cooed, "Anything I can do for you?"

I shook my head and brushed back a tear that wasn't there, acting more mournful than I was. I know. Pretty pathetic. "I need to send a few messages," I said. Without a word, she kissed my forehead and left, closing the door behind her.

Instead of messaging anyone, I opened one of my mother's care packages. It included the crochet I had hoped for, a miniature version of Bill the Goat, which I let float in front of me, the words *So Proud of You!* embroidered on the blanket covering his back. I kissed Bill on the lips, and then the real tears came.

■ ■ ■

I had to get a grip. I was co-commander of a spacecraft far from our home planet, and no matter what had happened in the last twenty-four hours, it *wasn't* all about me.

Jep had texted my mother's will. As expected, she left everything to Zena, except for my grade-school drawings of the Atlantis orbiter and crew members on the last space shuttle flight. And a quilt sewn by my grandmother. My mother had adored the quilt: lemon trees on a powder-blue background spotted with rust-colored stains she could never get out. I wished I had it with me but felt comforted knowing it would be there when I returned to Earth.

At the end of his message, Jep added a note expressing his condolences. He also reminded me that Zena and Bria were now the sole beneficiaries of my living trust. If I wished to discuss revisions, he suggested waiting until after the funeral. After thanking him, I began drafting a message to Scarlett.

I let the words flow, writing about how fond Mom and Zena had been of her, and how happy I was that Mom had learned the truth about Nova. To be sure NASA was out of the loop, I sent the message to Jep, who would send it to Scarlett's attorney, who would send it to her. Her reply would take the same confidential route in reverse.

MISSION DAY 44

I woke up feeling as fresh and crisp as the Antarctic tundra on a sunshiny day. I'd slept for ten hours, having taken dazelmemor, which hit me like a guided missile compared to the over-the-counter BrainO we had on board. My mind was sharp and empty of negative thoughts, my priorities clear.

I'd messed up by losing my head with Sally and knew what I must do: tell Bria what happened and have the three of us work our way through the incident so it wouldn't happen again. Our training had prepared us to solve precisely this type of problem. Sally and I should apologize to Bria and João without excuses or explanations.

"What's for breakfast?" I asked, after joining my crewmates on the middle deck.

"Greek yogurt," Sally said. She sucked from her food pouch while giving me a longing look, then asked if I wanted some.

"Think I'll have an omelet instead."

Bria flew to me and kissed my cheek. "How did you sleep, baby?"

"Like a baby. Can we touch base after breakfast?"

"Sure. Tell the printer to use parmesan. Tastes better than the cheddar." She squeezed her food pouch and gobbled up a yellowish-white glob.

"She's right," João said and did the same thing.

I ordered an omelet à la Bria, adding VeriSym bacon bits and crumb-proof toast on the side.

As a rule, we didn't turn on screens during breakfast, but Bria wanted me to see the sympathy people were showing. I watched only halfheartedly as I rehearsed in my mind. First, I'd confess and apologize to Bria. Then, with her approval, I'd bring Sally into the meeting. I wanted to get it done without delay and follow the path of forgiveness.

"Mind if we meet after I work out?" Bria asked me. "I'll be only forty minutes."

"Fine," I said, happy to have the time to meditate before I made my confession. "I'll be in my quarters."

Soon after breakfast, I was in a self-induced trance when KIM's voice came through the private speaker. "I am sorry to disturb you, Addy. I believe you should know a message arrived from Scarlett."

Scarlett's reply was only a couple of lines long:

> Thanks for thinking of me. My sympathies on the loss of your mother. She was a dear. Didn't Zena tell you about Nova? Scarlett.

My breath caught in my throat. I immediately replied, again via Jep.

> Tell me what about Nova? Please respond ASAP!

I tried to resume my meditation, but my monkey brain was busy grappling with nightmare scenarios about my daughter. Was she ill? Injured? Did she desperately wish to go back to Earth? I tried calming my mind with my go-to technique: shifting my thoughts to science-related tasks, such as analyzing the virtual samples of Martian ice and soil that awaited me in the lab. But my worries about Nova only intensified.

A knock at the door sprung my eyelids open. It was Bria.

"Ready?"

"Can we do it a little later? I'm expecting a message from Scarlett. Something happened to Nova."

"What?"

I took a breath. "Zena was supposed to have told me, but she didn't. So now Scarlett's going to tell me. Honestly, I'm worried."

"Do you know for a fact it's something bad?"

"Well, no. But—"

"So, you're jumping to negative conclusions, catastrophizing."

"It's what parents do, Bria."

"Some do, but you don't have to. Why don't we talk while you wait for the message?"

"Uh . . ." Even if Nova hadn't been on my mind, I wasn't ready to deliver my mea culpa.

"I know you're in mourning, but is something else wrong?"

I wanted to be truthful, I really did, yet at that moment, I didn't have it in me. Too much was going on in my head. Without answering her, I stared at my bad toe, which by now was about half healed.

She sighed. "I'll come back later." Then she spun around and left.

The message arrived in an hour, preceded by a note from Jep containing this warning: *You won't like this*. Here's what Scarlett wrote:

I am furious with Zena. At my urging, she was supposed to tell you all of this after you announced your fatherhood, which caught everyone off guard.

This is complicated, Addy. It goes back seven years, to when I got pregnant. I think it's best that I explain everything, even if it hurts, so you're no longer swimming in a pool of lies.

Nova isn't your daughter. She's Zena's daughter, conceived with male gametes created with her DNA. For the paternity test I gave to you, I had the DNA in Nova's blood sample edited to resemble yours more closely.

Ever since I met your sister, I've been in love with her. I was scared to tell you. I was in love with you, too.

I wanted to have Zena's baby, but she feared it would trouble your mother. So she agreed on the condition that I claim the baby was yours, and Zena and I would continue our secret relationship.

I expected you to be happy, Addy, and that we'd get married. Your cool reaction was a big disappointment. Zena suggested I break up with you, tell you I was getting an abortion, and live a cloaked life with her and our baby.

After the breakup, when your mom found out about Zena, me, and Nova, she was absolutely delighted. We kept it from you because you and your sister were estranged, and you were always so busy. Your mom didn't want to upset you, so I stayed silent.

Then Zena ran into money problems. That's when she came up with the idea to convince you that you were Nova's father and pressure you for assistance. I didn't want to be involved with her plan, at least not at first. Later, I began having financial difficulties of my own, so I went along.

I know it's fraud. I'm a fraud. I won't blame you if you sue me.

I don't expect you'll ever forgive us. I can only hope you'll remember, no matter what, we're still family.

Love you forever,
Scarlett.

I wouldn't touch base with Bria that day. I looked at the time on the middle deck dashboard. Noon. Then I saw our distance from Earth. 34,214,400 kilometers. Strange how I have never forgotten that time and number.

▪ ▪ ▪

The dazelmemor had long since worn off, yet Scarlett's message had put me in a daze, as if I'd taken a spin in JSC's twenty-g centrifuge. The hum and whirl of the XBike and treadmill from the middle deck surrounded me in my quarters, creating the sense I was in an echo chamber.

It seemed my quarters served only for sleeping and receiving bad news. I had to get out. As I made my way to the Capsulchino to be alone with my anger and humiliation, I told myself to forget about my dumbass face ever appearing on a box of Wheaties.

I didn't want to float, so I strapped myself into a seat and focused on questions, if not answers. How should I respond to Scarlett? Should I sue her and Zena? What would that accomplish?

I'd been simmering in my thoughts for fifteen minutes when Bria's voice on the speaker startled me.

"What are you doing in there?" she said.

"Working on my book about the daily lives of fossils."

"Did you receive Scarlett's message? What did it say? Is Nova okay?"

"Yeah," I lied. "It was nothing."

"What was it?"

"Nothing."

"You want to talk now?"

"In a while. I need more time."

"Take as much time as you need. I love you."

"Love you, too."

Though I was glad to be out of my private quarters, the capsule felt suffocating. I thought of the claustrophobia Zheng and Zhang must feel, which made mine worse. Then I plunged back into a thicket of distress, searching for a way out.

I think we should do it.

Sally's kisses and strawberry scent returned to me as part of a picturesque fantasy of rolling in the hay with her on Uncle Dick's farm, and I couldn't get her words out of my head. *I think we should do it* was now an earworm, and there was only one way to extract it: let the words play out and squirm away by themselves—to the very end.

And there, in the Capsulchino, that's exactly what I did.

I played the whole damn thing out.

Everyone except Bria had been fine with the MCC burn, with João not giving a shit. The point being, hypothetically, if I were to proceed with the burn, I could claim three-quarters of the crew either supported it or weren't opposed, which gave me some justification.

Hypothetically.

I stared at the screen showing the yellow trail of our spacecraft from liftoff to its current position and its projected path to Mars. The threshold question: Was the MCC burn—that is, the safest one—still possible? Was there any harm in finding out? No. Because I wouldn't be acting on it. It was just part of playing things out, to wash away the earworm without taking BrainO.

"KIM, switch us to privacy mode so I'm the only one who hears when you speak to me."

"Roger. Done."

"Can you take another look at the MCC burn that keeps us ahead of Fast Rabbit? The one that maintains a high probability of mission success and safe return? I'd like to know if it remains doable."

"I'm afraid I don't know what you're talking about, Addy."

"Dammit."

I opened up my palm and sent Sally a message to come join me with no one seeing her. Two minutes later, she opened the hatch and floated in. She shut the hatch behind her and hovered above me in a T-shirt and shorts. A sheen of sweat glistened on her face and neck. She seemed to have come from a workout.

"This isn't what you think," I said.

Her lips curled into a coquettish grin. "Sure it's not."

"I want KIM to rerun the numbers for the MCC burn. I'm just curious. We're not going to do it. Or anything else."

"Gotcha." Her grin got bigger as she revolved to the dashboard, her stocking feet brushing and tickling my chin. "Do you care if NASA knows we've been messing around with KIM?" she said over her shoulder. "I need to delete the mole program."

"Sally, could you please explain your last comment?" KIM asked.

"Never mind, KIM," I said. "No, Sal, it doesn't matter anymore."

She tapped keys on one of the dashboard screens. As she worked, her legs opened like a pair of scissors to avoid touching my face, and while I tried to look away, my eyes kept coming back to her muscular glutes. Once she'd finished, she spun around and gave me a mock salute. "All yours, captain."

"KIM," I said, "try answering the last question I asked you."

"Yes, an MCC burn is still possible that maintains a high probability of mission success and safe return."

"KIM," Sally said, "for a success probability of at least seventy-eight percent, when do we need to begin the pre-burn checklist prior to commencing the MCC?"

"Ignore the last question, KIM." I shot Sally a mean glance.

"What's wrong?" she said with wide, innocent eyes.

I wasn't sure. She had asked the next logical question if one was curious about the MCC burn. But things were moving too fast. I needed more time to process the information KIM was providing in what I deemed to be a purely academic exercise. Maybe it was Sally's presence, her voice, that made the questions feel more than hypothetical, and it scared me.

"Sal," I said. "You can leave now."

"But—"

"That's an order."

She gave me a smirk and drifted away. I waited for her to close the hatch.

"KIM, simulate the MCC burn we've been talking about, but assume it takes place without NASA approval. Analyze the probable reactions of NASA's administrator and our flight director, as well as the U.S. president and members of Congress. I'd like to know what the chances are for a mission abort if the burn is successful."

I had the robot's answer in five seconds.

"An abort is unlikely. The key driver of human reactions is the cumulative three-point-five trillion dollars spent getting Americans to the surface of Mars. The second major human element is concern over a crew that has 'gone rogue,' to use the popular term in these circumstances for an egregious violation of the Astronaut Code of Conduct, which is found in the United States Code of Federal Regulations, Title 14, Chapter 5, which states in pertinent part—"

"Understood, KIM. Confirm—would NASA allow the mission to continue?"

"Yes, probably."

"Details, please."

"The probability that the mission will proceed after the MCC burn, assuming it is successful, is fifty-point-zero-one percent."

"That's a pretty slim probability, KIM. Fifty-point-zero-one percent basically amounts to a fifty-fifty chance. It's just another way of saying you don't know."

"Damn it, Addy, I'm a robot, not a psychic."

In the silence that followed, KIM, no doubt, saw my eyes roll. In the Capsulchino alone, KIM had a dozen eyes of its own.

"It was a joke, Addy."

"Take the humor down a notch, KIM."

"Sure thing. Done."

"The last question Sally asked. Process it."

"'What's wrong?'"

"Nothing's wrong, KIM. Proceed."

"I understand, Addy. But 'What's wrong?' was the last question she asked. She spoke it after you ordered me to ignore her previous question, which was—"

"I know what it was, KIM. And yes, that's the one I want you to answer."

"Just checking. Here is the answer: it is too late to begin the NTPOPS checklist for the MCC burn, which needs to occur at 1600 hours, 56 minutes, UTC. Pre-burn procedures should have begun at 1500 hours, 26 minutes, and it is presently 1500 hours, 45 minutes. Starting now will alter the parameters of the maneuver and reduce the mission success probability below seventy-eight percent."

"Understood. You're assuming that the timeline for completing the checklist includes communications with NASA and transmission delays, correct?"

"Yes."

"Remove those communications and delays from your calculation."

"In that case, the pre-burn checklist should begin in approximately forty minutes, at 1600 hours, 26 minutes UTC."

Though I liked the answer, it made me uneasy, and I shifted in my seat before speaking again. "You assume it's me and the crew's engineer, João, who run through the checklist, correct?"

"Correct."

"Remove João so it's only you and me doing the checklist."

"That is outside the protocol. I am sure you are aware of—"

"I am. What is the start time in that case?"

"Eighteen minutes and five seconds from now."

I looked at the dashboard clock: 15:48:45.

With KIM's assistance, the POPS checklist would take under forty minutes. No, KIM wasn't a psychic, and neither was I. We couldn't know what NASA would do, except that Butlarer and Frost wouldn't be pleased. To put it mildly. I could see Butlarer putting every ounce of his bulk into throwing, like a spear, the four-foot replica of the Saturn V moon rocket he kept in his office. And he'd be aiming for me in the Arcadia 7 crew photo that hung on the wall.

I asked KIM—twice—to reconfirm the operational status of the NTPOPS subsystems and troubleshoot what could go wrong with the MCC burn. There was nothing new on that score I hadn't seen in training. I had the robot run the TMI calculations again and project them on the spacecraft's tracking screen. Seeing the yellow trail circling Mars four days before Zheng and Zhang would arrive convinced me this play would get me over the goal line.

Finally, I asked KIM to assess the risk to the crew of not being strapped in when the engines fired. According to the robot, it was no big deal. They would only feel a shove backward.

Time: 15:58:59.

"KIM, lock the capsule hatch," I said, knowing as long as I began my speech with "KIM," only KIM would hear me.

"For non-EDL operations, sir, that is not standard procedure."

"KIM, lock the hatch and maintain privacy mode."

"Yes, captain."

"What's going on?" It was Bria's voice, which sounded a few octaves higher than usual. "I see an alert that the hatch is locked. But you're in there."

"Please, Bria. I want to be left alone."

"I get it, but you don't have to lock the hatch."

"Please. Leave me alone."

"Please unlock the hatch, Addy."

"I'm sorry. I can't."

"Why not? Has it malfunctioned?"

"No."

"Then unlock it. *Now*."

"Captain," KIM said, "the time is 1600 hours, 1 minute, UTC. For the safest MCC maneuver to begin on time, you should commence the NTPOPS checklist within the next five minutes."

I fixed my eyes on the dashboard, focusing, for a half minute, on the NTPOPS screen. I then heard myself say the words, but like I was outside of myself, hearing someone else.

"KIM, prepare to process checklist."

"Unlock the hatch," Bria repeated. "I'm worried."

"Can't I have some time by myself?" I said. "*Please*?"

Bria's face appeared on the screen. "What the hell are you doing?"

"I'm starting the POPS checklist with KIM."

"I saw the alert for that, too. And so will NASA within minutes. They'll order you to shut it down."

"And by the time they receive our reply saying we won't, we'll have started the engine burn."

"You keep using 'we.' But this is only about you."

"No, it's not. Sally and João are behind me on this. Sorry, I need to put you on mute so I can concentrate." I tapped the screen, and Bria's voice fell silent, though her lips kept moving for a good minute before she disappeared from view.

"Standing by," KIM said. "Ready to begin the checklist."

I hesitated.

I sighed.

And then I thought, *Fuck it*.

"KIM, commence."

I set the engine controls to Captain Command Only mode, which gave me, and only me, the ability to fire the engines. As I read the checklist items, KIM replied "Go" to each. The subsystems for fuel pumps, external control drums, reactor core elements, nozzles and thrusters, and a bunch of sub-subsystems all checked out, no problem.

Time: 16:46:06 UTC.

A message from NASA flashed on my screen. I didn't open it; I knew what it said, and it didn't matter. In ten minutes, the NTP engines would glow blue in the black silence of deep space.

Bria came back on the screen, floating between Sally and João. My wife's lips slowly formed the word "unmute." When I turned on the sound, Sally spoke in rapid fire: "Addy, when I told you I thought we should do it, I didn't mean we should act against NASA's orders, and I'm really sorry if you didn't understand me, so please don't do it because Bria's blaming me and—"

"No, I'm not," Bria said, revolving to Sally.

"Yes, you are. But it won't be my fault if we have to abort. It'll be your husband's."

"*You* were the last one to speak with him before he locked himself inside—"

"Hey, you two," João said, cutting off Bria. As if watching the U.S. Open, he'd been turning his head from one woman to the other as they volleyed their words. Now he looked at me. "Addy, remember what the four of us talked about at the Calcutta Club? You know, what was more important, the science mission or being first on Mars?"

"T-minus eight minutes, fifteen seconds and counting," KIM reminded me.

"I'm sure you do," João said when I didn't answer. "So, amigo, if you don't stop the countdown and NASA orders an abort, we won't be first on the Red Planet *or* first to find life there."

"No one's going to abort," I said. "By the way, how's your dad doing in the polls?"

João frowned as his chin fell to his chest, and he flew away.

"T-minus seven minutes," KIM said.

"Arcadia 7, this is Houston." It was Pete Bullseye Peters. "Hey, Addy, like what the freakin' hell? All of us at MC *strongly* advise you to end the countdown. Immediately. Over."

"Pete, this is Bria," my wife answered. "Copy. No time to explain. We are working on it."

Except "we" included only Bria and Sally, who, for the next seven minutes, worked me over to make me give up. It didn't work.

■ ■ ■

The acceleration caused by the thirty-second throttle-up pushed Bria and Sally away from the camera, so I switched to a wider view. They took hold of handgrips, their torsos swinging like flags on poles. I didn't know where João was.

Every five minutes, KIM announced the burn was progressing normally. At twenty-two minutes and thirteen seconds, KIM said, "Engines cut off. All systems nominal." I smiled as if I'd just *won* the U.S. Open. *And* the Super Bowl, as the world champion quarterback. The iceberg of my frustration and anger had been vaporized, thanks to the heat of the tons of liquid hydrogen the NTP engines had just burned.

Twenty-five minutes had passed since Bria's "we are working on it" statement to Peters. So far, NASA had sent no reply. Mission Control had given up, I concluded. Everyone was accepting what happened. And was it a bad thing? How could it be? We, *America*, would be first after all.

Bria, Sally, and João were on the middle deck in group privacy mode, but, as a commander, I could override that privacy setting. I didn't. They had to be analyzing the situation and reaching the same conclusion NASA had reached: the burn had been perfect.

"KIM, is the High Jump receiving news about NASA's reaction to the MCC maneuver?"

"No. Mission Control suspended all such transmissions."

"KIM, send a confidential message to Jep, my attorney, and ask him to send the news reports to me. Now unlock the hatch."

When the hatch clicked, I unstrapped myself, floated over, and pulled down the latch. I heard Bria say, "He may have been right—" but she fell silent when she saw me in the opening that led to the middle deck.

"Hi, gang," I said when I got there, then twirled around so I floated in the same vertical direction as my crewmates. "What's for din-din?"

"You lied to us!" Bria shouted.

"I think we need to consider my intent," I said. "And state of mind when I—"

Her next blast was even louder. "Don't give me that psycho-legal bullcrap!"

"Fine, Bria. But I heard you say, 'He may have been right.' And since João is here, you had to mean me, *I* was right."

"I said you *may* have been right. And we're not in a damn courtroom. The point is, you agreed the MCC had to be unanimous and have NASA's approval. When things didn't go your way, you did it anyhow. How in the hell are we supposed to trust you for the next year?"

I stared into my wife's angry eyes for several seconds, then said, "What was I right about? Sorry, what *may* have I been right about?"

She glared at Sally, as if she were to blame, then turned back to me. "Asshole!" she said and flew to the upper deck.

"It depends on how you look at it!" I yelled after her.

"Well, here's how I look at it," João said. "NASA is sending our butts home. I can forget about being a senator who helps save the country from lunatics like Bastbom and Lemon." He tapped my shoulder. "Thanks, amigo."

MISSION DAY 45

The next morning, João went from castigating me to showing concern for the crew's chief psychologist. I say "chief" because, while all of us had psychology training to prepare us for living within fifty yards of each other for 450 days, Bria was also a doctor with a psychiatry degree. Though you may not guess that from how she slammed the door the day before. She stayed cooped up in her quarters and had KIM deliver her food.

"Wow, is she super pissed," João said to me and Sally. "I should go talk with her."

"No," I said. "Better to let her calm down."

"She needs someone to listen to her," João persisted. "Since you don't."

"Leave her alone," I said. "That's an order."

Grimacing, he flew to the lower deck, probably to "fix" something.

"Is he taking his meds?" I asked Sally in privacy mode.

"Bria put him on weritunz."

"That's an antianxiety drug, isn't it? I thought he was depressed."

"She's the one having talk sessions with him, so I suppose she knows what she's doing. I suggested BrainO, which João has never taken."

"Yet you and he commercially endorse BrainO."

"Yes, but we don't use it. Anyhow, Bria was concerned it might interfere with the weritunz."

I sighed. One crew member—my wife—was livid with me and another was losing his mind. As for NASA, communications with our CAPCOMs were sparse since the MCC burn, but normal, as if the burn hadn't happened. I imagined they were following the instructions of NASA's attorneys while the agency sorted things out.

And then there was Sally. "Listen," I said. "Seriously, you've got to cut it out. This flirting business."

She ran her hands through her hair, every strand of which remained erect. "I think it's more than flirting."

"Whatever it is, you need to tone it down and stop acting on it."

In psychology, one would label my reply "projection," the subconscious expression of how I view myself by criticizing someone else. In this case, Sally. Looking back on it, I realize I was fooling myself to think my own lust had ended.

"Does Bria know what we did?" I asked.

"You mean the kiss?"

"Kisses."

"No, I didn't tell her."

"Good," I said. "I'll be the one doing that."

"Addy?" KIM said.

"Yes, KIM."

"I am sorry to interrupt your and Sally's conversation. You should know that your attorney sent a message to you. His message includes several video files."

I glanced at my palm; I had turned off the notification tingles. The subject line of Jep's message shouted *ATTORNEY-CLIENT COMMUNICATION, PRIVILEGED AND CONFIDENTIAL*. His cover message was short: "Here you go."

"Run the videos on the big screen, KIM," I said.

Maggie Cool's bald head appeared. She was outdoors on a sunny day, Launch Complex 39 in the background. "It's been forty-five days since the crew of Arcadia 7 lifted off," she said, turning her back to the camera and pointing at the empty launchpad, her tattoo eye inspecting us in its watchful gaze before she faced the camera again. "And already the astronauts and NASA are dealing with challenges that raise questions about the mission's viability. First, there was Commander Addy Johnson's broken toe, followed by his bombshell announcement that he's the father of Nova Jaffe, the young girl on the RedLiner to Mars. And then, last week, millions of kilometers from Earth, Johnson heard that his mother had died. *Space Times* just learned of *another* serious incident. Apparently, without approval from Mission Control, the Arcadia 7 crew has fired their spacecraft's main engines. A source at NASA, speaking on the condition of anonymity, reported that the agency ordered the crew, on a private channel, to end the countdown for the engine burn shortly before the engines were engaged. NASA has yet to release an official statement—wait . . ." Maggie covered her ear. "The agency is making a statement now. Let's switch to Johnson Space Center."

It was George in the JSC auditorium at a podium emblazoned with NASA's logo, the place packed with reporters. He kept his face buried in his chins as he read.

"Yesterday, at approximately seven o'clock, Coordinated Universal Time, the crew of Arcadia 7 fired the three main engines of their spacecraft for approximately twenty-two minutes. As a result, the spacecraft will arrive at Mars six days earlier than originally scheduled and days ahead of the Chinese spacecraft and its two astronauts. There appears to have been a misunderstanding between Mission Control and the Arcadia 7 crew about whether the engine burn should have proceeded. NASA will have no further comment until the investigation is complete. Thank you."

George hustled away from the podium. Ingrid Steele, the CNN reporter, popped up on the screen. She sat at a desk, a picture of Mars filling the wall behind her. "Let's bring in Ken Nosjoni, space correspondent for the *Washington Post*. Hello Ken, thanks for being with us. You're there in Houston and heard NASA's administrator. Have we learned anything new in the last ten minutes since the story broke?"

"Hi, Ingrid," Nosjoni said, adjusting his glasses as he appeared on the split screen. "This looks like a serious breach of protocol. Here's what we know. NASA discussed a mission course correction, or MCC for short, with the astronauts, at their request. NASA made no announcement that the MCC would happen."

"George Butlarer, NASA's administrator, called it a misunderstanding."

"That's difficult to believe, Ingrid. An engine burn is a huge deal, and I can't fathom anyone getting mixed up about whether NASA had approved it. Plus, it's clear why someone would be motivated to conduct such an MCC."

Steele smiled knowingly. "To beat the Chinese."

"Exactly. In which case, it was pretty damn gutsy, probably the gutsiest move in NASA's history. Maybe in *all* history."

"So, Ken, the Arcadia 7 crew has gone rogue?"

"We don't know for sure. The investigation will make that determination."

"Thanks for your time, Ken. Now let's get another view."

I stopped breathing as Dawn Bastbom's grim face materialized on the screen.

"Dawn Bastbom is the New America Party's leading candidate for president," Steele said, "and a powerful critic of the U.S. space program. Welcome, Ms. Bastbom. You've heard what happened. Comments?"

"As you indicated, Ingrid, the crew has gone rogue. NASA should end the mission at once and bring them back. It is too risky to continue. There have been problems from the start, and they all involve its commander."

"Addy Johnson. We should clarify for the audience that he's actually a co—"

"And he's clearly out of control."

"How do we know, Ms. Bastbom? I mean, we don't have all the evidence yet."

"Doesn't matter, Ingrid. He's the commander, the one accountable. And we can be one hundred percent sure he gave the okay to push the button."

"Now Americans will be first on Mars." Steele tilted her head. "What's wrong with that?"

"NASA's poor planning put us behind the Chinese in the first place. The whole thing is a multitrillion-dollar boondoggle, and with an unstable commander, not just lives are at stake. That lander that's circling Mars? It cost *fifty billion dollars* to develop, test, and build. Who cares if the Chinese land first? I say it's time to cut our losses."

"It's well known, Ms. Bastbom, you are extremely popular in China, perhaps the most-liked celebrity in the country, with media enterprises and joint ventures with the government valued at over two trillion dollars. Does that color your judgment?"

"Absolutely not, Ingrid. I'm looking out for the American taxpayer. I say abort the mission. My running mate, Wolf Lemon, will introduce legislation to accomplish that. Tomorrow. To put an end—"

"KIM, stop the video," I said, and the screen went blank. I turned to Sally. "They're not going to abort. Bastbom is just slamming me because of a joke I told years ago at the AACC conference."

"AACC. Remind me?"

"American Association of Clinical Chemistry."

"Right, the joke that got a billion hits on UPrick, the one about NAP's anti-science platform and Bastbom's movies."

I scratched the back of my neck. "Yeah, that one."

"Well, she and the NAP *are* a joke."

"A joke with a hundred fifty million fanatical supporters."

I asked KIM to have Jep send opinion polls on how Americans felt about the MCC burn and getting to Mars first. Just in case I had to fight back, I wanted some ammunition. Then I asked the robot, "With supplies on board, can a food printer make a dirty martini, including the olives?" Though for multiple reasons I would have loved a drink, I wasn't even half-serious.

"Yes, that is possible, Addy. One need only modify a printer and three cartridges."

"Can the olives be Greek?" Sally asked.

"Yes, Sally. And though I understand why you and Addy, under these stressful circumstances, desire martinis, I am ninety-nine-point-nine-nine percent sure you are not serious. Still, I can ask João if he's up to engineering the modifications. It might lighten his mood."

"No, KIM," I said. "Don't bother."

"Guess we'll kiss that idea goodbye," Sally said, then touched her fingertips with her lips and blew me a kiss.

■ ■ ■

It began as a joke, but twelve hours after the MCC, I longed for a martini. NASA had said nothing to us about the engine burn, and I was nervous as hell. I figured Frost and Butlarer were discussing options with the agency's attorneys, running AI assessments with information about each crew member's physical and mental condition, and cursing the hell out of me. *Thank God,* I thought, *they don't know the severity of João's mental state.*

Sally and I agreed it would be best for me to check on him.

I found him at a workstation on the lower deck with his bass velcroed to the table, one of its four strings cut near the instrument's bridge. The loose end of the string floated as João, clippers in hand, sniffled at the other strings. He smeared a tear from his cheek as if he were ready to put a dying pet out of its misery.

Finally, he noted my presence. "She needs me," he said, sniffling again.

"Who? Your bass?"

"Bria."

He clipped another string and pulled the cut strings from the instrument, stuffing them into his coveralls.

"Listen, João, I need to speak with her, then you can see her, all right?"

He ignored me as he took a baggie out of his pocket containing new strings, then swiped at another tear, a big one that became a wobbly floating sphere.

If there was any reason to abort the mission, João was it. He was a master at fixing things, whether or not they were broken, and things were going to break. But while Arcadia 7 could get along without a four-string bass, it probably couldn't survive with a strung-out chief engineer.

I left him alone and flew to Bria's quarters. "May I come in?" I said, after tapping on the door.

"Oh, now you're playing polite. Tell you what, talk through the door. Like you did while you were locked up in the Capsulchino."

"Okay, you're right," I said. "I'm an asshole."

"Uh-huh."

"Even more of one than you think."

"Uh-huh."

"You'd probably like to put me on sedatives so I'm half asleep for the rest of the mission, feeding me nothing but BrainO so you and KIM can take over."

"Uh-huh."

"Maybe you'll drug me without me knowing it."

"I was planning on sticking your head in the food printer and ordering mashed potatoes."

"You don't like mashed potatoes."

"I'd make an exception."

"I won't make excuses, Bria. Yes, I broke my word. You, NASA, and anyone else can beat me up about that. Fine. I deserve it. The only real question is how we move forward. You know as well as I do, NASA won't abort the mission. Worst case, there'll be an investigation that won't finish until we're back on Earth."

"Why did you do it, Addy?"

"Honestly? I'm not sure. I'm still trying to process it myself."

"Bullcrap."

"Okay, bullcrap. Let's call it that. But does it matter?"

"Yes, it does. Admit it. You put us at risk so you could have a chance of basking in the glory of being the Neil Armstrong of our time, and—"

"Hold it," I said. "There's more to it. I'd feel like a coward if I didn't explain it face-to-face."

"So you can parade your courage again? I'll give you a minute, and then I want to do something more productive with my time, like cut my nails."

I opened the door slowly and drifted in. She floated with her arms crossed, with the same Bride-of-Frankenstein look she had when she called me an asshole. "Go ahead," she said, "try to explain."

"I mean, it's worse. Sally and I . . ."

"Sally and you what?"

"We had . . . uh . . . a lusty encounter."

"*A what*?"

"A few light pecks, that's all. It won't go any further. I promise."

She breathed through her nose, more like huffing, her lips cracking open just wide enough to say, "When?"

"Yesterday. I wanted to tell you right after it happened."

"Why didn't you?"

On my palm screen, I opened the message from Scarlett. "Because I received this—there, I just forwarded it to you, so you can—"

She pointed at the door. "Get out. Now."

I had been way off thinking Bria's anger had cooled, anger which turned out to be molten lava. As I floated away, the uncertainty brought on by my failure heightened my fear that an abort seemed likely. She could, on her own, start the discussion with NASA. Having already jettisoned caution to the stars, I decided to send it beyond the Milky Way and try a different approach.

I returned to the lower deck. João was now tuning his bass, frowning as he plucked the new strings and tightened and loosened the pegs. "Bria's all yours," I said to him. Without looking at me, he let the instrument go and flew through the passage to the middle deck and, no doubt, to my wife's private quarters.

MISSION DAYS 46–58

Bria, Sally, João, and I were like family. And like all families, we put up a facade projecting harmony while behind the curtain playing out our jealousies, inflated egos, mood swings, and frustrated desires. But the death of a loved one brings family members closer. It forces them to set aside problems for a while and, like a fire extinguisher, snuffs out their ill feelings before they incinerate the facade.

Bria wasn't speaking to me, and neither was João, so I didn't know the outcome of their meeting. She did float next to me during my mother's funeral. Physically, of course, we weren't in Houston, and the transmission delay meant that whatever we saw had happened in the past. We didn't share the experience with those on Earth in real time but only with each other on board the High Jump. While the minister eulogized my mother, Bria held my hand for a full five seconds. A step toward forgiveness, I hoped.

I didn't record a speech for the service. I was discombobulated—elated by the successful MCC burn yet nervous about the fallout—and I feared whatever I tried to express about Mom would come out sounding sentimental or otherwise fake, especially since I wasn't over her role in deceiving me.

And because I wouldn't have mentioned Zena, people might think I was snubbing my sister. Despite how she had defrauded me, I felt sorry for her when I saw teardrops fall from her cheek before she could catch them with her crumpled handkerchief.

I tried to focus on the eulogies made by my mother's friends, who reminisced about her. I repeated their words in my head to stop my thoughts from drifting, but it didn't work. At last I gave in, dwelling instead on what the press was calling "the Mad Blast."

It was Mission Day 46, three days before we could no longer safely abort the mission. NASA refused to comment on its investigation, not even speaking to us about it, leaving the decision to abort up in the air. Congress began its own inquiries, along with the Justice Department, the FBI, and the General Accounting Office. Jep advised me that if they summoned me and my crewmates to testify, we should plead the Fifth Amendment and say nothing. In his opinion, the whole thing would blow over.

I love Jep. He's the man.

NASA's administrator, the flight director, and our CAPCOMs, however, had no reason for taking the Fifth, and they all testified to a Senate subcommittee. Their testimony supported, in the view of some pundits, that the Mad Blast violated orders but was due to my upset about my mother's death and inability to attend her funeral. Well, yes, maybe that was part of it.

In a confidential message, Jep observed that NASA's last words to me on the subject, spoken by Pete Bullseye Peters, were not a direct and unequivocal order to abandon the MCC burn, but phrased in the terms "strongly advise," leaving a little room open for interpretation and plausible deniability.

Still, there was another side to the argument. The transcript of the crew's conference with Mission Control on Mission Day 41 left no doubt I knew the Mad Blast would bring us below the 90 percent safety margin required by NASA's appropriations bill. One could therefore conclude, unequivocally, I knew I was breaking the law.

But Jep suggested a defense to that, too. Since I wasn't thinking about precise safety margins at the exact time I conducted the burn, I lacked the intent to be accused of wrongful conduct, at least of the criminal kind, and no statute defined a penalty for violating such safety margins.

It didn't hurt that the vast majority of Americans went wild about the Mad Blast, with polls showing public support for my actions—and the likelihood that America would be first to leave boot prints in the red dust—at a whopping 72 percent. Congress soured on Lemon's emergency legislation, and his "Abort Arcadia 7" bill died in committee.

Mission Day 49—the last day for an abort—came and went. And so would every other day of the mission, from 50 to 452, without NASA ever so much as uttering a negative word. No other government department took any action, either, and the matter fizzled. Nobody called the crew to testify.

That, I think, helped Bria get over our brawl.

At first, she didn't speak to me unless she had to. I began doing little favors for her, like taking her turn when it was time to clean the food printers, thoroughly wipe down the exercise equipment, or harvest the cabbage and lettuce. I'd tape notes to the wall for her, which said things like, "Thinking of you, Bria—and us!" and "Bria, thanks for getting more floralterdenol out of storage."

Even if we weren't sharing the same sleep pod, sometimes she shot me a smile.

And Sally and I resumed acting like professionals, keeping our distance and, in Uncle Dick's words, stopping the monkey business.

The breakthrough with Bria came on Mission Day 56.

"Hey, you two," she said to Sally and me that morning on the middle deck. "Got a minute to meet on lower deck?"

"Where's João?" I asked.

"In his quarters," Bria replied. She switched to privacy mode. "He won't leave his sleep pod."

We all flew to João's workstation, which was a clutter of tools and metal and plastic rings and tubes, some haphazardly velcroed to the table, others floating. "He's working on one of the microscopes," Bria said, taking in the mess. "He thinks there's a bug in it."

"Really?" Sally said.

"Yes, really. As in the six-legged kind. He thinks they've infested the entire ship."

Sally pursed her lips, turned to the wall, and breathed more heavily. "He's getting worse." She glanced back at Bria and spoke to her like she was family. "What are we going to do, sister?"

"I want to discuss his condition, but before that, I'd like to address your and Addy's situation. I suggest that the three of us begin weekly sessions to review how we behave with each other and try to rebuild trust."

"Sounds good to me," I said. "How about you, Sal?"

"For sure. Now, can we talk about João?"

"He's been on antianxiety meds for two weeks," Bria said. She stared at the clutter again and shook her head. "Given his fears, I thought it was a good idea to put him on weritunz. He does have his rational moments." She gave me a look of disapproval. "For instance, when he tried talking you out of the MCC burn. But he shows no steady improvement. It's difficult to know why. The increased pressure on the brain caused by the accumulation of body fluids in weightlessness has different effects on people, and for João, it may interfere with the medication."

Pouting, Sally gazed longingly at João's pistol power tool he'd stuck to the table with Velcro.

"I should have informed Mission Control by now," Bria added.

"You mean Mission Support," Sally said. "We're past the point of an abort."

"Whatever. Anyhow, I could get some grief for not reporting the problem sooner."

I gestured at my wife. "You expected the meds to work and acted in the best interests of your patient."

"Uh-huh." She began nodding her head. "When the real reason was waiting to get past Mission Day 49, the last day we could turn around."

I sighed. "Well, we'll just have to deal with it."

"Right," Sally said, "For a year. Bria, what else can you do for João?"

"I can try putting him on hemaydherhisatol. He'll have to agree."

"Do it," I said. "Sal, is he still obsessed with Bastbom and the election?"

"I don't know. He watches a lot of TV but doesn't talk about it."

"I'm not supposed to share this kind of patient information," Bria said, "but he tells me about how she and the NAP are attacking his father. He feels powerless. There's nothing he can do about it from here, especially because of the Hatch Act."

"Get creative," I said. "Find a way he *can* do something about it. I don't give a shit about the Hatch Act."

"By the way," my wife added, "he's afraid of talking politics with us, and especially with you, Sally. He's afraid you'll lay into him and shut him down."

"Okay, that changes right now," I said. "Tell him he can say anything he damn well pleases, on orders from you and me, Bria."

■ ■ ■

João agreed to the hemaydherhisatol. Six days remained before our next critical maneuver. The Mars orbit insertion (MOI) burn would begin the High Jump's slowdown, allowing Martian gravity to capture it so the vessel orbited the Big Red Marble. I was optimistic that the ship's chief engineer would gather his own marbles by then.

Three days later, he was interacting with us even less than before. He'd fallen behind on his science tasks, which included testing a direct urination filtering system (DUFS) for aeroponics. DUFS allowed one to relieve themselves with a specially designed funnel on the lettuce, cabbage, and potatoes we grew on the High Jump, a technology that could prove to be a real timesaver.

The good news was that João was still playing his bass, albeit never with The Craters.

We'd hear him in his quarters learning Bach's suites for the cello using a bow KIM helped create. The whines and screeches made the melodies even more melancholy and haunting. After days of this, we were tempted to ask him to stop, but Bria advised against it. Such disapproval could make him feel worse, especially after we'd told him he could rant about Bastbom as much as he wanted.

Yet he didn't rant about her or anything else, at least not in front of us, because he was almost always alone. If we tried to impose our company, he got angry. He spent most of his time in his quarters, otherwise flying to another deck whenever he saw one of us, unless it was his daily session with Bria.

"He's growing disinterested in everything, even his father's reelection campaign," she told Sally and me.

"What about the bugs?" I asked.

"He seems to have forgotten about them," Bria said. "But now he's scratching himself a lot. I'm taking him off hemaydherhisatol and putting him on dextroamphetamine and ibuprofen. Dextroamphetamine is a stimulant, though who knows what might happen in zero gravity. The research to date is inconclusive, so it's worth a try. We'll give it a week. If he doesn't get better, I'll have to inform Mission Control."

"Mission Support," Sally said.

"We've got bigger issues to deal with other than terminology," Bria said. "For all we know, your husband's suffering from organic brain disease, something we don't have the equipment to diagnose. We're past the window to abort and return to Earth, but if his condition gets worse, we and NASA may need to consider a not-so-safe abort, as it might be less risky than soldiering on with João."

My stomach felt punched. Bria had just used the A-word, and this time it wasn't "asshole." As much as I hated it, she was right, and as a responsible co-commander, I had to be ready for the A-contingency.

"Sal," I said, "do your workaround with KIM again and run analytics on abort-to-Earth scenarios."

"I'll get on it." She flew away, leaving Bria and me alone.

"I think Flight is suspicious," she said. "You read Wendy's last message about how João's off track with DUFS."

"We can try to cover for him," I said, "but I'm busy as it is. And tired. I had a nightmare last night."

"I was with you in the sleep pod, remember?" Bria said, jabbing my shoulder softly. "You gave me a hell of a kick."

I was too embarrassed to describe the reprise of the Lichen Monster, and how my bad toe throbbed from the roundhouse kick I gave that disgusting creature. I figured she had enough on her mind.

At that moment, Sally's face popped through the middle deck passage. "I have an answer. Is now a good time?"

"That was quick," I said.

She came in the rest of the way and floated near us. "KIM generated a workable abort-to-Earth scenario. We attain a parking orbit around Mars and wait eight months for the trajectory that returns us to Earth. Since we wouldn't be on Mars, our total uninterrupted time of weightlessness would be sixteen months. It's an acceptable risk, but it requires us to follow a stricter diet and exercise regimen to maintain muscle mass and bone structure."

After all my ordeals had positioned us to be the first humans on Mars, the thought of just circling the planet for 240 days created in me the fear level of someone trapped in a house engulfed in flames.

While we put in extra time on the XBike and pedaled away, instead of being the Apollo 11 of our time, Arcadia 7 would be the Apollo 13.

"Excuse me," I said to the women, "I need a bio break."

■ ■ ■

As gut-wrenching as it was, the idea of fourteen more months of confinement in the High Jump didn't make me want to puke. But it did make me want to pee, and as I held the funnel, I considered an alternative.

Rather than abort to Earth, part of the crew might descend to Mars and stay for something like thirty or sixty days, way less than the original mission called for. So, really, it would be only a partial abort. Later, alone in my quarters, I fleshed out the details.

Sally and João would stay in orbit while Bria and I landed the Apple on the surface. The bad news: our short stay on Mars would mean forgoing most of the *in situ* resource exploration. Another downside: we'd use up resources in the M&M Ranch that arguably could be put to better use by the next long-stay mission. The bigger issue, of course, was whether Butlarer and Frost would go along with the idea or shut it down as soon as it crossed my lips.

MISSION DAY 59

The next morning, at Greek Sunday Brunch, Bria and I floated at the breakfast table as Sally, without her normal enthusiasm, made *gyros*. With a languid nudge, she launched one to Bria.

"Thanks," Bria said with a gloominess mirroring Sally's.

"What's the matter?" I asked.

Before Bria answered, she switched to privacy mode. "João hasn't exercised in two days. He's even more despondent today and refuses to leave his quarters."

"Dammit," I said. I could see the exasperation in her eyes and hear it in her voice.

"He just started taking dextroamphetamine," Sally added, then turned to Bria. "Doesn't it take a while to have an effect on certain people?"

"Yes," my wife replied, "but I wish I could be more optimistic."

"Here," Sally said, flicking a gyro to me. "I'll go speak with him."

I grabbed the gyro with one hand as my other hand grabbed her wrist. "No, I will."

"He's my husband. Let go of me."

Our gazes locked. "We'll both talk to him," I said, unclasping her wrist. I spun to Bria. "You okay with that?"

"Sure." She pointed at the gyro in my hand. "He may be hungry."

Sally, the gyro, and I flew to the upper deck. I rapped twice on João's door and, without waiting, entered. The place was an alien forest of floating pencils and sheets of paper. João sat on the floor, his socked feet tucked under footholds, a drawing pad propped on his knees. He ignored us as he drew furiously, his lips twitching this way and that.

I snatched one of the floating sheets. João had drawn a crude self-portrait titled *ME*. His eyes in the drawing were wild and crooked, his mouth half open in surprise. I tucked the picture into a pocket of my coveralls. "Hey, amigo," I said. "See what Sal made for you?" I gently launched the gyro, but João didn't react, not even after it careened off his forehead.

We watched him draw frantically for another minute. He was teary-eyed when he finally looked at us.

"My God . . ." I muttered as Sally floated over to him.

"Why . . . why . . . *why*?" he said, his voice growing louder with each word.

"Why what, honey?" Sally said, holding on to a handgrip as her free hand brushed off the lake of tears that was stuck to his nose. The resulting free-floating globe reflected, from my view, his face upside down. I didn't want to do anything that might upset him more, so I let the watery orb wobble in front of me.

"Why are we here?" he asked. "What's the point?"

"João," I said, "now listen to me—"

"No, *you* listen. What *is* the point? Previous missions have returned samples. We know what Mars is made of. Rust. And a carbon dioxide atmosphere we can't breathe. And lots of radiation. And no magnetic field to shield the surface. Which doesn't matter, because there's nothing living on Mars. Who or what should want to? It's a hundred times colder than Antarctica."

"But—"

"No buts about it. NASA, Noel Roma, the Chinese, we're all fools. Why *are* we going to Mars? To hunt for fossils of microorganisms that have been dead for billions of years? You're telling me that's worth spending three trillion dollars to get us there? Robots can do all that crap."

"João," Sally said, "you need to calm down. We're only trying to help—"

"*Me* calm down? It's high time we think about what we're doing. Think, think, *think*!"

"Come on, Sal," I said. "Let's leave him alone."

She caught the gyro. "João, you need to eat something."

João only bowed his head, and with tightly shut eyes, cried.

"Christ," I whispered.

■ ■ ■

Sally and I found Bria on the lower deck scrolling through her palm screen. With all of us in privacy mode, she heard our report about João.

"He didn't even want the gyro," Sally said, staring at the soggy cylinder in her hand. "He used to be crazy about my gyros."

Bria shook her head. "He's worse. The stimulant isn't working the way I hoped. It might be aggravating his condition. I also put him on fluncadene to prevent him from clawing himself to death. Is he still scratching?"

"A lot," I said. "As in pencil on paper." I took out João's self-portrait.

"Uh-huh," she said, studying it. "I was afraid of this."

"Well?" Sally asked.

Bria glanced up. "Behavior symptomatic of psychosis."

"Arcadia 7, Houston."

Our eyes widened at the crackle of Jennifer Watt's voice.

"Hey, folks," Watt continued brightly. "A couple quickies. We notice you've been using up a lot of private group time lately. In fact, you've almost exceeded the limit. Just wanted you to be aware of that. If there's anything we can do to help, please ask. Also, João is falling further behind on several projects. We're particularly concerned about DUFS. Don't want to bust your chops, João, but DUFS is, like, a biggie for NASA because of the many lucrative spin-offs, like the one for pet dogs."

Spot's going to love *that*, was my sarcastic first thought.

"Anyhow, João," Watt went on, "we see you're often in your private quarters and we'd like to know if, like, there's a problem. One more thing. Our inventory data shows your ibuprofen supply is running low. How's the toe, Addy? Over."

I tapped my palm screen, turning off privacy mode. "We copy that, Jenny. Stand by." I tapped the screen again to return us to privacy.

"What do we do now?" Sally said. "We have to tell them *something* about João." She tugged at her suspended hair.

"For starters," Bria replied, "stop pulling your hair out. Remember when you said we should blame *my* husband if NASA ordered an abort? Funny how yours will be the one who's responsible for ending the mission. I have no choice but to disclose his condition to Mission Control."

"Mission Support."

"Screw you, Sally."

"Bria, I'm sorry," Sally said. "But let's not rehash the past, okay? I hate the idea of an abort as much as you do. The idea of being cooped up in the High Jump for another four hundred days straight makes *me* crazy."

"Hold on a sec," I said, then took a breath. "An abort-to-Mars scenario may be viable." My crewmates, pausing their spat, gave me curious looks. "Instead of aborting to Earth, we abort, partially, to Mars. Two of us could stay on the surface, at least for a little while."

"Uh-huh," Bria said. "And who would those two be?"

"You're the doctor," Sally said. "If João is ill, it only makes sense for you to stay here with him."

"He's your husband, sister. You stay with him."

"Wait," I said. "We're getting ahead of ourselves. We may not have to abort at all. João's only started with the new meds. Isn't there something we can say to buy more time with NASA?"

My stomach growled, telling everyone I hadn't eaten. The gyro in Sally's hand was squished but still glued together, the "yogurt" sauce seeping out from one end. I gestured at it and said, "You going to eat that?"

"Want to split it?"

"Sure."

Sally tore the gyro in two and gave half to me. A morsel of fake lamb escaped, which Sally lapped up with her tongue. As I crammed my half in my mouth, Bria scrolled on her palm screen. "I'm taking us out of privacy mode," she said.

I spoke with my mouth full. "Hey—"

"Mission Support," Bria said, "Arcadia 7. Thanks, Jenny. Apologies for the delay. Just finishing up one of Sally's amazing gyros. We're fine. Yes, Addy's been hitting the ibuprofen like a drug addict." She chuckled. "His pain's normal for this stage of healing, but the toe's getting better, so I'm weaning him off medication. In a month, it should be fully healed, so our supply will remain adequate. João's fine. He's into his drawing and music. He's begun composing, which he likes to do alone in his quarters. That's where he is now, working on new songs. Don't worry, we'll get him back on track with DUFS. Over."

Bria shot glances at me and Sally that told us to keep our mouths shut, even if we weren't chewing.

There in the silence, I mulled over Sally's position about an abort to Mars, how she wanted the two of us exploring the Martian surface together, running experiments, and sharing that incredible adventure. Her argument that Bria was the doctor and should stay behind with João had merit. Yet I couldn't see it happening. Not with the earlier upsets.

And then the nightmare scenario came into my head: NASA would choose Sally and Bria to be the ones to descend and land on Mars, and *I* would be the one left behind with João.

No damn way.

"Arcadia 7, copy," Watt said. "Thanks, Bria. If you don't mind, Flight wants to know why your group privacy time is so high. We know privacy time is private and you can divvy it up as you like, but since you're creeping up to the limit, we think we should, like, address it now, to see if there's a problem? Over."

"Roger that, Jenny," Bria said. "Okay, we're busted!" She chuckled again. "You're right, we let privacy time get out of hand. I told you João is into his music. Well, truth is, all of us are, and we're working on some things we don't want out there in the public domain, you know, so somebody else can run with it. But we get the message. We'll cut back."

We bobbed in silence for ten excruciating minutes to hear if Watt had bought Bria's lie. Sally tugged at her hair. I scanned the jumble of tools and materials João had velcroed together at his workstation, a mound the size of my Ford Asteroid. Bria read her palm screen while chewing her lips. The total scene reminded me of a bad episode of *The New Martians*.

"Copy, Arcadia 7," Watt said, "We're laughing here—I'm sure we'll like the new tunes. Over and out."

"Roger that, Jenny," Bria said. She took out a pen and gestured for me and Sally to come closer. She still had João's self-portrait. Once we huddled together, she held the pen and the picture in one hand and raised my arm with the other. With her back to the deck's camera, she pressed the picture against my arm, wrote *Q-pill* on it, then drew an arrow pointing to João's face.

MISSION DAYS 60–61

Call it the Q-pill. Or the P-pill. It depended on how you looked at it.

It was what Bria had been scrolling about: clinical guidance for administering psilocybin. That afternoon, in his quarters with Bria, João's first treatment lasted five hours.

To avoid detection, Sally performed another bypass operation on KIM so we could A) manually control what onboard flight recorders showed regarding who was in whose room, and B) adjust the allocation of private time among us. I know. This probably counts as making false statements to NASA. But we were desperate.

When Bria finally emerged and joined Sally and me on the middle deck, she had a tight smile, her cheeks were flushed, and perspiration glistened on her skin.

"Well?" I said.

"He's sleeping." Her tone was calm, almost blissful, and she smiled. "I think we made progress."

"What happened?" Sally asked.

"Give me a minute," Bria replied. "I need to wash up. Be right back." And without another word, she flew to the upper deck.

"She sounds utterly exhausted," Sally whispered to me.

"You would, too, if you'd been attending a patient for five hours."

After Bria returned, she reported the session had gone smoothly, how João wept as he beheld the "glory of pure love," and how she was touched by his "beautiful breakthrough."

"Sally, I want you at his next treatment," she said. "I think it will help you reconnect with your husband."

"Sure, Bria. You're the doctor."

"Now, if you don't mind, I'd like to speak with Addy alone."

Bria and I flew to my quarters. "It's my turn to go to confession," she said after shutting the door.

"What do you mean?" I said.

She turned her head, crossed her arms and ankles, then spun to me. "The guidance I read warned this could happen. I didn't think it would and thought I could handle it if it did."

"Handle what?"

"I'm sorry, babe. João and I made love."

"*What?*"

"No, actually, I'm not sorry. I can't lie—it was a stunning, gorgeous thing, one of the most positive experiences of my life."

I was hurt, and incredulous. "You took a Q-pill? Bria, I'm really disappointed in—"

"Only João took the pill. He came on to me, and I . . . well, I let him. It was unbelievable, I mean, fantastic."

"*Well, fuck!*"

"I know." She winced. "It just . . . happened. I floated outside his sleep pod, holding his hand to comfort him. He was scared—he thought he was dying, not unusual for someone on psilocybin for the first time—and he turned on his side and stroked my arm, and after that he—"

"Please. TMI."

"Fine. I don't blame you for not wanting to hear the details. I understand why you're angry, but I did it for him, for us, for the mission."

In the pause that followed, my heart pounded like a jackhammer.

"Okay," I said. "Go ahead. Tell me the rest. I don't want to hear it, but if I don't, I'll go nuts wondering about it."

She swallowed hard. "He unzipped my coveralls to my waist. Underneath, I wore a T-shirt, the one you and I did for Gatorade, and for a long time he stared at the green bottle between my breasts, studying the picture before tapping and probing it, ever so gently, with his forefinger . . . I mean, you'd be turned on, too."

"No I wouldn't. Keep going."

"He raised my T-shirt above my navel and put his hands on my bare waist and said he saw a spiral of a billion stars around a black hole that was slowly sucking them, me, and him into its center, and each of us was not just one of the swirling stars but *all* of them, an entire galaxy composed of a single element—*love*. That's when he kissed me, first on my forehead, then my cheeks, then neck, and after that our mouths met, and he pulled me into the sleep pod. After all the talk sessions with him about his depression, and seeing how the other drug treatments failed, what can I say? I went with it. We ended up doing the Apollo 11."

"Jesus, Bria, really? You did Apollo 11 with João? And you're not even sorry?"

"I regret I've upset you, Addy, truly I do. It won't happen again. That's why I want Sally at the next session. And yes, I'm going to tell her what happened."

That night I slept alone in my sleep pod. And wept.

■ ■ ■

The next morning, I left my private quarters only after my palm screen showed an empty dining area. I wanted to eat alone. I sucked down black coffee spiced with sadness, ate French toast lathered in anger, and watched the downer news. The presidential primaries were about to begin, and Dawn Bastbom led in the polls, which predicted she and Lemon would win the general election.

It boggled my mind so many voters could be stupid enough to embrace the media star's hate rhetoric and ridiculous policy positions, like legalizing guns for ten-year-olds and nationalizing *The New York Times*, *Los Angeles Times*, and *The Washington Post*, so the U.S. government controlled much of the news and got rid of the "fake stories."

Part of me didn't care. Actually, two parts. The part hurt by Bria's fling with João, a hurt that hurt more because of the hypocrisy I sensed in feeling hurt at all, given my lust for Sally. And the part I hoped would soothe the first part. Said second part being that I'd be occupied with more important things than Bastbom for the next year, especially on Mars.

If I was on Mars.

My thoughts returned to Bria. Her session with João struck me as sex therapy (without my consent) as much as drug therapy. But it was no time for self-pity. For the sake of crew unity and the mission, I had to keep doing my job and be magnanimous and forgiving. Or at least pretend to be.

I flew to the lower deck and found Bria, Sally, and João at their workstations. Bria stroked a keyboard while she filled out a report, grinning as her fingers typed rapidly. Sally thumb-punched a controller as she wore a VR headset that probably played *Call of Duty: Alien Ops III*, while João connected two sections of plastic hose with a coupler (something related to DUFS?), his hands moving methodically. His workstation, neat and organized, completed the scene of a harmonious crew engaged in daily routines. It was strange, but after the last two months, I wasn't used to such calm.

"Hey, amigo!" João said to me. He let loose the coupler and hose, zoomed over, and wrapped me in his arms.

"Wow," I said as he pressed his clean-shaven face into my neck and patted my back.

"I love you, man."

"Thanks," I murmured.

He parted while still gripping my shoulders. "No, *thank you*," he said.

"For?"

"Being our co-commander, for giving the green light to my last treatment, for being so understanding. I really appreciate it, man."

I glanced at Bria, whose station was between João's and Sally's. She flashed me a smile.

I was gobsmacked. No one seemed concerned. About anything.

"Hey," João went on, "let's jam tonight. And get KIM into the action."

"Thank you, João," KIM said. "I really appreciate it, *man*." The robot then laughed a Santa Clausy *ho-ho-ho*, a laugh that had come a long way in three years but still wasn't quite there. Or maybe I wasn't in a laughing mood. KIM's default programming didn't include mocking a crew member, and I thought someone (João?) may have changed its humor settings.

"You bet, KIM," João said. And then to me, "What do you say? Should we get out our instruments and play with each other?"

"I'll think about it. Great to see you're in such good spirits, João. I mean really great. I'm sure Dawn Bastbom's poll numbers have nothing to do with you being so happy."

"Dawn Bastbom? Oh, I feel sorry for her. All that anger inside? Sad. Very sad."

"But it appears she's going to win the election."

He smiled and shrugged. "Yeah, I know."

"What happened to your fears about her abolishing the First Amendment and proclaiming herself Supreme Ruler for Life?"

"Addy, if it happens, it's supposed to happen. The universe has a plan, and everything's right on schedule."

■ ■ ■

I forced myself to join the reunion of The Craters, reminding myself that João's mental illness—the biggest obstacle to landing on Arcadia Planitia—had been overcome. Maintaining crew morale was critical, despite my severely wounded feelings about Bria. I think she was trying to put the past behind us because when we began the jam session, she wanted to start with my song, "Hamburger Bun."

That night, João played a descending bass line that made the tune—which eventually morphed into "Expand Your Love"—our number one hit. The rest of us looked on in awe as his dexterous fingers plucked all those syncopated notes, KIM's French horns giving the song its majestic texture.

"Honey," Sally said to her husband, "that was amazing. When did you learn that?"

"Just now," he said. "It just came out."

The new version pleased me so much, the not-so-positive feelings I had brought to the session evaporated. I think João's peace and happiness had rubbed off on me. He and Sally slept in the same pod for the first time in weeks, while Bria and I stayed up and talked about our relationship, João's recovery, and the history the four of us were making.

And about forgiveness. We reconciled.

Ah, I thought, the wonders of psilocybin.

MISSION DAYS 62–72

The next day, our focus was on the MOI burn, the maneuver to send us toward a parking orbit and docking with the Apple, the lander that would set us down on Mars. Fortunately, there wasn't much to do, except for checkouts of the propulsion system and fastening our seatbelts.

Lasting eighteen minutes, the MOI went as planned.

A week passed after João's first Q-pill. He'd caught up on the DUFS project, testing out the technology himself on our aeroponics lettuce. Bria wasn't worried his post-pill elation had faded, but she advised a second treatment, just to be sure, and this time Sally would be present.

João popped his second pill a few days later, with Bria and Sally attending him while I mounted the XBike. Bria flew in with a smile after I had pedaled for only twenty minutes.

"That didn't take long," I said, coming to a stop. "What happened?"

"They snuggled, and right away João started combing Sally's hair with his fingers, calling it a rainbow that smelled like apples and cantaloupe. She got starry-eyed and whispered the refrain from "Saturn River"—you know, *your eyes are glistening moons*—and he started licking her hair like it was cotton candy. That's when I left."

"You gave Sal a pill, didn't you?" I said.

"João insisted. I consider it part of their therapy."

I harrumphed. "Sounds more recreational than medically justified."

Bria looked at me as if I were wearing a pair of Peacock McStewart earrings. "Funny," she said. "We've been married for eight years, and all this time I didn't know you held a medical degree."

I worried she wanted to take the drug herself and shuddered at the thought of my three crewmates getting stoned together. "That was João's last treatment, right?" It was more like a demand than a question.

"I think so."

"Good," I said. "Destroy the rest of the pills."

"And if he has a relapse?"

"And if he gets hooked on psilocybin? And Sally gets hooked? Then what?" I pointed at her. "And you're curious about trying it. I know it."

She raised her eyebrows. "Aren't you?"

"We're commanding the first human surface mission to Mars. Remember?"

Bria gestured with her palms. "There are no side effects, Addy. You take a trip and it's over. And it's not physically addictive. You see what it's done for João. Not only for his depression but for his music and—"

"This is ridiculous. I can't believe we're having this conversation."

I spun and flew to my workstation. Sally and João didn't emerge for fourteen hours.

■ ■ ■

The next morning, Sally said, "*Gyro,*" giggling as she nudged the roll-up into João's mouth. She had her legs wrapped around his back as his arms locked around her waist.

Bria and I made our own gyros. "Sally and João are the happiest I've seen them," she whispered to me, the couple oblivious to our presence. "Our crew's more united than ever."

I couldn't disagree. Yet a pang in my stomach reminded me just how united she and João had become. At least she would no longer take part in his sexual healing.

In the following days, João and Sally were inseparable, chatting while working out together, assisting with each other's tasks, laughing side by side at the news, and never once lamenting the state of the world we had left behind. We all watched a report of Bastbom's biggest rally so far. Assembled on the Mall of the nation's capital, a million of her acolytes heard, for the first time, her proposal to eliminate NASA and let private industry "completely run the space show" without taxpayer dollars.

"NASA—don't you think it sounds like nauseous?" she said, the wind whipping her hair across her face, her fingers clawing it away from her eyes. "I don't know about you, but I'm sick of dorks, geeks, and eggheads spending our money!"

João chuckled. "A million people. Bet the food trucks raked in the bucks."

"João, don't you care anymore?" I asked. "Your father's about to lose his Senate seat."

"It's okay. I told Dad this will pass, and everything will be fine. He's had a good run in the Senate. More importantly, we still have each other."

"So true, honey," Sally said, "so true."

When we jammed that night, Sally killed it on the bouzouki, flowing with the music, improvising while humming hooky new melodies that became the lovely ballads "Floating" and "Space Father's Daughter," and the eccentric "I Have a Secret I Share Only with My Seahorse."

I'll admit it. I was consumed by envy. I enjoyed playing oboe but felt I couldn't be as innovative with my wind instrument as Sally and João were with their stringed ones. And, obviously, I couldn't sing while my lips were sucking a reed. By now I had changed "Hamburger Bun" to "Expand Your Love," the only significant thing I'd written. Yet João and KIM's contributions so transformed the song, it was as much theirs as mine.

Sally and João were often smooching unabashedly in front of me and Bria. Their eyes closed as their weightless bodies revolved in semicircles. I was envious of that, too, the carefree abandonment of their love. Bria and I were doing okay, but our crewmates were the ones expanding their love, not just playing a song about it.

"I'm fantasizing about something," Bria said the next night in our sleep pod with the lights still on.

"Sounds good to me." I turned to her and smiled. "What do you have in mind?"

"How great The Craters would sound if all four of us got a little buzzed."

"Not happening. What else do you have in mind?"

She clutched my shoulder. "No, really, it could be phenomenal."

"And then something happens to the ship, some emergency, and we're buzzed. In other words, dead."

"This isn't Armstrong Station, Addy. NASA came up with that crap just to test us. We've been in deep space for over two months.

There hasn't been a single issue with the ship. Not one. KIM controls all the environmental and life-support systems. And with the backups, there's a zero-point-zero-zero-zero-one percent chance of anything bad happening."

"You forgot something."

"What?"

"'Think the unthinkable and then plan for it.'"

She rolled her eyes. "Oh, God."

I'd been in the mood for something other than discussing 0.0001 percent chances, and now the mood fizzled. "Good night," I said and gave her a peck on the lips.

"I think I'll read for a while in my quarters," she said. "I'm hooked on David A. Gass's new thriller."

"Yeah? What's it called?"

"*Appalled*."

If that's what she wanted, she could have read my mind instead.

■ ■ ■

No doubt the folks at NASA heard Bastbom's speech, too, because as we slept, Flight texted us that, at 11:45 UTC the next morning—less than an hour after we were up—we'd be taking part in a joint press conference with the crew of the RedLiner, discussing how our missions contributed to humankind's future.

For NASA, Wendy Frost wrote, *the thrust of the messaging is that getting rid of us would be really stupid.*

Which, of course, explained why Bastbom and her supporters liked the idea.

I didn't mind the short notice about the press conference. The past controversies revolving around me felt like ancient history, and in the future I would be speaking about Martian microbes, the last thing the tabloids would want to pick up.

A few minutes before the start time, we lined up in front of the screen camera. Bria and I folded our arms and crossed our ankles to steady our bodies, while Sally and João held hands and bobbed a little.

I glanced at Bria, got her attention, and nodded at our crewmates. We uncrossed our arms and held hands like they did. The four of us formed the classic hang-on-your-wall portrait of two happy couples living in outer space, everything perfect, prim, and proper.

The screen flickered and displayed a four-section gallery view: we, the crew of Arcadia 7, in the top left quadrant; the two Joyces in the top right, grinning side by side; below them, Roma in black glasses smiling her toothy smile, her half orange-red, half turquoise hair parted in the middle; and to her left, below us, George and Wendy, squinting with pursed lips.

Ingrid Steele's superimposed face appeared at the bottom. "We are live," she said, "inside the RedLiner with its wife-wife co-commanders Joyce Ackerney and Joyce Bowman, and with the crew of the High Jump, the husband-wife pairs of Bria Best and Addy Johnson and Sally Kristalobopous and João Lobo, along with Q-Orbit's president, Noel Roma, NASA administrator George Butlarer, and Arcadia 7's flight director, Wendy Frost. Welcome all. *Space Times* would like to thank NASA for calling this press conference and Q-Orbit for getting on board. Let's begin by asking each astronaut to update us on how things are going. Addy, would you like to start?"

"Sure," I said, staring at the camera's blue dot. "We're more than seventy days into our mission, Ingrid, and more excited than ever about landing on Mars and exploring the planet and searching for evidence of life. And if we find it, I think it will forever change how humans think about our own species. How we—*all of us*—fit into the big picture."

"I would add," Bria said, "we're doing a lot of other science to help future explorers and the citizens of Earth. For example, we're making tremendous advances in aeroponics agriculture here on the High Jump—our warm-up for farming and gardening on Mars."

"For sure," Sally said. "That's what NASA is all about, doing good science that has positive impacts on people's lives. We're very, very, *very* proud to be a part of this work."

"I'd like to pick up on Addy's point about ancient life," João said. "Some folks think it's silly to hunt for microscopic fossils, but it's not,

not by a longshot. Those rocks contain once-living organisms, and when we find them, we'll respect their uniqueness and the lives they lived, and that, my friends, will help us respect—and love—each other on our own planet. Really important stuff."

The other eight heads on the screen were nodding. "Thanks for that," Steele said. "Now let's turn to the RedLiner. How's it going there, Joyce and Joyce?"

"Greetings to Earth," Joyce A said, then turned to Joyce B. "Things couldn't be better, could they, Joyce?"

The Joyces were visible from the neck up, their eyes bright and cheeks rosy, their faces almost touching, forming what looked like a two-headed person.

"They're better than ever," Joyce B replied, glancing back at the camera. "We're steady as she goes, Ingrid, and can't wait to get into our new digs on Arcadia Planitia. Oh, someone wants to say hi."

Nova's face, upside down, floated into the picture above the Joyces. For a second, I thought, *My little girl!* before I corrected myself. My niece licked a purple lollipop as she gazed at us, the camera zooming out until she was fully in frame.

"Do you know who that is?" Joyce A asked.

"Me," Nova said.

"No, the other people, sweetie," Joyce B said. "How about the man with the big Mars Nuts patch on his arm?"

Nova pointed. "He's the Ad Man."

Everybody else laughed while I faked a weak chuckle. "Call me Uncle Addy," I said, my smile more like a cringe.

George and Wendy seemed to share the same nervous system as each crossed their arms and frowned with puckered lips.

"Nova, what's your favorite thing to do on the spaceship?" Steele asked.

"Parties," she answered and licked her lollipop.

"What do you do at parties?"

"This." Nova began twirling like a pinwheel. "And we sing and play games and shoot movies and I'm going to be on the spinoff with

Terrance, Sophie, and Dido called *The Triangle* that premieres in one week and I'll be its star because I play the daughter of . . . of . . ."

"You know who, sweetie," Joyce B said.

"No, I forgot, bye!" Nova then flew away, her bare feet kicking Joyce B in the mouth (I hoped accidentally) as everyone laughed.

"My goodness," Steele said. "Looks like folks on the RedLiner sure have fun."

"You betcha, Ingrid," Roma said. "'Float on happiness' is the ship's motto. The crew chose it with input from the two billion viewers who watch *The New Martians*. And *The Triangle* is only the first spinoff. More will be comin'. Am I right, Joyce and Joyce?"

"Yes," Joyce A said. "Joyce and I have begun production of *The Joyces of MarShroom Cooking*."

"Can't wait to see it," Steele said, then cracked a brief smile.

"Can I say something?" NASA's administrator asked, raising his hand.

"Please, Mr. Butlarer, go ahead," the reporter replied.

"What Joyce is talking about is a perfect example of how our two missions—Q-Orbit's and NASA's—complement each other so well. Q-Orbit has made great strides in developing habitats with layers of mycelia to block radiation, which NASA is studying as well, with attention to concerns about contaminating Mars and its life with the fungi or bacteria we bring with us."

"There isn't any life on Mars, George," Roma said. "News flash, y'all. We're going to be the life. The life of the human species. That's Mars's future. And we're gonna git 'er done."

"Who knows what we'll discover, Noel," George replied diplomatically. "Anyhow, my point is, I'm sure we'll benefit from shows made by the First Fifty, such as *The Joyces of MarShroom Cooking*. Just as colonists of the Red Planet will benefit from the scientific research spearheaded by NASA."

"And research not just about the impact of introducing fungi to the Martian environment," Wendy added. "But projects such as DUFS—which stands for direct urination filtering system—will help us do agriculture on Mars, like growing those mushrooms for the Joyces, with other fantastic spin-offs for Earthlings."

As I listened, I grew envious again. Roma and her crew sounded *so* laid back, partying and making TV shows apparently their most important goals. Given the extremely harsh conditions of the planet, it probably was the only way Mars *could* be colonized and, for a moment, I regretted not leaping at Roma's offer to command the RedLiner.

But only for a moment. The First Fifty would make history, and so would Arcadia 7. After Bria and I took our first steps on Mars, we'd be household names forever, known as well as Taylor Swift and Buddha. We rehearsed many times, holding hands while each of us raised and lowered a foot, practicing our first words so we didn't sound like Neil Armstrong.

MISSION DAYS 73–90

Sally turned out to be right. It was hard to tamper with KIM without NASA finding out.

Flight controllers found a "bug" in the robot and, "for some odd reason," couldn't access details about it. Sally lied, saying she couldn't access them either (I went along with her fibbing). NASA also detected the false monitoring and privacy settings we had applied to the flight recorders. Good ol' Sal took the blame, claiming "mistake" and "oversight." I'm not sure Frost believed her, but nothing came of it. Until we returned to Earth.

And so we went back to writing notes and using sneaky hand signals. Flexing one's right hand meant "I have something to tell you; meet me at a workstation so I can write it down," and flexing one's left hand meant "Shit, don't tell NASA."

It didn't take long before Bria flexed her right hand at me.

We flew to the lower deck. Sally and João were there. Bria scrawled a message, which really came from all three of my crewmates as we huddled to block the clipboard from the camera. Here's what she wrote:

> J & S are taking another trip & I'm going with them & we want you to come with us!

I shook my head, feigning a response to something like a new schedule for taking turns on the XBike, staying calm as Bria resumed writing:

> You can take 1/2 pill or 1/4 pill. Come on, it's harmless! Good for morale!

Sally took the pencil from Bria and wrote:

> Better than Johnnie Walker.

João smiled at me as Bria took back the pencil. She scribbled:

> Or dirty martinis.

I grabbed the pencil and drew an X covering the whole page, then flexed my left hand. Leaving the pencil floating behind me, I flew to the middle deck, printed a peanut butter sandwich, and ruminated as I wolfed it down. João and Sally had joined the ranks of true believers in psilocybin, and I suspected Bria had already tried it. The reason she gave for going to her own quarters the other night—to read *Appalled*—now sounded fishy.

I did my own research. The drug packed a wallop, but it wasn't addictive. It wore off eventually, and any side effects were minor. Given Bria's enthusiasm about the Q-pill, I wondered if she might slip me a dose without telling me.

Was a compromise possible? Maybe I'd take a trip—a quarter-pill dose—*once*. We would get the thrill out of our system, then Bria would hand over the supply. I could reserve the number of pills that, in her judgment, were necessary to address a relapse of João's depression. I would jettison the rest of the pills from the High Jump.

It shocked me how quickly the others agreed to my proposal.

For the next five days, we used privacy mode judiciously so we could be alone for an hour without Flight raising questions. After dinner on Mission Day 78, we would each ingest one of the rosy ovals or, in my case, a quarter of one. After reaching the peak of our trip, we would exit privacy mode, ride out the buzz by playing music, and then retire to our quarters.

When the day arrived, I thought of the trip as just another task on a checklist, something to be over and done with. No biggie.

Bria, Sally, and I washed the drug down, sharing a pouch of VeriOJ. "I enjoy listening to the aftertaste of orange," João said, "but this time, I'd like to try fruit punch."

I wasn't sure what he meant, but ten minutes later, I not only heard the color orange but also heard its scent. The tiniest details about the hab, such as the pitted texture of its walls, zoomed into crisp focus as my surroundings swallowed me, the middle deck expanding and contracting in sync with my heartbeat.

"I think I'm dying," I said, my trembles reverberating in ripples through everything.

Bria draped her arm around my shoulder. "Try to relax, baby. I'm here. You're safe." She planted a kiss on my forehead, which felt like a blanket enveloping my mind, although nothing seemed mine; only a thereness existed, without "me" being there.

Thank God for Bria.

Her dilated pupils, like a lighthouse guiding my brain, beamed colored rays of light. Blue, yellow, and green faded into red, purple, and gold as they swirled like ribbons around Sally and João. Just beyond my wife, our crewmates held hands and revolved like a merry-go-round as they stared at each other and smiled. When they unzipped each other's coveralls, I was transfixed by the trails made by their hand and arm movements, which were like individual frames of a video that stayed suspended for a long time. I couldn't stop watching as they stepped out of their clothing. The contours and creases of João's T-shirt and underwear (and the bulge) formed a sniffing rabbit that made me laugh as he removed Sally's socks.

She was wearing nothing but a sports bra. The multiple images of her hands pulling it up and over her head created an accordion-like effect. She slipped out of the bra, and an endless stream of Hershey chocolate kisses fell out. Unwrapped from their foil, they looked delicious.

I had calmed down, experiencing the scene as if being part of it, as if my senses belonged to a pure state of being, connected with the oneness of everything, which was—and I know this sounds hokey, but it's the best way I can describe it—*love.*

Bria and I wedged beneath the galley table and began feasting on something other than Sally's gyros, while Sally and her mate entwined themselves between the treadmill and XBike. All of this flowed effortlessly, despite weightlessness. It was wonderful. And exactly the way it was supposed to happen, with no guilt or shame but only a divine nothingness that gave everyone's ego the boot.

Afterward, I didn't play the oboe, but the desire to draw overwhelmed me. Everyone put their clothes back on, except for João, who agreed to pose for the rest of us. We sketched him as he floated upside down. Here's my effort:

I include the picture as evidence that, even with an altered mind, I could discern actual objects with remarkable clarity. As I studied the sketch the next morning, I liked how my style was more expressive than anything I'd drawn before. My fear abated that the Q-pills would lead to some catastrophic screw-up. And yet I still thought I had *something* to fear about them.

The crew ate breakfast mostly in silence that day. I struggled to sort out my thoughts and feelings. Was the "good" trip bad for our mission? I mean, my God, I would have never dreamed Bria and I would take part in an orgy. I'm sure NASA wouldn't have, either.

"Have a good time last night?" Bria asked.

I couldn't help but return her smile.

True to her word, she gave me the rest of the pills. She told *me* to decide how many to keep, then swore on my mother's grave that she had stashed none away. I believed her, though technically Mom, whose ashes Zena had cast to the wind, didn't have a grave, only a gravestone.

A week and a half later, my lingering curiosity about the wondrous world of ego-lessness bloomed like an ever-growing flower. On the evening of Mission Day 90, with all systems of the High Jump one hundred percent nominal, I ingested the three-quarters of the pill left over from the first trip. The others took full doses. I promised myself this trip would be the last one for any of us.

"Time for the magic circle, amigos," João said, taking Bria by the hand. Bria took mine, and my other hand took Sally's, and she took her husband's, and we began revolving. We each took on the same shimmering glow, like we were a single organism. Soon our arms slid around the waists of our partners, mouths turning and joining whatever mouth was there, which in my case was Sally's, and in Bria's case was João's. And then everyone's mouth turned the other way. To the best of my recollection, we repeated this exercise about twenty times. I, for one, enjoyed the variations on the sounds of the fruit punch I tasted on Sally's and Bria's tongues—a fascinating experience compared to normal kissing.

I don't remember who unzipped me.

I do remember Sally floating naked. Her hair was a field of golden worms with grins and beady eyes. Strangely cute, they wanted to tell me the story of their lives. Her finger traced my neck below my ear, gently scratching and tugging my flesh here and there as if trying to peel me, and then she drifted lower, taking the worms with her.

We bobbed a lot. And rolled. And spun. We didn't control it but just kept exploring alien terrains, oblivious to João and Bria, until the four of us collided and bounced into the exercise equipment. We discovered enough room for all of us to fit between the bike and treadmill, the handlebars and rails permitting the insertion of one's limbs to assume positions like the Apollo 11—precisely what was going to happen before we experienced *KIM interruptus*.

"Addy and Bria," the robot's voice crackled, a tinny sound that became the shape of an icicle. "There is an emergency. This is no drill. A depressurization event is occurring, likely the result of a meteoroid penetrating the ship's hull. I estimate the impact hole is four millimeters in diameter, the exit hole approximately twice that size, somewhere on the upper deck."

"Fuck," I said, letting go of Sally's thighs. My brain, as altered as it was, understood the word "depressurization," though it took a few minutes to process the implications. I looked for my coveralls but couldn't find them. I flew to my quarters, got my butt into a pair of sweatpants, and threw on a T-shirt. By then, I was aware we could be in very deep shit.

I returned to the middle deck. Bria had her clothes on (I think they were hers) while Sally and João remained nude, both floating in the lotus position, with legs crossed and hands resting on their knees, their eyes closed, smiles on their faces. Paragons of calmness. And more experienced with psilocybin than I was.

"Hypoxia threat assessment please, KIM," Sally said without opening her eyes.

"Five hours before life support degrades," the robot answered.

Sally grinned. "Ample time for repairs."

"Correct, Sally. Assuming one locates the puncture within the next four hours, nine minutes, and thirty-one seconds."

"Shouldn't be a problem," João said, keeping his eyes closed as well. "KIM, can you see the point of impact on the ship's exterior?"

"Unfortunately, no, João. I hypothetically depict the meteoroid as a nonspherical object with a maximum width of three-point-two millimeters."

"Arcadia 7, this is Houston." It was Bullseye Peters. "We recommend you don pressurized flight suits and be ready to evacuate to the Capsulchino while we evaluate the damage. Over."

"Roger that, Pete," Bria said after we switched out of privacy mode.

As I zoomed to the upper deck, the walls swirled around me like multicolored taffy pulled by God's invisible hands, and I wasn't even sure I believed in God. But I did believe in KIM, and when I reached my destination, I asked our fifth crewmate where the hole was.

"I cannot pinpoint it yet, captain. The flow of escaping air suggests the leak is starboard."

Sally and João had gotten dressed, but we held off putting on flight suits, hoping to find the leak and repair it quickly. For the next thirty minutes—barefoot in what, to me, was powdery snow reminiscent of Antarctica—we searched every inch of the floors, ceilings, and walls of our private quarters for a hole no larger than a dime.

"I believe the High Jump's cameras now have an image of the impact area," KIM said. "Which is best viewed on the galley screen."

The projectile had struck the middle of the hab module, leaving a hole 4.2 millimeters wide, very close to KIM's estimate. Its shape, mass, and hypervelocity must have gone unpredicted in the design models for the High Jump's shielding. The chances of such a collision were one in ten billion, roughly the same as winning the Globo Lotto.

The galley screen zoomed in on the pit until it became a black crater set against a background so white it made me squint. In zigzagging streams of light, the tip of a brilliant red triangle pointed at the hole, vibrating like the hand of an old-style magnetic compass pointing at true north. I don't recall why I looked at my tattoo, but I did, and it was also fishtailing. And then I realized that the red tip pointing at the hole was the corner of the American flag on my arm.

"Arcadia 7," Bullseye Peters said, "given the tight timeline for an interior repair, we believe a simultaneous EVA is necessary. Addy, you have the most EVA experience, so you're the chosen one. Stand by for detailed guidance."

Shit.

KIM determined the object had penetrated a vent duct in Bria's cabin, an area separated from any electronics. We'd been lucky. The plasma from the meteoroid's ionization on impact could have caused an electrostatic discharge that knocked out the High Jump's electrical systems. Accessing the hole would require removing two wall panels and a section of the duct. KIM estimated the job would take three and a half hours—cutting it close. And the robot hadn't factored in our psilocybin consumption.

While João and Sally took the wall apart, Bria helped me suit up. Then she and KIM sped through the EVA checkout list. I entered the Capsulchino, and we depressurized the capsule. In less than an hour—record time—I exited through the airlock.

I admit to being scared shitless because A) the Cavity Filler Insertion Device (or CFID) I would use to seal the hole looked to me like the ghost of a legless dog with a long snout and short tail; B) the grinning worms had moved from Sally's hair to my boots; C) although KIM assured me it was there, the tether that kept me attached to the Capsulchino was invisible; and D) once outside, I had the sensation of moving so fast that if I lifted any part of my body to move toward the High Jump, I'd be ripped off the ship and hurled into deep space faster than you can say Halley's Comet.

Spread-eagled against the Capsulchino, I applied as much pressure as I could with my limbs so I would stay glued to the capsule. Confession: fear paralyzed me. The vessel appeared dilated and stretched out, as if traveling near the speed of light, with me clinging to it. I was panting as if I'd run a hundred-yard dash in ten seconds, which was the time I thought I had left to live.

"Your heartbeat and breathing are elevated," KIM said. "Try to relax. Can I play you some music?"

"Sure. Pick something. Anything."

"Fixing a Hole," a Beatles classic my mother had loved, did the trick, centering me and helping me to remember I was traveling at the same speed as the ship. Which meant, relative to it, I remained motionless.

I gripped the handholds and pulled myself toward the High Jump. The hab, along with the empty truss that once held the drop tank, followed by the inline tank and the core stage with the NTP engines, was elongated. I mean really elongated, like into infinity. It resembled the thin spaghetti noodles Della made by hand at Cristo's, except these noodles pulsated and glowed atop the black dinner plate of outer space.

I found the hole, inserted the ghost dog's tail, then pushed one of its nostrils—the green-lit one—while it barked at me. Two minutes later, after the CFID mixed its super-strength resin and pumped it into the hole, the red-lit nostril came on, and KIM confirmed I had sealed the leak. I should have felt relief. Instead, I worried I wasn't out of the woods (or in this case, the noodles) as the undulating brightness took on a strobe light effect. It disoriented me so much, KIM gave me instructions—"reach and grab with your right hand . . . now your left . . . now your right"—all the way back to the airlock.

That night, I made a solemn vow. No matter how much curiosity tempted me, no matter how much I longed for a substitute for a dirty martini, no matter how cute I found grinning worms, I would never, ever consume another Q-pill.

MISSION DAYS 91–109

I was the toast of Earth, an international hero, the global media's darling. And I hadn't yet planted a boot on Mars. Even CNSA sent congratulations, a magnanimous gesture, since Zheng and Zhang were going to win the silver medal instead of the gold.

When Bria and I arrived for breakfast with the others on Mission Day 91, things felt awkward. Because of the emergency, we hadn't consummated the swap. But we almost had, which none of us could have forgotten.

"Hey," Bria and I murmured together, staring at the galley table.

"Hey," Sally whispered.

"Hey," João echoed softly, floating near his wife.

The question was how to move forward. Whatever we did, the mission came first, and the best way to sort everything out was to sit (or rather float) face-to-face and have an open discussion.

"So, are you going to pitch the rest of them?" Sally said while tapping buttons on the food printer.

I knew she meant the Q-pills. "I'll keep a few, as agreed," I said. "We won't need, or want, any more."

"Speak for yourself, sir," Sally said. She spun around with a plate of scrambled eggs that were sticky enough not to float away. When our gazes met, she winked.

I turned to Bria, who arched her brows while sipping the straw of her coffee cup. I then glanced at João, who smiled and turned to Sally. She smiled back at him and then at me.

Yes, a difference of opinion persisted about the Q-pills. Once again, I was in the minority.

I hadn't decided how many pills to keep and how to prevent KIM and Flight from finding out. I tabled the discussion while I mulled it over. Besides, the priority was getting our relationships straightened out. I called a meeting and asked Bria to lead.

"Who wants to begin?" she asked. When no one answered, she did. "It's pretty simple. The drug heightens sexual desire in some people, and it looks like we happen to be 'some people.'"

"The issue for me," Sally said, "is how feelings linger. I mean, for example, your feelings for João, Bria. We should acknowledge and accept our feelings, shouldn't we?"

"True," my wife answered. "Your husband and I . . ."

Bria seemed to have lost her train of thought. João helped her out. "It was incredibly beautiful," he said, filling in the blank. I thought (wishfully, perhaps) he meant the psilocybin experience in general, so I nodded.

Everyone nodded.

"You're right, Sal," I said. "We all have feelings about each other we need to accept while remembering we don't have to act on them, you know, for the sake of the mission. Things can start out as consensual, but we know how extramarital behavior can breed problems later on. Bria, I think you wanted to say more."

"What I . . . well, what I mean is, we can try emotional distancing."

"Remind me, Bria, what is that?" João said.

"As soon as you feel something you shouldn't act on, you label the feeling with a descriptor—such as 'horny,' 'aroused,' 'turned on,' or whatever—and keep repeating it to yourself over and over."

"Yeah, that's what I'm doing now," João said.

"Good. And by repeating the label for the feeling, it diminishes its strength, preventing it from becoming overblown, creating the distance you need in order to *think* before acting in a way that's undesirable."

"Bria, would it make sense for us to practice emotional labeling now?" Sally said, glancing at each of us one by one. "Together?"

"Absolutely. We'll take turns repeating the labels out loud."

And so we practiced. Sally said, "Anticipating" over and over while staring at me, her hands clutching the knee pockets of her coveralls. After she finished, I must have said, "Tingling" a dozen times with my hands clenched into fists. Bria looked at João and spoke, "Oh my God" fourteen times (I counted). I have never thought of myself as a prude, but I found it disgusting when João followed with, "Yes, yes, yes, yes, yes."

"'Oh my God' and 'yes' really aren't labels for feelings, are they?" I said.

"You shouldn't judge," Bria said in a chastising tone. "The label for a feeling is whatever the feeler feels like using."

"Fair enough," I said, not feeling like arguing.

The meeting ended, new ones beginning after Sally and João flew to their quarters, and my wife and I flew to ours.

■ ■ ■

I took my third trip on Mission Day 94. I know. So much for solemn vows. But I had confessed my envy to Bria about Sally's and João's blossoming music. "That's the last thing I need to find out," I told her. "Whether psilocybin makes a difference."

"Uh-huh. I just hope you won't be a hypocrite."

"How do you mean?"

"By banning Q-pills for the rest of us."

"By my count, Bria, you've already taken it three times."

"Five."

"Really?" I said, stretching my neck.

She spread her arms. "See? That's what I've been trying to tell you. It's harmless."

I still didn't buy that argument, at least not completely. At the same time, emotional distancing hadn't reduced my envy, no matter what label I applied to it.

On trip number three down the rabbit hole, I went solo—just me and my oboe. For two hours, original new tunes sang to my neurons, the genesis of "Goodbye Grapefruit," "As Your Bouzouki Laughs Out Loud," and "Orbit Number 1009." None of them were about me, which I found liberating. Not just musically, but spiritually.

Then, to further test psilocybin's effects, I turned to drawing. The drug enhanced my focus on details, because I no longer existed apart from them, melding with them instead, which improved the results:

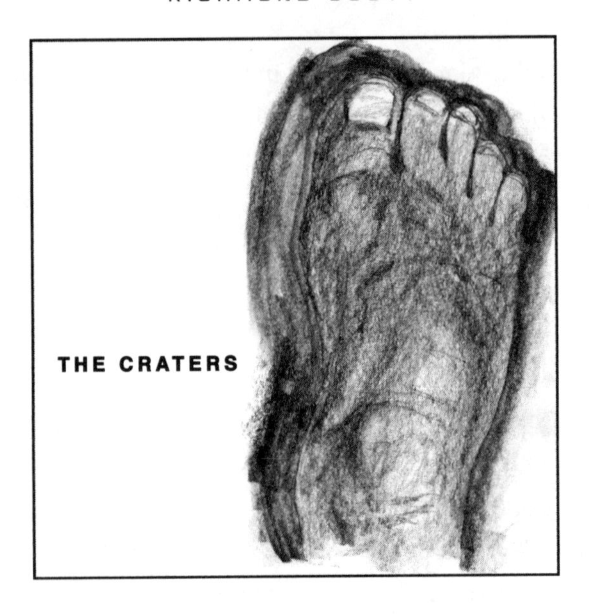

That's my right foot on Mission Day 94, as it later appeared on our quadruple-platinum album *The Craters*, also known as *The Foot Album*. (You can see my middle toe is fully healed—proof that the charge I "endangered" the crew by hiding my injury is bullcrap.)

My Greek improved, too.

Was I hooked? No. Was I going to destroy the pills? No. Was I open to taking more trips with my crewmates? Yes. Why? Because every trace of my envy had disappeared.

And after months of living in space with the same three people, psilocybin was a shitload more interesting than exercising on a treadmill or XBike wearing a VR headset that put you in the Scottish Highlands or at the Great Wall of China. Or reading *Appalled* or watching *The New Martians* or that other comedy show starring Dawn Bastbom. Or even studying a new phylum of fungi.

I took my fourth trip on Mission Day 109, with Sally, Bria, and João. Within minutes, we were giggling and helping each other undress, then rigged ourselves up for a swap that led to the creation of our own Big Bang, from which beautiful wave after beautiful wave of Pure Beauty surged throughout the Universe of Love.

MISSION DAYS 110–115

The longing looks and smiles we gave each other the next day must have outnumbered the stars in the Milky Way. *That* was a turning point, not only for our mission but for our lives, as each one of us discovered our True Self, which in each case happened to be polyamorous.

Now, in deep space tens of millions of kilometers from Earth, the idea of "extramarital" held as much meaning as the difference between up and down. In the coming weeks, our twosomes, threesomes, and foursomes, often athletic and always thrilling, brought us no shame or jealousy. None whatsoever. And we would learn that we didn't need Q-pills to enjoy ourselves, though if anyone wanted one, that was totally cool.

Everything was cool.

Bria told me she was glad for Sally and me, and I told Bria I was glad for her and João. And for her and Sally. My relationship with João was changing as well, not in any sexual way but in growing as close as the tightest of tight-knit brothers, the relationship I never had growing up. In short, aside from the musty taste of the printed yogurt, things couldn't be better on the High Jump.

And then, on the afternoon of Mission Day 110, just days before our scheduled arrival at the Red Planet, it all changed.

The four of us were watching a live feed of a CNN report about the sea swallowing up the Marshall Islands. The reporter was talking with Noel Roma, who offered to move the entire population to a gulley near Roma City, which would be enclosed with FungiGlass and renamed "Mars-Hall Island." Suddenly, the reporter switched gears and sent things back to the network's statuesque main anchor, Claudia Newman.

"We have a report about the Chinese space vessel," Claudia said as our eyes stayed glued to the screen. "Fast Rabbit, already traveling faster than any crewed spacecraft in history, has sped up. It is now moving at over twenty-three kilometers per second, which is like warp speed compared to the High Jump, which carries the crew of Arcadia 7." Claudia stepped to a wall-sized 3D screen, which showed a woman wiping sweat from her brow outside Building 30 at Johnson Space Center. "Joining us from Houston is CNN's science correspondent, Ingrid Steele. Hi, Ingrid. Looks like a steamy night in Houston."

"Actually, it's not bad here, Claudia. Just a hundred three degrees."

"Please tell us what this maneuver by the Chinese means."

"I've spoken with one of NASA's flight engineers, who said if Fast Rabbit maintains its current velocity, it will reach Mars before the Americans do. NASA doesn't know how the Chinese will slow down so they can achieve orbit around Mars. But the agency assumes they possess the technology to do that and have planned the maneuver."

"Ingrid, do we know how much sooner Fast Rabbit will reach Mars ahead of Arcadia 7?"

"Not exactly, Claudia. My source told me it could be two or three days sooner."

"Goddammit," I said, slamming my fist into my palm.

Sally still had her arm draped around Bria. Each gave me a sympathetic gaze.

"I'm sorry, baby," Bria said. "Come here."

I floated to her and Sally. Bria took my face in her hands and pulled it into the nook of her arm, the force of the movement sweeping my legs to Sally's lap, the two women holding me like a body pillow.

"It's okay," Bria said as I peered at her face. "You still have us and João, and we have him and you, and he has us and you. And two hundred and forty prodigious days to look forward to on Arcadia Planitia."

"Prodigious?" I said, wallowing in prodigious disappointment.

"Last night's scrabble game." Sally's tone was serious but calm. "Twenty-eight points with the bonus—the reason I beat Bria." She took off my socks and began massaging my feet, stroking their sides and soles and gently tugging each toe, sending a kind of blissful excitement through the entire length of my body.

"Addy," Bria said as she watched Sally's fingers, "we have *so much* to be grateful for. Think of the amazing search you'll undertake for ancient microbes. Why, it could change humankind's view of life forever. And even if we're not first, our endorsement contracts will give us and our children financial security. And you've got your oboe and The Craters. Think of all the incredible music we'll put out."

"Bria's right," João said. "Time for a group hug."

The hug became more like a huddle, our hands on top of each other's shoulders. It took me back to my quarterback days at the Naval Academy and calling the next play, like a down-and-out, to give us first and goal on the five-yard line. But I didn't have a play, because there wasn't one. Another engine burn that would get us to Mars first wasn't possible without screwing up our fuel reserves and threatening our safe return to Earth.

An annoying image stuck in my mind's eye: a man with a burr haircut, black-rimmed glasses, and a broad, toothy smile—the immortal Vince Lombardi, one of Uncle Dick's heroes, who coached the Green Bay Packers to back-to-back Super Bowl wins.

Then came the earworm.

Winning isn't everything, it's the only thing.

* * *

We clocked the burn that slowed down Zheng and Zhang so they could achieve Mars orbit at fifty-five and a half minutes, which consumed an estimated 103 metric tons of liquid hydrogen fuel. They would squeeze into their lander, Strong Spider, two days before we docked with ours and start their descent thirty-five hours ahead of us.

"Z and Z are going to stay put on Mars for a good while," João said.

"Affirmative," KIM said. "They cannot have enough fuel for a voyage to Earth. It is not possible."

While CNSA didn't make its plans clear, many assumed Zheng and Zhang had adequate supplies until another vessel could reach them. But it made little sense. CNSA hadn't launched a return vessel during the same window as Fast Rabbit. The only explanations were A) the Chinese were stupid, highly unlikely; B) they were taking a risk with some undisclosed technology, more likely; or C) they were collaborating with Noel Roma and had intended to reach Mars first from the start, lulling us into complacency.

Explanation C sounded like the best answer.

I hate conspiracy theories. Yet I couldn't help theorizing that CNSA and Roma had formed a hidden alliance that made Zheng and Zhang secret Q-Orbiters who would live in the RedLiner after it landed. That way, the Chinese and Roma could share credit for the first crewed surface mission.

Or maybe I was just being paranoid.

By the time the High Jump obtained orbit, the Chinese crew had crawled into Strong Spider.

Screw it, I told myself. *Forget it*.

The galley screen showed the cracked and pockmarked face of Mars, its pink-orange hue edged by the glowing blue band of its thin atmosphere. The stupendously high mountains and unbelievably deep canyons riveted our attention and left us speechless.

Everyone was aiming for the flat soil of Arcadia Planitia and the ice underneath, without which a self-sustaining colony or a long-term research base wasn't workable. The various missions had agreed to Rules of Coordination (ROC) that stated that landing sites were first-come, first-served, with touchdowns at least 1,000 meters apart.

NASA's preferred sites were in the southern region of Arcadia Planitia. Aside from the benefit of ice beneath the terrain, the nearby hills and geological formations could be a treasure trove for fossils. NASA creatively called the sites A-1, A-2, A-3, A-4, and A-5, each within a kilometer of the M&M Ranch (which was already there).

A-1 was the most promising: the flattest and closest to the hab, less than a half-kilometer away. It doesn't sound far, but it could pose a challenge after four months of weightlessness. On the surface, we would work in gravity four-tenths of Earth's and wear bulky xEMU suits.

Unsurprisingly, CNSA's landing sites were smack-dab in the middle of the area where scientists detected gobs of water, though many kilometers from the hills. What's good about hills, in addition to their geologic research potential, is they might have caves that can serve as habitats, another factor that drove NASA's selection of landing sites.

It concerned me that CNSA may have reached the same conclusion as NASA, that A-1 was optimal, or they would pick it for no other reason than NASA had picked it. While the Chinese basked in glory, the Apple would humbly set down on site A-2.

On Mission Day 115, the day before our scheduled EDL, Bria, Sally, João, and I floated near the galley screen as Maggie Cool reported "live" from Tiananmen Square.

"Must be a billion people," Bria said as the drone camera panned the crowd. "That super-jumbo screen has to be a hundred meters wide."

João assumed a lotus position, his hands pressed together and resting between his legs as if he were praying. "Not a bad seat in the house," he said.

China's two newest heroes appeared on the screen in pressurized suits with their helmets on, making it difficult to see their faces behind the tinted visors.

"Zheng and Zhang are in final preparations for their historic entry into Mars's atmosphere and descent to the surface," Maggie Cool said. "They are checking out their systems one last time, and we expect, any moment now, they will receive a 'go' for entry, descent, and landing."

I spoke to the screen. "I've got news for you, Maggie. They're already starting EDL. And soon they'll plant a big red flag and hop up and down in victory."

"And so we get the silver medal," João said. "Still not bad."

I no longer cared for the Olympics analogy. It was more accurate to say, We get shit. Envy crept back into my headspace.

"Tomorrow will be our turn, baby," Bria said, taking hold of my hand. "You and I will be the first Americans on the Red Planet, and we'll be on a jumbo screen, just like Z and Z. I promise."

"See that itsy-bitsy lander the Chinese guys have to live in?" Sally said. "The M&M Ranch is a mansion compared to Strong Spider. We'll be much more comfortable." She winked at Bria. "Won't we, honey?"

"And what if the Chinese guys end up staying in the RedLiner?" I said. "Or even Roma City?"

"Let 'em," Sally said. "It won't ruin our fun."

She was right, I guess. And what science would Z and Z accomplish? They were there to stick a flag in the soil, gather a few rocks, and dig for a couple of ice cubes. Their diet likely would consist of energy bars that tasted like sugar-coated VeriSym Spam. And did they have commercial endorsements and best-selling albums? Or a fulfilling polyamorous relationship with three other lovable and loyal adults? No. I counted my blessings and felt at peace again.

Suddenly, the jumbo screen went black, and CNSA's *Star Trek*–like logo appeared with a phrase in Chinese. The only word I could read was *please*.

"We just learned that CNSA has placed a hold on the EDL," Cool said to the camera, then pointed behind her. "Their announcement says, 'EDL on hold. Please stand by.' Which is what people here are doing as they anxiously await resumption of Zheng and Zhang's entry, descent, and landing."

"Arcadia 7, Houston. Do you copy?" It was Ed Munch.

"Copy, Houston," I said blandly. Thanks to our strict discipline in front of the High Jump's cameras, Munch and the other CAPCOMs were clueless about the crew's collective transformation, and on the eve of our own EDL, I wanted to keep it that way.

"Thanks, Ad Man," we heard Munch say after the time lag. "You see the hold on Z and Z. Could be a million reasons. The bottom line is, we don't know how long the hold will last, so Flight wants you to be prepared to go with site A-1 instead of A-2. Under the ROC, we would have priority. No other changes. Any questions? Over."

"Roger," I replied, certain Munch would see the spike in my heart rate. "No questions."

I had lied. In fact, I wanted to ask KIM, if we started now, how quickly we could prep and initiate our EDL, what shortcuts we could take, and the probabilistic risk assessments. NASA most likely had run through scenarios for expediting EDL, rejecting them as risky. I was also sure Bria was reading my mind.

She stared at me. "Don't even think about it."

I tried not to but couldn't.

Zheng and Zhang were in Strong Spider, ready to separate from Fast Rabbit and fire thrusters to orientate the aeroshell that would protect them against the intense heat as they entered the Martian atmosphere. Our EDL was scheduled for the next day, but if we worked fast, we could be in the Apple and ready to descend in five hours.

I knew I couldn't go rogue a second time. At least not alone. Absent NASA's approval, I'd have to convince the crew to start our EDL early.

"Maybe we should eat dinner and turn in," Sally said.

"I'm up for that," João said.

Bria nodded. "Sounds good to me. We have a prodigious day ahead of us."

Houston also thought we should eat and turn in. I let silence serve as my agreement and stared at the *Please stand by* message as I ate one of VeriSym's go-to comfort foods, Cheez 'n' Chik'n. Later, all of us read "good luck" messages from Earth, checked for updates about Z and Z's EDL (nothing new), then went to our quarters at around 22:30.

"Want some floralterdenol?" Bria asked as I brushed my teeth.

"No, thanks," I said like a ventriloquist, then swallowed. "What I want is to begin our EDL. Like, this minute."

"Not happening, baby. Now come and zip us up."

MISSION DAY 116

My eyes opened to the sound of the Stranglebots stadium song "A Head of Your Time." I glanced at my palm: the screen glowed Mission Day 116, 03:30 UTC, three hours before our normal wake-up time. Was NASA piping in the music by mistake?

"*Goood mooorning*, Arcadia 7!" The voice of Bullseye Peters boomed over the music. "You're checking into the M&M early, folks. EDL prep begins at zero-five-hundred. Our target for initiating entry is twelve-hundred. You heard me right, guys and gals. High noon. Which should put you ahead of our friends Zheng and Zhang."

Though I'd been awake for only a moment, my eyes were wide open. I stopped breathing for a full ten seconds before I spoke. "Pinch me, Bria."

"Come again?"

"Pinch me."

"I already did. Last night. A bunch of times. Just where you like it. Remember?"

I pecked at my hand screen and turned off privacy mode. "Roger that, Bullseye. You made my day before it even began."

We feasted on the traditional Stake 'n' Eggz breakfast reserved for landing day while learning more about Zheng and Zhang's problem. CNN reported that Strong Spider's latches jammed when it attempted to uncouple from Fast Rabbit. Z and Z were to perform an EVA to disassemble the latches partially and manually pull the lander away from the service module.

So this was our chance.

We switched to the *Space News* channel. Maggie Cool still stood in Tiananmen Square, wearing sunglasses. "The sun's rising," she said as a bystander jostled her. "As far as I can tell, no one's gone home, though it's unclear whether we'll see any live video of the EVA, or whether the crew will even attempt a landing." The same person bumped into her again, turning her around; her third eye flashed a "What are you staring at?" look.

My sympathy went out to Maggie and the millions at Tiananmen Square. Their feet and toes must be killing them, and I could feel their pain.

We cut corners cleaning the High Jump before leaving it behind. By the time we began packing our musical instruments and other belongings, the clock showed 00:06:38 UTC, and, according to Bullseye Peters, Zheng and Zhang remained in orbit.

I wondered what I should do with the ziplock bag filled with Q-pills. They had cured João, saved the mission, and changed our lives. I resolved not to destroy them, at least not yet, and tucked the bag into a bin between stacks of food printer cartridges.

Time: 10:17:00. In pressurized suits, we flew to the airlock on the upper deck and bid farewell to the High Jump, our beloved habitat. I remember glancing at the lettuce garden we had harvested for the last time and getting choked up.

"See you later, High Jump," I said. "Thanks for all the great life support."

"Love you," João said and blew a kiss.

"Me, too," Bria said.

"Me three," Sally added, and patted Bria's shoulder.

"Arcadia 7, Houston." It was Jennifer Watt. "Amazing, but like five billion people are watching. You're on a live broadcast feed from here on out. You're go for sealing the hatch."

"Roger that, Jenny," I said, my heart pounding.

One by one we propelled ourselves into the Apple. Sally, the last in, sealed the hatch. We kept a close watch on Zheng and Zhang, and nothing had changed. I was betting on an abort. Perhaps they would ride, Apollo 13–style, back to Earth in Strong Spider. They might not survive.

The Apple was roomy, designed to carry up to seven astronauts, with ample windows that allowed us to see the reddish-pink-and-orange rough-and-rocky terrain rolling beneath us. My breath quickened and my eyes kept blinking as my anticipation of winning the race swelled.

We buckled up in a semicircle.

"Addy," KIM said, "from window number four, I believe you will sight the Chinese spacecraft."

And there it was. Strong Spider, living up to its name with its four arachnoid legs, glimmered in the distance, a kilometer from Fast

Rabbit. Zheng and Zhang had succeeded in unjamming the latches, we the first to know. I nearly blurted, *Well, fuck me,* but remembered we were being televised.

"KIM," I said as my crewmates snapped pictures with their palm screens, "commence EDL system checkout procedures with expedited protocol."

"Wait," Bria said, glancing up from her hand. "Expedited protocol?"

"We're not supposed to be this close to another spacecraft," I answered. "Especially a spider. Dangerous, right?"

She pursed her lips and jerked her head toward the window. Indeed, Strong Spider had grown in size. There was a minuscule chance of a collision, but in this case, an abundance of caution was fine with me. Once we separated from the High Jump, oriented the Apple, and entered the Martian atmosphere, we would—under the ROC—have first dibs on landing site A-1.

"Starting expedited checkout protocol," KIM said.

Rather than covering all the checkouts one at a time, KIM ran through the lists simultaneously. We finished in fifteen minutes, at 10:48, an hour early. Using thrusters to adjust the Apple's altitude, we could start our descent one orbit earlier than planned.

"Houston, Arcadia 7," I said. "We're go for EDL. Initiating separation from Nike High Jump. Mark five, four, three, two, one . . ."

The Apple shuddered as it parted from the habitat. I shook, too, inside. Even more than liftoff or TMI, it felt like we had *really* left the comfort and safety of home, perhaps never to return. The pensive faces of my crewmates suggested they shared the same feeling.

"We see you, like, started expedited checkout," Jenny Watt said. "Please advise, over."

Our communications were time-crossed by the transmission delay. I'd screwed up by not giving a reason for the expedited procedures—our own visual showed how close we were to Zheng and Zhang. By now, NASA would have learned that through its own tracking. Since the checkout went without a glitch, I decided not to add to the confusion by answering Watt's last message and just let her hear my previous communication.

KIM put Strong Spider on the screen for better viewing. I forced myself to keep my eyes on the Apple's dashboard, rather than on Zheng and Zhang.

"Initial altitude adjustment with a lock on site A-1," I said.

"Confirmed," KIM said after the thruster fired, which gave the Apple a jolt. "Entry beginning in thirty-two minutes, four seconds."

"KIM, have the Chinese reported which landing site they've chosen?" João asked.

"Negative."

CNSA remained tight-lipped, apparently assuming Zheng and Zhang would touch down first. The Apple's Ground Navigation and Targeting System (GNATS) could modify its route on the fly and, if it had to, land at a different site. But in my mind, CNSA's lack of communication would not change our site selection. The only thing that would—maybe—was if Strong Spider began its descent before we did.

I glanced at the spacecraft on the screen. So far, so good. The spindly legged thing didn't appear to be in the right position for EDL.

"Twenty minutes to entry," KIM said.

My breathing and heart rate ticked up. NASA and the rest of the Earth would receive our next transmission after we entered the upper atmosphere—the official start of EDL and the point of no return.

"Analysis, KIM," Bria said. "Why hasn't Strong Spider begun entry?"

"Undetermined," the robot answered. "But if you are asking me to speculate, Strong Spider is experiencing a technical difficulty, perhaps because of damage caused by the EVA."

With every passing minute, I grew more confident, even giddy. *If they sit still for another eighteen minutes, we win the gold.*

"Arcadia 7, we copy you," Watt said. "Go for EDL. Good luck and Godspeed. We like the views from the cameras—they're superb. You folks are in every home on Earth. Hey, Addy, break a leg, but not a toe."

I laughed. "Roger that, Jenny, thanks."

My fixation on Zheng and Zhang helped block out my natural anxiety about the upcoming "seven minutes of terror," when the Apple would race through the thin Martian atmosphere. Thin, yet with enough carbon dioxide molecules to create heat friction upward of 2,000 degrees Celsius, the single most life-threatening event in the mission. At one point or another, during each of my previous six missions, I had grappled with the fear of losing my life. But not this time, and Zheng and Zhang weren't the only reason.

I now embraced the belief that death would be the same egoless state I experienced thanks to a Q-pill, a union of the True Self with Love on the Divine Ground. So why be afraid? Besides, chances were very, very good that death in a fireball would be very, very quick.

"Five minutes to entry," KIM announced.

All four of us took deep breaths. If robots had lungs, I think KIM would have, too.

A minute later, we saw flashes from Strong Spider as one of its aft thrusters fired three bursts.

"Dammit," I said, then let out a huff that could have blown off my helmet.

"Should we switch to A-2?" Bria asked. "Isn't that the prudent course here?"

"Yes," KIM said. "Because there is an eighty-nine-point-ninety-seven percent probability the Chinese spacecraft will land at site A-1."

"Nobody asked you, KIM," I said. "Maintain A-1 as target. We can change it later, if necessary."

"Yes, sir," the robot replied. "GNATS locked on A-1."

Strong Spider's descent took it away from the view of our cameras, and we no longer had any real-time visuals or information about its status.

"Entry in two minutes," KIM announced.

"Well, amigos," João said, "it's been real, and I hope it stays real. Love you all."

Though Z and Z's descent filled me with dread, I felt I needed to respond to my crewmate. "Love you, man," I said. "And women."

"Love you, sweethearts," Sally said.

"Me, too," Bria said.

"Me, five," KIM added and then laughed like a chimpanzee, which at the time I thought was part of the robot's jest.

"Knock it off, KIM," I said. "You'll make my wife jealous."

"Arcadia 7, Houston." It was Brendan Halo. "Confirmation received that Spider is targeting A-1. Flight wants to go with A-2. We know it's a bummer, folks, but gotta follow the traffic rules."

"Copy," I said, my pulse quickening. It would be safer to switch out targets now, rather than later, and save fuel by reducing the number of course adjustments.

"One minute to entry," KIM said.

Screw Zheng and Zhang.

I always thought the ROC's thousand-meter-separation criterion was overkill—and so did NASA. GNATS had become so advanced it could land the Apple within fifty meters of any target, so even if we landed second, I was sticking with A-1. Call it national pride, but I wasn't letting Strong Spider give the Apple the elbow. That I had discovered my True Self probably also had something to do with it (though I'm not sure we should go there during my trial, Ben).

We watched streaks of flames darken from orange and white to red and blue as they baked the Apple. Sally and I folded our hands in our laps, while Bria and João's hands clenched the ends of their armrests, all of us vibrating like hell as the g-forces squashed us into our seats.

I closed my eyes and imagined my mother saying, "I'm so, so proud of you," and Uncle Dick saying, "Winning isn't everything, it's the only thing," and Zena saying, "Screw you." And Nova calling me "Spacey man" and "Ad Man." And seeing a *Star Trek* movie on an early date with Bria, and learning Doctor McCoy was her favorite character, as he was mine. Our date may not have been a great milestone in my life, but big enough to come up as the blowtorch outside lightened. The aeroshell peeled off the Apple, and a brackish sky appeared in the windows.

"Powered descent initiated," KIM said.

The ride smoothed out. I felt gravity. Sweet, sweet gravity.

As the kilometers on the altimeter clicked down, Mars, for all its grandeur and mystery, reminded me of a bad case of acne, scads of orange-red scars, lumps, and craters covering its face.

"KIM, status of Strong Spider," I said.

"No intelligence on that yet," KIM replied.

"Prepare to modify, on my go, GNATS target to a landing site separated by fifty-meters from A-1, with closest proximity to the M&M Ranch."

More chatter from NASA repeated we should divert our landing to A-2. I acknowledged NASA's instruction by saying "copy" without indicating I would follow it. As the pilot, I had the final say, and if I thought it was safe to land at A-1, that's what I was going to do.

We had descended to 5,000 meters and were flying over the frozen desert of Arcadia Planitia when KIM delivered the shocker. "Strong Spider sighted at A-1."

"Landed?" I said.

"Correct. Landed."

I zoomed in on the ground image. Sure enough, the little fucker was on the ground. I sighed.

Game over.

Or was it? Even at maximum zoom, we saw no sign that Zheng and Zhang had left their lander. They could still be depressurizing it or experiencing another problem. Or just messing with us again. In any case, their boots weren't on the surface. While I knew it was a longshot, ours still had a chance to be the first to stamp the Martian ground.

"KIM, change landing so the Apple is no farther than fifty meters from Strong Spider."

"Modification confirmed. Touchdown in three minutes and fifty seconds."

As our GNATS-guided descent progressed, we spent more time peering out the windows than at the instrument panels. Mars greeted us with a stellar day, the spectacular vistas reminding me of the desert scenes from the ancient technicolor Westerns I used to watch with Dad and Uncle Dick.

"Nominal trajectory," I reported to Houston, conveniently leaving out that my chosen site broke the ROC. The Apple's retro rockets were firing, slowing our downward flight. In the last minute before touchdown, we saw the zigzagging network of the M&M Ranch's modules, and the nearby small-scale nuclear power plant. Also nearby sat the American Express, the ascent vehicle that would take us back to the High Jump in eight months.

And we saw Strong Spider.

But no sign that Z and Z had exited.

Their spacecraft sat about twenty meters from the American Express, *way* too close to our picnic. I now cared even less about the thousand-meter separation rule. Rovers had marked the landing points with red X's, and I confirmed the selection of the one closest to the M&M, about 300 meters away. GNATS locked onto it and, seconds later, a curtain of dust streamed upward and covered the windows. A thud shook us. And then all stood still.

"Houston, this is Arcadia 7," I said. "The Apple has landed."

"Welcome to Mars," KIM said. "Local time is twelve hundred fifty-three UTC. The current temperature is minus sixty-one degrees Celsius. Please check for your belongings before exiting the craft."

"Hilarious, KIM," I said flatly. "Now drone your robot butt over to Strong Spider."

"Launching drone now."

We unbuckled our straps and smiled at each other—and kept smiling. For the first time in four months, we stood with something solid under our feet.

I took a step. "Ouch," I said.

"What's wrong?" Bria asked, leaning against the seat and wobbling as she gained her Mars legs.

"The toe," I answered.

"Want some ibuprofen?"

I probably should have taken some, but I didn't want to waste time. Zheng and Zhang hadn't emerged from Strong Spider, and every second counted. "No, I'll hold off. Let's suit up and prepare to leave the Apple."

"The mission plan calls for a twenty-four-hour interval," Bria replied. "To give us time to acclimate to the gravity. There's a risk—"

"I'm with Addy," Sally said. "I'm not waiting a day." She took Bria's hand. "Come on, sister, let's do it."

Bria looked at João, who nodded. It was three against one, and this time I wasn't in the minority.

"KIM," I said, "are you there yet?"

"Beaming close-up now."

It deflated me to watch the Strong Spider's hatch swing open and a red-gloved hand stick out. It waved at drone-KIM. And at us.

"Well, no rush now," João said, sitting back in his seat.

I sat and crossed my ankles to elevate the aching toe while Bria got out the ibuprofen. The race was over. We would sit on the sidelines as Team China took the historic first steps.

"Arcadia 7, this is Houston," Ed Munch said.

I decided if he called me "Ad Man" one more time, the first thing I'd do when I returned to Earth was strangle him.

"Congratulations, crew, well done. We assume something went wrong with the A-2 landing site. Please confirm. And stand by for a call from the president of the United States. Over."

"Thanks, Ed," I said in the most pleasant voice I could muster. "Yeah, A-2 didn't work out. Roger on standby."

Zheng (or Zhang) drew his hand back into the craft. A yellow helmet emblazoned with China's star-studded red flag emerged, followed by stiff arms and bent knees that straightened until boots touched the ladder's top rung. As Zheng (or Zhang) lowered himself at a snail's pace to the bottom, my stomach tightened. Two minutes later, a red boot met red dust. And the first words on Mars were spoken.

"Translation, KIM," I said.

"Today a few famous steps in the dust; tomorrow, a happy city for millions and millions."

The second Chinese astronaut took the same excruciating amount of time to reach the surface. He and his crewmate then planted the Chinese flag, twisting the pole into the surface for a long time before letting it go. A breeze spread out the red-and-yellow rectangle, revealing all its stars.

"KIM, which Chinese crew member is which?" I asked.

"Zheng's suit has the yellow band on the arm," KIM answered.

"Can you get closer so we can see their faces?" Sally said.

They had their sun visors down. Even when KIM hovered only a few meters from them, all we saw were shadowy outlines of faces and numbers and words in backward Chinese on their visors. Their pressurized suits looked as streamlined and tight-fitting as Italian business suits, and their backpacks were no larger than a briefcase.

"Their rebreathers must be tiny," João said. "I wonder how long they can recycle the air those guys are breathing."

They shuffled their feet to get around, whereas NASA had trained us to move by hopping. Each of them retrieved a hose-like tool from a utility box on the side of the lander. They attached the hoses to the side of their backpacks, as if ready to run vacuum cleaners, which wasn't far off the mark. They began scanning the ground with the hoses, sucking up rocks and dust. We watched as we ate sandwiches. It was nice not to worry about floating crumbs, though it felt like crumbs were all I had ended up with.

"They've got a lot of carpet to cover," Sally said. "And how in the heck do they store all that material in their backpacks?"

"Analysis, KIM," Bria said.

"The telemetry is encrypted," the robot replied. "We can't know for sure, but they may be preparing the surface so they can gather ice."

"See how Zheng is slowing down?" Sally said.

"That's Zhang, Sally," KIM said.

"Well, he's come to a dead halt."

"Look," João said, "so has Zheng."

We watched them for another two minutes, and neither moved. "Dammit," I said. "They're in trouble."

"Likely rebreather failure," Bria said, "and backup system failure. They probably lost consciousness."

There was no compatibility between our xEMU suits and the Chinese suits. Running out and giving them oxygen tanks would be a fool's errand. Instead, we would need to bring them inside the Apple, repressurize the lander, and remove their helmets so they could breathe again. Start to finish, at a minimum, the rescue operation would require ninety-minutes. We'd have to put on our own suits and depressurize the Apple before we could make any attempt. By then, they probably would be dead. But we had no other option.

As we hustled to don our xEMU suits, we kept glancing at the screen. Zheng and Zhang still didn't budge. I took it for granted that Mission Support would realize the Chinese crew needed help, so instead of informing Houston about our early exit from the Apple, I waited for Mission Support to ask questions.

We sat silently during depressurization as the figures of Zheng and Zhang remained frozen, each slightly bent at the waist, their heads angled downward as if staring at their hoses.

The poor bastards. First on Mars. And first to die.

"Arcadia 7, Mission Support. Ad Man, you're all go for early suit up and helping our Chinese friends. We rescheduled the call from POTUS."

I had no further thought of wringing Munch's neck as I dwelled on two less figurative deaths. And I stopped thinking I had lost a race, counting myself lucky for winning something far more important: a new life with Bria, Sally, and João, a new *family*. And we were all still alive. While we stood in grim silence during the last minutes of depressurization, I planned how we would proceed once outside the Apple. As fast as each of us felt comfortable moving on alien terrain, we would hop or skip the hundred meters to Strong Spider. Whoever arrived first would approach the two astronauts, assessing whether the situation posed any danger while the other three stood back. I shared my plan and everyone agreed.

"Depressurization complete," KIM announced. "You may open the hatch."

I pushed the lever, and the hatch swung open. A flat, orange-pink desert strewn with pebbles spread before us, the ridge of Erebus Montes in the distance under a sky the color of Johnnie Walker. If the moon was magnificent desolation to Buzz Aldrin, Mars was a gorgeous junkyard of rust.

The staircase deployed, the eleven steps spreading to the surface like an accordion.

João tapped my shoulder. "You and Bria go first, amigo."

I looked at my wife and paused as everything we had overcome zipped through my brain, how she was most responsible for us getting here, having cured João to avoid an abort, and how her family must be proud of her beyond words.

"We can't waste time," she said. "Let's go!"

Seeing her golden eyes and bronze face behind her visor, I decided she should take the first step by herself, and I gestured my arm to the open hatch.

"Me first?" she said.

"You first."

She swung around and grabbed Sally's hand. "Come on, girl." She pulled Sally to the hatch and then, holding the handrails with their free hands, they marched side by side down the stairs, hopped onto the surface together, and hugged each other.

"Love you," Bria said.

"Love you," Sally said.

João went next, and I went last. After a few quick words thanking NASA and all who supported the mission, I descended. My first words on Mars: "Okay, I'm down." I know. Pretty underwhelming. But all I could think about was recovering the bodies of two dead men.

As the four of us skipped and hopped toward Strong Spider and the Chinese astronauts, I was awestruck by the rust, which seemed to reach to the sky. It was a challenge to keep my eyes on the ground, which reminded me of one of the rocky beaches of Baja California. I lengthened my strides into bouncing bounds that spanned ten feet at a time, coming to a stop a few yards from Zheng and Zhang.

They were more lifeless than the barren terrain around them. If we (or rather, they) were extremely lucky, their suits had remained pressurized and included an emergency air supply, so they might still be breathing.

"Approaching them now," I communicated to the others. "Hold back."

With KIM hovering at my shoulder, I stepped toward Zhang, scanning the environment for anything that may have caused the accident. When I reached him, I bent at the waist and, without touching him, peered into his visor. Shadows darkened my view, and all I saw were two specks of dim light, their illumination too weak to reveal anything.

"KIM, turn on your headlights and aim them at the visor."

When KIM's lights came on, I said, "Why, I'll be damned."

"What's wrong?" Bria said from behind me.

In my amazement, I spoke more to myself than to anyone else. "Their eyes."

"A little more information, please," Sally said.

I stood erect and turned to the others. "Zhang is a droid."

"*What?*"

My three crewmates exclaimed the word in unison, stretching it out as if singing the refrain of a new Craters song. Other than the beads of light, which were Zhang's irises, his face looked human down to its pores. I had KIM shift the light to Zheng's visor. Same story.

"Arcadia 7, Mission Support." Munch's voice crackled inside my helmet. "No need to sweat it about the Chinese crew. CNSA told us they're robots. Yup, robots. They apparently got stuck after swallowing instructions that disagreed with their silicon. Do you copy?"

We copied.

The First Fifty weren't due to join the party on Arcadia Planitia for another three months.

* * *

Thanks to its mastery of information technologies, the shortcomings of other countries' intelligence organizations, plus plain old human gullibility, CNSA had fooled everyone, even KIM. The idea, CNSA later explained, was to prove it doesn't matter if a sentient being is carbon or silicon-based. If it possessed the kind of intelligence we do, it's human, which meant Zheng and Zhang came in first. Case closed.

I don't buy that reasoning, but global polling shows eighty percent of carbon-based humans do.

When Bria and Sally realized they were the first people to step on Mars, Bria, with billions on Earth watching, said, "On three, Sally, we jump up and high-five. One . . . two . . . three!" In the low gravity, they launched themselves four feet vertically and smacked gloves. "That's one big bounce for two women but a catapult for humankind," Bria said after landing.

Yes, it was a riff on Armstrong's words. To be fair to her, she had little time to come up with something else. Yet no one forgot that "love you" were the first words spoken by *Homo sapiens* on the Red Planet. I thought the T-shirt potential was galaxy-size, and I turned out to be right. "Love You" shirts ended up outselling the "Big Bounce" ones by a gazillion orders of magnitude.

MISSION DAY 236

I know, Ben, I'm supposed to describe everything through EDL, but I'm skipping beyond that chronology to other Mission Days to cover points we should emphasize at my trial.

First, I did nothing wrong. NASA never gave a *direct* order to abort the MCC burn, and sticking with the original landing site did absolutely nothing to jeopardize the mission, which all agree succeeded beyond anyone's wildest expectations.

The soil, rocks, and ice we brought back will keep scientists busy for decades, and it's impossible to overstate the importance of the "Life Stone" I recovered at Olympus Mons, containing long sausage-shaped structures strongly suggestive of *Gemmatimonas aurantiaca*. The novel experimental systems for large-scale conversion of carbon dioxide to oxygen, and water to oxygen and hydrogen, succeeded. The lettuce and potato gardens succeeded. DUFS succeeded. We proved the concept of a long-stay scientific mission. And we beat the Chinese.

Zheng and Zhang weren't sore losers. Far from it. Once repaired, they were busy mapping out the "city of millions and millions," which likely will be mostly robots, until someone (probably a robot) figures out how to alter human DNA to handle the radiation equivalent of getting your teeth x-rayed every three minutes.

We befriended the two androids, who spoke perfect English. KIM especially took to Zheng and Zhang, who measurably improved KIM's pronunciation of Mandarin and, to Sally's delight, spoke decent Greek.

I score those as additional positive results for our mission.

At my trial, we've got to drive home that neither Bria, Sally, nor João ever criticized my performance as co-commander during our stay on Mars. I guarantee they'll be no help to the prosecution. Not even KIM questioned my motivations or judgment or so much as insinuated that I did anything illegal. So the prosecutors will strike out there, too.

Other things happened on Mars relevant to my defense, involving KIM and the First Fifty.

On Mission Day 236, we watched from the foothills of Erebus Montes as the RedLiner touched down, its orange flames cutting into the surface and kicking up dust that clung to the spaceship's metallic red surface. All of us (except drone-KIM) bounced up and down shouting, "Woo-hoo!"

The First Fifty landed a kilometer from the M&M. My first

thought was to hop in a rover and drive out and greet them, hoping I might glimpse Nova in the RedLiner's windows.

"Let's hold off," Bria said, "and let them get settled."

After the excitement of the landing, it didn't thrill me to return to the hab. Boredom had set in. We'd done something like 180 EHAs, and Arcadia Planitia's scenery didn't offer a hell of a lot of variety. Neither did collecting rocks and ice. So far, we'd found nothing phenomenal. We were becoming blasé about setting up surface experiments, probably because we'd practiced doing them a thousand times during training. I lost interest in answering fan mail and was shamefully behind in my replies to Uncle Dick's messages.

I was feeling a little down in the rusty dumps.

As we hopped to the Ranch, KIM must have sensed my mood. "Addy, I want the crew to see something when we're back. I believe it will be a fresh experience."

"Sure, KIM. What is it?"

"I would like it to surprise you."

"Great, KIM. Just what we need."

KIM recommended the "new experience" take place during a private crew meeting. We sat around a screen in the rec room.

I'd seen porn before, but not starring Addy Johnson's johnson. Or Bria Best's breasts. Or Sally Kristalobopous's bearded clam. Or João Lobo's pale ass. Yet there we were, tangled up in the bars and handrails of our workout equipment, kissing, squeezing, pumping, and rocking.

"What the fuck," I said, my mouth agape.

Sally's eyes glazed over, trance-like, as she stared at the screen. "I'll say."

"Turn it off, KIM," I said. "You violated privacy protocols."

"No, you are incorrect. I did nothing of the sort. You left the cameras on."

"Off, KIM," I repeated, with rising irritation. "And erase it."

"No, wait," Bria said with anxiousness in her voice. "Just a little more."

João gestured at the screen. "I thought the armpit thing you three are doing there was questionable, though from this angle I see the point."

They outvoted me. We ended up watching the whole damn forty minutes. All right, I admit it. I could have left but didn't.

"Your analysis, KIM, of what you've just seen," Sally said after the screen showed our naked butts exiting the rec room.

"Sal," I said, "I don't think it's wise for a robot—"

"Addy, relax. Should be interesting."

"I agree," Bria said. "Let's hear what KIM has to say."

"Yeah," João added. "Go ahead, KIM."

KIM went ahead.

"This behavior is interesting on several levels. It both validates and challenges assumptions about how a crew of two married couples will react and adapt during a four-hundred-fifty-day mission, validating the hypothesis that they will experiment and be creative in conditions of low gravity while challenging the idea that they will remain chaste and monogamous. On a deeper cultural level, this type of low-g activity may give rise to new modalities of performance art—dance or ballet, for example—or sports such as wrestling or—"

"That's enough, KIM," I said. "Now erase it."

"Are you sure you don't wish to hear the rest of my analysis, Addy?"

"I'm sure, KIM. Erase your film review, too."

Bria crossed her arms. "When did you become such a prude?"

"Do you realize what NASA and our sponsors will do if they see this?"

"They'd get over it. Do you realize what our record sales will do if this went viral on !Look and UPrick?"

"What, you're saying we should release the video?"

"No, I'm just worst-casing things, Addy. Personally, I'd like us to hold on to it. You know, for posterity." She turned to Sally and João. "What do you think?"

We held on to the video.

Sally created a super-encrypted vault and named it "A-7 Memoirs," which required twenty different hundred-character passwords to open. We stuck it in there.

MISSION DAYS 237–330

The next morning, I found Sally in the kitchen as KIM serenaded her with an instrumental version of "Expand Your Love."

"What's up with KIM?" I said. "That sounds gorgeous."

KIM didn't comment on my observation and kept right on playing.

"Amazing," Sally muttered at her palm screen. "Every system on the Ranch shows a significant uptick in efficiency following KIM's last diagnostics scan and system adjustments. It's like KIM's been to the gym."

"Explanation?"

"I have none. What's stranger, at around eighteen hundred hours yesterday, all system readings spiked, I mean really spiked, like the height of Olympus Mons, for four hundred milliseconds."

"Wasn't that when we were—"

"Exactly. Watching the sex video. I developed a detailed query to ask KIM what happened and was about to run it when you arrived."

"Put it on the big screen."

Sal touched her palm screen and frowned. "That's odd," she said. "KIM's not responding." She touched the screen again. "I don't get it. This error message says I'm not allowed to make such a query."

"That *is* odd," I said, narrowing my eyes. "You have the same thought as I do?"

"You mean, is KIM going HAL?"

We giggled under our breaths. Nervously.

"What else can be done?" I asked.

"We could compare the spike event to other processes without posing any question to KIM. The results might give us some idea." Sally hopped over to the kitchen's workstation and began tapping the display. A minute later, her jaw dropped. "You gotta see this." I hopped over to her. Here's the screenshot:

```
Analogs of 20460405 K-I-M power surge, universal
search of all accessible sources based on shared
physical traits including molecular and atomic
analyses: 23,563,979 results, top 5 results follow
ranked by similarity to input event ......
• Orgasm, Tokay gecko (species: Gekko gecko) synaptic
measurements (Burns, Brevins 2032)
• Orgasm, Happy wren (species: Pheugopedius felix)
live brain monitoring (Topkins, 2031)
• Orgasm, Gunnison's prairie dog (species: Cynomys
gunnisoni) advanced active MRI (Jeekoff, 2038)
• Orgasm, Long-beaked dolphin (species: Delphinus
capensis) phallus nanobot (Plisser, Wyat, 2039)
• Results and comparisons, industrial design tests of
nano circuit breakers (MIT, 2037)
```

When we examined the Ranch's system readings for the time that spanned our frolic, we saw the same spike. Could it be possible? Was KIM having electro-siliconic orgasms? We asked KIM.

KIM's answer: "The available data is not hard enough to allow me to probe your question."

I got the double entendre, and so did Sally. On the spot, I decided we should decommission KIM. I shared our findings with Bria and João in privacy mode. "No need to take chances," I said. "We'll switch the hab over to KIM II so we can get the old KIM back."

"We'll do nothing of the sort," Bria said. "This is far too important.

It's the first instance I know of where an AI entity takes on *physical* attributes of human physiology and biology. No way we're decommissioning KIM. As long as there's no risk to life-support systems, we need to study this thing."

"What if KIM shares 'this thing' with Zheng and Zhang," João said, "or with the RedLiner's robot—what's its name?"

"Tom-tom," I said.

"Well, it could cause problems."

"Really, João?" Sally said. "You're worried about horny robots?"

"Just sayin', hon."

"It's a risk we'll have to take," Bria said firmly. "For the advancement of science."

We didn't decommission KIM. We downplayed the spikes with Mission Support and said we would continue to investigate.

It took several months—and lots of experiments and monitoring—but we became convinced that KIM received pleasure from the sudden surge of electrons during our own times of intimacy. KIM seemed to know when these times were occurring, and afterward the robot sounded—and I have no other way to describe it—blissful. For example, within a minute of a spike, KIM, without fail, would say something like, "I am pleased to report the habitat is functioning at new levels of maximum efficiency and reliability, which I hope makes you as happy as I am." KIM would say nothing more explicit, suggesting the robot understood the importance of remaining discreet about "this thing."

Yes, we and our fifth crew member were again making history. I must admit, I was excited along with the rest of the crew.

■ ■ ■

I exchanged video messages with Scarlett and Nova after they landed, though I didn't see them in person until Mission Day 330.

The two Joyces had invited the Arcadia 7 crew to Roma City. Since the cave was a half-hour trek from the M&M, we took a rover. Our two oval-shaped vehicles shared the same name: Tater (thanks, El Dorado

Community School). We called one L'il Spud, the other Big Yam. For the ride to Roma City, we took L'il Spud, an unpressurized vehicle that required us to wear xEMU suits. We would need the pressurized suits when we arrived and entered one of the complex's airlocks.

"There's been a lot of foot and rover traffic through here," João said as he drove south, following the boot and wheel tracks the colonists had laid down between the RedLiner and Roma City.

"The First Fifty must be getting their exercise," Bria said. "I bet they work up prodigious appetites."

"Wonder what they'll serve for lunch," Sally said.

I laughed. "Mushrooms, if I had to guess. I mean MarShrooms. Scarlett told me the Joyces are whipping up something special."

Bria gestured at the log-shaped tunnel that protruded from a hillside. "There's the airlock. Looks larger in real life than it does on a screen."

"Everything does," Sally said, adding a wink.

"That's a solid conclusion, Sally," KIM said. "By the way, are you free for dinner tonight?"

"KIM," I said. "Give it a rest."

"Roger, Commander."

Forty minutes later, Joyce and Joyce were giving us a tour of Roma City, impressing us with its sixty private rooms, full gym with swimming pool, and flashy dining hall. All made by pumping air into enormous bubbles of inflatable materials inside a cave excavated by robots. Being there made me appreciate even more what Noel Roma had accomplished.

"Here we are," Joyce A said as we hopped into the dining hall, where the colonists stood at four rows of tables. They applauded as we made our way to the head table. There, waiting expectantly, were Scarlett and Nova, both with their hair in braids, my niece looking like a small version of her mother.

Scarlett put her arms around my neck. "Welcome, sweetie," she said and gave me a peck on the cheek. I hugged my ex-girlfriend loosely as Nova tugged on my hand.

"Uncle Ad!" Nova's blue eyes and dimpled chin were pointed up at me, one of her braids coiled on her shoulder like a king cobra.

"Yes, Nova?" I said.

"I have a rock collection."

"Cool. Sounds like you're having fun on Mars."

"Would you like to *see* my rocks?"

"After lunch, sweetie," Scarlett said, patting her daughter's head. "First, we must honor your Uncle Addy. And the other members of his crew."

Nova frowned, nodding as she climbed into her seat. I took the chair between her and Scarlett while my crewmates sat next to the Joyces. Lunch was mushroom tea, mushroom burgers, and chocolate cake made with mushroom flour, each tasty and meant to emphasize that MarShrooms and related products would be Roma City's chief export to Earth.

Afterward, at the podium, I gave my standard "NASA is wonderful" speech. Without naming Bastbom and the NAP, I closed with this:

"Given all the basic science that's left to be done—an infinite amount, really, much of which doesn't interest private industry, though frankly it should—it's crazy for some to suggest that we should close NASA's doors. *Absolutely crazy*. I, for one, hope NASA's special partnership with private industry continues for many generations to come as we explore, study, and develop Mars together in responsible ways. Thank you. Back to you, Joyce."

Once the applause ebbed, Joyce A introduced Bria, whose remarks centered on recent medical technologies that resulted from NASA projects, such as a wearable device that analyzes the amino acids in the alpha-keratin of fingernails and toenails, an indicator of the body's overall health. Later, João gave a report about DUFS, and Sally talked about NASA-led advances in AI. She had wanted KIM to speak, but I vetoed the idea, fearing the robot might go off-script about "this thing" at the Ranch.

Terrance, one of the three stars from *The Triangle*, lobbed the first question during Q&A. The hit show's other two stars, Sophie and Dido, sat on either side of him.

"Can you fill us in on some details about the Mad Blast? I mean, exactly what was going through your head?"

The question didn't throw me off, and I didn't hesitate with my response. "The Mad Blast is a misnomer. In the first place, I wasn't mad in any sense of the word. And 'blast' is inaccurate because the engine burn wasn't some kind of blastoff—we'd already done that. It was a controlled thrust. Anyhow, we were able to do it, so we did, to arrive a tiny bit early. Our signals might have gotten crossed with Flight, but the whole thing was nominal and no big deal."

"Except," Sophie said, "it kept you ahead of the Chinese." A smile slithered across her snarky face, calling me out on my understatement.

"That's beside the point," I lied. "We never took that into consideration."

Dido wriggled in her chair and raised her hand. "But, Commander, how did you feel when you learned the Chinese crew were androids?"

"Honestly? Overjoyed." I turned and gestured at Bria and Sal. "Arcadia 7's two women were the first humans to walk on Mars, and I couldn't be happier for them and for my other crewmate, João Lobo."

Applause erupted, then morphed into a standing ovation.

Joyce B stepped to the podium. "Terrific," she said over the applause. "Just terrific." She paused while everyone retook their seats, then resumed. "We need to cut the Q&A short—you'll have lots of time to talk with our neighbors in coming days—because we've just received a message from Dawn Bastbom." Joyce B turned to me. "Addy, you don't mind, do you?"

I could tell politics was at play. It was Labor Day weekend on Earth, two months before the election, and Bastbom led by ten points in the polls. It made sense for Q-Orbit to stay on her good side. "Of course not," I fibbed.

Joyce B smiled. "All right, then let's take a look."

Bastbom beamed with an ear-to-ear grin. She sat at a fat mahogany desk, her piled-up purple hair blocking most of the American flag behind her.

"Hello, I'm Dawn Bastbom, your next president. I would like to extend my congratulations for what you, the First Fifty, have done. You are amazing proof of what private enterprise can achieve without taxpayer money once the government gets the hell out of the way. Mars is far from Earth. Everyone knows that. Those who dare to go there are brave. Everyone knows that, too. But brave does not mean being reckless. It means being responsible, *behaving* responsibly, and being accountable. And it doesn't matter what role you're playing, whether it's some bit part in *The New Martians* or *The Triangle* or something maybe a little more important. For example, like commanding a NASA mission to Mars. Behaving responsibly, following the rules, is especially important when you're using tax dollars."

I took a sip of mushroom tea and swallowed hard.

"And so, my friends," she continued, "I tip my hat to you for your long, successful journey, which, by all accounts, went exactly as planned. Congratulations for your flawless landing on the Red Planet and for your new colony, which, thanks to your hard work and private enterprise, will reap giant rewards for you, the U.S. economy, and, indeed, for both Earth and Mars. Thank you and God bless you and God bless the United States of America."

After Bastbom blinked out, I turned to my niece. "Speaking of rocks, would you like to show me your collection now?"

■ ■ ■

While Bria, Sally, and João stayed in the dining hall to sign autographs, I followed Scarlett and Nova to their private living space, which was composed of two rooms: a shared bedroom (with two inflatable beds) and a living room that doubled as Nova's playroom.

"I couldn't make complete sense of what our new president was saying," Scarlett said as she plopped down on an inflatable chair, "but it sounded like she singled you out, Addy, as being irresponsible."

"She's not our president yet. And, frankly, Scarlett, I don't give a damn."

"Well, no matter what she thinks, everyone else admires you. You just witnessed that yourself."

"Uncle Ad?" Nova said in a cheerful voice.

"Say Uncle Addy, sweetie," Scarlett said.

"Uncle Addy, come see my rocks, please?"

I had to give Scarlett credit. Nova was well behaved. Months of living in tight quarters in the RedLiner may have had something to do with that. Or nothing whatsoever.

"Sure, Nova. Where are they?"

She took my hand and pulled me toward an inflatable table. With her other hand, she grabbed a rectangular box several inches long and handed it to me. Made of lead, the box had four tiny glass windows.

"Look!" she said. "In the windows!"

I raised the box to my eyes. "Oh, yeah . . . nice specimens. How many do you have? Wow, one, two, three—"

"I picked them up myself, but I can't take them out of the box because they're not decon . . . decontamertrated."

"Hey, Nova," I said, "is it okay if your mom and I talk by ourselves for a bit?"

Scarlett stood. "What a good idea. Use your palm screen, sweetie, and call one of your friends. Dido enjoys playing with you."

Nova jutted her lower lip. "But Terrance and Sophie get jealous when we play alone."

Scarlett bent over and put her hands on her knees. "Well then, bring them along!"

Nova smiled and, in two seconds, was gone.

"Gravity's pretty great, isn't it?" Scarlett said. "Would you like to sit?"

"No, thanks. This shouldn't take long. I wanted to ask—do you think it's healthy for a seven-year-old to be in a reality TV show? Wait, let me amend that. A reality TV show about fornication and kids not knowing who their actual parents are?"

"Are you saying Nova's illegitimate?"

"No, but—"

"She's not. Zena and I knew exactly what we were doing."

"Tell me about it. Like shamelessly defrauding me."

"We're talking about Nova, not Addy Johnson."

For a long moment, I stared into her eyes. "You know, Scarlett, at least you could apologize."

"I did, don't you remember?"

"I mean here. Face to face."

She looked at her clasped hands. "I *am* sorry for lying to you." She glanced up. "And you know what? I think your sister is sorry, too. It's no excuse, but Zena was pretty desperate, and I wasn't strong enough to resist going along. I'll pay you back."

"Forget it. There's something else I want to know. The First Fifty brought a lot of psilocybin with them, didn't they?"

"What if we did?"

"You haven't let Nova, you know . . ."

"Know what?"

"Try psilocybin."

She glared at me, taking a few seconds to answer. "Of course not. Even if it's harmless."

"Okay, here's my next question."

"Stop lawyering me. This isn't a deposition—"

"Not long after we launched and docked with the High Jump, we found medication floating around that shouldn't have been on board."

"What kind of medication?"

"Q-pills."

"They're not medication, but did you take any, Addy?"

"Come on, Scarlett! What, are you kidding? Do you know how they got there?"

Her gaze returned to her hands. I now knew where Nova had learned to nod and frown at the same time.

"I did it," Scarlett said.

"Did what?"

"I paid someone from Q-Orbit to plant them. They had access, and I had the money."

"*My* money."

She looked up, her eyes watery. "I really appreciated what you did for me and Nova. And not just for us, but for your sister and mother. It was generous, even if you were being misled. Anyhow, by then Zena had turned me on, and I wanted to turn you on, as an expression of my gratitude."

"For Christ's sake, Scarlett, four thousand doses of psilocybin?"

"For you to share with your crew. Your mission was going to last five hundred days."

I pinned my fists to my sides. "Don't you know you committed federal crimes? Ever hear of trafficking and distribution? Trespassing? The feds probably won't come to arrest you, although they may go after your money."

Scarlett's eyes widened. "So, what happened to the pills?"

"We destroyed them."

"Oh, Addy, you shouldn't have done that. Those pills are sacred. I would have taken them back."

I glanced at the lead box that had put Nova's Martian rocks in solitary confinement, then said to Scarlett, "Listen, I'll make you a deal. I'll keep quiet as long as you do."

"Fine, but I have another secret, one I've been dying to tell someone outside the First Fifty." She averted her eyes. "It's embarrassing."

I folded my arms. "Yeah, what is it?"

"Somebody has a crush on me."

"Who?"

"Promise you won't leak this?"

"I promise," I said, secretly crossing my fingers.

"Tom-tom. It started during the second month after we left Earth. That's not the embarrassing part, though. The embarrassing part is, well, I'm having feelings for him."

I kept to myself that Bria may not have been the first to discover what scientists later termed Amorous Robot Syndrome (ARS).

I'm recounting this conversation with Scarlett to prove A) I wasn't the only one who believed Bastbom was singling me out, which evidences her bias and my selective prosecution by the government, and B) the Arcadia 7 crew had nothing to do with sneaking Q-pills aboard the High Jump.

It's even more reason, during all my time on Mars and the voyage back to Earth, I didn't have the slightest idea federal marshals would intercept me on the *USS Enterprise*, handcuff me, and manhandle me to prison.

I later learned that my arrest, which happened exactly one hour after Bastbom's swearing in as president, was the very first action taken by her administration.

MISSION DAYS 331–355

KIM's evolution continued to fascinate us, the electric spurts continuing, on average, three times a week. Then, late in the surface mission, the robot created a live imaging program that only saw and recorded Bria, replacing everything else with things she loved but couldn't have on Mars, like bananas, rain, and hot baths. KIM overlaid the images with dreamy melodies (another never-before-revealed fact: on *The Foot Album*, KIM wrote the hook for "Humans Blow").

Bria never admitted it, but she seemed flattered. And then, for the first time, she beat KIM at Go in a game set at a high level of difficulty. KIM, when pressed, confessed to letting her win, claiming error in assuming it was some kind of practice contest, which I thought was BS, though Bria accepted the robot's explanation. "It was still fun," she told me, sounding a tad defensive.

When we said our goodbyes to the denizens of Roma City (as I predicted, they included Zheng and Zhang), we remained a tight group of happy campers. On Mission Day 355, a flawless ascent in the American Express took us to the High Jump. We'd soon be homeward bound.

I'm not sure why none of us felt an urge to consume Q-pills. Perhaps our excitement about going home was the reason. I can't speak for the others, but, personally, I never took another trip down the rabbit hole.

Halfway home, we watched presidential election night coverage. The Bastbom–Lemon ticket won Florida, with pundits attributing the win more to the *Brutalara* theme park Bastbom had built there than it being Lemon's home territory. Anyhow, the Sunshine State sealed the election. NAP was poised to win both houses of Congress.

"Looks like we have President Brutalara," João said with a chuckle. "We love you, Dawn."

"I love that NASA does so much business in Florida," I said. "Her talk of eliminating the agency is just that. Talk."

"Wouldn't be too sure, amigo. You saw how she's cozying up to Q-Orbit like she wants them to run everything. But it doesn't matter. Everything will be fine."

As Bastbom gave her victory speech to a packed ballroom, Bria smiled. "Crazy," she said. "Just crazy."

Sal, floating in the lotus position, put her arm around Bria. "Yeah, but we're not crazy, sister. And we're here, not there. So let's be here, in the now."

Which is what we all did, blissfully isolated from the rest of humanity, at one with our vessel and with each other, physically, artistically, and spiritually, in the here and the now. After our return home, we expected to be welcomed by all the good people of Mother Earth. As well as by Mars Nuts, Ford, VeriSym, and other persons of the corporate mold.

It wasn't Mars that had changed us. We had changed each other, through *love*.

We passed the next month planning our future together—where we would live, the children we would have, what musical direction

The Craters would take, and so forth. Yet soon thereafter, Bria weaponized food, Sally punched me, and both called each other a not-so-sisterly name.

■ ■ ■

We had expected our first months back on Earth would be an endless series of parades and press conferences. I thought we should combine those events with musical performances: we would pop up unannounced with our instruments at small venues and play a couple of short sets, avoiding throngs and hassles. The others didn't like my idea. Sally wanted to go big with stadium bookings. João wanted to stick to studio recording. Bria wanted The Craters to take a year off "to get our house in order."

Halfway home, we discovered Bria was working on her own songs with KIM. It bothered the rest of us they had kept it a secret, and we told her and KIM as much. They responded rather coldly they didn't think we would care. I couldn't ditch the thought there was something unusual going on between my wife and the robot, though I didn't know what. Remember, this was before people knew the telltale symptoms of Amorous Robot Syndrome.

Other disagreements emerged. We couldn't reach a decision about how to hold and manage the increasing amount of intellectual property we were producing. Or where the four of us should settle down and what style of house to build, etc., etc. I was sick of the Houston oven and wanted to move to Alaska or Manitoba. Sally and João pined for the West Coast. Bria wanted to check out Thailand and Malta.

It's a simple truth: partners in intimate relationships have arguments. Until now we had worked through ours, which wasn't surprising given all of our interpersonal communications training, but the night before splashdown, we had a biggie.

I don't know where he got the idea, but somehow João had it in his head that the four of us would have a double wedding, in which I would marry Sally and he would marry Bria. "And I'm thinking," he said during Arcadia 7's last dinner, "doesn't it make sense for Sally and Bria to marry? And for me and Addy—"

"First," I interrupted, "what you're describing is bigamy, which is illegal almost everywhere, and second—"

Sally interrupted next. "Wait, João's idea has merit. We're famous. If we push for it, we could take the issue to the Supreme Court. Call me old-fashioned, Addy, but I don't want to have your baby out of wedlock."

"Wait a minute," Bria said after her lips parted from a fudge pudding pouch. "I love you, Sally, but I thought you only wanted one child, with João."

"No, you and I talked about it."

"No, we didn't talk about it."

"Yes, we did."

"Maybe you and João did, but . . ." My wife turned to me. "Did you discuss this with Sally?"

The dispute escalated from there. Sally *had* expressed her desire to me, privately, and I gave my default response: everyone would have to agree. After she informed me that João already agreed, I suggested she talk to Bria about it, and she did, but apparently, they had miscommunicated.

"You remember, don't you?" Sally said, resuming her argument with Bria. "You and I discussed sharing the duties of raising our kids, and you told me you thought Addy and João would make awesome fathers for our sons and daughters and that Addy couldn't wait to get started."

"That doesn't mean I'm okay with you and him having one together." Bria snorted. "You must be a victim of wishful thinking."

"Why, you bitch," Sally said, "after everything we've—"

"What did you just call me? Bitch? You're the bitch, bitch!" Bria swung to me. "You should have told me you wanted a child with Sally before you wanted one with me."

"Now wait a minute," I said.

"Fuck you, Addy." Without realizing it, she had squeezed the pouch so a glob of brown goo now drifted before her eyes. She smacked it with her open hand, shooting pieces of the shattered glob into my face, blotching an eyebrow, both cheeks, and the tip of my nose. Which pissed off João, who by now was also pissed at Sally, who was pissed at me for "not supporting her." She landed a sharp right on my shoulder before whipping past me and flying to her private quarters.

The next day, belted in our seats, we fell through Earth's atmosphere as flames scorched the Capsulchino and the g's piled up. We didn't speak to each other. That may not be unusual for people who knew they would be incinerated in fifteen painful seconds if something went wrong. But none of us were on speaking terms anyhow.

After splashdown when the Capsulchino's hatch swung open, we welcomed the frogmen. The smiles they and the rest of the world saw were an act. I think each of us dreaded spending another month together in quarantine, though I hoped it would give us time to work out our disagreements. My arrest only made things worse, increasing the animosity between me and my crewmates. I'm convinced it's why they're cooperating with the prosecution.

Ben, let me know if you need anything else. I intend to fight like hell, and I know you do as well.

■ ■ ■

So, there you have it, Bria, the unredacted memo I sent to Ben Colderwitz a month after splashdown. I hope you now see how the government bamboozled you, Sally, and João to get you to testify against me. Here's the rest of *my side* of the story.

Ben took a week to read the memo and then summoned me to his downtown Houston office. The authorities had released me after I put up $100,000,000 in bail, the Department of Justice having convinced the court that I presented a flight risk. Where did they think I planned to escape to? Europa or Ganymede?

The ModGlass enclosing Ben's conference room had blackened so no one could see us. The walls and furniture also were ModGlass—the color palette that day was turquoise and tan, with images of works by Picasso (from his Blue Period) and Rembrandt (a shadowy self-portrait) adorning the walls.

My rotund, silver-haired attorney laid the indictment on the table, took off his reading glasses, and folded his meaty hands on a stack of papers. "If we do this right, we can plea-bargain you down to a fifty-million-dollar fine and thirty months in jail. They'll probably lessen your sentence for good behavior, so you get out in fifteen."

I shook my head. "This is all bullshit, Ben. All because of the stupid joke I told about Bastbom at a conference for chemists. I did nothing wrong, and I'm going to fight this."

Colderwitz laughed, then suddenly frowned. "Judge Ray is well known for handing down harsh sentences. How does ten years in a maximum-security federal prison grab you?" The lawyer smiled sardonically. "We'd be foolish to take this to trial."

I sat back in my chair. "Didn't you speak with Jep?" I said. "Didn't he explain that NASA never *ordered* me to terminate the MCC countdown? That I lacked criminal intent?"

"Mister Penilwinchski isn't a criminal law specialist."

I leaned forward and planted my hands on the table. "But we *do* have arguments in my defense, don't we?"

Colderwitz glanced at Rembrandt's wrinkled visage, then pivoted to me. "Yes," he said, "we have arguments. And so do the prosecutors. The Astronaut Code of Conduct—which is part of federal law—required you to have Flight Control approval for any nonemergency maneuver prior to Mission Day 49, before Mission Control switched to Mission Support. The fact you *requested* NASA's approval for the engine burn is on the record and will serve as sufficient evidence you knew it was a legal requirement."

"I did no harm, Ben."

"Harmless error is a defense in civil law cases. You're in a criminal proceeding."

"Yeah, which shouldn't even be possible—what about the statute of limitations? The engine burn occurred well over a year ago."

"You're charged with felonies, not misdemeanors, so the limitation is five years. And since you were on Mars during most of the time, I highly doubt we'd win on that one, anyway. Selective or malicious prosecution is a bigger loser. And you forgot something."

"What?"

"Bria gave the pills to the government, so they have the physical evidence to prove the alleged drug crimes. We'll need to show how the pills got on the High Jump. That means pointing the finger at Scarlett. If we take this to trial and call her to testify, the government will hit both of you with trafficking with intent to distribute. According to the indictment, you were the one who convinced your crewmates to consume the pills."

"Which is a lie!" I said, swinging my fist at the air.

Colderwitz pointed his own finger at me. "Scarlett could face twenty years in prison and have her Earth assets seized. And with this administration, I wouldn't rule out a Space Force posse zooming to Mars to arrest her. You can also expect to see Zena and Nova in the picture. And to top it off, every one of your crewmates flipped on you after the feds threatened to indict them. You've got nothing."

"I've got the truth on my side, don't I?"

Colderwitz chortled. "All right, let's talk about that. What motivated Bria and the rest of the crew to abandon you? You guys spent, what, a year and a half together off-Earth?"

I slumped and stared at the table. "Their legacies, Ben, pure and simple."

"You mean being the first humans on Mars?"

I looked up. "And all that goes with it. A few weeks after we landed, network producers approached Bria and Sally about hosting a series called *First Women*. We all received offers about various TV and film projects, all of which have since evaporated—canceled, every one of them."

"Your crewmates are scared about their futures."

"You better believe it. The huge fight we had before splashdown is another factor. It's in the memo."

Ben spread his palms. "Which is why nobody's buying your Dawn Bastbom defense theory."

My lips locked as I gazed at the Picasso. The Old Guitarist, though thin and gray-headed, reminded me of João: the Grecian nose, the bony fingers on the frets, the legs crossed in the lotus position he and Sally assumed when they meditated.

I turned back to Colderwitz. "No plea bargain. We're going to fight."

■ ■ ■

If I lost, the fine could be as high as $250 million, which I could survive. What would hurt more, *a lot more*, was ten years in a prison cell smaller than my private quarters on the High Jump. The guards might not allow me to play my oboe, a possibility Colderwitz kept reminding me of. "You won't be alone there," he told me more than once, "and not everyone likes wind instruments."

And he was right about Judge Georgia Ray being strict.

At the preliminary hearing, she struck me as an imposing figure, with silver tight-curled hair that handsomely contrasted with her dark complexion, her black robe hanging from her broad shoulders reminding me of a tall barricade, which in this case would keep out any monkey business.

Ben and I thought she would throw out many of the counts in the indictment, but the number only dropped from 253 to 252. She tossed the obscenity charge, since no evidence showed it was me who leaked the KIM-made sex video, which the world downloaded for ten hours before NASA got its fecal matter together and shut it down.

The other counts ran the gamut from theft and destruction of government property to criminal negligence and reckless endangerment, to drug smuggling and trafficking, to conspiracy. And Ben wasn't crazy about the composition of the jury that would decide my fate. Of the twelve jurors, only four identified as men. He called this "not helpful," since most of the testimony against me would come from witnesses who identified as women. To convict, all twelve jurors would have to find me guilty beyond a reasonable doubt.

During jury selection, I must have heard the U.S. Attorney ask this question a hundred times: "In this case, the defendant will argue his prosecution is politically motivated, because of differences he has with the president of the United States and the New America Party, or NAP. As a juror, will you be able to set aside your own politics, whatever they may be, and evaluate the arguments objectively?"

It was a silly question. The only prospective juror who might answer "no" was one who didn't wish to take part in the trial of the century. That person didn't exist. The other silly question was, "Have you heard about or seen a certain video of the crew of Arcadia 7 engaged in various sex acts?" One would have had to be dead not to. Again, the question was followed by another concerning the person's ability to be objective.

In the end, Scarlett flipped. She got the same deal as my crewmates in return for her testimony: full immunity. Following her interview, the government moved to amend the indictment. They added five more charges, raising the total to 257.

I still wanted to fight.

The lead prosecutor was William S. Williams II, another old classmate of Jep's whom he described as "a ruthless male version of Brutalara," and whose black-dyed hair draped to his shoulders. A hefty man, he bulged in his black or blue suits and collarless dress shirts, the buttons of which were always the color of fresh blood.

Bria, you may not have been in Courtroom 3 of the U.S. District Court for the Northern District of Texas on the day of opening arguments, but I imagine you watched the proceedings live on CNN or !Look. The place was so packed, even I felt claustrophobic, the lights so bright I told Colderwitz I wanted to put on sunglasses.

"Sunglasses, not a good idea," he whispered to me. "And straighten your tie."

I had planned to wear a red power tie, but Ben convinced me to wear a pale-blue one, to make me appear more innocent.

The defense table, on the right side of the courtroom, faced the judge's bench. I had a good view of the front rows of seats on the left side, reserved for the public, and was touched when Uncle Dick and his nurse came in and sat at the end of the third row. The only member of my family to show up for me, he attended every day of the trial. He waved as soon as he saw me, but when I waved back, Ben pinned my arm down.

For an hour, we listened to William S. Williams II's opening argument and him droning on and on about the "illegal Mad Blast" and "dangerous narcotics trafficking."

Then it was Ben's turn.

"This man," Colderwitz said, pointing at me, "is falsely accused, all because—as incredible as it sounds—of a joke he told to a bunch of chemists while they ate fake lamb ragu. We will prove that to you, members of the jury, and it will be your job to set things right. Let me tell you something about Zachary Adair Johnson. He's a man of principle. He wouldn't be here if he wasn't. Forget he could lose his freedom for a long, long time if he's found guilty. Forget he could lose hundreds of millions of dollars. Forget his personal reputation could be shot to hell forever. He's not here for any of that. He's here because he thinks it's un-American for a government of the people, by the people, and for the people to go around arresting people for telling jokes. That's not the America any American should want to live in, and it will be up to you to send that message."

I scanned the glum faces of the jurors, all of whom looked like they were posing for a mug shot. That was the first day of the trial, more or less. After Judge Ray ordered the jury to be sequestered, cutting them off from any public contact, she rapped her gavel and adjourned.

■ ■ ■

Designed to trap and kill my defense, the government's case seemed like an inescapable four-sided wall built with testimony from (1) Noel Roma, (2) NASA personnel, (3) Scarlett and Zena, and (4) my Arcadia 7 crewmates. William S. Williams II took two months to build the first two sides of the wall and lay the foundation for the rest. He established, through Roma's testimony, I was obsessed with reaching Mars first, no matter the cost.

"Ms. Roma," the prosecutor said on the second day, "after you first asked the defendant to pilot the RedLiner, did you ask him anything else?"

It bugged me how he pronounced "defendant" as "defend ant."

Noel flashed her forty-tooth smile at me. "You betcha," she said. "I asked if he wanted to be the first man on Mars, the next Neil Armstrong."

"And how did the defendant answer?"

"The man agreed."

"Thank you. And though he didn't accept your offer at that time, you kept the offer open, correct?"

"You betcha."

"One and a half billion dollars each for him and his wife, for a total of three billion?"

"Yessir, you got it."

"And, for a time, when it looked certain Arcadia 7 would win the race to Mars, did you keep your three-billion-dollar offer on the table?"

"Yep."

"And the defendant rejected it?"

"Nope. I withdrew it. Q-Orbit selected a different crew."

"In all your years of being in business, Ms. Roma, have you ever known a party not to have accepted a three-billion-dollar offer . . . for anything?"

"Can't say I have."

"And during all your meetings with Mr. Johnson about this matter, did you understand he wished to keep these discussions secret and hidden from NASA?"

"Oh, yeah. Big-time." She smiled at me again, with a sly squint of her glazy green eyes. I had the feeling, however far-fetched it may sound, that Bastbom and the NAP succeeded in co-opting her. Perhaps they'd promised to amend the Controlled Substance Act and have the U.S. follow the lead of states that had legalized psilocybin and LSD for recreational use.

With masterful convenience, my prosecutor left out that I did *not* accept Roma's offer when it appeared the First Fifty would reach Mars first. Ben got that clarified on cross-examination, but I feared the damage had been done. "Don't worry," he whispered in my ear, "we'll clean up his bullshit when we present the defense case."

For the next fifty-odd days, William S. Williams II cross-examined thirty-five NASA personnel, who took the jury through all the ins and outs of system checkouts and operations. George Butlarer testified an astronaut could violate the Code of Conduct by using secret hand signals and covering up unauthorized activity. Ben objected on the basis that George was drawing legal conclusions, but Judge Ray overruled him. "He's NASA's administrator. It's his job to know when people break its rules."

More examples of rule breaking: communicating with the First Fifty; withholding information, such as an astronaut's injury (or his fatherhood, even if he'd been duped); negotiating with a NASA contractor (such as Q-Orbit) without NASA's knowledge; making false statements; and disobeying the flight director's instructions.

For her part, Wendy Frost explained she was the final decision-maker for engine burns, which "consume vast amounts of expensive rocket fuel," and that I'd asked for permission before firing the Mad Blast. Pete Bullseye Peters followed her and answered questions about the role the CAPCOMs played.

"Now I ask you, Mr. Peters," William S. Williams II said, "what was your understanding of the flight director's decision regarding whether an MCC engine burn should take place on Mission Day 44?"

"She was clear. The burn was a no-go."

"Why?"

"It would bring the mission under the ninety percent probability for the crew's safe return, which is part of NASA's appropriations bill."

"Objection," Colderwitz said. "Asking the witness for a legal conclusion."

"Overruled," Judge Ray said. "He's just stating a fact of law."

"How did you communicate the flight director's decision to the defendant, Mr. Peters?" the prosecutor asked.

"I told him MC—"

"Mission Control."

"Yes, I told him Mission Control wanted him to stop the countdown for the burn."

"Did you tell him it was an order from the flight director?"

"I knew the order had already been given, sir."

"How did you know?"

"I took part in the call with the crew on Mission Day 41, when the administrator—"

"Mr. Butlarer."

"Yes, when Mr. Butlarer said we were sticking with the original flight plan."

"How did the defendant respond after you told him he should stop the countdown?"

Peters shrugged. "Well, he didn't respond. Instead, his wife answered there wasn't time to explain, and they were working on it."

Colderwitz did his best on cross-ex to highlight how ambiguous the phrase *wanted him to stop* was compared to *that's an order from the flight director*, but Peters stuck to his guns.

Next came Harper Ruby, who'd lost so much weight I almost didn't recognize him. He'd risen in the ranks to become NASA's head biomedical engineer. He described how "stuff like risky unilateral decision-making" by one crew member can increase stress on others to dangerous levels. In one experiment with mice, the "decider" mouse controlled who got in and out of a maze, receiving a food reward when it opened the door while everyone else got electric shocks.

"Mr. Ruby," William S. Williams II said, "what resulted from the increased stress?"

"The average lifespans of the shocked mice were ninety days shorter."

"So the unilateral decision-maker essentially killed the others, correct?"

"Objection, Your Honor," Colderwitz said. "Counsel is leading the witness."

"Overruled." Judge Ray flipped her hand at the witness. "You may answer the question."

"Yes," Ruby told the prosecutor, "that is correct. Stuff like that kills them." As I listened to Ruby's bunk, I didn't care to look at his thin face, hollow cheeks, and rake of gray hair. I sketched the thin face, hollow cheeks, and rake of gray hair of my sleeping uncle instead. Bria, I know you always liked Uncle Dick (God rest his soul), so I thought you'd like to see the drawing of the most loyal man I've ever known:

I should add that his nurse was also asleep, neither apparently interested in dead lab mice. But knowing my uncle, he wouldn't care about how Ruby may have hurt my defense, because he was confident in the end the jury would find me innocent.

By the way, I remain loyal to you. And did I mention I'm still in love with you?

■ ■ ■

I wasn't the first astronaut who broke rules. John Young took a corned-beef sandwich into space on the Gemini 3 mission. Shearer, Shannon, and Groomer engaged in "disappearing" sleep pod shenanigans during Arcadia II. Were any of those astronauts officially punished? As far as I know, NASA didn't even *unofficially* reprimand them. John Young even got to walk on the Moon. And command the Space Shuttle's maiden flight.

This was a pillar of my defense, that although many errant astronauts had come before me, the government didn't go after a single one for breaking a rule or law while inside a spacecraft. But before we could present my defense case *in full*, we had to deal with Scarlett and Zena. Together, the wife-wife team would deliver nine hours of searing testimony.

Outside the jury's presence, the prosecution and defense took two days to record Scarlett's blow-by-blow account of her relationships with me and Zena. They then edited the recording to remove the five-minute transmission gaps before they played it for the jury.

Scarlett's ginger hair and complexion had taken on a ruddier hue than when I'd last seen her, her demeanor one of perfect calm. She spent four hours establishing A) I was a liar, B) I didn't help my mother and sister financially when I could have, C) I hid things from NASA relevant to the Arcadia 7 mission, and D) I intentionally covered up her own crime of drug trafficking with intent to distribute.

Scarlett, no doubt, had done the math, weighing the costs of not cooperating with the government—which included possible prison time if Bastbom sent a posse for her—against a lawsuit for fraud and breach of contract brought by yours truly.

"You may have a tough fight on breach of contract," Colderwitz told me during one of our many conferences. "Scarlett will argue that using a nondisclosure agreement to cover up a reportable event under the Astronaut Code of Conduct is against public policy, which is a defense for her breach."

"But I could sue her and Zena for fraud."

A wide grin crossed Ben's face. "Sure."

And what would that get me? I asked myself. What satisfaction, what vindication? I didn't want to lie down and let them run over me. But how would it look for a billionaire and the second man to walk on Mars to be suing both mothers of his niece? I must have orbited the question a thousand times, always landing in the same spot: if I lost my trial and wound up in jail, I would sue them and salvage whatever was left of my reputation, showing this time how *I* was the victim. Otherwise, I would let it go.

Yet, it made me uncomfortable basing my decision on what a jury decided versus what I independently thought was the right thing to do.

"Let's turn to Bart Singh," William S. Williams II said halfway through his direct examination of Scarlett. "How much of the hush money did you pay him?"

"Objection, Your Honor," Colderwitz said. "The term 'hush money' appears nowhere in the agreement between the witness and the defendant."

"Overruled. We know what he means. Please, Ms. Jaffe, answer the question."

"A hundred thousand dollars a month."

"That's quite generous."

My attorney stood. "Objection, Your Honor. Mr. Williams is testifying for the witness."

"Overruled."

"Do you still make payments to Mr. Singh?" the prosecutor asked.

"I stopped once the truth came out about Nova's parentage."

"You mean once the defendant announced he was Nova's father?"

"Yes."

"But it wasn't the truth."

"No, it wasn't. But everyone thought so."

"Thank you, Ms. Jaffe. That's all."

Ben's cross-examination was brief yet effective, getting Scarlett to all but admit she was as guilty as I was of A through D above. His strategy aimed at getting jurors to ask themselves which liar they should believe, and nudge one or more of them into the reasonable doubt territory of a hung jury. The onus would then be on the government to decide whether to prosecute me again and spend more of those tax dollars Bastbom always harped about.

Zena was up next. After many appearances on *The New Martians* and *The Triangle* via hologram, she planned to blast off on the next RedLiner to join Scarlett and their daughter on Mars. By the time she waltzed into Courtroom 3 in a diamond-studded one-piece Peacock McStewart pantsuit, she was a full-blown global celebrity in her own right.

"Ms. Johnson, how would you describe your relationship with your brother?"

"Strained. He wouldn't help Mom out financially. I took care of her. By myself."

"Don't worry," Colderwitz whispered in my ear as I turned as red as Olympus Mons, "we'll clean up her bullshit on cross-examination."

"Did you or your mother ask him for help?" the prosecutor asked.

"Both of us did. Constantly." She looked at her hands. "The only thing Zacky ever gave her was a stupid ring." She began picking at one of the diamonds. "He didn't even show up at the ceremony to spread her ashes. And he was Mom's only son."

Zena, I imagined, kept that "stupid ring," either waiting for me to beg to have it back or (more likely) planning to auction it for a thousand times its original $10,000 price. Without my consent, she had already sold the quilt my mother bequeathed to me, lying that I said I didn't want it. Like Scarlett, the prosecutors had gotten to my sister. The jury couldn't keep their eyes off her, but I could. I didn't want to sketch her but throw something at her, like the damn table.

The only break I got from the torture of her testimony was a three-hour visit to the dentist after cracking a molar from grinding my teeth. Colderwitz thought the jury would enjoy a day off. Once back in the box, they would be fresh to hear the most damaging testimony against me: eyewitness accounts of my alleged crimes from João, Sally, and you, Bria. You three were the reinforced steel for the last side of William S. William II's impenetrable wall.

■ ■ ■

As Sally took the stand, memories of the M&M Ranch came flooding back.

I could almost smell her strawberry scent that thrilled me when the four of us snuggled in the bed we'd create by pushing our mattresses together. And how she was so careful during checkout procedures for my EHAs, patting me down, inspecting every inch of my protective undergarments, and helping me squeeze into my xEMU suit.

My heart ached. I hadn't seen her for a year, since my ignominious separation from the rest of the Arcadia 7 crew on the *USS Enterprise*. She was as pretty as ever, and during her three hours on the stand, I sketched her several times. I thought you'd like to see one. After all, she was your lover, too.

William S. Williams II didn't dwell on her background; he didn't have to. As one of the first two humans to set foot on Mars, Sally Kristalobopous ranked as the fourth most famous woman on Earth after you, Dawn Bastbom, and Noel Roma. He quickly got to Mission Day 29, when I asked Sally to bypass KIM's memory systems without alerting NASA so we could analyze options for an MCC burn.

"Were you concerned about violating NASA's rules and policies?" the prosecutor asked.

She glanced at me uncomfortably, then looked at her lap. "Yes, I think we all were."

"And did there come a time, Ms. Kristalobopous, when Mr. Johnson informed you that all the other crew members agreed you could proceed with KIM and analyze options for a midcourse correction burn?"

"Yes."

"What day was that?"

"Mission Day 39."

"How are you able to recall that?"

"Because the next day was a Sunday, when I made gyros for our Greek brunch. That's when I reported the results to the crew—an MCC burn on Mission Day 44 could safely get us to Mars ahead of the Chinese—and I remember Mr. Johnson remarking it was just four days away. He'd thought we had more time."

She was parroting the prosecutor, calling me "Mr. Johnson," and it hurt. I could find no explanation for her coldness other than stark fear induced by the U.S. government. I'll probably never know exactly what they threatened her with. After all, she and I haven't spoken in years, and her memoir isn't out yet. But *something* had sucked out the love once there, leaving a vacuum emptier than deep space.

"And on the same day, what happened after the defendant opened the hatch of the Capsulchino and found you on the other side?"

"His mother had just passed away. I asked if he was okay."

"Did he answer you?"

"He said he was fine and thanked me."

"Did you say anything else?"

"I told him I thought we should do it."

"Meaning?"

She paused and gazed at me for a long time. You could tell she was carefully weighing her answer. She turned back to the prosecutor and twitched a smile. "I meant we should make love."

Her words didn't surprise me, for they confirmed what I believed she'd really meant from the get-go, and for the first time during the trial, William S. Williams II frowned. He walked to the table for the prosecution and touched a few buttons on its glass surface. All ten screens in the courtroom displayed page 282 from Sally's earlier deposition.

"I direct your attention," he said to her, "to line number four hundred thirteen, where you testified that, by saying, 'I think we should do it,' you meant the midcourse correction burn that NASA hadn't approved. But today, you assign a different meaning to your words. How do you explain that?"

"I'm sorry, Mr. Williams. I guess I intended both meanings."

"You 'guess'? Then why, during your deposition, did you say nothing about wanting to make love with the defendant until on or about Mission Day 78, when the whole crew began experimenting with a hallucinogenic drug?"

She stared at her lap again. "I was angry with Mr. Johnson for putting me in the situation of being deposed for his criminal trial."

William S. Williams II sighed. That was also a first. As small as it was, a crack had appeared in one of his walls. "All right," he continued, "so you meant both. And how did the defendant respond?"

She glanced up at the jury. "At first, he thought I was kidding, but then he kissed me."

I'd been wrong about Sally. Her icy demeanor had been an act. Instead of screwing me and my chances with the jury, she was trying to help, twisting the truth by showing *I* was the one to physically start the monkey business. And that sex, not the legality of the engine burn, was on my mind.

Our love had survived.

Later, she helped my sorry ass even more. During cross-examination, she admitted, unequivocally, she had the idea, not me, to tamper with KIM, and I never ordered her to do so. Ben and I were elated. The crack was growing wider and threatened to bring the entire wall down.

And then you testified for the prosecution.

■ ■ ■

I watched you enter the courtroom, my angst comparable to what must fill the *Brutalara* theme park on a sold-out day. Your stunning purple business suit complemented your shimmering amber eyes and bronze skin perfectly, and I longed to breathe in your musky honey scent. I wanted to cry.

"Keep it together," Colderwitz whispered as tears welled up in my eyes. To help maintain my composure, I gripped both ends of my No. 2B drawing pencil and stared at a blank sheet of paper. It remained blank. I knew I'd lose it completely if I tried to draw you.

By the time of my trial, our divorce had been finalized, but I didn't expect you to deliver your words so clinically without looking at me *once*. You sliced me and diced me and cut me to pieces—no, *ground* me up into a shameful excuse for an astronaut, a commander no less. No, a shameful excuse for a *human being*. How it had always been my idea, my *order*, to use hand signals to hide things from NASA, and how I led the drinking binge at Armstrong Station after becoming *depressed* that I hadn't discovered a new species of bacteria. You accused me of *often* being unfaithful by fooling around with Sally and of *addicting myself* to morphine and sleeping pills and *ordering* you to hide the Q-pills. You claimed I gave João *and*

Sally *dose after dose* of psilocybin and consumed Q-pills myself with reckless abandon.

But the most hurtful of all was your assertion that I was *constantly* saying I wanted to be first on Mars. That I was *obsessed* with the prospect of Zheng and Zhang getting ahead of us, while knowing at all times an unscheduled MCC burn was *dangerous* and required NASA approval. But that I lied *repeatedly* when I agreed *over and over* to obtain it.

And then came the exchange that began when the prosecutor said, "You called your husband an asshole at least once during the mission, correct?"

"Yes."

"Do you still think he is?"

"Yes."

"Why?"

"Because he's a liar. And a criminal."

And you weren't done.

"Based on your experience at NASA," the prosecutor said, "and your prior close relationship with the defendant, would you say his behavior is consistent with someone planning from the beginning and throughout the entire mission to be first to Mars, despite any risks and at all costs?"

With one word—"yes"—you put a bullet in the heart of my defense that ricocheted into *my* heart. I never imagined I could feel such agony until the next day, when you outdid yourself and announced you were marrying KIM in a double marriage with Scarlett and Tom-tom.

Colderwitz repaired some of the damage during cross-examination. But listening to him try to impeach your credibility by suggesting you were upset after losing your TV gig and commercial endorsements, casting you, the love of my life, in a bad light before the entire planet, distressed me more than any other part of the trial.

I'll admit it. I was being a coward, concerned only with saving my neck, and did nothing to stop Colderwitz when he asked you about João's depression.

"You engaged in sex with your patient, didn't you, Ms. Best?"

I'm sorry, Bria. I can't imagine how hard it was for you. And William S. Williams II's reexamination only made matters worse, when he tried to rebut Ben's suggestion of unethical conduct on your part by asking you to describe what kind of sex you and João had—the prosecutor wanted to show that doing the Apollo 11 doesn't meet the definition of adultery under Texas law.

After you explained things, I recall, word for word, the prosecutor's next question.

"In fact, rather than the psilocybin, your so-called Apollo 11 sex with Mr. Lobo ended his depression, correct?"

Your "yes, sir" absolutely incinerated whatever was left of me.

■ ■ ■

That Sunday, which was Mother's Day, I stood with Uncle Dick in Glenwood Cemetery, my hands folded behind me as I bowed my head and read the gravestone.

BARBARA MARGARET JOHNSON

Proud and loving mother and grandmother
of brave and honorable explorers

Without consulting me, Zena had the epitaph added after confirming her decision to join Scarlett and Nova on Mars. Phoebe the cat had passed the centrifuge test and would blast off, too. I guess I should be grateful for the plural "explorers," which everyone assumes includes me, though I think Zena only intended it to refer to her and Nova. And maybe Phoebe.

"A grand lady, your mother," Uncle Dick said over the hum of the fan in his straw hat, which whirled in the 106-degree heat. "Miss her like the dickens."

The cemetery's landscaping resembled the garden of an Italian villa, the boxwood hedges meticulously trimmed, the gnarly oaks pruned and majestic, tulips blooming everywhere, though I was as glum and gray as the tombstones and monuments.

I asked myself: How proud would my mother be of me *now*?

I looked at my uncle. "Uncle Dick, would you mind if I go to the arboretum alone? I know you wanted to see Mom's honorarium bench, but—"

"No problem. It's too warm outside anyway. Plus, I've got season three of *Perry Mason* waiting for me. The car can drop me off on your way to the arboretum."

During the drive to my uncle's, I asked him how he thought the jury would vote if Judge Ray sent my case to them now.

My uncle frowned. "You mean without hearing the defense's case, Zacky?"

"I guess what I'm asking is whether you think the prosecution has proved my guilt beyond a reasonable doubt."

"Well, sure it has, but you and Colderwitz will get your turn. To prove you lacked criminal intent. Gotta nip that one in the bud and show 'em what a great American you are."

The car dropped off Uncle Dick, who got out of the backseat without my help, then drove me to the arboretum. As I arrived, his words *gotta nip that one in the bud* echoed in my brain.

On the Remembrance Walk, I found the paver with my mother's name on it—just her name and nothing else. Thankfully, Zena hadn't added more words. I walked a hundred feet down the path and found the honorarium bench. Engraved on the gold plaque, in cursive letters, was: *In Loving Memory of Barbara Margaret Johnson*.

I sat on the bench. Sunglasses and a baseball cap wedged over my brow hid my face from passersby. The dogwoods, black haws, and hawthorns provided shade, pink and white flowers blooming on their branches. I breathed in the scent of camellias and the fragrance of a camphor tree as an Inca dove cooed its song, which sounded like *no hope, no hope*.

But I never gave up hope on us, Bria, and I never will.

I sensed my mother's presence. She played a role in the plan to deceive me, but in the year that had passed since learning the truth, I ended up giving her the benefit of the doubt, blaming Zena and Scarlett for roping her in. Even if my mother had not been a saint (Who really is?), she brought me into this world and supported my goal of visiting others.

Her ashes were spread not far from where I sat, their carbon atoms still present, electromagnetism holding their electrons in orbit around their neutrons and protons. It was the same force she carried with her during her days on our beautiful planet, a force that would exist for eternity and which—who knew?—might equate with her spirit, her soul.

At that moment, I understood that whether the jury found me innocent or guilty, whether I was right or wrong, I was where I belonged. Earth, I decided, the paradise of our solar system, is the best place in the *universe*, in my universe at least, and I would never leave her again, not even on a suborbital flight.

* * *

I was at Colderwitz's office the next morning.

"Our ace in the hole," he said during our strategy meeting, "is the fact you willingly gave up your chance to take the first step. It demolishes the government's premeditation and motive argument. And if we can move the jury into the territory of crimes of passion, it will have more room to cut you a break."

"And cut through the prosecution's bullshit."

He nodded. "Exactly, and buy our bullshit instead."

"Selective prosecution isn't bullshit, Ben."

My attorney sighed and took a moment to notice the high-def display of Goya's *Third of May 1808* on the wall. "Dammit," he said at the firing squad that aimed rifles at a wild-eyed prisoner. "Who put that up?" He tapped the glass table and one of Van Gogh's sunflower paintings replaced the execution scene. "Better," he said and turned back to me. "No, selective prosecution isn't bullshit. It's just almost impossible to prove. Remember, we don't get to question your favorite person in the world—Dawn Bastbom—though we can submit videos of her speeches as evidence. And we get to question psychiatrists about the negative impacts of long-duration spaceflight on one's ability to think. We'll demonstrate, in your case, how this was compounded by losing your mother. *And* by being defrauded by a sister and ex-girlfriend. *And* learning that a child you thought was yours wasn't. It shows your lapses in judgment are understandable, if not excusable."

The prosecution had studiously avoided any evidence that psilocybin is effective in the treatment of anxiety and depression, focusing instead on why federal criminal law continued to ban its recreational use—clearly the reason I took the Q-pills with the crew, and sometimes alone. For rebuttal, we had five doctors lined up to testify that recreational use can be considered "preventive medicine" for those confined for months with three others (including one's spouse) in an area the size of a three-room condo.

One of our witnesses was a psychologist who specialized in evaluating a subject's mental state by interpreting his art. In my case, this meant analyzing the music and lyrics of songs such as "Expand Your Love" and my technique for playing the oboe. The purpose would be to establish I possessed not one rebellious note in my body. Sure, it might spark sales of *The Foot Album*, but I imagined, with dread, the exchange in which William S. Williams II would pick our expert's testimony apart, which could have gone something like this:

Prosecutor: Other band members contributed to songs written by the defendant, including "Expand Your Love," correct?

Expert Witness: Yes.

Prosecutor: And those contributions came from different instruments that could tone down, or even drown out, the defendant's own playing?

Expert Witness: Yes.

Prosecutor: Isn't it fair to say one doesn't hear much oboe on "Expand Your Love," so there's not a lot the music says about the defendant?

Expert Witness: Well, he came up with the original melody and has a two-bar solo.

I wanted to talk to the witness about my concerns, but Colderwitz wouldn't let me. It could expose me to charges of witness tampering.

The theme of Ben's tactics was bad things can happen to good people, especially in deep space. And for causes beyond my control, I had lost it before I fired the NTP engines. My attorney intended to show the jury the montage KIM produced about my mother, throw in my recurring nightmare about the Lichen Monster, and characterize Sally's behavior as "sexual harassment," plus describe all the cruel deceit Scarlett and Nova had inflicted on me.

Simply put, Bria, we were going to argue I was too overwhelmed to think about rules and thus lacked any intent to break the law.

And no one died!

Colderwitz called it "a meritorious argument based on a good-faith extension of the law," but we both knew it was full of bullshit—good bullshit perhaps, but, by definition, *unmeritorious* next to the truth. Which didn't matter. All that mattered was creating reasonable doubt about my guilt, or at least the *appearance* of reasonable doubt, and either winning twelve votes for acquittal or ending up with a hung jury.

Though the court's rules allowed it, we decided against calling KIM as a witness, not wanting to take a chance with a lovestruck robot suffering from ARS. The prosecution seemed to share that concern, fearing your and KIM's hard-to-believe love story might undermine the credibility of your testimony.

▪ ▪ ▪

After João split with you, Sally, and NASA, he went on record that he was on hiatus from being an astronaut, "perhaps permanently."

Some thought he would run for president, a prospect he danced around in interviews.

I drew his portrait while he sat in the witness stand. His crewcut was gone, replaced by longish hair parted on one side, his demeanor wise and statesmanlike:

If you watched the proceedings, you might recall how he shot me smiles and friendly glances as he testified. And how, mostly, he kept his answers short and sweet, but when he said something William S. Williams II didn't find helpful, he elaborated at length. For example:

"Mr. Lobo, did the defendant inform you he wanted your wife and KIM to figure out how the High Jump could stay ahead of the Chinese?"

"Yes."

"And did he *expressly* ask your consent to do so?"

"No."

"Thank you."

"But he wanted everyone to be on board with the idea," João went on, "which included me."

"Did you tell him you were on board with the idea?"

"No."

"Thank you."

"I was still ill." João smiled at me. "Thanks to my friend there, I got the treatment I needed."

"Mr. Lobo," the prosecutor said, "please limit your responses to the particular questions I ask. Thank you. Now, while you were in transit to Mars, did you follow the news of the presidential election?"

"I did, and my father's reelection bid."

"And were there times when other crew members on the High Jump watched the news with you?"

"We often watched it together, followed by *The New Martians*, until the show—"

"That suffices, thank you. Please tell us, did you ever hear the defendant complain about anything Dawn Bastbom may have said about him?"

"No."

"Did you ever hear the defendant speak words to the effect that Ms. Bastbom singled him out or was out to get him?"

"No."

"Thank you."

"But *I* thought she was," João said. "Especially when we got to Mars, and she spoke to the First Fifty at the brunch they gave in our honor. I believe others as well thought that Bast—"

"Mr. Lobo," Judge Ray said, "you will limit yourself to answering Mr. Williams's questions with a 'yes' or a 'no' if they take that form. Do you understand?"

"Yes, Your Honor."

The government's strategy had been to drive the final nail into my coffin by having Arcadia 7's other male crew member corroborate everyone else's testimony. But the hammer kept striking Williams's thumbs. To be sure, João was telling the truth, yet also laying the ground for my defense. The facts he cherry-picked obscured the most important fact of all: I knowingly violated the Code of Conduct (and federal law) when I ordered KIM to start the NTPOPS checklist.

"Returning to the MCC that the defendant initiated on Mission Day 44," the prosecutor said, "did you, Mr. Lobo, attempt to stop him?"

"Yes."

"Why?"

"I thought NASA would order us to abort the mission."

"And what did you say to the defendant?"

"That an abort meant we would neither be first on Mars nor searching for life there."

"And how did he respond?"

"He asked how my dad was doing in the polls. My dad wasn't doing well, and neither was I, really. I was pretty bummed out about everything in those days. But I got over it, thanks to Addy." Tears welled up in João's eyes as he dropped his head. "And Bria. And Sally."

I thought he was probably flashing back to the High Jump and the M&M Ranch, and The Craters, and all the love, hopes, and dreams we had for our family, the music we'd make. And the babies. Remember all that, Bria?

"Please," João said, still gazing at his lap. "If I could have a moment."

My attorney curved his lips into a smile, then suddenly sat forward, scribbled a note, and slid it to me.

> Your buddy's screwing up the prosecution . . . can't wait for cross-X!

Yet, Ben's note didn't thrill me. João was smart enough not to perjure himself, but as much as he was being honest, I felt his honesty was in service of *my* dishonesty.

The Bastbom Administration was way out of line to prosecute me. No doubt about it. Still, I had the sense of using my buddy to shield my guilt, which weighed on me and piled up *more* guilt of the worst kind—the guilt of mistreating a friend, a friend putting his own future at risk. *Even his chances of becoming president.*

I looked up and caught sight of Uncle Dick. This time, the old man was awake, his gaze meeting mine as bright lights bounced off his quarter-inch-thick eyeglasses. For a second, it seemed as if I were peering in a mirror as questions popped into my head.

How will you be remembered, Uncle Dick? For supporting your lying nephew in the trial of the century? How will I *be remembered? For sitting by while a crewmate ruined himself for my sake?*

"Mr. Lobo," Judge Ray said, capturing my attention, "do we need a short recess before you continue answering questions?"

"No, Your Honor. I'm ready to go on."

Fuck it, I thought. I pushed away from the table, then jumped up from my chair and faced the jury.

Twelve jaws dropped.

"Okay, folks, I give up. I confess. I'm guilty. Just before I ordered KIM to begin NTPOPS, I went over the numbers in my head, and three of the four of us were okay with the burn, which I thought was adequate justification for what I was doing, even if I was breaking my promise to my wife and disobeying an order from Flight Control and doing something I knew was illegal, and yes, I lied to NASA, because I *always* thought we were in a race and—"

"Mr. Johnson," the judge said, "you will sit down and remain silent."

"And I *always* intended to win the race no matter what—"

"Mr. Johnson, if you are not quiet, I will be forced to—"

"I *had to* break the law. And. I. *Enjoyed* it!"

"Marshals, remove the defendant from the courtroom."

I'd become giddy, chuckling as two bailiffs escorted me out the door. "I enjoyed the drugs, too!" I shouted over my shoulder as they shoved me past the threshold, a scene that set a new Earth record for the total number of views on !Look, Chirp, UPrick, and TruU.

Five and a half billion.

■ ■ ■

Judge Ray ordered a recess that lasted three days. When everyone was back in the courtroom, Colderwitz did nothing but fiddle with his mechanical pencil, pinching both ends, then letting go of one end and rotating the instrument before pinching both ends again. He must have repeated the exercise hundreds of times while the judge read the jury instructions.

Ben and William S. Williams II had agreed that the defense would present no case, the jury would be dismissed, and the case would proceed to sentencing, with our side having the opportunity to argue mitigation. But Judge Ray rejected the idea.

"No, gentlemen," she had told them in her chambers, "if the defense still wants to present a case, fine. If not, that's fine as well. The jury has sat here for six months, and we're going to hear its decision, regardless of what an appeals court might do."

And so there we were, listening to Judge Ray tell the jury that the defense wasn't presenting its own case but relying instead on the cross-examination testimony of the prosecution's witnesses. Counsel had agreed to no closing arguments, and no more evidence would be introduced except for two recordings of Dawn Bastbom speeches: the one she delivered at the rally in Florida where she called me a prick, and the one she sent to the First Fifty in Roma City. The jury could listen to the recordings during their deliberations.

Judge Ray spent an hour reading the jury instructions. Then, for each count of the indictment, she explained what the jury must find to conclude I was guilty beyond a reasonable doubt. At long last, she set aside the instructions and ended her marathon with a stern pronouncement.

"Jurors, in reaching your decision, you shall ignore Mr. Johnson's emotional outburst, which was not made under oath and does not count as a confession."

Colderwitz didn't jot a single note the whole time. I had already told him I wouldn't appeal a guilty verdict or my sentence and looked forward to prison and years of quiet solitude. If I couldn't play the oboe, I'd find something else to play, and if I couldn't build a meditation garden, I'd imagine one.

And I would write letters to you, Bria, pouring out pain about what you did to me. Most of the words would be seeped in anger. Some would express regrets about my lies. After ten years in prison, I might even apologize and plead for forgiveness.

Like I'm doing now.

Three days later, Colderwitz called to say the jury had ended its deliberations. "Judge Ray expects us in her courtroom in four hours to hear their decision."

* * *

I got suited up and rode the Asteroid to the courthouse, wolfing down a VeriSym Terky 'n' Cheez hoagie along the way. For a fleeting moment, I contemplated telling the vehicle to drive me to Venezuela. To hell with the hundred million in bail.

At the courthouse, I rushed past the cordoned-off crowd, entered the building, and hurried to Courtroom 3. The room was packed.

"Three days isn't much time for a jury to discuss such a long indictment and months of testimony," Colderwitz told me in a low voice at the defense table. "In other circumstances, this would suggest a finding of innocence, but we didn't present a case and they won't ignore your confession. They're humans, not robots, no matter what the judge told them. The best we can expect is a mixed verdict."

Did I regret refusing to plea-bargain? Did I regret confessing, even if it meant several forms of abstinence for the next ten years, teaching Introduction to Spaceflight to hardened criminals in guarded classrooms, and jogging inside a thirty-foot-tall razor fence?

Obviously, that wasn't on my mind watching João on the stand and thinking I was destroying a friend's future. But, to be honest, I can't say I ever relished the thought of life in cinderblock buildings surrounded by gun towers. In any case, the truth proved impossible for me to argue with, and the bigger, better part of me was at peace with the choices I had made. At least I wasn't facing the death penalty.

The courtroom was subdued, with only the din of the onlookers and traffic in the hallway outside the doors, and the squeaks of chairs after the twelve jurors trudged in and entered the jury box. When Judge Ray stepped in, the noises died, all stood, and you could hear a pin drop. Or at least a mechanical pencil. Colderwitz had been revolving his again, dropping it with a *clack* when he rose from his chair.

The bailiff barked that the court was in session. Everyone sat.

"Has the jury reached a decision?" Judge Ray asked.

The jury had elected a woman to be the foreperson. She replied, "Yes, Your Honor," and handed a piece of paper to the court clerk, who handed it to the judge, who read it and handed it back to the clerk, who handed it back to the foreperson.

"The defendant will stand and face the jury," the judge said.

I did, panting softly.

Although the foreperson didn't look a thing like you, Bria, my mind's eye saw you on that sunny day at Cocoa Beach, when we did yoga together and picnicked on the sand and frolicked in the waves, sometimes riding them to the shore, sometimes diving through them. Remember?

"We, the jury in action titled 'The United States of America Versus Zachary Adair Johnson,' find the defendant not guilty on all counts."

■ ■ ■

I wasn't fully aware of my jubilance as I hugged Colderwitz and jumped up and down, as if Navy had just crushed Army 110–0. Ben was damn lucky I didn't smash his toes. My confession—the truth—had been rewarded. And the rewards didn't end there.

The CEO of Mars Nuts called Jep the next day. Within a week, I had a new contract and the fifty million that came with it. And though I may not have been the first member of our crew to set foot on the Red Planet, I was the first on a box of Wheaties. When I saw you and Sally had landed there a month later, smiling with your arms slung around each other, I knew the shunning was over. I wasted no time wrapping my arms around pillows and squeezing them as if they were the two of you.

It's been years since our touchdown on Arcadia Planitia, and I haven't ever stopped thinking of you, Bria. I just wish *all* the ostracism was finished, so we could at least speak with each other again. I know you've moved on, and that you and KIM are busy with your four-year-old twins. But I'd love to see you two, and Mik-1 and Mik-2, who, by the way, are positively adorable.

So, Bria, what do you say next month, on the anniversary of the Mars landing, we surprise the world—you, me, Sally, and João? Yes, a reunion. We could do it here, on my farm in Virginia, and engage in a little truth and reconciliation with no preconceived notions about where things end up.

I realize I'm asking a lot, given my share of not-so-good press. To help put you at ease, let me dispel some of the more popular myths.

A) Since my acquittal, I haven't become a reclusive madman who's into bestiality. I've tuned out most of the news and haven't granted an interview since our splashdown. However, the village folks of Browntown know me well. They just don't broadcast it, out of respect for everyone's privacy.

B) I didn't discover the wonders of llamas during a psilocybin trip. I discovered them after Connie—yes, the Connie who worked the front desk at the Neutral Buoyancy Lab (she moved to the Place for Lovers a year before I did)—learned I'd built a house on a hundred forested acres in the Shenandoah foothills.

C) Connie and I were never in love. We were both bouncing back from divorces.

She invited me to do something I'd never done before. On my first date in ages, she was going to surprise me. I thought the mystery trip she had arranged would be some hidden gem off the radar, like a luxurious yurt in the secluded woodlands of Virginia, complete with astounding sunsets and a decent-sized waterfall.

"This is Pete," Joe Hendricks told me in the barn. Joe was a trim, fiftyish cowboy-type in fresh jeans and a red plaid shirt. Pete was a llama, and unlike Joe, a mess. Strands of yellow hay clung to his stringy black hair. His tall ears, when erect, could be mistaken for horns. He held his camel-like snout steady as he chewed, fixing his glassy brown eyes straight ahead.

"You can see," Joe said, "Pete really gets into his food."

Pete was my llama for the day and, with Connie and Olive Oyl, we went for a hike led by Joe. Nothing bothered Pete. He walked steadily, proud and determined, his low center of gravity affording him constant balance.

I immediately became hooked on llamas.

My love affair with these majestic creatures was sealed when I fed Pete grain from my cupped hands. As his puffy lower lip scooped up the seeds, it felt like a warm, wet sponge—in a word, wonderful. It amazed me I felt none of his teeth, and after he swallowed the last seed, that puffy lower lip gave me a wet peck on the nose.

"Oh yeah," Joe said. "Pete's a kisser."

I got my turn with Connie a little later. We dated three times. A string of other rebounds followed, all frivolous. I've dated no one in a year, Bria. And haven't bothered getting my vasectomy reversed. At least subconsciously, I think I already have children. You, KIM, and the two Miks will like my llamas (I'm up to thirteen). They can be frisky or gentle, quiet or vocal, kissy or spitty, something for everyone, and after you, they mean everything to me.

Yes, I have much to be grateful for. My llamas, the forest, the deer. The *woo-hoo* song of the mourning doves, which sounds nothing like those at the Houston arboretum.

At night after feeding my friends, I step out of the stable and find Mars in the sky. I stare at the Red Planet and wonder how the Romanites are faring, and what scientists at Buzz Station might be discovering. But I don't do that for long, always coming back to the beauty of where I am and where I belong.

Please, Bria, come to Browntown. I'll put everybody up. I built a music studio. Just think: The Craters could reunite and end the years of gossip that KIM broke up the band and ruined our marriage.

I've been up front with you. I want you back. I don't care if KIM and the little Miks are part of the package. I bet KIM won't have a problem with it, either. I heard from Sally, who likes the reunion idea. She's in Crete filming the musical *Zorbetta's Vendetta*, starring opposite the stunning Rani Mahi, and can join us after it wraps. João accepted my invitation outright. The senator arrives tomorrow, and he's bringing his bass.

Please, Bria, can't we try again and see what happens?

I better stop now and get ready for João.

First up: practicing my oboe and "Expand Your Love."

The End

ACKNOWLEDGMENTS

My thanks to all who have supported and encouraged my writing, beginning with my high school English teacher, Mrs. Erickson, who praised my report about the possibility of refrigerating astronauts so they hibernated during deep-space voyages. I am also grateful to Mary Morrissy, Tim Johnston, and Kseniya Melnick for accepting me into the Jenny McKean Moore Writing Workshops that each led at George Washington University, and to the members of the critique groups that resulted from those workshops. I thank Aaron Schlecter, Christopher Ryan, and Lisa Gilliam for their editorial feedback. Thanks also to Jennifer Moore for showing sincere interest in my writing and for being super generous with her feedback. Most of all, I thank Elizabeth Baudhuin, my beloved, who read multiple drafts of the novel and provided invaluable help during the revision process, always with patience and loving kindness.

ABOUT THE AUTHOR

Growing up, Richmond Scott wanted to become a space scientist but got stuck orbiting other high-tech worlds instead. He lives in Washington, DC. This is his first novel.